THE MACKENZIE FAMILY SECURITY SERIES

SHADOWS AND SILK

SECRETS AND SATIN

SINS AND SCARLET LACE

LILIANA HART

Copyright © 2013 Liliana Hart

All rights reserved.

ISBN: 149103517X
ISBN-13: 978-1491035177

DEDICATION

To my readers: Because you keep asking for more MacKenzie books. Thanks for allowing me to keep writing the family I love.

TABLE OF CONTENTS

Shadows and Silk   1

Secrets and Satin   190

Sins and Scarlet Lace   343

About the Author   510

ACKNOWLEDGMENTS

A special thanks to members of The Indie Voice for your unwavering support – Jasinda Wilder, Dorien Kelly, Tina Folsom, Jana DeLeon, Jane Graves, Colleen Gleason, Denise Grover Swank, Theresa Ragan, and Debra Holland.

SHADOWS AND SILK

A MACKENZIE FAMILY NOVEL

NEW YORK TIMES BESTSELLING AUTHOR

LILIANA HART

LILIANA HART

CHAPTER ONE

Surrender, Montana

The frigid wind howled with fury, cutting through clothes and skin like a knife, and laying claim to a normally peaceful landscape. It was the first storm of what promised to be a long and turbulent winter. Gray clouds—pregnant with snow—roiled across the sky, and a blanket of white, soft powder would cover everything before morning.

The ground was bitter with cold, and the smell of fresh dirt and gunpowder lingered in the air long after the final shots had been fired. Dusk loomed on the horizon and Darcy MacKenzie watched as the last of the DEA cleanup team removed the bodies of Miguel del Fuego's men, wiping the violent scene from existence with the expertise of men who were good at making things disappear.

They loaded the remaining bodies into a black panel van and disappeared down the long, paved driveway that led off her property, and she was left alone with nothing but fading adrenaline and the one man put on this Earth to make her crazy.

SHADOWS AND SILK

Darcy shivered and hugged her arms across her chest. Her white cable knit sweater and jeans weren't enough protection against the weather, and added with the shock of what had just happened, she couldn't seem to control the shivers that wracked her body. She shifted on her bare feet, rubbing one foot on top of the other as she tried to warm them.

There hadn't been time to stop and put on shoes once the gunfire started, which was damned inconsiderate of del Fuego's men, considering they'd interrupted a cozy dinner by the fireplace and a whole hell of a lot of sexual tension. Brant had been a hairsbreadth away from finally giving into temptation and kissing her brainless, and though he'd landed on top of her once the first shots were fired, it hadn't been in the way she wanted. The way she craved.

"There are bullet holes in my house," she said, assessing the damage to her home.

The big farmhouse was made of gray stone and heavy timber, the porch going around on all sides. It was a postcard in the middle of acres of green fields, rolling hills and white fences. Except now there were bullet holes lodged in the mortar, the hanging baskets of winter ivy hung in broken clumps of wire and dirt, and the white curtains billowed from the shot out windows. Her parents were going to have kittens if this wasn't fixed by the time they got back from their trip.

"The agency will send a construction crew out to make repairs," Brant said. "It might be best if you go and stay with one of your cousins for a while until the mess is cleared away."

If he hadn't spoken, she wouldn't have even known he was there. He never made a sound when he moved—like a big jungle cat stalking its prey—only he'd made it very clear he had no interest in coming after her.

"Yeah, right," she said, laughing. "They all have so many kids that they can barely fit in their houses. The MacKenzies have no problems with fertility. At least on that side of the family. I'll just put plastic over the windows and make do. I've got an extra heater I can use in the bedroom."

Darcy finally turned to face him, remembering vividly how close she'd come to tasting him. She'd been in love with him since she was sixteen years old, and damned if it had faded like she'd been told those first infatuations would. She had a sinking feeling it was the real thing. If she hadn't been absolutely certain he was attracted to her in return then she wouldn't have pressed so hard.

But she'd seen him watching her when he thought she wasn't looking, and she'd seen the way his eyes had darkened with lust and his breathing had changed whenever she happened to stand too close. And she made it a point of standing too close often. None of the men she'd met in the last ten years had made her want like Brant Scott had. It was his face she dreamed of when she pleasured herself in the loneliness of her own bed, and his name that escaped her lips when she finally found satisfaction.

Even now, she was drawn to the magnetism of the sheer maleness of him. The gun at his side was as much a part of the man as the vivid green of his eyes or the slightly crooked tilt to his nose he'd received after a game of football with her brothers. His black cargo pants and shirt were dusted with plaster and small pieces of glass from the bullets that had ripped through the walls and windows. His blond hair was buzzed close to his scalp and the stubble of his beard was close to the same length. She also noticed he had a pair of her tennis shoes in his hand.

Death had come too close today. If Brant hadn't had one of those infamous moments of intuition he was famous for and thrown his body over hers in the nick of time, then she knew with certainty she'd be as dead as del Fuego's men. Nothing had ever scared her more than watching as he'd headed towards danger with his weapon drawn, and wondering if he'd return to her in one piece.

SHADOWS AND SILK

"It's your ass that's going to be freezing, sugar. If you want to stay here that's fine with me. I've already been called to another assignment." He smirked at her with superiority like he had when she was a teenager, trying to keep the distance between them. "I'll be soaking up the sun while you're freezing in the middle of nowhere by this time tomorrow."

Pain ripped through her at his declaration. Just once she wanted it to seem like it was hard for him to walk away from her. It could be months before she saw him again. But she'd known Brant for a long time and he wouldn't welcome her worry, so she covered the fear with false bravado and a lot of attitude, fisting a hand to her hip and giving him a sneer that was bound to ignite his temper. She loved to see that flash of wildness in his eyes, especially since he held himself so rigidly in check all the time. This was the last chance she'd have for a while. She wasn't going to let him walk away without breaking past that wall he'd built between them.

"Just make sure you get that crew here before you go basking in the sun. If this house isn't fixed by the time my mother gets home things aren't going to be pretty. She's no one to mess with."

"What's wrong, sugar? Afraid she's going to ground you for misbehaving?"

Darcy narrowed her eyes before she realized he was baiting her. He never stopped trying to remind her that there were too many years between them. At barely twenty-four, she was just finishing up her second Master's Degree—this one in Mayan Civilization—and she was about to start work on her PhD in the spring. And at eight years her senior, Brant had been an agent for Homeland Security since its inception and a Navy SEAL before that. Despite the sizzling attraction between them, the fact he'd lived his life and chosen a path that was wrought with danger was something he never let her forget. He didn't have room in his life for complications.

"I'm not the one who should be afraid. Someone is going to have to explain how her grandmother's mirror got broken. I'd be more worried about her hunting you down and unmanning you."

"Many have tried," he said. "None have succeeded."

Darcy took a step closer, so her breast brushed against his arm, and she smiled as his nostrils flared with desire. He'd been denying the chemistry between them for too long, pushing her away when the flame had been burning hotter and higher between them. And spending three weeks in each other's pockets had only intensified the flame to scorching proportions. She looked him up and down slowly, heat rushing to her cheeks at the obvious bulge behind his zipper.

"Maybe you just haven't met the right woman," she purred.

His eyes dilated to almost black and his nostrils flared as her hand skimmed down his arms and took the shoes from his hand. She pushed past him, putting a little extra swing into her hips as she headed toward the barn. She wasn't quite ready to face the disaster of the inside of the house just yet. What she needed was a hard ride at neck breaking speed to release the rest of the tension and, if she was honest, the anger over the fact that he was leaving again.

"You're playing with fire, sugar."

She laughed huskily, a seductive tone she hadn't been aware she possessed, and kept walking. "I don't think so, Agent Scott. You're the one who's afraid to get burned."

The game had gone on long enough. It was time for him to claim her once and for all or walk away forever and stop the incessant teasing. It was time for him to move on from whatever had happened in his past to give him such a grim view of relationships. If he didn't want her then she could put all her focus on her career. But it was time for him to make a decision or ride off into the sunset.

"Goddammit, Darcy." He cursed. "You're taking

things too far."

"And you're not taking them far enough. I never figured you for a coward."

She never heard him come up behind her. His grip stung her arm as he spun her around and pulled her close. His breath heaved in and out of his chest and she could see the anger etched in the lines of his face. Her eyes widened as the ferocity of his gaze bored into hers, and blood pounded through her veins. Her nipples tightened to hard buds and moisture pooled between her thighs at his dominance.

"You don't know what you're doing, Darcy."

"You underestimate me." She placed her hand on his chest and felt his heart thumping wildly beneath. "I know exactly what I'm doing. Just like I know that you want me so bad you can hardly breathe." Her hand trailed down his chest, across the taut ridges of his abdomen, and rested just above the waistband of his pants.

"You have to know this can't go anywhere. I can't give you what you want. There are no picket fences in our future. Just a night of mindless fucking to quench this need that's been pounding at us for years. Is that what you want?" he asked, shaking her shoulders as if he desperately wanted her to disagree and walk away.

She knew he believed what he said, but that didn't stop his words from hurting any less. There was still a girlish hope inside of her that he might stay. That he might love her the way she loved him.

"I know you'd rather tell me what I can't or shouldn't do than get me naked and writhing beneath you. Maybe you're not man enough after all."

Darcy tried to jerk her arm out of his grasp, but he held on to her like a vise. The war raged across the harsh planes of his face as his lips hovered just over hers, their breaths mingling.

"Well, sugar. I guess we'll find out."

His mouth crushed to hers and she let out a savage

moan as she finally tasted him—and after years of dreaming, nothing could even come close to reality. Heat sizzled across her skin and her sex moistened with anticipation. He tasted like decadence and sin and she opened her mouth wider and let him plunder. His tongue teased and tormented, and she could taste the wild hunger inside him. And, God, how she wanted that hunger to devour her.

"Christ, Darcy," he said, yanking up her sweater and pulling it over her head. He tossed it to the ground, and his eyes darkened as he reached out to skim a finger over the flesh above her bra. "Beautiful," he whispered, and leaned down to replace his finger with his tongue.

Darcy leaned back and let him taste, not feeling the cold that surrounded them any longer. His fingers kneaded at her back, and he expertly released the clasp of her bra. His lips trailed between the valley of her breasts and her bra slipped off her shoulders and dropped to the ground to join her sweater.

"Stop teasing me," she demanded.

"Patience is a virtue, baby."

"So is chastity. Virtues are overrated. Let's stick with the vices."

Brant laughed, and her head dropped back on a moan as his mouth found her nipple and suckled greedily. Her pussy throbbed, and her hips unwillingly arched against him, seeking release.

Desperate hands grasped at his shirt and pulled it up and over his head so she could feel the hard flesh beneath. His skin burned beneath her touch, and she ached for that heat to be inside of her. She pressed herself against him so they were skin against skin and raked her nails across his shoulders.

"This will be over before it gets started if you keep that up," he said.

His fingers tore at the snap of her jeans, and he kissed a wet trail down her stomach as he pushed them down her hips to pool at her feet.

"You'll just have to make it up to me. Again and again."

"I love that smart mouth of yours," he said, twirling his tongue around her bellybutton and nipping his way down south.

"I promise you're going to love it a lot more a little later. I've got an awful lot of fantasies stored up, and my mouth plays a big part in all of them."

"Jesus," he whispered.

Darcy didn't know if it was her words or the sight of her in nothing but the black lace thong that caused such reverence, but he sat back on his heels and stared at her with enough heat to make her go up in flames. His hands skimmed up her legs, and he brought his face to her cloth covered mound, inhaling the scent of her desire even as he placed small kisses over her swollen flesh. His fingers slid beneath the lace and she parted her legs as he probed along the creamy folds.

"So wet," he said, jerking her panties down and burying his face against her, not giving her a chance to catch her breath.

Darcy screamed and her legs almost buckled as he licked inside of her, taking the taut bud of her clit in his mouth and sucking her into a maelstrom of pleasure. He didn't take her easy, but shot her straight into delirium as tongue and teeth tortured the sensitive flesh.

Her fingers clenched in his hair and she writhed against him as her body tightened, just on the edge of release.

"Brant," she panted. "God, please."

Her eyelids shuttered and closed as he slipped two fingers inside of her, stretching her inner walls and probing against a spot that had flashes of light dancing behind her closed eyes.

"That's it, sugar. Come all over my fingers. Show me how much you want me."

She cried out at his words and clamped around him.

The pulses started deep in her womb, spiraling like bursts of electricity through her entire body, as the orgasm rocked through her. Wave after wave of pleasure shook her body with tremors as he drank in her release.

"Fuck," Brant hissed, kissing his way back up her body. His cheeks were flushed with need and his lips swollen and damp with her desire.

"Yes, please," she said shakily.

He picked her up and Darcy wrapped her legs around him. He started toward the house, his fingers kneading her ass and his tongue wreaking havoc against the sensitive spots on her neck.

"I want you in bed."

"It's too far," she panted. "We'll never make it."

She ground herself against the bulge behind his zipper and tightened her legs around his waist, causing him to stumble on the first step leading to the wide covered porch.

"You're right," he said, propping her against the railing and ripping at the button of his cargo pants. "We'll never make it."

Darcy watched, mesmerized, as the button popped open and the zipper spread easily. His cock sprang free—long and thick—the darkened crown flared and swollen, the tip moist with desire. He reached into his pocket and took out a condom, ripping the packet open with his teeth and rolling it on hurriedly.

"Pretty presumptuous of you," she said cheekily.

"I've been carrying it around for three fucking weeks. Wanting you so much it was everything I could do to not bend you over the nearest surface and claim you like I wanted."

Love and desire for this man brought tears to her eyes, and she buried her face in his neck so he wouldn't see the raw emotions. She'd wanted him for what seemed like her whole life, and now to hear he wanted her just as much was like a dream too good to be true. She loved him with everything she was—with the memories of a young girl and the darker desires of the woman she was now—and now that he'd touched her she knew she'd never feel for another like she felt for him.

She watched in fascination as he pushed the head of his cock inside her. The time for control was long forgotten, and she sucked in a breath as he stretched her to the limits of pleasure. He pulled out and pushed in again, working his way in until he was buried to the hilt. He pulsed inside of her and she clasped around him, milking his cock while he held still and tried to get control.

"Fuck," he swore savagely. "You're killing me. I'm trying to make this last."

"It's lasted for years. Stop being a martyr."

He laughed and began to move, hips bunching and flexing as he plunged in and out of her with undisciplined ardor. Darcy's nails dug into his shoulders and her mouth opened on a silent scream as the fight for control disappeared and all that was left was the feel of the two of them, joined together in the most intimate of ways, as a thousand exposed nerve endings sizzled like lightning and shot from one body to the other.

Perspiration dampened their skin and steam rose from their bodies as it evaporated into the cold. She arched against him, skin slapping against skin, as he pummeled inside her with fierce strokes and an urgency she'd feel in her muscles for days to come. Her head thrashed as he rode her hard and fast, and her hips pumped in equal fervor to the rhythm he set. She was determined that he'd feel her just as much in the following days—that he'd remember the magic they'd shared.

Darcy opened her eyes and got caught in the heated green of his gaze, lost in the need she saw there. She wanted him to love her, to remember this moment and know that no other woman would love him as she did. He shook his head as if he'd heard her plea, trying to clear his head from the spell she'd cast on him.

"Darcy," he whispered, almost apologetically. He took her mouth in a fevered kiss, his tongue thrusting in time with his cock. Her pussy pulsed with the need to climax, and she knew it wouldn't be long before it came.

She pulled away from his kiss and closed her eyes, pushing away the love she yearned for and trying to harden her heart against the pain. Wishing wasn't the same as getting. If all they could have was soul shattering sex this one time, it would have to be enough. She'd be damned if she'd ask him for more.

"Harder," she panted. "Fuck me harder."

His eyes flared in surprise at her demand and his fingers dug into her hips. And then he did as she commanded and colors exploded behind her eyelids as she screamed out his name. Her body went taut like the string of a bow, and then sensation washed over and through her as pleasure ripped her apart. Her pussy tightened around him and she shattered, drenching him with her sweet syrup. She'd never had an orgasm so intense—that it whipped through her body like a raging storm and left her heart and soul in tatters.

Darcy thought she heard him curse in the far off recesses of her mind, and then he thrust once more against her, stiffening in her arms as his release tore through him. She didn't know how long they held each other up during the aftermath of the storm, but when she finally had the strength to open her eyes, she saw it was full dark and the wind had died down.

She tried to think of something the old Darcy would say—something sassy or wicked—but nothing came to mind that wouldn't give her true feelings away. The cold of the night air finally penetrated through the heat they'd produced and she shivered in his arms.

"We should go inside," he said against her neck, nibbling at the sensitive flesh.

Her legs relaxed from around his waist, and she tried to push away from him, determined to keep a certain distance between them so it wouldn't be so hard when he left. But Brant shifted and slid back deep inside her, still hard, and she gasped as the need ignited in her once more.

"I'm not done with you yet," he said, kissing her gently. "Not by a long shot."

He wrapped her legs back around his waist and picked her up, carrying her into the house and crunching over broken glass until they reached a bedroom at the back of the house that hadn't been damaged.

"It's a good thing I kept my shoes on," he said.

"You're also wearing your weapon. I could have shot you during the throes of passion."

"It'd be a hell of a way to die."

Brant kissed her again, building the heat in slow increments, making love to her mouth with a tenderness that brought tears to her eyes. Kissing her as if she were the only woman on Earth—a kiss of claiming—a kiss of promise. He laid her back on the bed and proceeded to love her once more, this time slowly, savoring every inch of her as if he were committing it to memory.

Maybe he was.

Because after they'd found satisfaction once more and she'd fallen asleep wrapped in his arms, she felt him shift away from her and rise from the bed. His finger touched her cheek gently, and it was then she knew he was leaving. And he didn't plan on coming back.

She waited a few minutes until she heard the front door close, then slipped out of bed, pulling on a robe and sliding into a pair of shoes as she made her way to the front room. She parted the lace curtains and watched as he picked up his scattered clothes and finished dressing.

Her heart thudded wildly. She'd known he'd try to leave, but she hadn't thought it would be so soon—with her skin still reddened from his beard and her body still tingling from his touch.

He tossed his duffle bags into his Jeep and got in without looking back. He hadn't even said goodbye, and the girlish dreams she'd once cherished shattered like the glass at her feet.

CHAPTER TWO

Four Years Later

MacKenzies were nothing but trouble. Brant had known that for almost fifteen years—ever since Cade MacKenzie had dragged him to his home in Montana for Thanksgiving one year and shoved him into the freezing cold pond behind their farmhouse. They'd been as close as brothers ever since, and he considered the MacKenzies to be his second family, especially since his sister, Bayleigh, was now married to Cade.

But sometimes families were a pain in the ass, and this was one of those times.

He weaved in and out of the late night Georgetown traffic—the Harley rumbling beneath him—as a cool mist fell and collected in fine droplets on his riding leathers. Every instinct he had was telling him to turn around and go the opposite direction.

Unfortunately, he didn't have much of a choice when it came to this latest summons. The call from Declan MacKenzie had come early that morning—there was to be a meeting between all agents involved in the investigation of the del Fuego drug cartel. All agencies had been working together for the past four years to put an end to the cartel's reign of terror, and since Brant was the special agent in charge for Homeland Security, he had no choice but to be at the meeting.

He slowed and turned onto M Street, cursing the inaccuracy of the weatherman as a loud crack of thunder rent the air and the soft mist turned into a downpour. Headlights glared off the wet streets and impatient drivers blared their horns as this latest inconvenience kept them from their social obligations. He veered around a florist van to pull into the underground parking garage across the street from O'Malley's Pub.

With his helmet stuck under his arm, he sprinted across the street and into the warmth and familiarity of the long time hangout used by a mixed bag of federal agents. The smell of beer and the polish they used to wipe down the seats of the bar stools and booths hung heavy in the air. The floors were scarred and the wood paneling on the walls darkened with age. Music thumped steadily from the speakers, but not so loud you couldn't hear the person next to you. O'Malley's was a place to talk shop, let off steam, or sweet talk pretty waitresses—though not necessarily in that order.

Brant ran a hand through his hair, dripping water onto the mat on the floor, and wiped his feet.

"Agent Scott," Jimmy O'Malley said from behind the bar. "Haven't seen you in here in a while. What'll it be?"

O'Malley was a former FBI agent and had opened the pub after a bullet shattered his knee and he'd been taken out of the field. He always said he'd rather serve whiskey than start drinking it because he was bored out of his mind sitting behind a desk. Brant couldn't say he blamed him.

"The usual. And put it on Declan's tab," Brant said, causing O'Malley to laugh.

"I'll have Lily bring it to you. Your friends are upstairs." O'Malley jerked his thumb at the curved staircase that led up to the private room he sometimes rented out for parties or wakes, and Brant nodded his thanks and moved toward the back of the bar. He acknowledged a few of the familiar faces he passed on his way, and headed up the stairs.

"It's about damned time, Scott," Shane MacKenzie said, his concentration never wavering from the game of darts he was playing. "Devlin here already owes me fifty bucks. Can't play darts for shit."

Max Devlin was leading the DEA team assigned to the recent tourist murders that had been happening throughout Mexico as the cartels battled over their turf and the Mexican government's crackdown on drug trafficking. He'd been Cade's boss once upon a time, and since Devlin was a former Marine sniper, Brant very seriously doubted it was him that couldn't play darts for shit. Devlin punched Shane in the arm and called him an inappropriate name and then quickly made a bullseye on his next turn.

Seeing Shane reminded him of his own brother, Brady. Shane was Brady's SEAL Team Commander, and it seemed they'd been out of the country more often than not in the past couple of years. Considering some of the missions he suspected they'd taken part in, he was just thankful his brother was still alive. Shane's team was the best there was, so they got the most dangerous missions.

Brant narrowed his eyes as he took a closer look at Shane. The youngest MacKenzie had a hardness about him that hadn't been there the last time he'd seen him. He was a couple of years younger than Brant, and there was something about him that went beyond just being a SEAL. Brant remembered all too well the things he'd seen during his SEAL days, not that working for DHS was a walk in the park, but he no longer feared that any given hour could be his last.

Shane's dark blond hair was buzzed close to his scalp and there was a vicious looking scar at the base of his skull that was still puckered and red in its newness.

Brant caught Max's eye and raised his brow in question over the wound, but Max shook his head, signifying he didn't know and didn't ask. Not that Shane would even tell them how it had happened if they did ask.

Max looked like the odd man out in their group. Everyone was dressed down in jeans and t-shirts, but Max had on a pair of grey dress slacks and a white dress shirt with the sleeves rolled up, which meant he'd probably been stuck in meetings with his superiors all day.

Max was an anomaly. He looked like he belonged in the corporate world—like an Ivy League boy next door with his clean cut pale blond hair, and his face freshly shaven. His quiet nature and relaxed air made it easy to forget that he was deadly. Like he was the kind of man who got his muscles playing tennis and swimming at a country club instead of the MMA training he did to stay in shape. No one could gutter fight better than Max Devlin.

Brant stripped off his leather jacket and tossed it across an empty chair, laying his helmet in the seat. The noise from below was muted and the bass from the music vibrated the floor, but the room was private for all intents and purposes.

Declan MacKenzie sat in one of the wooden whiskey barrel chairs, his posture relaxed and his eyes hooded halfway in sleep. Brant knew as well as any of the others in the room that Declan was never fully relaxed, and he could be up with a weapon in his hand before most people could blink. He and Declan were the same age, though it was Cade, the oldest MacKenzie, who was his best friend.

He'd been crossing paths with Declan for years during different assignments, and he'd sat across from him at the dinner table for MacKenzie family dinners more times than he could count, but he still didn't know exactly what branch of the government Dec worked for. By the way he seemed to know every damned thing almost as soon as it happened, Brant was guessing CIA. The one thing he did know was that Declan was in charge of this op, whatever it was, and he was calling the shots.

Lily knocked on the door and came in with a tray filled with drinks. Dark haired and dark eyed, she gave Shane a smile that would have any red-blooded male's blood boiling, and went about passing out the drinks. She was efficient as she set them around the table, and Brant raised a brow as he saw her place a napkin and a beer in front of the fifth seat. As far as he knew, only the CIA, DEA, Homeland Security and the assigned Navy SEAL teams had active operatives searching for the del Fuego labs. It had been an assignment met with little success over the last few years.

"Ooh, baby," Shane said, as Lily gave him one last smile and closed the door behind her so they'd have privacy. "I think I'm in love."

"That's what you said last night, dickhead," Devlin said.

"There's love and then there's love," Shane said, waggling his eyebrows. "I think Lily could be the one. And she was real delicate about the way she slipped her number in my pocket." He held up the piece of paper from his pocket for them to admire.

"Jesus, sometimes I can't believe I'm related to you," Declan said. "How old are you again? Fifteen?"

"Jealousy doesn't become you, brother. Just because you've got a sex life that rivals great-aunt Matilda doesn't mean I'm ready to follow in your footsteps."

"Am I wrong, or did I miss the part where this was a MacKenzie family brawl instead of a government op?" Brant asked.

"You've been in the middle of enough MacKenzie family brawls to recognize when it's serious," Declan said. "Or have you forgotten the broken nose? Maybe I need to refresh your memory."

Brant flipped him off and took the seat next to him. "I knew you did that on purpose, asshole. A slip of the elbow my ass."

"All's fair in football. Suck it up, Nancy."

"Maybe if Cagney and Lacey are done playing darts, we can get this show on the road." Brant took a long sip of beer and felt some of the tension drain out of his shoulders. It had been too long since he'd just taken an evening to relax. "I'd like to have an entire weekend off at some point in my career."

"I've never had one of those," Declan said. "I don't see why you should get one if I can't."

"I appreciate that, Dec. You're nothing but heart."

"That's not what the ladies tell him," Shane broke in with a laugh. "They tell him he's nothing but—"

"Enough, Shane," Declan growled. "Take a seat, and lets get this done. Our guest will be here before I'm done with the briefing."

An uneasy feeling slithered up Brant's spine, but he pushed it away. His intuition had been infamous when he'd been a SEAL and that reputation had followed him to DHS. And right now, his intuition was screaming red alerts at him. He trusted Declan. Hell, he trusted all the MacKenzies. But something was going on, and he was pretty sure he was going to hate whatever it was.

Brant was an expert at reading people—at body language and the signs a person gave when they were in an uncomfortable situation. Declan wasn't giving away anything as usual, but he'd known Shane long enough to see the worry in his eyes and the tension in his shoulders. He hadn't stopped tapping his ring finger against his leg since Brant had walked into the room.

Declan tossed out sealed manila envelopes to everyone at the table. At Declan's nod, they each broke the seal and pulled out the papers.

"We've received new intelligence that the del Fuego cartel has in fact been taken over by Alexander Ramos and the whole operation moved to Mexico."

"Shit," Brant said, rubbing the bridge of his nose with his thumb and forefinger. They all knew of Alexander

SHADOWS AND SILK

Ramos. He was currently the leader for the Sinaloa drug cartel, which happened to be the most powerful and deadly cartel in Mexico. "He's expanding his territory."

"It looks that way," Declan said. "He's setting up the del Fuego cartel in southern Mexico, from the Yucatan to the border of Guatemala. He already controls almost all of western Mexico, and I think we can agree that controlling that much territory isn't going to go well once the Mexican government finds out and they start cracking down. The rumors are already spreading. The streets will be overflowing with the blood of innocent people."

"But according to this information, we still don't have a location for the new labs," Devlin said, shuffling through the intel quickly. "How are we any better off than we were?"

"We don't have the exact coordinates," Shane said. "But we do have information we didn't have access to before, and the new labs have definitely been set up in Ramos' territory. My tech wizard was able to ferret out the information while my team was doing surveillance. In fact, we think Ramos took control over what was left of the del Fuego cartel just weeks after Carlos and Miguel del Fuego were killed. We were focusing all our attention on Colombia, but Ramos was keeping things on the down low until he had everything in place. I'm assuming it took time to rebuild the labs in a place no one would find them. The new rash of killings in the Yucatan area suggests the cartel is up and running for business now. Whispers on the street are starting to strengthen."

Miguel and Carlos del Fuego had been the heads of the del Fuego cartel up until their deaths a few years before. Carlos had killed his father in a struggle for power, and Declan had killed Carlos with a shot straight to the heart while Cade rescued Brant's sister, Bayleigh. It had been sweet justice considering the del Fuego's had killed Cade's lover a few years before.

"How'd it come to your attention now?" Brant asked.

He didn't bother to read through the papers in front of him. He was waiting for the axe to fall. He took another sip of beer and kept his gaze steady with Declan's.

"Intelligence picked up an unusual transmission through satellite. It seems Ramos is a little smarter than your average drug lord. He's got brains behind the muscle, and that makes him even more dangerous."

"Spit it out, Dec," Brant said.

"The cartel has set up the underground communication system using Maya as their language of choice."

Brant was already shaking his head, knowing where Declan was going. His stomach twisted in knots, but Declan didn't let him get a refusal out before continuing his explanation.

"Ramos is a Mayan descendent and has managed to bribe enough native speakers to work for him. An underground network to pass along sensitive messages, much like the Navajo Code Talkers during World War II. Unfortunately for us, there are only a handful of people outside of the natives who are knowledgeable in the language. They're a closed culture, and they wouldn't want our interference. And Ramos is probably paying them handsomely or threatening their families to gain their cooperation, so we can't try to work our way in through them. They're loyal to him."

"No way in hell," Brant said, shaking his head again. "You're out of your fucking mind." He saw Max pass Shane a twenty-dollar bill out of the corner of his eye, but he ignored them.

"Told you," Shane said, taking the money and putting it in his wallet.

"You can't seriously be talking about bringing your sister into this mess," Brant said.

"She's been in this mess for years," Declan said. "She wants to help us destroy the cartel once and for all, and she has the resources we need to do it. She's an expert in the field. She speaks the language, and she can read the hieroglyphs. She'd be invaluable on a mission like this. We use civilian consultants all the time."

"No. Absolutely not. She's your sister, for fuck's sake. Has she pissed you off so much lately that you feel the need to take her into cartel territory and leave her to a horrible death? They'll make an example of her. She has no field training, and it'll endanger the entire team. Who's supposed to protect her?"

"From my understanding," Shane said, the perpetual grin he kept on his face in place as usual. "You did a fine job protecting her the last time. Surely you can manage it again. Besides, we drew straws before you got here and you lost."

Brant narrowed his eyes at Shane, wondering exactly what he knew about the time he'd spent with Darcy four years ago, and then he immediately dismissed the thought. If her brothers knew what had really happened between them, his body would've disappeared a long time ago.

He'd both cursed and congratulated himself on walking away from Darcy all those years ago. The further he'd driven from Surrender, Montana, the more he'd wanted to turn around and go back to her. She was his weakness. And in his line of work, there could be no weaknesses. Not unless you had a death wish.

A day hadn't gone by where he hadn't thought of her, and he'd kept track of her from a distance—making sure she was truly safe after her run-in with del Fuego's men. He'd done thorough background checks on the men she'd dated and he'd made sure doors had opened in her career. He had the power to do those things, and he used it without apology because he'd come to realize shortly after their one night together that no one was more important than she was, even if he couldn't be the man in her life.

Brant scooted back his chair and stood abruptly, planning to get his coat and walk out the door before the craziness of this conversation could go any further. The need to get away as soon as possible was getting stronger with every passing second. Being around Darcy again would be a mistake—he knew it as sure as he was standing there.

"We're going to take her into cartel territory," Declan said, the friend gone and the commander taking his place. "And she's going to do her job by deciphering whatever needs to be deciphered so we can find the location of the labs and keep hundreds, maybe thousands, of people from getting killed. She's an expert on the Maya. There's no one more perfect for the job. She's already familiar with the cartel, and she was the one who helped us realize how they've been communicating all these years. And she's not completely untrained. We've all worked with her since she was a kid. She knows how to protect herself, and I wouldn't hesitate to let her watch my back if things turned to shit."

Brant's hands fisted at his sides, and the lack of control brought his anger to the surface. Anger over the way he'd had to leave Darcy. Anger at himself for not being the kind of man who could ever have a normal life. And anger at Declan for pushing the matter when he knew damned good and well nothing good could come of it.

"This is a mistake," he rasped, his throat dry at the prospect of what his future held.

"Is there something you're not telling me about the real reason you don't want to do this?" Declan asked, narrowing his eyes and coming to his feet to look Brant eye to eye. "You clearly have a problem with Darcy. You haven't been to a family get-together since Cade and Bayleigh's wedding, and you left as soon as the ceremony was over even though you were the best man."

"I had food poisoning," Brant gritted out. "And I'm with all of you all the damned time. I'm surrounded by so many MacKenzies I can't piss without one of you holding my dick. What the hell is your point with all this?"

"Nothing. You're just being more unreasonable about this than usual. Darcy's an intelligent woman, and you've known how to handle her since she was ten years old. She's always listened to you more than the rest of us. I'd think finally shutting down the del Fuego cartel would be your top priority."

"No one knows about priorities better than me," Brant said.

Declan nodded somberly. Not many people knew the details about Brant's first wife, or that he'd even had a wife for that matter. He hadn't had her for long. Declan was one of the few who knew the real story.

"Which is why Darcy is going in with you," Declan said. "She's the only team you need on this op. Shane and the rest of his SEAL Team will be your backup, and Max and I both have agents already in the area. We trust Darcy's safety with you. I can count on one hand the number of people I'd say that about, and four of them are her relatives."

"Great," Brant said. The urge to put his fist right into Declan's face overcame him, and he could tell by his friend's raised brow that he was daring him to try. "Just great."

"What's the matter, Brant?" A silky voice called from the door—a siren's call that had his blood pumping and his cock hardening in an instant. "Afraid I'll be too much for you to handle?"

CHAPTER THREE

Darcy walked into the room like she owned it. Like a woman who didn't care that the man who'd broken her heart was only a few feet away.

She'd dressed carefully for the occasion—jeans appropriate for a night out at a bar, and a soft silk blouse in a watercolor floral print, topped with a cropped violet jacket. Her tan leather boots came up to the knee and fit like a second skin, and four-inch heels spiked to a sharp point. The underwear beneath the clothes had been selected with care—cobalt lace panties and a matching bra that were the same color as her eyes. No one would see them, but it gave her confidence all the same.

She looked good and she knew it—like a successful woman who had ultimate control over her sexuality. The naïve girl she'd once been no longer existed, and she'd decided if she was going to be forced into Brant Scott's presence, then by God, she was going to make him suffer.

"Cat got your tongue?" she asked, her smile devilish as Brant seemed frozen in his tracks.

"I don't think we've met," a man she didn't recognize said, holding out his hand for an introduction as he rose from his seat.

"Darcy MacKenzie," she said, liking the man instantly. He had a warm smile and a teasing glint in his chocolate brown eyes that told her he could probably hold his own with her brothers.

"Nice to meet you, Darcy MacKenzie," he said, lifting her hand to his mouth in a gallant gesture. "I'm Max Devlin. I've got an eighteen-foot sloop that rides the waves like she was part of the ocean. Maybe you'd like to come out with me some time?"

"No—" the three other men in the room said simultaneously, making Darcy smile even wider.

"Something tells me you say that to all the girls."

"Just you, sweetheart," he said, winking. "How can someone as beautiful as you be related to these assholes?"

"I'm pretty sure my mother had an affair with a Neanderthal. It's not something we like to talk about though," she whispered conspiratorially. "Shane's very sensitive."

She heard Brant snort out a laugh and she winked at Max Devlin, taking back her hand as she made her way to the empty seat next to Brant.

"Jesus, you still have that smart mouth," he said, shaking his head. "Nice to see you haven't changed."

"Oh, more than you can possibly know," she said, her eyes going cold as she met the shuttered look of his gaze. He wasn't giving anything away, and she'd be damned if she let him read anything from her but the loathing she felt.

Tension coiled off her in waves, and she cursed herself for thinking seeing him again after so long wouldn't affect her. But here she was, hating him so much she could have done violence and still so turned on that her panties were soaking wet.

He hadn't changed, was all she could think. He still made her breath catch and her heart stutter in her chest. It had been years since she'd seen him. His dark blond hair was longer, but it was still short, and he still seemed bigger than life—his chest broad and hard beneath the white t-shirt he wore—his riding leathers encasing the hard muscles of his thighs. The green of his eyes seemed electric, and she remembered how they'd darkened as he'd slid inside of her.

"Long time no see, Brant. What's it been? Four years since I last saw you?" The smile she gave him was meant to drive him crazy, and from the pressed line of his mouth, she could tell she was doing an adequate job. "One would think you've been avoiding me after our little adventure with the del Fuego cartel, but my brothers tell me you've been keeping busy. We'll have to catch up on old times now that we're going to be working together."

"Cut the man a break, Darce," Shane said, rolling his eyes. "Why you couldn't have been born mute is beyond me. There's a reason Brant gets the honor of carting your ass around the jungle—I'd probably strangle you within five minutes of crossing the border."

Darcy narrowed her eyes and turned to snap at the brother closest to her own age. There were only two years between them, and they were more alike than either of them wanted to admit. Their mother swore every gray hair on her head was because of dealing with her two youngest children.

"You know," Max broke in before a fight could start, "I wouldn't mind taking her in with my team. I have a feeling she and Jade are going to hit it off just fine."

Jade Jax was the lone female agent on Max's team, and she was one of the best damn snipers Brant had ever met. She was deadly. And the thought of her and Darcy teaming up was enough to make his balls shrivel in fear.

Shane clapped Max on the shoulder in sympathy and sighed. "Darcy has you trapped in her evil spell. Everyone wants to be with her in the beginning, my friend. And then she opens her mouth—"

"Enough, Shane," Brant said before he could continue to insult Darcy. "Leave her alone. She's here to do a job like the rest of us."

"Since when are you so quick to defend her?" he asked.

SHADOWS AND SILK

"You were the one telling boss man what a bad idea this is. I happen to agree with you. It's got disaster written all over it."

Darcy met Declan's cool stare and wondered what he was thinking. She could tell he was doing his damnedest to analyze the scene before him as quickly as possible. Nothing much got by Declan, and when his eyes narrowed and he looked between her and Brant, she had a feeling he'd come to some sort of conclusion.

"My decision is final on the matter," Declan said, standing and grabbing his leather jacket from the back of his chair. "Darcy goes in with Brant. The other teams will go in as planned, and we'll stay focused on them the entire time. Full disclosure between all teams. I don't want covert agency bullshit on this, or I'll make all of your lives miserable. And believe me, I can do it. Darcy can fill Brant in on what she's found so far."

Declan focused his attention on Max and Shane. "I'll leave it to the two of you to update your teams by 0800 tomorrow morning. I want everyone in place near Darcy's best estimate for the labs within forty-eight hours."

Darcy knew she wasn't going to like whatever orders her brother was about to give her. She could tell by that devilish gleam in his eyes that she'd seen so often in her childhood. She crossed her arms over her chest and glared at him, warning him of retribution if she didn't like what he had to say.

"Brant, you and Darcy will act as tourists," Dec said. "Newlyweds on their honeymoon who are interested in the ruins. That'll give you a good cover. I'm sure the two of you can manage to make it look believable."

Darcy's mouth dropped open, and before she could utter a protest she heard Brant mutter something that sounded like, "I'm going to kill you."

Declan's smile was sharp, so the ragged scar along his left jaw turned white. "All we need you to do is find and decipher the codes they're using so it will lead us to the labs. The teams will be there to back you up if you need us, but you're going to be on your own for most of the mission. We've got to stop that drug from being manufactured. I'm sure you can put aside your differences for the greater good."

She saw Brant's mouth clamp shut out of the corner of her eye, and he nodded once at Declan.

"Are you getting any closer with the hieroglyphs?" Dec asked her.

Nerves slid through her belly at the thought of how much they were depending on her. She'd done all she could with what she had, but she knew she wouldn't find the location from the bits and pieces of information she was being sent.

"I've narrowed it down to region," she said. "But it's at least a hundred mile radius."

"Keep working on it," Declan told her. "And bring Brant up to speed. I need you to narrow it down to a fifty-mile radius within twenty-four hours. That'll still give us enough time to get the teams in position."

Darcy nodded and watched as her brothers and Agent Devlin gathered their things.

"I guess we're done here for the night," Shane said, rolling his eyes. "I barely got to finish my beer."

"Look on the bright side," Max said. "You've got the rest of a Saturday night to yourself and a phone number in your pocket."

"There is that," Shane said as he closed the door behind them, leaving her alone with Brant for the first time in four years.

"I don't suppose I can talk you into changing your mind, can I?" he asked, breaking the tense silence.

"No," she answered. Her throat was suddenly dry, but she had no interest in the beer that sat in front of her on the table.

He shifted his body subtly, so only inches separated them, and she could feel the heat pouring from him and enveloping her in its hold. The strength of him hadn't diminished over the last few years. If anything he was bigger, broader, but the desire in his eyes was somehow hotter.

"Go home, Darcy. For your own sake. You know I won't be able to keep my hands off you, and then we'll be back exactly where we were four years ago. I can't do that again."

"What, you mean fuck me and walk away without looking back? I think I'll pass this time around. I've already seen the ending of that story."

He moved even closer, forcing her to strain her neck up to keep eye contact. "It was more than fucking and you know it. And I told you I had to leave. It shouldn't have been a surprise. You knew exactly what we were doing before I ever tasted that sweet pussy of yours."

Her breath caught at the memory his words evoked, and a bitter laugh escaped before she could control it. "I guess you're right. I shouldn't have been surprised that you ran as far and fast as you could. You've been nothing but honest with me since the first time you realized I'd grown breasts. I don't know what I was thinking." The sarcasm dripped from her tongue and she finally gave in and put some distance between them. Standing so close was muddling her brain.

"And you don't have to pretty it up," she said sweetly. "Fucking was exactly what we had between us. Nothing more. I've gotten over it, and I've mostly forgiven you for being an asshole and not even bothering to say goodbye. It makes things easier, I think. And it's not like you've been avoiding me on purpose these last few years."

"You're pissing me off, Darcy."

"Then I apologize. I certainly don't want to start this assignment out on the wrong foot. We're going to be spending a lot of time together."

"Which leads me back to my original question," he said, patience obviously waning. "How the hell am I going to keep my hands off you? I've thought of that night between us every damned day since I walked away. And I've regretted it more than you can ever know."

"Don't lie to yourself, Brant. You regret that things aren't what they once were—that the game was played out between us and the sexy banter and flashes of heat aren't at your fingertips any longer. You regret the fact that you alienated yourself from my family because you were afraid of what my reaction might be when I saw you. You didn't have to worry, you know. I wouldn't have made scenes or demands. You punished yourself for nothing. I forgot you as soon as you walked out the door."

"You lie," he whispered, his hand coming up and cupping the back of her neck, bringing her closer so she felt the warmth of his breath against her lips. "I dream of your taste, Darcy. It's like a drug that seeps into the system and stays there forever. And you're right. I did punish myself. I should have stayed and made love to you until dawn. But I knew if I did I'd keep coming back to sink inside that tight heat of yours, and it wouldn't be fair to make you believe there could be anything more than that between us. There are things you don't know about me. Things I'm not sure I could ever explain."

"Well, I guess it's a good thing you left. You did us both a favor. And it'll make working with you now that much easier."

"Wishful thinking, sugar."

Darcy trembled as his body touched hers ever so slightly, and her nipples tightened in response to his obvious arousal. His lips whispered over hers—a delicate touch that was barely a kiss at all—but she felt the tug and pull all the way to the sensitive bud between her thighs.

"We're both fighting a losing battle here," he said. "We might as well give in and see where it takes us. I need you so much I ache with it."

Darcy put her hand to his chest and pushed out of his embrace. "Maybe we should get you some cream for that."

SHADOWS AND SILK

She moved further around the table, putting more distance between them. She looked down his body to the obvious bulge straining against his zipper. She'd never gotten to taste him, and her mouth watered with the need to release his cock and take him into her mouth. She held in the shudder of longing and forced herself to look him in the eye.

"I don't belong to you, Brant. I never did. And you can keep your secrets and your past and your lame excuses for your behavior to yourself. I gave you something precious, though you didn't want to see it at the time. I loved you with everything I could have—since I was a girl—but you killed that without a thought."

"Darcy—" The look on his face was panic stricken, and she realized a tear had fallen down her cheek. She shook her head as he started to come around the table, holding him off. She couldn't let him touch her now.

"I would have given you the space your mind needed and the satisfaction your body craved if you'd cared for and respected me enough. But you didn't, and you don't if you think I'd be foolish enough to fall into your arms again after you left me before."

"You're right," he said. "You're right. But that pussy belongs to me, Darcy. I bet you're so wet I could slide easily inside of you. I'll have you again. It's inevitable, baby. And this time we'll see it out to the end. Until the need runs out and we're both ready to move on."

"You don't understand, Brant. This isn't about you." The words almost stuck in her throat, but she stuck out her chin and somehow found the courage to say them. She lifted her left hand so he'd see the sparkling diamond on her finger. "I guess I forgot to mention that I'm engaged to be married."

CHAPTER FOUR

Brant had to throttle back the rage that infused his body after Darcy's bombshell. He'd never felt so close to losing complete control of his sanity until faced with the possibility that she might belong to another man for the rest of her life.

He knew she'd had relationships since their night together. He knew she'd even taken a lover or two. But she hadn't been serious enough about them to consider marriage, and the threat of losing her forever hadn't worried him. But the sight of that ring on her finger made him even more determined to claim her. She was his, dammit, even though his mind and body were warring with each other over how he could possibly keep her. Love her the way she deserved. He could only hope the madness of their lust wore itself down.

Brant saw red as his anger grew, and her eyes widened in shock as the back of the chair he was holding on to snapped off under the force of his grip. He tossed it to the floor and stalked her around to the other side of the table. He saw the worry in her eyes, and he almost laughed as she stuck out her chin and met his gaze head on. Darcy was no coward. And damned if it didn't piss him off for her to think that he'd ever lay a hand on her in anger.

He was so hard he was surprised his jeans could

contain his cock. Darcy's eyes flared and she sucked in a deep breath as he stood in front of her, so their bodies were barely touching and the heat of his desire wrapped around her.

"Do you think for one second that ring would stop me from taking you?" he whispered. "Do you think it would stop you from giving in to me?"

"Why you arrogant son of a—"

Brant's hand grabbed her fist as she took a swing at him. His mouth cut off her words as his lips took hers in a savage kiss filled with four furious years of longing. Of remembering. He damned them both as her mouth opened on a sigh, and the hot, wet heat of her tongue welcomed him as he stroked against her. She fit perfectly against him, and his fingers gripped her ass and pulled her closer, rubbing the heat of her against his cock.

"Christ, Darcy—"

She moaned against his mouth, and her fingers buried in his hair. He shoved chairs out of the way and lifted her onto the table, her legs parting and wrapping tightly around his waist. He was mindless with the pleasure. Why did he ever think he'd be able to do without her? No other woman would ever do. Just Darcy.

She arched against him, cradling his cock between her jean-clad thighs, and he could feel the tight beads of her nipples beneath the thin silk of her shirt. He didn't care that there were dozens of people below, or that someone could walk in on them at any time. All he could think about was stripping her down and sinking into her. Of coming home.

She moaned as he kissed his way down her neck and marked her—claimed her. His fingers undid the buttons of her shirt, and he kissed a wet trail down to her lace-covered breasts. They were full and swollen, and her nipples strained against the blue lace. He covered her nipple with the heat of his mouth and laved her through the lace. Her fingers tightened in his hair and her hips pushed against him, searching for fulfillment.

"God, you taste so good." He flicked open the front clasp of her bra, and he had to hold back his own release as her breasts spilled into his hands. Christ, he was like a teenager. When was the last time he'd come in his jeans?

"Brant." Her voice hitched and then she screamed as his teeth scraped across her nipple. He soothed it with the flat of his tongue, while his other hand worked at the snap of her jeans.

He kissed his way back up to her mouth, not caring where they were, only how good she'd feel around him. But then he tasted the saltiness of her tears, and the need shattered as he fought to regain control.

He leaned back and looked at her face—a face that had been etched in his mind every day and night for the last few years. Her cheeks were flushed with desire and her lips swollen from his kisses. She'd closed her eyes and tears leaked slowly from the corners, trailing down her cheeks. The thought that he'd hurt her was enough to cripple him, but he didn't know how to fix it. How to right all the wrongs he'd done. He couldn't give her what she needed. What she deserved. But he couldn't make himself stay away. Not any longer.

"Darcy," he said softly, kissing the corner of her mouth. He wiped away her tears with his thumb, and she drew in a shaky breath before pushing at his chest. He backed away slowly and fell into the lone chair that had managed to stay upright in his frenzy to mate with her. Damned if he could find the strength to stay standing.

"Listen—" he said.

"Don't say anything, Brant."

The look on her face had his hands fisting against the arms of the chair and fear gripping his belly.

She sat up on the edge of the table and ran her fingers through her disheveled hair. She refastened her bra and buttoned her blouse with shaky fingers. There was no hiding the obvious—she looked like a woman who'd been thoroughly tumbled.

Darcy was the most beautiful woman he'd ever known. Even when she'd been a smart-assed teenager he'd had to fight his baser needs and the attraction and go elsewhere for a mindless release. And he'd had the pleasure of waiting for the woman he'd glimpsed in the teenager. She'd always belonged to him, whether he'd been able to admit it to himself or not. But he'd screwed up, and now the damage might be too severe for anyone to fix.

"I guess you were right," she said, sliding off the table and tucking her shirt back in. It took her a minute before she was able to look him in the eye, and he didn't like what he saw there. "The ring on my finger can't stop you from taking me. And I guess you proved that it can't stop me from giving in to you. Congratulations, Brant. You got exactly what you wanted."

She looked down at the diamond on her finger, and the sound that came out of her mouth was somewhere between a laugh and a sob.

"But it's just a symbol, Brant. A symbol showing me that someone out there does love and respect me enough to want to spend their life with me. And the symbol on my finger might not stop either of us from taking up where we left off four years ago. But it doesn't matter, because I'm going to stop us."

Her eyes sliced across him with all the anger and heartbreak she was feeling, and he hated himself more than she ever could for putting that look in her eyes.

"You had your chance," she said. "It's someone else's turn now. I'll see this mission out because I know it's the right thing to do. And I'll agree to this stupid cover Declan has thought up because in a twisted way I know it makes sense. But once we're finished I don't ever want to see you again."

Darcy headed to the door, and her hand was on the knob before he found the strength to speak.

"You're lying to yourself," Brant said. "How can you

give yourself to this man when you think you're in love with me?"

He watched her spine stiffen and the shudder that went through her body, and he felt like the lowest kind of bastard. But damned if he was going to let another man have what was his without a fight.

"Easy," she said. "You're the one that taught me that loving and fucking don't necessarily go hand in hand. I don't need one to do the other. And the last time I checked, that's how babies are still made. Thanks for the life lesson, Brant."

Darcy slipped out of the room while he was still frozen in shock. She wanted marriage and children, and sweat broke out on his brow as the thought of providing her with both of those things didn't terrify him as much as it should have. He'd wanted a family of his own once upon a time—with the wife who'd seduced him with her sultry looks and sharp mind. The woman who'd had him so tied up in knots that he'd missed the signs that she might be something more than she'd seemed.

He thought he'd loved Vivian. But he'd found out rather quickly that his instincts were unreliable when it came to the emotion. He hadn't even known that Vivian was really blond and green-eyed until the investigation had begun after her death. But she'd known of his infatuation with Darcy, even though Darcy had barely been eighteen when he and Vivian had married. He'd been twenty-six at the time, and if Vivian hadn't come along and bewitched him he would have ended up claiming Darcy much too young.

Vivian had caught him by keeping her hair colored black and wearing pale blue permanent contact lenses that were an agency standard for deep cover agents. She had looked so much like Darcy he almost hadn't felt guilty for thinking about her while he was buried inside his wife. He'd been young and stupid. And it was those similarities between the two women that had almost cost him his life.

SHADOWS AND SILK

If he'd hesitated just a second longer before pulling the trigger then it would have been him lying six feet under instead of the woman who'd promised to love and cherish him for eternity.

Brant took a long pull of his forgotten beer, and set it back on the table with vicious control. Darcy might have given up on him, and he couldn't say that he blamed her, but he'd come to realize that he couldn't live without her. And he couldn't stand the thought of another man claiming his woman. If he had to fight to keep her, then that's what he'd do.

He only hoped she'd be agreeable to taking what he could give her. He could give her marriage if she had to have it. And God knows if she wanted children then he'd be more than up to the task of providing them. But long gone were the days where Brant Scott gave his heart and soul to one woman. He'd learned that lesson the hard way—with a knife in his back and his illusion of love shattered.

CHAPTER FIVE

Darcy spent a restless night, her body primed for release and the heart she'd spent the last four years mending, cracked and bleeding once again. She'd been able to take care of the first problem—at least she'd taken the edge off—but the second problem wasn't something that could be fixed.

She lay in the oversized bed in her hotel room and stared at the patterns on the ceiling. The covers were twisted around her, and her sleep shirt was still rucked around her waist.

"Damn you," she whispered, not sure if she were cursing herself or Brant. Her body was hot with need, and nothing she'd done had put out the flames.

The ring on her finger was heavy, and she turned it round and round. It had been a stroke of luck Kenneth had proposed only a few hours before her meeting with Brant and her brothers. He'd driven down from his apartment in New York so they could spend the evening together. She'd had no idea he'd planned to propose. Kenneth was the kind of man who wanted stability. Unfortunately, she hadn't been as ready as he was to commit to something long term. They hadn't even been dating exclusively. But he'd been unfazed when she'd turned down his proposal, and he'd insisted she wear the ring for a few days and think about what she really wanted in her future. Unfortunately, what she really wanted was Brant.

There was nothing wrong with Kenneth. They shared common interests—he was Dean of the history department at Columbia where she taught, and they both came from large families. They kept each other mentally stimulated, and she'd had no complaints when she'd finally agreed to share his bed. But he wasn't Brant. And she'd stopped hoping for even a fraction of the pleasure she'd experienced four years before. She'd looked for it, and no one else even came close.

Quite honestly, Kenneth's proposal had taken her completely by surprise. She'd thought the relationship had been waning. They'd started spending more time apart, and she'd never quite gotten around to moving her things to his place like he'd invited her to do. She'd been busy with work, and she could admit she'd taken more lecturing jobs where she had to travel for weeks at a time, so she wouldn't have to make a definite commitment to their relationship. It had been months since she'd shared Kenneth's bed or had time for more than a casual dinner. And he'd felt her restlessness, thinking the cause of it was because she was looking for more of a commitment from him, when in fact it had been the opposite.

Darcy threw back the covers, deciding sleep was never going to come. The sun would be coming up in another hour or so, and there was no reason for her to lie in bed and pretend that the ring on her finger was the real problem. The real problem was Brant had put his hands on her again. And her body had come alive after four years of nothing but the memory of his touch.

He'd ruined her for anyone else. *Damn him.*

"To hell with it," she said, stomping into the bedroom and taking off the ring. She put it inside the little zippered compartment of her makeup bag, and tried not to feel guilty. She'd already tried calling Kenneth when she'd gotten in the night before, but he hadn't answered his phone. He'd probably known she was going to try to break things off for good. She'd just mail the ring back to him with a letter. It was the right thing to do.

Darcy stripped out of her nightshirt and stared at herself in the mirror. She barely recognized the woman she saw there. Her hair was tangled from a sleepless night, and her eyes were wide and full of unfulfilled heat. It hadn't mattered how many times she'd tried to relieve the pressure of Brant's touch through the night. She hadn't had him inside her to quench that need, and her eyes still flamed brightly with desire.

She winced as she saw the mark at her throat. At how he'd branded her. Her nipples beaded to hard points at the memory of his mouth suckling there. Was she stupid for not accepting Kenneth's proposal and spending the rest of her life with nothing more than contentment? Was she wrong to want more?

Darcy jumped in the shower and tried not to think about how sensitized her body was as she lathered the soap and rubbed it across her skin. She stood under the hot spray of the water and closed her eyes, bringing back the feel of Brant's hands and mouth. It was a torture that was almost impossible to ignore.

It wasn't hard to imagine the heat of Brant's mouth worshipping her breasts, suckling her nipples. She moaned as the pleasure ricocheted to the taut bud between the folds of her sex.

Her pussy was slick with need, and her fingers knew exactly where to touch—the right amount of pressure. But she drew it out, imagining Brant's tongue in place of her fingers. She could feel his broad, calloused fingers tracing the outer lips of her vagina before they'd sink inside.

"Yes. Brant," she cried as her fingers moved faster and faster. But nothing was as good as the real thing. His cock was large and thick, and she remembered the way he had to work the mushroom-shaped head inside of her, even though she'd been more than ready to take him.

The liquid heat between her thighs flowed thicker, sweeter, and her knees trembled as she felt the first tremors of her climax. She braced a hand against the cold tile of the shower wall to keep her balance, and when the heat gathered in her clit and spread through her body, it was Brant's name she yelled out as the orgasm rocked through her. Pleasure zinged down her spine, and she held the palm of her hand against her pussy to prolong the feelings.

The tremors finally subsided and she sucked in great gasps of air before dropping to her knees. The water rained down over her bowed head, and her chest was tight with the need to hold back the tears. What the hell was she going to do? She couldn't keep fighting it.

Brant was the only man she'd ever loved. Him walking away hadn't changed those feelings for him, even though she'd prayed she could come to hate him. Could she harden her heart and use him to fulfill the burning sexual needs inside her, and then move on as he had obviously done? She had a career. She was one of the top people in her field. Could she take what he'd offered her the night before and then live out the rest of her life without looking back with regrets? It was time to take care of herself and go into self-preservation mode. No more wishing for things that wouldn't happen, and no more tears.

Darcy turned off the water, her body weak and tired, and she grabbed a thick white towel, wrapping it around her twice as she headed back into the bedroom. Her eyes were heavy with sleep, and she planned to fall face first into the bed until she had to get ready to meet Brant later that morning. But those plans were shot to hell when she saw Declan sitting at the little table in front of the window, a fresh cup of coffee sitting in front of him.

"How the hell did you get in here?" she asked.

"If I told you, I'd have to kill you," he answered with a smile. "You look like hell. Bad night?"

"I can always count on you," she muttered, grabbing a pair of black leggings and an oversized knitted sweater in varying shades of blue from her suitcase. "If you're here to ruin my morning with more good news then I'd like to get dressed first."

Darcy didn't wait for an answer as she slammed into the bathroom and changed clothes. She brushed out her wet hair and decided to let it air dry, and she creamed on moisturizer. Makeup would be wasted on her today. Declan would have to live with looking at the dark circles under her eyes for a while.

When she came back out, he was still in the same spot, but he'd poured her a cup of coffee. She noticed breakfast had also magically arrived, and he took the liberty of removing the silver covers from the tray.

"That food is the only thing saving you right now," she said, sitting across from him and taking a long drink of coffee. The caffeine flowed through her veins, and she decided she might let him live to see another day after the stunt he'd pulled the night before.

"It's a good thing I know you so well," Declan said.

She looked up quickly, wondering how well he really knew her. It was one thing to grow up in a house full of boys who did their best to irritate you at every turn. It was another thing entirely when you grew to adulthood.

"You didn't tell me you were bringing him in for this?" she said, dropping her gaze to her plate so he wouldn't see what that decision had done to her.

Declan had changed over the years. She missed the precocious kid and the devil-may-care teenager he'd been. He'd barely been twenty-one when he'd come home with that jagged scar on his face, and he'd never really been the same since.

She and Declan and Cade looked the most alike of the five MacKenzie siblings—from the black of their hair to the dark gypsy gold of their skin. But none of them shared the same eye color. Hers were bright blue like her dad's,

Cade's were almost black like their mother's, and Declan's were an eerie gray he'd inherited from Grandfather MacKenzie.

"You seemed to handle yourself okay without the knowledge." His gaze was probing, and she busied herself by salting her eggs. "Why should it matter if he's here or not? You agreed to do the job. Is he a deal breaker for you?"

She cut into the omelet on her plate with controlled viciousness so she wouldn't be tempted to stab her brother with her fork. "I'll do the damned job. It just would have been nice to have some information. I don't like going into situations blind. I'm sure you can relate."

"Fine. Next time I need to bring you both in on the same job, I'll make sure to send out a memo."

Darcy all but growled at his highhandedness and stuffed more food into her mouth.

"I don't suppose you want to tell me why the two of you are so hell bent on staying away from each other?" he asked, starting on his own breakfast.

"Not really."

"Darcy—" he warned.

"I'm twenty-eight years old, Dec. You're not my father, and you have no business poking your nose into my personal life."

"Sure I do," he said, cheerily. "It's in the brothers handbook. For instance, is there a reason you're not wearing that giant rock you had on last night? Are congratulations in order for you and Kenneth?"

"You can go now," she said, pushing back from the table. "I've got things to do this morning before I have to start preparing for the honeymoon you so thoughtfully arranged."

Declan's lips quirked in a half smile, and he just stretched his legs out and crossed his ankles, telling her he was going to stay however long he wanted.

"It's probably for the best. Kenneth would've bored

you to tears in a month. You dodged a bullet there."

"Mom should have drowned you at birth."

"I'm sure she feels differently. I'm her favorite you know."

She didn't hear him get up and move in behind her, but she was used to the silent way her brothers moved. When his hand touched her shoulder, she let out a sigh and dropped her head.

"Tell me now, Darcy. Can you work with Brant? I'll kill him if you ask me to, but it'd be a shame to waste a damned good agent."

"I'm sure you think this is funny. All you adrenaline junkie hot shots stick together anyway." She tried to shrug off his hand, but he held tighter and pulled her around to face him. Her head fell to his shoulder, and she realized she'd missed her family over the past few years. She only went home once or twice a year because she was always afraid she'd have to face Brant. She was a coward. And she was tired of running.

"Baby, you're a MacKenzie. There's no one else I'd rather kill for. We stick together. Always."

"I know." Her voice was muffled against his shirt. "I'm sorry. I'm just tired."

"In all seriousness, Darcy. I need you to tell me if working with Brant is going to be a problem. I'm not stupid. I know something happened between the two of you four years ago. I won't ask for details, but this job is important. And it's dangerous. I trust him with your life. But you've got to trust him with it as well."

This was her chance. She could put that ring back on her finger and call Kenneth, agreeing to a lifetime of safety and monotony. Or she could tell Declan she'd spend the next few weeks agreeing to play Brant Scott's wife, sharing his bed and letting the thrill of the hunt feed her need for adventure. Her brothers weren't the only ones who needed that adrenaline rush.

And then she realized maybe Brant wasn't the only

reason to take or decline this job. She needed to do it for herself. She'd been living a half-life for the past few years. She'd focused on her career and building her reputation, but she'd changed as abruptly as Declan had once he'd gotten that scar. The only difference was her scars were on the inside. And it was time to reclaim the woman she'd been before she and Brant had shared more than their bodies.

She took a step back and faced her brother eye to eye. "I can do it," she said. "I *want* to do it."

Dec sighed and nodded. "You know I would have gotten anyone else if I could have," he said. "I looked for months after we'd gotten the intel for someone who fit the description. I'm putting you in danger, and I'm sorry for it."

"I can handle myself."

"Most of the time, I'd agree with that statement. We taught you well. But there are times when you'll need help, and Brant's going to be there to give it to you. I don't want anything to happen to you, Darcy. Shane and I have already come to blows over your involvement. He's really pissed at me right now."

"Tell me something I don't know. He's always the one to throw the first punch."

"In his line of work, that's a good thing. Believe me."

"I'm a big girl. I know what I'm getting into."

"You love Brant." He wasn't asking her a question, but she could hear the worry in his voice.

"I don't want to talk about it."

"There are things you don't know about him, Darcy. Things that make him the way he is."

"So he tells me," she said. "But that doesn't make the feeling go away. Because I know he cares about me too."

"Then you have two choices. You can fight for him and try to change his mind. Or you can enjoy the time you have and be prepared when he walks away."

She paused and looked at him carefully. "You think

he'll walk away," she said, the truth like a slap in the face.

"Yeah," he sighed. "I think he'll walk away."

Darcy felt herself go cold inside and she lifted her chin against the pain. "I can handle it. Like I said, I'm a big girl. I've got my own life, and what Brant Scott decides to do with his is none of my business."

Dec looked at her long and steady—the same look he got on his face whenever he was trying to untangle a puzzle in his head. "I could be wrong. Maybe it is your business. You're not the only one who's changed over the past four years. Brant needs stability in his life. The missions he's leading are getting more and more dangerous. It's only a matter of time before he doesn't come back from one. If you decide to fight for him, then my money is on you."

"There's such a thing as self preservation, Dec. Some things can't be fought for."

"The best things are." The regret in his eyes made her wonder if he knew what he was talking about from firsthand experience.

Darcy nodded and turned around so he wouldn't see the tears that filled her eyes. The expensive luggage and boxes with designer names in the corner of the room caught her attention. She hadn't noticed them before, which told her exactly how far away her mind was. She needed to keep her head in the game. She wasn't in covert ops like her brothers were, but they'd trained her for her own protection. She knew she needed to have her head a hundred percent in the game.

"What's all that?" she asked.

"Brant's been busy. That's your new wardrobe, and a few other things all honeymooners need."

"Fast work," she commented.

"We have all kinds of little tricks up our sleeves. You'll also be armed. Brant said you've been practicing with a Sig instead of the Beretta you used to carry."

"I guess it's stupid to ask how he knows that," Darcy

said.

"Probably. You've also got an assortment of ammunition and fun gadgets to play with. Try not to lose anything. The expense report for this op is ridiculous."

"Not a problem. And maybe when it's all over I'll get to shoot Brant."

"That's the spirit," Dec said, slapping her on the shoulder. "I've got a briefing in an hour. You might not see us down there, Darce, but Shane and I will both be close by. We'll keep you safe. Watch your six, little sister."

"Same to you."

Declan left her suite without a sound, and she went to put the deadbolt on behind him. Not that a deadbolt had kept him out earlier, but she figured most people weren't her brother.

She walked back over to the pile of boxes and saw the small envelope. It was attached to the smallest box—black and glossy with silver scrollwork and a name she didn't recognize.

Brant's handwriting was a bold slash against the creamy envelope, and she pulled it away from the box and then carried them both over to the bed. She had a feeling she'd need to sit down for whatever it was he had to say. With that thought in mind, she decided it might be better to open the box first.

She tossed the envelope aside and lifted the lid of the box. Inside was a smaller box that had her heart catching in her throat. It was a black square jewelry box, and she lifted it out with trembling hands.

Darcy flipped open the lid and gasped at the sight of the wedding rings inside. The wedding ring was a wide band of platinum, simplistic in its beauty. But it was the engagement ring that had her cursing Brant. It's exactly what she'd have picked if it had been her choice. The ring Kenneth had given her was flashy and expensive, but it wasn't her. Leave it to Brant to know her that well and make the wound a little deeper.

LILIANA HART

The engagement ring was a delicate design of small diamonds surrounding a square sapphire. It was old fashioned and unique, and she knew as soon as she put it on her finger that it would seem like it should've always been there. She stubbornly left them in the box and picked up the letter, sliding her finger beneath the sealed flap.

She pulled out the folded sheet of paper and read the short message from her soon to be fake husband, and she wondered if he realized how much of a tactical error it had been to provide her with weapons for this trip.

Darcy,
You'll not wear another man's ring while you belong to me.
~B

A slow death was too good for him. He thought this was a game. Darcy crumpled the note and tossed it into the wastebasket across the room with a shot that would have made Michael Jordan proud. She slipped the rings onto her fingers and wondered if this was what Cinderella had felt like when the slipper fit perfectly.

Brant didn't know what he'd gotten himself into. By the time she was through tying him in knots, he'd know she always played to win. It was never a good idea to underestimate a MacKenzie.

CHAPTER SIX

"If you keep glaring at me like that, no one is ever going to believe we're on our honeymoon," Darcy said, tossing the file she'd been reading into the empty seat next to her.

The back of Brant's neck had been itching and his cock straining since they'd boarded the little private jet back in DC. He didn't have a good feeling about this mission. His mind was so clouded with thoughts of the things he wanted to do to Darcy that he wasn't sure if she was the reason for his unease or some other unknown danger. Either way, he was starting to regret that he hadn't pushed Declan harder to find someone else. Not that Declan would have changed his mind. He could be a single-minded son of a bitch if the circumstances called for it.

"Sure they will, sugar. Everyone looking at us is going to know that you fit me like a glove. Want to try me on for size?"

She'd been driving him crazy for the past hour, seated across from him in jeans and a black sweater. Her hair was piled up on top of her head with little tendrils escaping, and the moment she'd slipped on those black-framed glasses his mouth had started watering. She looked like a sexy librarian.

His dick flexed behind his zipper as she licked her lips

and her gaze lowered to his obvious arousal. The only thing that had kept him from taking her on the plane had been the two-man cabin crew joining them on the flight. He knew damned good and well they'd been hand selected by Declan for a little extra protection. Whether it was protection from him or in case they met with trouble, he wasn't sure.

"Been there, done that—*sugar*," she drawled, making his dick spike even harder. That sassy mouth was going to get her in a whole heap of trouble. "You're a big talker, Brant Scott. But if I remember right, it was me that had to make all the moves four years ago. Maybe you should put your money where your mouth is for once."

Brant laughed softly and leaned back in the leather seat to ease the ache some. He'd always enjoyed sparring with Darcy, and he wasn't going to let her get away with teasing him a second more. But he was also on guard, because damned if that was the response he'd been expecting. She was up to something, no doubt about it. But he was more than willing to take full advantage of her agreeability for the time being.

He'd made a decision the night before. She was going to belong to him no matter what, and he'd give her everything she wanted—marriage and children—as long as she understood he couldn't give her anything more. He didn't believe in love, but he was willing to let her have her illusions. And he couldn't afford to let it break his concentration when he was on a mission. His job was dangerous, and he had no intention of stopping the work he did. It was too important. But going home to Darcy every night was starting to sound better and better.

"My mouth is going to be everywhere," he said, his voice low and laced with warning. "And I'll make you beg for mercy before I stop."

Her mouth opened on a soundless gasp, and he glanced to the front of the plane to make sure the cabin crew was out of sight. He was past the point of caring whether or not they'd run back to Declan and tattle. He moved quickly, unfastening her seatbelt and jerking her so she ended up in his lap.

Before she could protest, her legs straddled his hips and he pushed his erection against the heat of her. His fingers tangled in her hair and he forced her head lower, so he could bite at the sensitive spot at her neck. She moaned loudly, and he soothed the bite with his tongue, tasting her, sipping at her skin like the finest wine.

"Quiet, sugar. Your brother's spies will know what we're doing back here."

Her teeth nipped at his earlobe, and his eyes almost rolled back at the pleasure. He tightened his grip in her hair and pulled her back so they were eye to eye.

"Let's get one thing straight, baby. As far as you making the moves four years ago, I figured at least one of us needed to show some common sense, so don't get cocky. Considering common sense is something I've never heard of you possessing, it was left to me to try to be the voice of reason."

"Yes, I can see that now," she said, fluttering her eyelashes. "Nothing but common sense would've had you fucking me on a front porch in the dead of winter that had just been shot to shit."

His eyes narrowed at the way she so casually tossed off what had happened between them. He'd known from the moment he'd picked her up at the hotel that morning she'd made some kind of decision regarding their current circumstances. She hadn't protested at his touch, and she'd been tempting him like crazy, but she hadn't let him get too personal either. That was going to change. By this time tomorrow, he planned to get as personal as two people could.

"Then taking you on a beach under the hot sun should be a nice change of pace for the both of us. Don't think you can play me, Darcy. When I take you, I'll have all of you. No holding back, sugar."

"Don't think you can play *me*, Brant. When I give myself to you, I'll give exactly what I want you to have and no more. We'll both walk away satisfied. I'm no longer the naïve girl I once was. Now either finish what you started, or I'll do it myself."

Brant took hold of her wrists and kept them bound behind her back with one hand. She pulled and struggled against him, but it was a subtle reminder that she couldn't wrap him around her little finger like she did everyone else. He was the one in control.

"Don't threaten me, baby," he whispered against her lips. "I'll tie you to my bed and pleasure you for hours before I let you get off."

The tension skyrocketed between them, and the plane felt very cramped all of a sudden. He needed her. Desperately.

Darcy melted against him, and she nipped at his bottom lip before sucking it into her mouth. She kissed her way around to the corner of his mouth and up his jaw, her hot little tongue teasing him to the point that he swore he felt every stroke along his cock.

"I didn't get to taste you last time," she purred in his ear.

Come boiled in his balls at the thought, and he squeezed his eyes closed and tried to think of anything else so he wouldn't embarrass himself.

"I wanted to so badly," she said. "To wrap my mouth around you. To lick and stroke and suck until you spilled down my throat."

"Jesus—Darcy," he moaned. Perspiration broke out on his skin and he worked his free hand between them to loosen his pants and relieve the pressure. The thought of her mouth around him was too much to bear.

"Let me," she begged.

He didn't have the strength to say no, so he released her hands. She stroked him through his jeans and he dropped his head back against the seat in pleasure. That's when he felt the prick of the knife at his throat.

He opened his eyes and stared into the furious blue of hers. "I loved you once," she said. "And maybe what I felt for you isn't as distant as I'd like it to be. But gone are the days when you or anyone else will dictate my pleasure. Like I told my brothers, I can take care of myself."

She lied. To herself and to him. He could see the love she had for him was still there. In the way the blue of her eyes softened and her gaze got a little sad. Or maybe that was disappointment. Who the hell knew?

"Maybe you can take care of yourself," he agreed. "At least for a while."

He gripped her wrist, and it went limp in his hand as he hit her pressure point. The knife dropped into his other hand, and he stabbed it into the seat next to them. "But there will always be someone out there you'll lose against. It's the way of the world. Trust no one and take care of yourself. That way you're never disappointed."

Darcy pushed out of his lap and dropped back into the seat across from him. "If you believe that, then you're worse off than I thought. What about my brothers? Your own family? Are you waiting for them to stab you in the back? They love you."

"It's a stupid word that no one knows the real meaning of," he spat out. "It's a fucking fairy tale. I prefer to face reality."

"So you believe Cade and Bayleigh are delusional?" she asked sarcastically. "Your sister and my brother are just caught up in the *fairy tale*, and eventually they'll realize their mistake and go their separate ways? Too bad they're about to bring a child into the world to share their misery. When's the baby due? Another three weeks, right? I guess it's too late now to tell them the truth."

"You're pissing me off, Darcy."

"I guess I wouldn't want to do that," she said, all innocence. "Not when you have my knife."

"Cade and Bayleigh made a promise to each other," he

said. "They'll see it through because that's the kind of people they are."

He hated that she was backing him into a corner. Maybe love was an option for some people. Or even the illusion of love. But not for him. It wasn't worth the cost in the long run.

"And that's all it is? A promise with nothing but vows behind it?"

Darcy stared out the window and fiddled with the rings on her left hand, a nervous gesture he'd rarely seen from her. But the sight of those rings—rings he'd picked himself, even though he'd known he shouldn't make it so personal—made him feel as virile as any male laying claim to a mate. He knew he couldn't love her the way she wanted. But he needed her anyway.

"You're living an illusion," he said softly. She looked up, and what he saw in her face only made him more determined to make her see the truth. "You think you love me. I've seen it in your eyes since you were too young to know any better. But you're fooling yourself if you think it's real. Nothing is forever, sweetheart. And human nature is a fickle thing. You're asking for heartbreak if you think you can give a person everything you have—your heart and soul—and not expect them to trample it to dust."

"I know. It's what I got from you," she said, the aim of her arrow hitting true. "But I still believe in it. I guess if I'm guilty of living an illusion, then you're just as guilty of living in the past. You must have loved her a lot."

Brant's fists clenched tight, and his nails bit into the palms of his hands. The last thing he needed was for Darcy to find out about Vivian. On second thought, maybe that was the best way for her to see the truth. The fact that he'd killed his wife would shatter any illusions Darcy had of true love.

"I need to change clothes," he said abruptly. "We'll be landing in another hour."

Brant grabbed the clothes he'd hung on the back of the

door and escaped into the bathroom. He couldn't force her to see the truth, and he couldn't let himself give into the illusion. Not even for Darcy.

Darcy struggled to push away the anger—the envy of knowing another woman had gotten the love she'd always wanted. She couldn't remember her brothers ever talking about Brant being in a relationship, and he sure as hell never brought a girlfriend around whenever he visited her family. But there had been someone. And Darcy wanted to know what the woman had done to him.

She grabbed her knife out of the seat and put it back in the sheath inside her boot. Declan was going to have questions about the damage to his plane, and she'd never hear the end of it if he learned the truth.

Her body was strung taut, and her silk panties were soaked with the need for fulfillment. Damn him for bringing her so close, only to ruin it at the last minute.

She was lying to herself. She'd never stopped loving him. And the attraction between them was even stronger than it had been four years ago. They'd both changed individually, and those changes had only intensified the sexual chemistry.

The glimpses of danger she saw in him didn't scare her away. She loved the way he touched her, the way he demanded that she surrender. Even now, her breasts felt full and heavy and her clit throbbed, begging for attention. And there was nowhere she could go to find relief. Not without him knowing.

She gathered her files and went to the long conference table that sat on the opposite side of the aisle. If anything, Declan always made efficient use of his time and work space, so his plane was set up much like a boardroom. Maps and photographs lay in rigid order on the mahogany surface, and she added the new pictures she'd found after Declan had left her hotel room earlier that morning.

More women were dead. The body count had only increased over the past months since she'd been deciphering the glyphs. The problem was they were always a step behind. Ramos hadn't put the drug *Rabbit* out on the worldwide market yet. It wasn't even the exact same drug the del Fuego cartel had been distributing four years ago. But it was still just as deadly. Even more so, if such a thing were possible.

The Sinaloa cartel and Ramos had made their name and fortune from cocaine distribution. And once he'd successfully taken over the del Fuego cartel and moved the labs, he'd had the scientists experiment with the original formula. They'd targeted individual women at first. Mostly American tourists.

The core of *Rabbit* was the same. It was a date rape drug, plain and simple. It was topical, which is what made it different from other date rape drugs. Only a small amount had to touch the skin for it to be effective—easy for anyone to administer by jostling or bumping the victim in a crowd or dancing too close at a club. It took less than a minute to take effect—for the vicious heat to take hold and the lust to compromise all rational thought. It was a drug that made the victim seem like the willing, even though those who'd survived had heard their own screams of refusal in the backs of their minds even as they'd welcomed the next waiting man into their arms.

But Ramos had decided to cut the drug with a little cocaine, and the results had tripled the death count. The cocaine added a violence and adrenaline rush to the victim. The crime scenes had been horrendous. She'd seen some of the photographs. At least the ones Declan had cleared her to see. The damage a hundred and twenty pound woman could do to a full grown man—several full grown men—with the right mix of chemicals in the system was jaw dropping. The victim had killed more than one of her attackers before her body had finally overtaxed itself and she'd gone into cardiac arrest.

Ramos had had to readjust several times over the last year before he had a saleable product, and it looked like he'd finally found the right amount of cocaine to lace in the drug. It was just enough to make the victim think she was having a good time, and keep her alive a few hours longer than the original drug. Until her heart finally gave out from exertion. The lust didn't dissipate over time. The more orgasms you had, the more you wanted.

Darcy took off her glasses and rubbed her eyes. The deaths were increasing in frequency, and she knew it was because Ramos had perfected the formula and was ready to hold an auction for major buyers all over the world. And that's where her expertise came into this. She lined up the pictures of the newest hieroglyphs—nothing more the crude graffiti drawn onto the side of a building. The note Declan had attached said they were only two days old.

Ramos's men were using the glyphs as coordinates for drop locations. It was part of the reason Ramos hadn't been caught. He had thousands of men to take the fall for him. The glyphs were a map of sorts. Ramos would deliver the drug to his cartel members, and then they'd use the glyphs as a map to find the location of the buyer. It was a well-organized network. No two people doing the same job twice. Unfortunately, the bodies they'd been finding also matched the coordinates of where the buys were taking place. They were testing out the merchandise on site and then disappearing like rats back to their holes.

The bathroom door opened and Darcy watched Brant from the corner of her eye. He didn't look at her, but she knew he was aware of everything she was doing. His shoulders were tense and his jaw clenched in anger. She'd struck a nerve asking about the other woman. At least she knew for sure that her hunch had been right.

He'd taken the time to shave, and he'd changed into natural linen pants and a green island shirt the same color as his eyes. He wore loafers without socks, and she noticed he wore a wedding band on his finger that matched hers. The sight of it gave her a little thrill she couldn't explain, even though she knew they were pretending. She couldn't help but drink in the sight of him. He was so big. So—male. He dominated every space he was in. No one should be that sexy. He turned her on in ways that should be sinful, but it didn't stop the wanting. She lusted for him. Ached for him.

The muscles in his shoulders and back bunched as he pulled a heavy case from an overhead compartment, and she had to roll her eyes at the distraction he presented. It was a damned good thing he hadn't been around the last four years or she never would have finished her doctoral dissertation.

Her eyes widened as Brant unlatched the case and pulled out a pistol. He checked it over thoroughly and then popped in a magazine before putting it at the small of his back.

"I didn't realize we were going in armed," she said, turning to face him. He kept his back to her and his attention on inspecting the other weapons. "I don't think I have a place to put my gun in any of the outfits that were packed for me."

"*We're* not going in armed. *I'm* going in armed. Always be prepared for the worst. Even at five star resorts."

"I'm sure that'll be a great relief to the masseuse when we get our couples massage. Let's hope she doesn't pull the trigger on that stick up your ass."

Brant stopped what he was doing and turned to face her, his expression thunderous. If she'd had room to back away she might have given in to the temptation. He was pissed. Though the day had been pretty varied so far, so she wasn't sure what, exactly, he was angry about.

"One day, Darcy," he said menacingly, stalking her like a big cat, "You're going to push me too far. And I'm going to be forced to bend you over my knee for the spanking you deserve."

Her ass clenched and the throb between her legs quickened. It took everything she had to let amusement cross her face instead of the lust she was feeling.

"In your dreams, lover boy. Now if you've finished your dom fantasies, I've finished deciphering the glyphs Declan left me this morning."

She should have been warned by the thin smile that spread across his face that she was in deep trouble. Some day she was going to learn to keep her mouth shut. Her brothers had been warning her for years that it was going to get her into trouble one day.

He kept coming toward her, and she had to lift her chin to keep eye contact.

"They're not just fantasies, baby," he whispered. "Your sweet ass is mine. It's going to burn red from my hand, which is nothing more than you deserve after all the stunts you've pulled. You think you're hiding how much the thought of that turns you on? I can read you like a book, sugar, and your nipples are hard enough to cut glass. Now show me what you've found before I bend you over this table and give the babysitters your brother sent something to report."

"What makes you think I'd protest?" she purred.

His nostrils flared and a growl rumbled in his chest. "You are so fucked, baby. The minute we get to the hotel." He inhaled deeply and took a step back. "Now tell me about the damned glyphs, and stop distracting me."

Her heart thudded in her chest and her pussy was weeping anticipation. Damn him for being able to do that to her. Just a look. Barely a touch. And she was ready to welcome him between her thighs like the Prodigal Son. She braced her hands on the table and pointed to the map.

"The resort we're staying at is here." She'd already circled the location in red marker. "And the glyphs were found at the ruins at Bonampak, about an hour or so away. The wording is vague, but I think we're either looking at

Chiapa de Corzo or San Cristobal for their next location. The outer limits of the towns are sparsely populated and there are miles of nothing, so it would be very easy to transfer the drug without being seen. Or they might have been seen and no one cares, because those cities are in Ramos territory."

"Shane reported in that a body was found in Chiapa de Corzo early this morning," he said. "I just got off the phone with him a few minutes ago. His team is already checking out the area, but they're lying low so no one suspects they're there. We can't let Ramos find out we have men in place."

A sigh escaped before she could stop it and she dropped her head. "I was hoping I could relay the message in time to get someone in place. Before they killed someone else. Too many lives have been lost, and I can't stop it."

"Those deaths lie on Alexander Ramos's shoulders," he said. "Not yours. We'll get him. And then we'll make him pay."

"That won't bring these women back to their families."

"No," he said, running his hand down the back of her hair in a gesture so gentle it almost brought tears to her eyes. "But it'll save the ones he hasn't gotten to yet."

"The resort we're staying at is in a good location. We've got the ocean to our backs, and the cities where each of the hieroglyphs were found are no more than a two or three hour drive in any direction."

"But we need to find the lab site, not go over old ground," she protested. "They haven't repeated any of the drop locations and Ramos wouldn't have his men making the drops too close to where he has the lab set up. I think I've got the lab possibilities narrowed down to two locations. Both within the fifty-mile radius Declan asked for. But it's impossible to know for sure. Ramos has had four years to build the labs, and there hasn't even been a whisper of suspicious activity for a project of that magnitude anywhere in Mexico."

"The lab won't be far from where these hits are happening. It takes about twenty hours to drive from one end of his territory to the other, but only a couple of hours by plane. Ramos isn't known for his delegation skills. He likes to know what's going on in his cartel on every level. And visiting the drop locations is exactly what we need to do. It won't take them long before they start noticing how closely we're tracking the coordinates. Ramos will have eyes on us within a couple of days. And then we'll have fireworks."

Brant traced his fingers across the map—along the routes she'd plotted—and the image of how those hands had touched her so skillfully had her biting back a whimper.

"Ramos is smart. He's been patient and he's kept low. After Carlos and Miguel del Fuego were killed, all the street traces of *Rabbit* were found and discarded. Or so we thought. We kept our eyes on Colombia, because we knew that's where the del Fuegos had set up their original labs, and the del Fuegos were enemies of both Mexican cartels, so we knew they wouldn't have moved their operation into enemy territory.

"There were rumblings Ramos had slowly gained control of the cartel, but no solid proof. Some of the del Fuego cartel's top lieutenants were found dead, but once again, we couldn't prove it was Ramos behind the killings. So after a year of no new movement or related drug deaths, the DHS and DEA were ordered to cut the number of agents they had in the area because of budgetary issues. And now we don't have the men we need in place to bring them down as easily."

"Well, there's us," she said, raising a brow.

"That's what scares me." He moved in close, trying to intimidate her with his size, but she stood her ground. "You don't understand how fucking dangerous this is, Darcy. We're bait, sugar. And I'm going to strangle your brother the next time I see him for putting you in this position. You think I can't see the need for the thrill in your eyes? I hate knowing that you're going to be a moving target if they get wind of what we're doing, and it scares the hell out of me that I might not be able to save you."

"Brant—"

He touched her lips with his fingers, stopping her from reminding him that she could take care of herself. He leaned in closer—so close that she felt the breath of his words against her cheek.

"Listen to me, and listen close, because I'm only going to say this once. There's something about you, baby. Something that's always drawn me closer to you, even though I knew damn good and well I should be pushing you away. You filled my mind with thoughts I shouldn't have been having when you were too young for me to act on them. And now you've got me so twisted up inside I worry that I won't see the danger until it's too late."

The truth of his words slammed into her. He was telling her that he understood they belonged together, but he didn't like it, and he'd continue to fight it.

She drew the finger touching her lips into her mouth. Her teeth nipped at the calloused pad of his finger before drawing it further inside. His breath grew heavy, and she could feel his erection growing against her stomach.

"You were too young for me then," he said. "And in ways, you're still too young for me. I should have never touched you four years ago, but I couldn't seem to help myself. Just like I know I'll touch you again before it's all said and done."

The whimper escaped before she could control it, and her eyes fluttered closed as his other hand traced the underside of her breast.

"I know I'm no damned good for you, and your brothers should have shot me for touching you. And believe me, baby. They know I've touched you."

She jerked back, her breath heaving and fire in her eyes

as she heard him try to explain that he wasn't good enough for her. That was a bullshit excuse if she'd ever heard one. Something much deeper was keeping him from loving her the way they were meant to love. She placed her hand over his heart, the steady beat a comfort beneath her palm.

"But you've always been a light to my darkness, baby. And if anything happens to you I don't think my soul can survive it. If I think for one second that you're in danger while we're on this mission, I'm going to throw you over my shoulder and hide you away for good, Ramos and your brothers be damned."

He backed away and the softness that had been in his face for that brief moment was gone, replaced by the determined hardness of his jaw. She was pissed off and turned on in equal measure, and she was just about to open her mouth to let him have it when he turned his back and walked away.

"You'd better get dressed. We're already starting our descent."

She stalked into the bathroom and slammed the door behind her. It was either that or start screaming.

CHAPTER SEVEN

"**O**h, hell no," Brant said, as Darcy came out of the bathroom fifteen minutes later.

The cobalt blue bikini top was nothing more than two tiny triangles and string, showcasing her firm, round breasts to perfection. The matching sarong she wore barely covered her ass, and he had a feeling if he ever saw the bikini bottoms he'd go into cardiac arrest. Her black hair fell down her back in waves, and if the sway of her hips was anything to go by, she knew exactly how damned sexy she looked.

"You're changing the minute the wheels touch the ground. You can't traipse around Mexico half naked."

"Don't worry, sugar. I found the perfect place for my knife."

The teasing glint in her eyes and the images that one statement brought to mind had all the blood pooling below his waist. He sucked in oxygen and stared hard at her as she calmly strapped herself back into her seat to prepare for landing. His gaze ran up the length of her legs, from the tips of her scarlet toes all the way up to the smooth, dusky thighs that felt like silk when wrapped around him. The sight of her had stolen his breath, and he was so hard he could barely sit to strap himself in.

"You're changing," he growled. "And that's final." His

voice sounded like a stranger's—broken and husky.

She picked up a magazine and started flipping through it. "Everything in the boxes you dropped off for me looks like this. I guess you weren't the one to select all my clothing?"

"No," he scowled. But he was going to murder Jade the first chance he got. The agencies had every want and need right at their fingertips, and Jade had been the only available female in the area since the plan had been for her to arrive in Mexico with Max as another couple at the resort. Brant had only had one request—that she pick a lot of blue. Darcy looked like a goddess in blue. But Jade, sick sense of humor that she had, decided to make his life a living hell by clothing Darcy in as little blue as possible.

"I got the impression I'm supposed to play the part of trophy wife." She smirked at him over the top of her magazine. "I'll tell everyone I'm your much younger second wife since you've always been so worried about our age differences."

If only she knew how right she was. His back teeth clenched together and he knew the expression that came over his face—the one the other DHS agents called his killing mask. Thoughts of his first wife never made him feel anything but anger. Or the need to kill her all over again for ruining the one thing that had brought innocence and purity to his savage life.

Brant hated the hurt look he'd put on Darcy's face. Of course she didn't understand his reaction to what should have been a simple joke, but even the mention of his wife made him freeze. He didn't speak another word to her as the plane finally landed, and he grabbed the emergency bag with extra cash, passports and guns, and slung it over his shoulder. Their bags would be brought to the resort by their "guards," and he and Darcy would drive separately.

Their covers were firmly in place and fairly straightforward. As Brandon Kane, he'd earned his money the old-fashioned way—by inheriting it. And then he'd tripled his wealth by making healthy investments and buying up real estate. Darcy had been right about her cover. She was his much younger third wife, and the only thing she needed to worry about was staying barely dressed and trying to seduce him. The high profile cover was the easiest way to fly in his own personal entourage and use Declan's private plane.

"Here are your keys," one of Declan's men said. "The green Jeep is yours. We'll follow behind you in the black one." The agent stared down at Darcy, an uncomfortable look coming into his eyes. "I'm supposed to give you a message from your brother."

"Why am I not surprised by that," she said, narrowing her eyes. "What is it?"

"He says to ease off your new husband and stay out of trouble."

Brant recognized the look that came into her eyes, and he took a step closer just in case he needed to protect the man.

"Since you've done such an excellent job of spying for my brother, why don't you give him a message back for me." The agent took a small step back and Brant couldn't say he blamed him. "Remind him mom and dad still don't know who hid the firecrackers under the wood in the fireplace. Last time I checked, mom was still mad that her brand new leather sofa was burned down to the stuffing."

Brant's lips twitched because he'd heard the story told a million times at different MacKenzie gatherings, and it was still a sore subject that no one would ever confess to, though it had happened almost twenty years before.

Darcy left Declan's agent shaking in his boots, and Brant followed the twitch of her hips down the stairs and into the bright sun. They both slipped on their sunglasses and into the dark green Jeep that had been left for their use. He couldn't see her eyes behind the dark glasses, but he could tell by the stiffness in her shoulders that she was still upset about his reaction earlier. And when Darcy was hurt, she got pissed. They were in for a long drive.

The resort where they were staying was an oasis in the desert—a mile long driveway lined with palm trees, and the ocean playing as backdrop to a white stucco palace that promised luxury at every turn.

They were greeted at the door by men dressed in matching khaki shorts and white flowing button up shirts with the hotel logo over the heart. Drinks appeared in their hands, and the cold air in the lobby was a welcome respite after the three-hour drive they'd just made.

Brant put his hand at the small of Darcy's back and she stiffened under his touch, only to relax immediately once she remembered the roles they were playing. She downed the fruity concoction in her glass and then turned to smile up at him, though he could see the strain around the edges.

An older man dressed in khakis and a white polo approached them. He had a distinguished look about him, and Brant knew from the dossier gathered about the resort that they were about to meet the owner himself.

"Mr. and Mrs. Kane," the owner said, his smile genuine. "I'm Marco Luna, and I'm happy to welcome the both of you to La Luna Resort and Spa. Congratulations on your marriage. Everything has already been taken care of for your arrival. You have the honeymoon beachside villa for the duration. Please let us know if we can do anything for you."

Brant took advantage of the moment and pulled Darcy closer, sliding his hand around her bare waist. Her skin was warm and smooth as silk, and he smiled as he felt her breath catch. Her body never lied when it came to the effects of his touch.

"We'd like to get settled as soon as possible" he said. "It's been a long drive, and I'm sure my wife would like to freshen up and rest for a while."

"Of course, of course," Mr. Luna said.

He had to give the owner credit. He kept his eyes on Darcy's face instead of checking out her body like every other man in the hotel. The possessiveness Brant felt had him scowling in warning at those who looked her over a little too long. Including Max, that bastard, who was having a drink at the bar with a woman who was as scantily clad as Darcy.

"Your luggage has just arrived, and our bellmen will have it delivered to you shortly. My son will be over soon to personally take you to your villa." Marco looked around and his smile dimmed. "If you'll excuse me, I'll go get my son. Please, enjoy another drink," he said, signaling to a waitress from the bar.

Brant waited until Darcy had another drink in her hand before he spoke. "The first item on the agenda is to find you something decent to wear," he said. "It appears I'm the jealous sort after all. And if I have to stand here and watch one more man stare at you like you're his greatest fantasy, then I'm going to end up killing someone."

He flinched as she pinched his side and wiggled that hot little body closer. His cock responded immediately, and he turned slightly so she hid his erection from public view. His heart thudded painfully in his chest as he felt the softness of her breasts against his chest.

"You'll just have to deal with it," she purred, kissing his chest as she cradled his hardness against her belly.

"You expect me to deal with it? I'm not Kenneth, sweetheart. You won't walk all over me." Things were about to get out of control. He could feel it.

Darcy's hand slipped under his shirt and her nails scraped across the rigid muscles of his abdomen. "I'll walk wherever I damned well want to. Stop acting like a caveman. It's ninety degrees outside in October, and we're at a resort. Look around you. I'm wearing more than a lot of the women here, including that woman by Max who looks like she wants to stab him with the toothpick in her martini glass."

Brant grunted, but couldn't seem to tear his eyes away from the vixen in front of him to see what was happening between Max and Jade. "Stop wiggling that sweet pussy against me or that's about to change. My control is at its limit, Darcy."

"Speaking of wiggling," Darcy said, running those long, slim fingers up and down his arm. He caught her hand and kissed her palm before nipping at each of her fingers. Her nipples spiked to hard points beneath the excuse for a bathing suit top, and if someone didn't come and show them to their room soon, he was going to look for the nearest dark corner so he could relieve the ache in his balls.

"Who's that woman with Max?" she asked, her voice breathy.

"I haven't noticed any other women since we walked in. Just you."

Brant skimmed his fingers over her bare middle and slid them under the fabric of her bikini top, rubbing slow circles on underside of her breast. They were pressed together in the middle of the hotel lobby, the stolen touches hidden from the smattering of other couples scattered around, but it was obvious that *something* naughty was happening between them. Her hands clenched against his shirt, and he could see the pulse pounding in her throat.

"Liar," she moaned against him. "You always notice everything."

"That's Jade. You'll get a chance to meet her later."

"Stop teasing me," she moaned. "Unless you're living out some exhibitionist fetish that I don't know about."

He chuckled and removed his fingers from her bikini top. "You're the tease. And I'm past the point of caring who's watching so long as I can be inside you." She shuddered against him and he held her close as their bodies settled down.

"She's beautiful," Darcy said out of the blue. "Jade, I mean."

There was no doubt that Jade was a beautiful woman. She was tall, a couple of inches shy of six feet, and she had a lean muscular body and arms like Linda Hamilton's in Terminator 2. Her skin was the color of dark caramel and her black hair was cut in a pixie style around her angular face. Her green eyes matched her name, and the exotic tilt of them reminded him of a sorceress ready to cast a spell. You couldn't tell by looking at her that she could kill a man with only the touch of her fingertips.

"What's beautiful is the way that woman handles a weapon," Brant said. "You'll never meet a better sniper. She's saved all our asses at one point or another."

Darcy shifted again, and he had to bite back a groan at the way she fit against him. He leaned down and kissed his way up her cheek to her ear and whispered, "You know you're driving me crazy, don't you, sugar?"

He felt her smile against his chest. "Of course. But if it makes you feel any better I want you so bad I can barely breathe."

"God, Darcy," he groaned. "We need to talk before we let this go any further. There's no doubt I'm going to be sliding into that hot pussy before the day is out, but there are things we need to discuss."

"There's no need to discuss anything," she said, her eyes wide and serious. "I've made a decision, and I think we can have fun these next weeks without any of the baggage you despise. And if you don't have me naked and screaming in the next forty-five minutes, I'm going to cause a riot. I'm a big girl this time around, Brant. I don't expect anything more than you can give me. And when you walk away, I'll finally be able to move on to the next stage of my life without any regrets."

"Will it be so simple to move on, Darcy?" he asked, his heart clutching at the thought of how cold she sounded.

How final. "I've made some decisions of my own. What if neither of us walk away this time?"

She pulled back so there was a hairsbreadth of space between them, but he couldn't read her expression for once. "What are you saying, Brant? That you want to get married and live happily ever after? Has an alien taken over your body or something?"

He swallowed and nodded his head. "I'll marry you. I can give you that promise. We both keep our promises. And I can give you children."

Her lips trembled with emotion and she shook her head in denial. "What about love, Brant? Can you give me that, or are you making some magnanimous gesture just so you can get your cake and eat it too? Because really, it's not a problem. I'll give you the cake for free, *and* let you eat it."

Something terrible felt like it was ripping inside of him, but he knew that more than one set of eyes were on them, so he pulled her back into his arms and buried his face against her neck to hide the sudden tension between them. He got the feeling that she was mocking him, but he hadn't seen any humor in her face.

Isn't this what she wanted?

"So you're telling me you won't marry me unless I pretend to give you an emotion that doesn't even exist?" he asked, fury touching his voice. "I could just lie and say the words you wanted to hear. That's what most people do, isn't it? I thought you of all people would want to approach something like this with honesty, but I can say the words if you need to hear them that bad."

"We should talk about this later," she said. "People are staring at us."

"They're staring at you because you look like sin and sex. And I think we should definitely talk about this now."

Brant felt something close to panic rise up and grip his heart, and he looked around for a place where they could talk privately. He caught Max's eye and the other man raised his brow in question, but Brant ignored him. He'd never thought Darcy wouldn't want to marry him. It wasn't an option now that he'd made up his mind, and that might make him the worst kind of arrogant bastard, but he was giving her the future she'd spoken of less than twenty-four hours before. What more could she want from him? He never thought he'd be able to offer her even that much.

"Stay here," he said, leaving her alone as he headed to one of the bellboys who was loading up their luggage on a cart. He got directions to their cottage in broken English, but he got the general idea, and tipped him twenty bucks for his help.

Something more was driving him now, and he was sorely afraid it was because Darcy had set the stakes higher and he was at risk of losing something he hadn't known he'd had. He cared for her, and the thought of her belonging to him forever was starting to sit comfortably on his shoulders. He could trust her. She wasn't like Vivian, no matter how much they resembled each other in looks.

Brant made his way back to Darcy and grabbed her by the hand, leading her out into the tropical gardens that surrounded the resort. The pathways were mostly deserted, but just to be safe he veered off to one of the lesser-worn areas.

"Brant, you're overreacting," Darcy hissed. "You don't really want to marry me, so what the hell is all of this about? I told you, I'm happy to scratch your itch. You'll be doing me a favor by scratching mine right back. You're acting like a spoiled child who isn't getting his way."

Brant lifted her over a fallen palm tree, and he slowed his pace when a pink stucco building came into view. He pushed her towards one of the two wooden doors, not caring which one they entered.

"Are you insane," she said, her voice strangled. "This is the ladies room. Someone will come in."

He looked around the small space and grunted,

satisfied that the room was empty. He was losing his mind. There was no other explanation. Of course, he'd lost it four years ago when he'd been buried deep inside the spitfire beside him.

"No they won't," he said, locking the door behind them. "This is a lot nicer than the men's room. No wonder it always takes women so long."

The floor was square adobe tiles and the countertop was a quartz granite that picked up the colors in the floor and walls. A small wicker loveseat and two chairs sat against the opposite wall, and lotions and tanning oils were lined across the counter. It was clean and smelled of lemons, and best of all, it was private.

"I think you're insane," she said. "I don't understand this at all."

"Men tend to lose their minds when women are involved. Now answer my question. Do you need to hear the words before you'll marry me?"

Her eyes narrowed and her hands fisted at her waist. "Of course I need to hear them, you dumbass. But what you don't understand is that I need you to mean them. That's why I won't marry you. Now let me the hell out of this bathroom so I can go enjoy my goddamned honeymoon."

He caught her as she tried to walk past him and lifted her against him, dodging the knee she tried to jab between his legs and the elbow that glanced off his jaw. He hoisted her up on the counter and pushed her legs apart. The kiss he gave her was rough, a kind of conquering, and his teeth nipped at her bottom lip once before his tongue slipped inside and devoured. His hand fisted in the back of her hair and he yanked so her mouth was tilted higher, and he felt triumph as she moaned into his mouth.

Her nails raked over his chest and her fingers gripped his shirt and ripped it open, sending buttons scattering across the floor. They broke apart, panting for breath and staring at each other as if they were strangers. He shouldn't take her in anger—he knew that deep down—but dammit, he *was* angry. And hurt. Her logic didn't make sense to him.

She licked her swollen lips and leaned up so she could kiss her way across his chest. And then she bit him—hard—and he lost the rest of his control completely. Maybe she was a little angry too.

He pushed her thighs wider apart and growled at the sight of the G-string that was barely covering the folds of her pussy. The fabric was dark with her desire, and he slipped his fingers beneath the fabric and touched the syrupy folds. They both groaned at the touch, but he wanted so much more. He wanted to brand her—to make her his in every way. His hand fisted around the fabric and he tugged sharply, tearing it from her body and letting the tatters fall to the ground.

"Fucking beautiful," he rasped, pushing her legs further apart so she was completely bared to him. "Look at that sweet cream waiting to cover my cock. I want to taste you, but that'll have to wait. I'm too impatient."

"Brant," she cried as he slid two fingers inside of her without warning, thrusting hard and fast and taking her right to the edge of pleasure before she could draw a breath. He pulled the cups up her bikini top down so her breasts were exposed and his mouth clamped over a turgid nipple, sucking it with hard stroked that had her pussy rippling around his fingers.

"You'll be the death of me," he said, kissing his way to her other breast and this time scraping the nipple with his teeth. "My greatest distraction."

"So walk away," she said through gritted teeth. "Take what you want and then leave."

His fingers pushed deep inside of her and then he stopped moving, feeling the way she clamped around him and the pulsing tissue that signaled she was about to come.

He kept his hand still, his thumb pressing over the hard bud of her clit, and he slowly curled his fingers inside of her until he found the raspy tissue that made her eyes roll back in her head.

"There, baby," he whispered. "There it is. You're so fucking tight. So wet." He rubbed his fingers over the spot in slow circles, and her body jerked like it was being shocked.

"Pl—please," she begged. "I can't stand it."

"Is this all we have between us, Darcy? This endless need to fuck? I thought you loved me."

Her hips moved against him—thrusting and undulating—searching for release, and his fingers stilled until she opened her eyes and looked at him.

"What do you care?" she said. "According to you, my love isn't real anyway. It's a lie, right? So just fuck me and let's move on."

Something snapped inside of him. He'd always found comfort in the way she'd loved him. In the way he could count on her to be there through the years and warm the cold places in his heart. But when he looked at her now, he couldn't see that warmth any longer, and it terrified him. Because the look on her face reminded him of the way Vivian had once looked at him, when he'd been buried balls deep inside the woman who was supposed to love and honor him. He'd been too caught up to realize what she had planned until she stabbed him in the back with the blade she'd hidden under her pillow. The way she'd climaxed around his cock while she waited for him to die was imprinted in his nightmares forever.

He closed his eyes and pushed the memory away. Vivian wasn't Darcy. He knew that deep down. He also knew what it felt like to be on the receiving end of Darcy's love. And now he knew what it felt like when it disappeared.

"Damn you," he whispered. "Don't shut down on me. I want everything."

His fingers moved faster inside of her while his thumb rasped over her clit with every stroke. Her head banged against the wall, but she either didn't notice or didn't care. Mewling cries escaped from her throat and her arms collapsed so she fell back against the counter. He took a nipple between his thumb and finger and squeezed, and then shot her into ecstasy.

He was wild and hungry for her, an animal who needed to give her the sharp edge of pain and pleasure to justify his own. And then he felt the ripples start from deep inside her. Her pussy clamped around his fingers like a vise, and she cried out in delirium. Her nails dug into his arms as liquid pleasure coated his fingers and ran down her thighs. The climax milked his fingers and all he could think about was how it would feel against his dick.

"Fuck, yes, baby," he groaned, jerking at the button on his pants and freeing his cock. He gripped the base tight in his hand, holding back the come already boiling in his balls, and he slowly withdrew his fingers from her vagina. She whimpered and went lax, her body melting against the counter.

He moved between her thighs and lifted one of her legs so if rested on his shoulder. Perspiration glistened on their skin and he rubbed his dick against the folds of her sex, causing her to moan with aftershocks from her orgasms.

"Look at that, baby. Look how I'm going to stretch you."

The head of his cock was dark and angry looking, swollen and flared, and he waited until her eyes opened and traveled down the length of her body to where their flesh joined. He pushed the head of his cock inside and gritted his teeth. She was wet, but her tissues were swollen from the orgasm, so he still had to work himself inside of her. The muscles in his thighs strained to hold back, and then he remembered the condom he had in his pocket. He never in his life resented the use of protection more than in that moment.

"Look at me, Darcy," he said, pulling out and then pushing his way back in, going deeper this time. Her eyes lifted to his and he saw arousal and defeat in their depths. "This thing we have between us isn't going to go away. Why wouldn't you want it forever if you could have it?"

Brant repeated the motion—pulling all the way out and pushing in twice more until he was finally seated to the hilt. Even completely still, he could feel her vaginal walls milking at him, undulating against him in a torture bound to make him lose his mind.

He cursed viciously and pulled out, reaching for the condom in his pocket. He tore the packet with his teeth and rolled the condom over his shaft, praying the thin layer of latex would help him last longer than thirty seconds. Her breasts were framed and pushed together by her swimsuit, and her breath heaved in and out of her chest as she lifted her hips to meet him.

"Answer me, Darcy," he said.

"You wouldn't understand," she said. "Stop torturing me and just do it, dammit."

He heard the frustration and tears in her voice, and he didn't know what made him keep prodding her for an answer. The answer he wanted.

"Tell me what I don't understand, baby." He pushed inside her slowly, watching as her flesh sucked him inside, and a wave of heat stole his breath and tore through his body. "Tell me," he demanded.

Her head dropped back and she closed her eyes, so he couldn't see to deep inside of her. "You are what you are. I can't change that, no matter how much I once loved you. Marrying you and loving you would destroy what's left of the feelings I have for you, Brant. And I'd wither away waiting for you to return those feelings."

"You don't know that." He pushed her knees up so they rested by her shoulders, and he knew he couldn't wait much longer. "We could be happy." He felt her hands reach down and take hold of his hips, and before he understood what she was going to do, she impaled herself on his cock, and he sank into the greedy depths of her pussy.

"God, Darcy," he groaned.

"No more talking. Just fuck me, Brant," she panted. "Please."

Her words pushed him past that last edge of control, and he slammed inside of her over and over again. She refused to look at him, to make that connection that had once been so special the last time they'd come together. Hopelessness and anger built up inside of him and he was relentless in his pursuit for her pleasure. Her screams echoed in the tiled room and she grabbed her breasts, tweaking the nipples between her fingers and making his balls tighten at the sight.

"Is this what you want, Darcy?" he said, the violence barely restrained. "Nothing but a good fuck now and then, and then we can all go back to the way things were? Like it never happened?"

His hands went beneath her ass, and he lifted her, changing the angle so his cock hit something that made her go wild beneath him.

"Yes, damn you. It's all I want."

"Then so be it." His hips jackhammered inside of her, and her pussy clenched around him in one long shuddering pull. They cried out together as they came. Electricity shot down his spine and pleasure thundered though his veins as he jerked against her one last time, semen shooting in powerful spurts that left his knees weak but his heart cold and empty.

His body trembled and his cock flexed within her, still spilling into the condom he knew had just been torn to shreds by his release. He'd felt the power behind his orgasm and known the second the latex had burst open.

"And sometimes it all comes down to fate," he whispered, feeling the stickiness of his come between her thighs.

"Wha—" Darcy said, barely coherent. Her face was pale and she struggled to get her eyes open. He thought she would have slept just where she was if he hadn't pulled out of her body.

"Are you on birth control?" he asked.

Her eyes opened a little wider at that and she looked down to the shredded condom he was discarding.

"I—um—I'm on a light dose. To keep my periods regular."

"If you get pregnant, you'll marry me. I mean it, Darcy. That's not something I'll budge on. My child will have a father around."

"Fine, but you don't have anything to worry about. The timing's off, and you'll have to ask fate to lend you a helping hand some other time. Or maybe I should buy the condoms next time," she said, pushing him back so she could slide off the counter.

He moved back and shook his head at her denial. Her hands trembled as she retied the sarong and tried to cover the fact she no longer had on a bathing suit bottom, and he knew the sudden show of nerves was because she knew as well as he did how powerful that release was. She couldn't *not* be pregnant after that. And she knew it as well as he did, timing be damned.

He adjusted his pants and left his shirt hanging open since it no longer had buttons, and he waited patiently as she wet some paper towels and tried to clean away the evidence of their passion.

"So you agree?" he asked just to make sure. "If you're pregnant you'll marry me?"

She straightened her shoulders and lifted her chin. "Yes," she finally answered. "But if I'm not, I want you to agree that both of us will walk away after a certain amount of time. We'll walk away forever with no hard feelings and no regrets. I want a life with a man who can give me everything I need."

"And how long is a certain amount of time?" he asked incredulously.

"I figure a month should be long enough for us to fuck

ourselves into oblivion and be ready to move on."

"A year," he heard himself say, his back teeth clenched so hard he was surprised they didn't turn to dust.

She walked past him and unlocked the bathroom door herself, but he kept her from going out until he'd looked to make sure there were no threats. She turned to look at him, her hands on her hips as if she were thinking through the positives and negatives of their negotiation.

"Six months," she countered. "With the option that if either of us decides it's not working then we can move on."

She'd be pregnant before the month was out. He'd make damned sure of it. That was a loophole he was going to make sure wasn't covered.

"Fine," he said, smiling. "Six months. But our time doesn't start until after this mission is over. I want six months of undivided attention. I've got a lot of vacation time saved up, and we're going to spend all of it naked."

"That ought to give my family a cheap thrill," she said, raising a brow. "The holidays are just around the corner, though I'm almost positive your idea of a Thanksgiving spread and mine are completely different."

He cracked out a laugh before he could help it and felt some of the tension ease inside him. Six months was plenty of time to convince Darcy that the sweeping love she believed in was nothing more than contentment between two satisfied people. And he planned to make her very satisfied.

CHAPTER EIGHT

Six months was going to have to be enough time to convince Brant that he loved her. If her plan failed, she'd have no choice but to move on. She was making a gamble, and it was all or nothing.

Darcy had made a decision after she'd thought on Declan's words that morning. She could fight or she could let go. It was really that simple. And she wasn't ready to let go. The plan that came to mind had butterflies bouncing in her stomach, because it could just as easily backfire.

But she knew Brant. Knew how he approached and handled things. And the only way she could see to reach him was for him to get a taste of his own medicine. For her to be the one who only wanted a casual fling and nothing more. To make him realize how cold sex and intimacy could be when the love was held back.

The only thing she had to worry about was not letting him see past the deception—the way his touches and their bodies became one really affected her.

Darcy stayed to the edges of the main path, feeling more than exposed without her bathing suit bottom, slight as it had been to begin with. And she could feel the burn of Brant's gaze from behind her, no doubt checking out her ass. A look over her shoulder told her she'd been right about where his eyes had been looking, and she raised a brow when she saw he was already hard again. If this plan didn't work, the sex alone might kill them.

"Maybe I should let you walk in front next time," she said. "It's been awhile since I've gotten to ogle your ass."

His mouth quirked and his eyebrows raised in question. "When was the last time you ogled my ass?"

Her smile was mischievous, and she cocked a hand to her hip so the split in her sarong showed more of her thigh. "You mean other than watching your naked behind walk out of my house in the middle of the night four years ago?"

He scowled at that reminder, but there was no heat in her words. She was starting to understand why he'd thought he'd had to leave. He had feelings for her, and he was scared to death.

"You stopped coming to the house as much as you used to," she said. "But about ten years ago, I guess Cade had talked you into staying with us for a few weeks one summer. I spent that time checking out your ass, and every other part of you, while you helped my brothers bail hay and repair the fences. You wore jeans and no shirt, and all those muscles flexing made my young heart go pitter-pat."

Darcy placed her hand over her heart and fluttered her lashes, and Brant smiled again. He didn't do that nearly enough. She knew he had a great family, parents and a brother and sister who loved him, but Brant had always been a little bit of a loner. And there was a sadness inside of him that always hovered just around the edges.

"I remember," he said. "You spent that summer traipsing around the house in tiny shorts that barely covered your ass. I thought your brothers were going to kill you."

"I was nineteen. My brothers are overprotective asses."

"They had every right to be. They knew the way I tried not to look at you."

"Don't worry, sugar," she said, using one of his endearments. "I noticed. And I looked right back.

SHADOWS AND SILK

Especially that time you went skinny dipping down in the stock tank. I got an education for sure." Her eyebrows waggled and she turned back towards the hotel, twitching her hips a little.

"You little brat," he said, the amusement obvious in his voice. "Someone should have spanked you more as a child."

"I thought you were going to do that?" She smiled as she heard his low growl and then thought back on that summer. "Tell me something, Brant. When you came to stay with us that summer, you seemed angry with me. More angry than your usual self, I guess. But it was more than the sexual frustration that always seemed to be between us. It was like you hated me. You had a fresh scar on your back, and you'd lost weight. I remember how red and angry it looked against your skin, as if it had barely healed before you'd come to us."

"I remember," he said softly, and she could tell by the sound of his voice that the smile and playfulness she'd sensed in him earlier was gone. "Just like I remember you getting pissed at me over not giving in to you, and then you started dating that Freeman asshole."

She stopped walking and turned to face him again, but this time she only saw the cold hard side of him that had been taking over more frequently. "I believe that was the summer you told me it'd be a cold day in hell before you put your hands on me, and that I should just go and find a college boy to tempt. Then you said some other horrible things and kissed the daylights out of me. And then you didn't look at me for the rest of the summer. I just did what you told me to. And a girl has to lose her virginity at some point."

Brant went completely still, the green of his eyes turning almost black as he stared her down. "Jesus, you gave your virginity to that prick? What the hell were you thinking?"

"Well, you didn't want it, so I figured he was as good as

anyone. Of course, I know better now." She sighed and shrugged her shoulder. "But I guess you live and learn."

He opened his mouth to say something else, but footsteps coming up the path had him jerking her to his side. A young man of around seventeen came around the bend, his dark hair and eyes slightly familiar. He looked sullen and a little angry, but he still gave them a smile when he saw them.

"Here you are," he said. "I'm Enrique Luna. My father sent me to find you in case you got lost on your way."

His eyes trailed a slow path over Darcy from head to toe, and the very adult look in those young eyes made her shiver. He then took in Brant's torn shirt and he smirked. "I guess you had a reason for getting lost."

She couldn't see Brant's look since she was standing partially behind him, but she saw the younger Luna pale considerably and take a step back.

"You can follow me this way to your cottage," the boy stuttered out. And without another word he turned on his heel and headed back up the path.

"Ah, men never change," she said, feeling better now that those creepy eyes weren't turned on her. "Is there ever a time in life when you don't have to compare dick size? You all make things very complicated in a woman's life."

"The size of my dick is the only one you need to worry about, sweetheart. And if you weren't practically naked, it wouldn't be an issue in the first place."

The Luna kid was practically running down the graveled path towards the beach, but they walked at a normal pace behind him, forcing him to slow down and wait for them to catch up, giving them impatient glares all the while.

Darcy sighed as Brant kept moving her slightly in front of him and to the left. She assumed it was so his shooting hand would be free, just like her brothers always did when they were out together.

"Jesus, you're just like my brothers," she finally said.

SHADOWS AND SILK

"That's not what you were saying twenty minutes ago."

She snorted out a laugh, and he relaxed a little beside her.

"I mean it's impossible to go anywhere with them without feeling like your life is on the line. You guys are always looking for bad guys in hidden corners and the closest escape routes. It makes me itchy. One day I'd like to take a normal walk with a normal man and not have to look over my shoulder."

"Is that what you had with Kenneth?" he asked. "Normalcy?"

Her brow furrowed and she thought about it for a second. "Sometimes normalcy is nice. And sometimes it just feels good to be with someone who cares about you."

"You don't love him," he said with confidence. "Why waste your time?"

"Because being lonely sucks. I grew up in a town of three thousand people and four brothers. Friends were few and far between, and my brothers stuck together like glue. I just don't want to be alone anymore."

"So get a cat. Don't keep tying yourself to men like Kenneth just because you're lonely. You're a MacKenzie, babe. You can't live without a little excitement in your life."

"I guess it's fortunate I have you for the next six months to keep me occupied. Maybe you'll cure me of my need for adventure, and then I won't mind having a man like Kenneth in my life. Six months was a good idea, love," she said, patting him on the arm.

She was playing with fire, and she knew it. Brant was nothing if not competitive, and the thought of her leaving his bed at the end of their time together and going to a man like Kenneth wouldn't sit well.

They followed Enrique in silence—off the graveled path and through the manicured tropical gardens—both of them lost in their own thoughts. The beach opened up suddenly in front of them for miles in each direction—

white sand and crystalline blue waters. Thatched roof huts were built at the ends of docks that were spread every few hundred feet down the shoreline, but Enrique headed in the opposite direction and up a narrow sandy path lined with palm trees and flowers in bright pinks and yellows.

Darcy was starting to think the boy was leading them in circles when they finally came upon the honeymoon villa. It sat high up on a hill—a small white stucco replica of the main hotel. The windows and doors were arched and the roof was red tile. It was completely secluded from the rest of the resort.

"Here it is," the boy said, handing Brant the key. "My dad said your luggage is being brought up. Enjoy your stay." And with that, he started back down the hill without looking back.

"Little prick," Brant said. "I guess he didn't want a tip."

"I think you scared the hell out of him with your macho display earlier." She grabbed the key from his hand and was just putting it in the lock when he put his hand over her wrist.

"Let me go in first. Stay behind me."

Darcy rolled her eyes but she stepped back and let him do the honors. Brant pulled the heavy black pistol from the small of his back and kept it down at his side while he unlocked the door with his left hand. It opened on smooth hinges, and she followed in close behind him into an open foyer. She inhaled the tangy scent of citrus and moved to Brant's side so she could see the room better.

The cottage was larger than it seemed from the outside, and it was dominated by shades of white. Two long white couches faced each other and a wicker coffee table sat between them. The little kitchen off to the side had a coffeemaker and a large basket of fruit on the counter, and a wall of floor to ceiling windows were all that separated them from the beach.

Darcy assumed the arched doors on each side of the main room went to the bedrooms, and she sighed in relief at the thought of taking a shower and changing clothes. She tried to move around Brant, but he held out an arm to stop her.

When she looked at him, she could see the tension in his shoulders, but he shook his head at her.

"Come on out, Dec," he said. "I won't shoot you. Yet."

"What—" Darcy said, confused. Until she saw Declan come out of the bedroom.

He was dressed like one of the resort guests—navy blue swim trunks, a loose white t-shirt and flip-flops—except for the weapon he had in his hand. The scar on his face stood out against the darkness of his skin as he frowned while looking her over from head to toe. And then he took in Brant's open shirt, and Darcy took a step in front of Brant because Declan looked like he wanted to use the gun in his hand.

"Don't ever try to stand in front of me," Brant said from behind her. "It's not your job to protect me from anyone, much less your brother."

"Of course not," she said, a little hurt by his brusqueness. "I don't know what I was thinking, little ole me trying to protect a big, strong man like you."

"Why don't you go find something decent to wear?" Declan said. "I need to have a word with Brant."

"Why don't you both blow it out your smokestack," she said, heading over to the little bar just off the kitchen. She poured herself two fingers of whiskey and took a healthy drink, enjoying the burn as it settled in her stomach. "Let me ask you something, Dec. Have I ever given you the impression that I need any of you to make decisions for me? Or judge the decisions I do make? I don't recall saying a word that time you brought Lisa Helmsley to Thanksgiving one year."

"You don't want to start in on me right now, Darcy. And you had plenty to say about Lisa Helmsley if I recall. But I think you're the one who has some explaining to do this time around. Or maybe I should just ask the SEAL team I have watching you guys for protection. I'm sure they enjoyed the show."

"Enough, Dec," Brant said. "It's none of your business, and you're not giving either of us enough credit."

"Don't bother to try and protect me," she said, giving Brant his own words back. Having each other's backs was only something a *real* couple did. She'd forgotten that when she'd stood in front of him before. Brant didn't want anything from her but sex. Not her protection and not her love. He'd made that clear. "He's been lecturing me a lot longer than you've been around."

She looked at her brother and Brant and then knocked back the rest of her drink. "I guess I'll go take a shower and change. I wouldn't want to interrupt whatever important business you have to discuss."

She'd always been on the outside in her family. Always the one they saw as weak and unable to fend for herself. The one they saw as reckless who should do nothing more than stick to her studies and her books. Growing up in a house with four older brothers who were all domineering and bossy had made its mark on her, and all she'd ever wanted was to feel like she could stand on equal ground with them.

Declan took her arm as she walked by and she could see the warning in his eyes, along with the worry and love. She knew he meant well, but she didn't need any more unsolicited advice at this point. She'd already made her decision.

"The beach is secure," Declan told her. "SEAL Team 2 has watch over this area of the beach. You'll need to watch yourself and your behavior."

"I'm twenty-eight years old. I can take care of myself. And I didn't sign on to help with this mission to have my private life spied on. Tell SEAL Team 2 they'd better watch for threats and nothing more. After all, I'm on my honeymoon."

She smiled sweetly and glanced over her shoulder at

Brant, giving him a look hot enough to melt butter. She could practically feel Declan vibrating beside her.

"We just want to keep you safe, Darcy," Dec said evenly. He was one of those people whose voice got softer and more level the angrier he got. "Don't try to make our jobs harder by being stubborn. And if you're going to act like a child by cavorting around the beach without thought or care to your safety, then you deserve what you get."

"Sure, Dec. You know I live my life just thinking of different ways to make you guys miserable. I guess I should apologize for not having enough common sense to do what's right and for being such a fucking burden all the time."

She hated the tears in her voice, but she'd had a hell of a last twenty-four hours. She chalked it up to exhaustion and realizing she had a long road ahead of her where the men in her life were concerned. If she didn't love them so damned much she wouldn't have bothered.

With her chin held high, she pulled her arm from Declan's grasp and made her way into the bedroom.

"I'm assuming you have a reason for being here," Brant asked Declan, going over to the bar to get his own drink. He'd heard the tears in Darcy's voice just as he was sure that Dec had.

"You're really walking the edge to the limits of our friendship," Dec said.

"Like Darcy said, it's none of your business."

"No, but I'll be the one still here when you walk away again. Do you think we didn't know something happened between you four years ago? None of us are stupid. You practically disappeared off the face of the planet after you were sent to protect her from del Fuego's men. We should have sent someone to protect her from you."

"Yeah, maybe you should have," Brant said softly. "You don't have to worry this time. She's making the rules."

"She's not Vivian," Dec said.

"You think I don't fucking realize that?"

"I think you don't realize that Darcy has loved you with everything she has for years, and you've given her nothing in return because you're so caught up in the past you can't see what's standing in front of you."

"I asked her to marry me," he finally said, his frustration bordering on the edge of violence. Nothing would feel better than slamming his fist into Declan's jaw at that moment. "What more do you want from me?"

"What did she say?" Declan asked, his mouth twitching in what looked suspiciously like a smile.

Brant stared at Declan, trying to read the other man's thoughts, but that was like trying to read a book without pages. "She said no," he finally said, giving into his frustration and slamming his fist against the bar. Bottles and glasses rattled, but none tipped over. "So like I said, Darcy is calling the shots this time."

"Good. You deserve to have to work for it a little after what you put her through the last time. Whatever happened between the two of you changed her."

"I'm assuming you broke in here for a different reason than busting my ass over your sister."

"That's just a secondary benefit," Declan said. His face went back to the unreadable mask he normally wore. No one could accuse Dec of letting emotions get in the way of a job. "We've got a hell of a problem."

"Of course we do."

A knock sounded at the door and Brant and Declan both pulled their weapons up, the air going still and silent around them. Declan slipped back into the bedroom and Brant went to the door. Two bellmen waited on the other side with their luggage, and he put the gun away as he opened the door.

"Just leave it in here," he said. "My wife is in the shower." Brant tipped them well and locked the door behind them.

"The *my wife* certainly comes off your lips easily," Declan said, coming back into the living area with a manila envelope in his hands.

"Shut up, Dec."

Declan shrugged and poured the contents of the envelope out on the kitchen bar, flipping on the bright overhead lights. Brant knew the news was bad when he saw the photographs of five innocent faces.

"A group of girls disappeared from their hotel about three o'clock this morning. They're here with their school for two weeks to study the ruins. A very exclusive private school that had excellent security and brought along their own guards. Three of the guards are dead. The other two critically wounded. The girls were taken from their beds, and we can't find any witnesses who are brave enough to speak up. The youngest was fourteen. The oldest is eighteen. Five girls total."

Brant closed his eyes in horror at the thought of what would happen to those girls if they weren't recovered soon. "Ramos is suspected?"

"More than just suspected at this point. And it proves he's getting ready to make waves in the worldwide drug market. In that group of girls are the daughters of a U.S. senator, a member of British parliament, the Canadian Prime Minister, and a Supreme Court Justice."

"Shit."

Dec nodded and said, "We expect a ransom demand at some point. There's a bill on the Senate floor right now about sending more agents and soldiers into Mexico to help crack down on the cartels. It's backed by Senator Robert Mitchell, and he's taking a no leniency stance against those caught."

"Let me guess," Brant said. "Senator Mitchell's daughter was one of those kidnapped."

"Two daughters, actually," Dec said. "The bill has the full support of the Mexican government, but I think Ramos is going to ask for that bill to be expunged in exchange for the lives of those girls. We know for a fact he's bought most of the local authorities in his territory. The poverty level is so great that they almost have no choice but to accept his offer and turn the other cheek when he runs the drugs."

"Have any glyphs been found to lead to a drop site?"

"Not yet. Shane's SEAL Team is scouting the area where the girls were taken. He'll let us know when they find the glyphs, and we'll need Darcy to decipher them as soon as possible so we can get to them before it's too late."

"That's a hell of a lot of pressure to put on a person. She'll make herself sick trying to get to those girls in time. And she'll blame herself if it all goes wrong."

"Which is why we're not going to tell her about those girls," Dec said. "I don't want that on her conscience if we don't make it in time."

"You can't keep that information from her," Brant argued. "If you have the balls to pull her in on a mission like this then you need to have the balls to keep her apprised of what's going on and tell her the truth."

"You don't want to lecture me on the truth, my friend. When are you planning on telling Darcy about Vivian?"

A cold sweat broke out on Brant's body at the thought of Darcy finding out the one thing that would really make her walk away for good. "Never," he said, almost choking on his fury.

"That's what I thought."

Declan turned his back and went to the sliding glass doors that led out to their private beach, and Brant watched him impassively, wondering for the first time if he could really trust the MacKenzies to keep his secret.

"I won't tell her," Dec said, reading his mind. "But you don't give her enough credit. She loves you. And maybe you need someone to listen."

Declan slipped outside and was gone from view before he could blink, and Brant rubbed his hands over his face and head, wishing to God he knew what was right and wrong anymore. The lines had become blurred somewhere along the way.

CHAPTER NINE

Darcy knew the moment he came inside the bathroom. She could feel his presence like she could feel her own skin, and already her body was responding to his nearness.

She kept her back turned, scrubbing away the hours of travel and lovemaking, but she stopped as his arms came around her. His lips kissed her shoulder while his hands caressed her stomach, working the lather of soap across her skin, down her thighs, avoiding the swollen folds between her legs.

Her head dropped back on his shoulder and she pushed against him, feeling his erection against the small of her back. His hands worked their way back up her body until he held the heaviness of her breasts in his hands.

"You feel so good," he whispered against her ear. "I always want you. Even when I'm away from you. You hold that power over me, Darcy."

"Then we shouldn't waste the time we have," she said, turning in his arms. Her nipples rubbed against his chest hair and he turned them so she was backed against the shower wall—his cock already probing as he pulled her leg up to surround his hip.

"Not yet," she moaned, shivering as he barely pushed inside of her. "It's my turn."

SHADOWS AND SILK

The heat in his eyes had her licking her lips in anticipation, and she pushed him away, kissing him once on the lips before beginning her exploration. The first time they'd been together, he never gave her the chance to touch and explore, and the last time had been too fast and furious. But this was her time, and she wanted—no needed—to touch him in a way she'd always remember.

She placed light kisses across his chest, circling his nipples with her tongue, and feeling the low growl of appreciation deep in his chest. And then she knelt slowly in front of him, nipping gently at the small indentations above his hipbones and licking a trail down his thigh.

"God, Darcy," he said, turning so the water hit his back. "You drive me crazy."

The laugh that came from inside her was deep and seductive—the call of a temptress. "I hope so," she purred, rubbing her cheek against the length of his rigid cock.

Her hand grasped him at the root, and he sucked in a breath as she licked over the head with small, fiery kisses, tasting the small drop of come that had gathered at the tip. She looked up at him—up the hard ridges of his abdomen to the muscular chest, past his clenched jaw, and into half-closed eyes that were almost black with desire.

And while they were connected eye to eye, she opened her mouth and took him inside, circling her tongue over the head before relaxing her throat and taking him down as far as she could. She closed her eyes in pure bliss, and her nails scraped across his bunched thighs once before he took hold of her wrists and held them captive.

She used her tongue as she took him down and sucked and swallowed, tightening the hold she had on him, going down as far as she could until he became too big for her mouth to fit around.

"Just like that, baby," he crooned. "It's so good."

She tried to pull her hands away from his hold so she could touch him, but he wouldn't release her. Her mouth slid off him and she looked up at him.

"You never let me touch you," she said, her voice raspy. "You always try to hold my hands down. Why do you do that? I need to touch you as much as you need to touch me."

Darcy watched as something came into his eyes that looked almost like fear, but he slowly loosened his grip from her wrists. There was something in his eyes that warned her she needed to take care of the power he was giving her, and she kept her gaze steady on him as she grasped his cock with one hand and held the tight sac below with the other.

His eyes fluttered closed, and he seemed to give in to whatever struggle he'd been waging with himself, because his hands went to the shower wall and he threw his head back in surrender.

Darcy felt her own juices running down her thighs as he gave her control, and she took him back in her mouth with a determination meant to blow his mind. Her tongue worked up and down the rigid shaft, sucking and slurping, one hand pumping as she massaged his balls with the other. Saltiness coated her tongue and she knew he couldn't hold on much longer.

"Darcy, I can't—" he trailed off, his hips pushing against her face of their own accord. "If you're going to stop, now's the time."

A lone groan came from her throat and vibrated around his cock, and she grasped his ass in both hands, opening her mouth wider as he fucked into her. His pleasure was what mattered most at that moment, and when his buttocks clenched against her hands and his cock seemed to swell in her mouth, she knew he'd reached that pleasure.

Salty liquid shot down her throat, and she kept swallowing as spurt after spurt of semen filled her mouth. Her fingers stole between her thighs, pushing into the syrup that coated her pussy, and she moaned as her fingers flicked over the taut bud of her clit.

"Oh, no you don't," Brant said, pulling his cock from her mouth slowly, his whole body shuddering in the aftermath of his orgasm. "My turn. Though I'm not sure my legs are working properly."

Darcy would have laughed, but she was too close to the edge herself. Her fingers dipped inside her pussy as she felt the water go off in the shower, and then strong arms were lifting her from the floor.

"I need you now," she heard herself beg, too far gone to care about anything but release.

"For once we're going to make it to a bed," he said, lifting her into his arms.

He didn't bother to dry them off, and he carried her straight into the bedroom, laying her on the white cloud of a bed that dominated the room. The sheets were soft and smooth as he came over her, and her legs parted automatically to pull him in.

She was already wet and ready for him, and the push of his hot flesh against her entrance had her holding her breath as she stretched around him. His eyes held her captive as he kept pushing into her, and she watched as a bead of water dripped from his hair down to his cheek. The feel of him inside her was almost too much—she was too full—too stretched. But he didn't give her a respite. He worked his way inside until she felt his testicles resting against her vaginal lips.

Her lungs burned and she inhaled sharply, taking in the oxygen she'd been depriving herself. She felt him throb, hot and hard inside of her, and the fact that he'd just come hadn't seemed to affect his desire for her. She lifted her hips and her legs, circling them around his lower back, and she felt him jerk inside of her as she clenched her internal muscles.

"You're not playing fair, baby. This will be over before we even get started."

"I'm about two seconds from coming, Brant Scott. I

don't have the patience for you to get more started than we already are."

He laughed softly, and she felt the rumble all the way between her legs. Her eyes fluttered closed as the sensation washed over her and she flexed around him again, determined to take the edge off.

He pressed her hips to the mattress with his own, keeping her from being able to move, and he stroked his hands up her sides, trailing briefly across her breasts before he continued the path up her arms. She didn't realize what he was doing until he held her hands above her head.

Her eyes snapped open, and she tried to buck against him, but he was too strong.

"I want my hands," she panted as he started to move—one long stroke—before he held her hips captive again. "Give them to me now. I won't be restrained by you. We either go into this as equals or not at all."

The struggle on his face was almost painful to see, but she held her ground. They were going to get to the bottom of this sooner or later. Sooner if she had her way about it.

Brant's hands clenched tighter around her wrists for the briefest of seconds, and he took that opportunity to pull almost all the way out—until the head of his cock was barely inside of her—and then he gave her another slow thrust that had her writhing with frustration and need.

She was just about to demand he release her again when he rolled them across the bed, and she found herself sprawled on top of him. Her wet hair trailed over her shoulder and lay like ropes on his chest, and she slowly sat up, watching his eyes and some internal struggle the entire time.

When they'd been together four years ago, she hadn't paid much attention for his need to dominate her in the bedroom. Their first time had been a wild frenzy of lust. The second time just as crazed as the first, but even then he'd held her captive beneath him while he'd almost dared her to do something about it.

SHADOWS AND SILK

"Brant," she said, shaking her head as she sat up. She was still impaled on him, and her breath caught as he seemed to go deeper inside of her, finding an internal place that hadn't been explored yet. His stomach and chest muscles were rigid beneath her, and she moved to get off of him. Making love shouldn't put a look of panic into your lover's eyes.

"No," he said, holding her hips so she couldn't move. "Ride me."

She shook her head again, but he wouldn't be deterred. He pressed her down until she was seated to the hilt, and her head dropped back on her shoulders at the sensation of him filling her.

"That's it, baby. Just feel me. Milk me with that sweet pussy." His hands relaxed against her hips and he moved them to her breasts, tweaking her nipples between his fingers as she began to ride.

It wasn't long until she was lost in the pleasure, until the heat suffused her and electrical currents were shooting up her spine. Her knees clutched his hips and her hands found purchase on his chest, and she rode up and down the thick length of his cock with nothing but that end goal of release in mind. She felt his fingers move to her clit, and one touch was all it took before she clamped around him. Liquid heat poured from her core and she shuddered and trembled above him as the climax claimed her.

She would have crumpled to his chest, her muscles were so lax, but he sat up beneath her and his mouth clamped around her nipple.

"Ahh," she moaned as another spasm moved through her.

His fingers would likely be imprinted on her skin, they were holding her hips so tight. His cock swelled inside of her and he slammed home one last time as she felt his come shooting deep inside of her, coating her walls with spurt after spurt of semen.

"Darcy," he cried out as he shuddered one last time.

His arms came around her and she buried her face in his neck. Their hearts beat as one, and there were no words for the emotions rioting through her body.

If he couldn't see and feel the love she had for him, then it was hopeless, because she hadn't been able to hold it inside once she'd seen that look of vulnerability cross his face. Tension seeped into the bliss of the aftermath, and she finally pulled away, gasping as their bodies disconnected, and she rolled to her side away from him.

She expected him to get up and go to the other room. To put some physical space between them to go with the emotional distance that was sure to come, but she felt the bed dip beside her as he lay down. Her body was stiff as he put his arm around her and snuggled close, their bodies fitting together like spoons. It seemed like hours before he finally spoke, and she found herself disappointed that he wasn't going to explain what had happened while they'd been making love.

"We need to get up and moving," he said. "A new situation has developed. Five girls were kidnapped early this morning by Ramos and his men. They're being held for ransom, but there's no telling what Ramos will do to them in the meantime. He likes to try out his drugs on his victims and give them to his men to share. We need to find them fast. Which means we need to get a first hand look at some of those glyphs and see if there's something you might have missed in the photographs."

Darcy put her own problems out of her mind. She and Brant would have time to come to terms later, but those girls might already be out of chances.

"Have they found any new glyphs that might lead to the girls?" she asked, scooting out of his arms and getting out of bed.

She looked back at him and her heart fluttered in her chest. He was so beautiful. He lay without covers in the middle of the bed without any self-consciousness at all, his body hard and muscled, his cock twitching against the sheets as she took her time looking him over. The sigh escaped before she could help it and she forced herself to go to the suitcases in the living area they had yet to unpack.

A pair of olive green shorts and a matching halter were folded at the top of her suitcase, and she grabbed a lacy white thong from the selection of lingerie packed. She wouldn't be able to wear a bra with the halter top, which was just as well, because it was too damned hot for extra layers.

"Where are we going first?" she asked, pulling on her clothes and then pulling on thick socks and her hiking boots. She knew from experience that some of the ruins were an arduous hike. Her hair would be in the way while she was working, so she pinned it up in a knot on top of her head and watched Brant pull on khaki shorts and another loose button-up shirt.

"Let's drive into Chiapas," he said. "That's where the coordinates for the last victim were found, and it isn't too far of a drive. We'll be able to get back before dark, but we'll take a driver for extra precaution."

Darcy didn't like the fact that all of her clothing was too minimal to effectively hide a weapon, but she slipped her knife and the Sig Brant had acquired for her into her backpack along with a camera, her notebooks, and a couple of bottles of water. She watched Brant gather up a bunch of pictures Declan must have left, and he put them back into an envelope before hiding them in a hidden compartment in his suitcase.

"That's handy," she said, wondering what else he had hidden in there.

"Better to be safe than sorry. Who knows if any of the staff have ties to Ramos indirectly?"

"I was actually wondering if you'd smuggled anything interesting into your suitcase," she said, giving him a cheeky grin. "You know, maybe something you might not have wanted to go on the expense reports for my brother."

He arched a brow, and he took a minute to look her over—from where her nipples were plainly visible beneath her shirt to the smooth expanse of stomach that wasn't quite covered. And then over the tiny shorts that barely covered more than some bathing suit bottoms. She was going to have to thank Jade in person, because as much as Brant might hate the thought of others seeing her so scantily clad, it was obvious he was enjoying it for himself.

His lips twitched once before his eyes came back to hers. "I might have a trick or two up my sleeve. Maybe if you can stay out of trouble I'll let you look in my secret compartment."

She laughed and gave her hips a little extra swing as she walked out the door. "Been there done that, sugar. Looks like you'll have to step up your game."

CHAPTER TEN

An hour later, Brant started to get a tingle in his gut that maybe things weren't going to go according to plan.

Their driver and bodyguard were the two agents who'd accompanied them on the flight into Mexico—named Smith and Huxley—and they were both armed to the teeth.

Brant was starting to wish he'd brought along some more artillery himself. By the way that Smith was gripping the wheel in a white-knuckled grasp, Brant thought maybe his gut might be tingling too.

He'd worked with Huxley before, and he knew that he and Declan were actually really good friends. In fact, Declan had been best man at Huxley's wedding. But Brant had never seen Smith before, and working with someone new was a crapshoot. He had to trust that Declan wouldn't have sent anything but his best to protect his sister.

Darcy sat calmly beside him on the way into Chiapas, reading over her notes from the glyphs they'd discovered and re-examining the pictures. The drive had been straightforward—the highway turning into a one-lane dirt road the closer they got to the ruins where the glyphs had been discovered—but the place felt abandoned when there should have been tourists roaming the shops along the road or hiking their way up to the ruins. Granted, it was October, and high season was long past, but there still should have been someone.

"I don't like this," he said as they pulled past a sign that said the ruins were closed to the public because of crumbling rock. A couple of temporary wooden barriers had been erected, but nothing that looked permanent.

"That's odd," Darcy commented. "I've been to these ruins hundreds of times, and this is the first time I've seen them closed."

"The sign was placed there by the local police two days ago," Smith said. "They didn't give a reason other than safety issues, but they said it would reopen by the end of the week."

"Has the site been cleared by our guys?" Brant asked.

"Shane's SEAL Team was called away to the latest kidnapping site before they could do more than slip in and out to photograph the glyphs and send them to Dr. MacKenzie. Max wasn't able to get any of his agents in either without rousing suspicion, so they've held back."

"So we're on our own?" Brant asked.

"We have a satellite shot, and there's been no suspicious activity in the last two days. There are two undercover DEA agents in the village, but we're only to signal them in case of emergency so their covers aren't blown. Declan said to give him and Max about half an hour to come around from the opposite direction. They'll be your cover from the back."

"Half an hour," he said, blowing out a breath. "I hope we don't need them sooner."

"Huxley and I will guard the front side, so you can protect Darcy while she's studying the glyphs. Boss man says she's your priority."

"I know what the hell my priorities are," he growled. "But you'll excuse me for being paranoid, especially since my neck's been itching for the last forty-five minutes."

Brant tried reaching Declan on the satellite phone, but

there was no answer, so he pulled his weapon and made sure a bullet was in the chamber. Darcy's hand touched his knee and squeezed reassuringly, and he realized that she was more than just a priority. If anything happened to her he didn't think he'd survive it.

"I don't even know how this all started," Darcy said. "Declan just showed up on my doorstep with a picture one day and asked me what it said. Some of these ruins are in bad shape, and there are markings all around the area that date back centuries. It wouldn't be an easy thing to discover for the untrained eye. I asked him where he got them from, but he never would give me a straight answer."

"It was safer that way," Brant said. "Max had an agent who'd worked his way up in Ramos's organization, and he fed us the information about the glyphs."

"What happened to the agent?" Darcy asked, more perceptive than he was comfortable with.

Brant sighed and looked out the window for threats as he answered. "Donovan Jax was tortured and killed by Ramos. Someone sold the information to Ramos and blew his cover. We know it was internal, but we don't know from what agency."

"Jax?" Darcy asked. "Isn't that Jade's last name?"

"Donovan was her husband. There was hardly enough body left for her to bury by the time Ramos finished with him, but they didn't break him. He was a good agent. A good friend."

"It has to be hard on her to keep working in the same field."

Brant turned to look at her, and he didn't know if he was trying to scare her away or give her a warning, but she paled at his words. "We all know the risks of this job. Life is finite no matter how you live it. You can either move forward or you can let the terrible things you see bury you. Donovan Jax knew the chances he was taking, and he knew there'd be a possibility he'd leave his wife a widow. And she knew them too. Jade has more reason than anyone to want to capture Ramos."

"Too bad that won't bring her husband back."

"Sometimes justice is all there is," he said.

The road past the police barriers was deeply rutted, and dust flew up and coated the sides of the Jeep. The jungle speared up all around them, completely circling the ruins on all sides.

"Bonampak is much smaller than the site of Yaxchilan just down the road," Darcy said. "But the site itself is just as important. The Temple of Murals is here." She shivered next to him. "It's like a ghost town. I've never seen it deserted before."

Smith drove the Jeep through the trees and finally parked about a half a mile from the site so no one would see their vehicle if the police were doing drive-bys.

"Let's make this quick," Brant said as they got out of the car.

Smith and Huxley split in opposite directions, and Brant pushed Darcy towards the site, his weapon up just in case. The quiet was unnerving—just the occasional chatter of birds.

"Shane said they drew the glyphs at the top of the Temple of Murals on the outside wall facing east. Bastards," she muttered. "They obviously have no care for preserving their heritage."

Brant looked at her incredulously as he kept her in the cover of the trees. "Darlin', these men would kill their own mothers if they were paid enough. I think their heritage is the last thing they care about preserving."

"Well," she said primly, making his mouth twitch, "They should."

They stood in the trees about twenty feet from the base of the Temple of Murals—a long structure with a pyramid base where crumbling steps on all four sides led to the temples on top. Brant knew as soon as they started climbing the stairs they'd be sitting ducks for anyone wanting to take a shot at them until they reached the enclosed rooms at the top. Work was being done on some of the lower structures, and support poles and tents were set around them.

"Are we going to the very top?" he asked, assessing the situation and then catching Smith's all clear signal from the corner of his eye.

"The very top," she affirmed. "You can see for miles from up there. It's very beautiful."

He grunted and grabbed her elbow, his steps quick as he ushered her to the base of the structure. "We'll use the tented areas for cover if you can't make it to the top without a break."

"I beg your pardon," Darcy said, clearly offended. "I'm in excellent shape."

"Lead the way, sugar. I'm right behind you." Which might have been the worst mistake he'd ever made, come to think of it, because keeping his eyes off Darcy's ass and on the surrounding areas was a lot harder than it should have been. But she'd been right about one thing—she was in excellent shape—and by the time they reached the top of the temple and ducked into the first room, he was so hard he could barely walk. The combination of adrenaline and the thought of cupping those round globes in his hands and sliding into her from behind was enough to make him insane with lust.

"Here we go," she said, moving through the room with familiarity.

There was another door in the opposite wall from the one they'd come in, and she slipped out and knelt down near the area Shane had marked on the map for her. Brant knelt beside her, so they were smaller targets, but kept watch across the jungle. It wouldn't be long before Max and Declan were into position, but he wouldn't be able to find them in the dense trees. He just trusted that they'd be where they said.

The glyphs were small, and drawn in what looked like charcoal. Darcy dug through her bag and put her glasses on, and he felt the slow burn of desire roll through his stomach and to his loins.

"What's wrong?" she asked.

"Nothing." The reply came out terser than he'd meant.

"Do you see someone?" Her voice lowered to a whisper. "Why'd you get so still?"

"For God's sake, Darcy. Just stay focused on the glyphs. You'd argue with the Pope."

"I have a right to know if we're in danger."

"If you must know, I get hard as a rock every time you put those glasses on, and if you don't hurry up so we can get out of here I'm going to bend you over that altar in the middle of your precious temple."

Her mouth opened in a silent O, and her pupils dilated so only a thin rim of blue showed. Color flushed her cheeks and she lowered her gaze back to the glyphs while he tried to find a comfortable position without strangling his cock.

"The jaguar runs to the north," Darcy murmured under her breath, tracing the glyph. "The hawk flies from the west. And the deer is sacrificed at the temple of our brethren."

"What the hell does that mean?" Brant asked.

"They're making it a game. Like a scavenger hunt. The jaguar and the hawk are the dealer and the buyer. The deer is the victim. And the temple is where she was found. They laid her out right on the front steps of Santo Domingo. These glyphs here," she said pointing to the last four, "are coordinates. In case they can't decipher the riddle. We've missed some."

"Missed what?" Brant asked, following her back inside.

"Glyphs. There have to be more Donovan Jax didn't know about before his death. How long since he was killed?"

"About six months," Brant said, watching as she pulled her map out of her backpack and went back inside the temple. She spread it the map across the altar he'd threatened to take her on.

"Look," she said, grabbing a pen. "We're here, and the clue leads to Chiapa de Corzo, more than a six hour drive away. But that's where our victim was found early this morning. A couple of hours later, five girls were kidnapped from their resort near the ruins at Lagatero." She placed big X's over the two areas. "Now let's go back over the past few months."

She mumbled under her breath while she checked her notes and kept making marks on the map. They were there long enough for the sun to change positions, and he ignored the heat as he kept watch while she worked out the puzzle. And then he finally saw the pattern.

"Son of a bitch. We missed some of the clues," he said, shaking his head. "But only after Donovan died. No wonder Ramos paid so much to have the mole in organization brought forward. When Donovan was feeding us intel, Ramos wasn't able to test the drugs like he needed to."

It seemed obvious now that he was looking at it. It was like a scavenger hunt. The clues were drawn, sending the dealers to the new locations where the buyers would be met and a victim taken, and then the dealers would leave a new set of clues in or near the location where they left the body, probably at Ramos's instruction, leading the next group of dealers to the next drop spot. He never used the same group of men in a row, and if you didn't find the glyphs marking the spot, then the killings couldn't be anticipated.

Excitement poured off Darcy in waves, and he realized he had a great deal of pride in her for what she'd discovered. Declan had been right after all. They'd needed her on this mission.

"Don't you understand?" she asked, her eyes shining with hope and everything that was good and honest. "We need to search the area where the girls were taken. They'll have left instructions for where they're taking them for the next set of dealers."

She had him under a spell. That was the only explanation he could think of as he felt his chest bursting with some foreign emotion. Darcy belonged to him. And he belonged to her. If she didn't want to get married then that was fine, but she'd be the one to explain to their children why she wouldn't marry him. He wasn't going anywhere at the end of six months. He could trust her. And that was as good as love in his book.

"Brant, are you listening to me?" she asked, a look of concern crossing her face. "Are you okay?"

The sun casting shadows now, and the orange glow shot shafts of brilliant light into the small cutout door of the temple, distorting the colors of the faded frescoes on the wall and spotlighting the altar in the center of the room, just as it was meant to. Sunset was a sacred time of the day. A time for worship and reflection. And he wanted nothing more than to see Darcy bathed in the light from the setting sun.

His hand touched just above her wrist, and he circled his fingers over the pulse there, making gentle strokes until he felt it racing beneath her skin. Her eyes opened wide and her lips parted on a soft gasp as a realization of what he wanted heated her cheeks. Her nipples were erect beneath the thin shirt she wore, and perspiration glistened across her skin from the heat inside the temple.

"Brant." She breathed out his name like a sigh. "We can't. The others—"

"I need to taste you." He pulled her into his embrace so their bodies touched, and he knew one taste would never be enough. "Just for a little while. We're safe for now. It's just you and me on top of the world. There's no one else."

They were words meant to convince—to seduce—but he was the one falling under her spell. She had that power over him. He wanted to remember this moment—the way the sun kissed her skin and the way her breath hitched when his hand touched the sensitive skin at the crook of her elbow. The way she melted against him when he bent his head and touched his lips to hers, as if it were the first time.

The taste of her went to his head. She was ambrosia and heat and sex, and he couldn't help the way his body responded—the way he deepened the kiss and insisted on her surrender. But Darcy wasn't one to give in without a fight. Her tongue stroked his, sucking him into her mouth, and he groaned as he felt her hands slip under his shirt. She traced the scar on his back and he froze, feeling the control slip from his grasp. He shook his head, fighting against the need to hold her arms down, and then her fingers moved on as she began placing light, teasing kisses across his jaw and down his neck.

"God, Darcy," he groaned. "Touch me." He craved the heat of her hands against his skin, the way she could soothe or incite with a glance of fingers.

His mouth fused to hers and he lifted her, setting her down on the stone altar. His fingers threaded through her hair, pressing her closer, closer, and he knew whatever feelings were rioting inside of him were something he'd never experienced before. This was making love at its most basic—the joining of two bodies and two souls to become one.

"You make me dizzy," she said, her words slurred as if she'd had too much champagne. "What are you doing to me?"

"What I should have done the first time we were together," he rasped out, his heart pounding in his chest. He unbuttoned his shorts to give himself room, but this wasn't about his pleasure or how fast he could find it. It was about hers.

He flicked open the button of her shorts and slid them down her legs and over her boots. The white lace panties she wore were damp, and he could smell the musky scent of her desire. His fingers trailed up her legs and she shivered beneath his touch. Her flesh pebbled and she gasped as he stopped just short of touching the lace covered mound between her thighs.

"Please," she begged.

"Patience, love," he whispered. "I want to see all of you." He grasped the bottom of her shirt and pulled it over her head, baring her breasts. Her nipples were dusky pink and tightened into small buds, and her chest heaved as her anticipation grew.

"Lay back," he commanded, and watched her while his cock grew painfully hard at the sight of her stretched out on the stone slab. "You're so beautiful. You take my breath away." Her skin glowed in the fading sunlight, and she looked like a Pagan goddess stretched out before him.

He wanted to wait—to savor—but he knew their time was short. He knelt between her thighs, breathing her in before placing a soft kiss on the damp lace.

"Mmm," she moaned, her hands clenched around each side of the stone slab.

His fingers found the elastic band of her panties and he pulled them off quickly, letting them drop to the ground. The soft curls covering her mound were dewy and he could see the cream of her desire coating her pussy lips. Just a little taste, he thought. It would have to be enough.

His tongue swiped through the folds once—twice—and he spread her legs wider as her hips began to push against his face.

"So sweet, baby," he rasped. "I've never tasted anything sweeter." His tongue circled her clit and then dipped down into the dripping slit of her pussy, spreading her juices all around. And then his mouth clamped over the taut, swollen bud and he began to suckle, flicking his tongue as fast as he could and bringing her to a screaming climax.

"Shh," he crooned. "You don't want me to stop, do you?" He slowed his licks, building the tension inside her once more.

"Don't stop."

His finger joined his tongue, and he slid it inside of her to the first knuckle, loving the way she clamped around him. She was so tight, and she was swollen from her first orgasm, and even the thought of working his cock into that vise-like heat had him breaking out in a sweat. He joined a second finger to the first and scissored them, stretching her for his invasion.

Her body began to tremble, and he knew she was just on the edge again. He gave her clit one last kiss and then removed his fingers.

"Nooo," she moaned, sounding close to tears as he left her.

"Just for a second, baby." He stood between her splayed thighs and pushed his shorts down around his hips, his cock springing free from the confinement. He didn't think he'd ever been this hard in his life, and his balls were drawn up so tight to his body he didn't know if he'd be able to last past the initial thrust.

He gripped his cock at the base and squeezed tight, and then he began kissing his way up her belly and over the swollen mounds of her breasts. His teeth grazed each nipple, and her hips began to buck wildly beneath him.

"Now," she begged. "Please—"

Brant pulled her to the edge of the stone slab and pushed her knees back so they rested on either side of her breasts. She was wide open to him, and when he stood straight his cock was at the perfect position. He placed her hands on her knees so she was the one holding them in place, and then he took his cock in his hand and rubbed the head through the glistening juices of her vagina.

And when he speared through the waiting lips and began to push inside, he wondered how anything could ever feel more perfect than this woman wrapped around him—how he'd ever thought anyone else could be more than a paltry substitute.

"You're so tight," he said through gritted teeth, his hips flexing with each push into her body. She was slick with desire, more than ready for him, and impatience finally got the better of his control. He slid to the hilt with one strong push, and she gasped and cried out as he filled her.

"Put your legs around me," he said.

Sweat ran down his temple as he leaned over her, kissing and suckling at her breasts as her ankles crossed behind his back. He kissed his way up her neck, and each time he kissed a new place on her body it somehow pushed him deeper inside of her. Her vaginal walls fluttered around his cock, and he knew she could come without him thrusting at all. Just by being full and heavy inside of her.

"Open those eyes, baby. I want to watch you climb." Their bodies were bathed in the orange glow of the fading sun, and he held her face between his hands and kissed her lips gently as her eyelids fluttered open. Brilliant blue stared back at him, and then he began to move, thrusting in long, measured strokes that were more of a caress than a coupling.

The flutters in her womb turned to ripples, and their breaths became more labored as he pushed them both closer to the precipice. But he kept his hands on her face, and his eyes steady on hers. He didn't know what she saw in his eyes, but she began to shake her head, to try to break hold of his grasp. But he didn't budge.

"Darcy," he whispered as his hips began to pump faster and her legs tightened around his waist.

And then her mouth opened on a silent scream and she threw her head back as the ripples turned into waves of undulating ecstasy around his cock. Her pussy tightened around him to an almost painful degree, but he still kept his strokes steady, wanting to give her every last drop of pleasure before he took his own.

"I love you," she cried out, lost to her own desire. She repeated the words over and over again, and that was all it took to send him over the edge.

Her love was a heady sensation, going straight to his head as he felt the come shooting from his cock and filling her womb. And as his strength gave out and he collapsed on top of her, he realized that there was still hope of her not walking away after all.

CHAPTER ELEVEN

They dressed quickly and in silence, and Darcy didn't dare look at Brant as she gathered her belongings and stuffed them back in her backpack. How could she be so stupid as to say the words aloud? The slipup left her without any protection for her own heart, and she waited, the tension coiling in her shoulders, for Brant to denounce her claim as unreal. As a lie. As if she didn't know what the hell she was feeling.

Her mood turned black the more she thought of it, and she kept as much distance between them as possible as he led her back down the multitude of stairs to the base of the temple and back into the jungle.

The sun had almost completely set, so once they were in the dense cover of the trees, it was almost black and Darcy could barely see the hand in front of her face. That didn't keep Brant from pushing her along and helping her to avoid fallen limbs or vines she might trip over.

Two long whistles sounded to her left and then two answering whistles sounded to her right. Her clothes were damp from perspiration, but a decided chill had settled once the sun set, and now she was shivering with the cold. She could feel Brant's seed still wet between her thighs, and she was grateful for the darkness so the others couldn't see how disheveled she looked.

SHADOWS AND SILK

Smith and Huxley were standing outside the Jeep, a small green glow stick in each of their hands to provide a little light. Darcy's heart pounded as Brant helped her in the back seat. Smith navigated the Jeep through the jungle and back to the main road without headlights, and she had a fleeting thought that that might be a helpful skill to acquire at some point. All three of the men in the car seemed to have eyes like cats, while she was fumbling around like an idiot.

"We received the all clear from Declan a few minutes before you guys came back down," Huxley said to Darcy. "He and Max didn't see anything out of the ordinary, but he wants you to call him and give him an update."

Brant dialed in the number on the sat phone and passed it to her. The shivers were starting to become uncontrollable—a combination of the cooler temperatures and fading adrenaline—and she huddled in the corner of the backseat even though Brant had tried to pull her closer to share his body heat.

She realized someone was speaking to her through the phone, and she shook herself out of the fog.

"Darcy?" Dec asked. "Darcy, answer me."

"I'm here," she said, softly.

"Are you okay?" he asked, perceptive as ever at reading emotions.

She didn't answer him, but instead went into what she'd discovered from the glyphs at the temple. "You need to start searching the area where those girls were taken. The glyphs are like a scavenger hunt. It's a game to them," she said, her voice breaking. She cleared her throat and refused to look at Brant.

"What do you mean?" Dec asked.

"I found the pattern once I started connecting the glyphs on the map. They leave a new set of glyphs after each drug drop for the next team of Ramos's men to find."

She noticed Smith and Huxley become very alert at the mention of the pattern, and Huxley turned in his seat so he could listen more closely.

"Damn, how did we miss that?"

"When Donovan Jax was still alive he was messing up the game because he was feeding you information, and the drops weren't being made like they were supposed to. After he was killed, that's when the pattern becomes more noticeable. If you go back and look, every time glyphs were found, there was eventually a body found in the corresponding place. I didn't always understand the clues, and your guys didn't always find glyphs at the drop locations, but they were there somewhere. We just missed them, and we didn't know exactly what we were looking for."

"And now you do?" he asked.

"Yes. Wherever those girls were taken from will have the next set of glyphs. They're not always going to be easy to find, so we'll need to look in obscure places at times. The sooner we find those glyphs, the sooner I can decipher them and we can get to those girls."

"Good work, Darce. Put Brant on the phone."

She handed the phone over to Brant, but still refused to look at him. If she was honest with herself, she was embarrassed because he'd made her lose her control, and not once had he ever shown that she had the same effect on him.

Brant took the phone, and she could feel his eyes on her as he answered her brother in monosyllabic tones. He hung up and handed the phone to Huxley in the front seat.

"Dec says it's time for you to relocate for the night," Brant told the two men. "We've got a sneak and peek at 0 dark 30."

They nodded, but no one bothered to interpret for her. Exhaustion seemed to come from nowhere, and she slumped down in her seat, knowing she needed to be alert when they went to look for the glyphs.

Her eyes drifted closed, and she must have dozed because she woke in Brant's arms. She stiffened against him and looked around, recognizing the path that led to their villa. She'd slept for longer than she'd thought if they were already back at the resort.

"I can walk it," she said, her voice husky with sleep. The moon was bright and full in the sky—a cloudless clear night that smelled of salt and sea.

"I know, but I'd rather carry you."

She could tell he was on alert, constantly searching for someone who might be lurking, and he didn't relax until they were inside. He laid her down on the bed and then went into the bathroom to turn on the shower.

He came back out to get fresh clothes, but didn't do more than glance over at her as he said, "You should go ahead and get some sleep. It's been a long day, and you're exhausted."

The fact that he thought she'd go to sleep in sweaty clothes with the sex still drying on her body alerted her that something was up. He'd been quiet ever since he'd talked to Declan, and she pushed off the bed and went to her suitcase to grab clean underwear and something to sleep in. She should probably unpack at some point, but Brant hadn't exactly given her time.

The bathroom was luxurious, and the shower was big enough for multiple people and surrounded by frosted glass that went from floor to ceiling on three sides. Steam billowed behind the glass, and she could barely see Brant's outline. She tossed down her clothes on the counter and stripped out of the ones she'd worn to the temple, and then she opened the shower door and watched as he looked up at her in surprise.

Her curiosity at his sudden odd behavior was stronger than the embarrassment she felt for making a fool out of herself earlier.

"Want me to scrub your back, sugar?" he asked, giving her the grin that had made her heart melt as a teenager.

She stepped beneath the spray and let the hot water rain down on her—her muscles welcoming the heat, and the stickiness from her body washing away.

"You can do my front too," she said, answering his grin with one of her own.

His eyes widened and his grin turned sensual. His cock bobbed against her hip, and she raised a brow in question, as if to say *again?*

"Always with you," he said softly. "But I have to say I'm much more interested in your back for the time being. I haven't been paying it near enough attention."

His hand slid around her hip and squeezed her ass, and she gasped as his finger ran down the crevice and slid into her pussy from behind. Her nipples grazed his chest, and she held completely still as he worked two fingers inside.

"I haven't taken you from behind," he said, kissing her temple and trailing down to her cheek. "I dream of bending you over and holding on to that fine ass as I slide inside of you."

She shuddered against him, but felt like she should be remembering something—focusing on something important—but he stole her senses.

"And what about here?" he asked, removing his fingers from her pussy and back to the puckered star of her anus. "Have you ever been taken here?"

A gasp escaped as he circled the hole once before pushing the tip of his finger inside.

"Mmm," he said. "I don't think you have. I like that I'll be the first, and that sweet ass will belong only to me."

He removed his fingers completely and reached for the soap, squirting some into the rag he pulled from the towel bar. Darcy was surprised as he began washing her as if he hadn't been teasing her for the last few minutes.

"Change your mind?" she asked.

"When I take you like that it won't be in a shower. I'll need to prepare you first."

"Hmm," she said, her mind working over the way he was acting. Almost as if he were in a hurry. "So what's a sneak and peek? And when's 0 dark 30? I'm assuming this is something to do with looking for the glyphs."

He finished scrubbing her and then started on his own body while she washed her hair. "A sneak and peek is just a term for a recon mission. 0 dark 30 is any time after dark. Not such a puzzle," he said.

"So when are we leaving?"

"I'm going in with Shane's SEAL team. They'll be here in another half hour. It'll take some time to get there and be briefed before we get into position." He paused as he rinsed the soap from his body. "Jade's going to be here to stay with you, and SEAL team 2 is still keeping watch from the water. You'll be safe until I get back."

Darcy finally realized what he'd been trying to keep from her until the last minute, and she shook her head in denial, turning off the water with a flick of her wrist.

"You can't leave me here. I need to go with you so I can decipher the glyphs, and you know it. I'm going."

He sighed and opened the shower door, and the steam billowed out into the air conditioned room. He handed her a towel and then grabbed one for himself.

"It's too dangerous. We don't know what we're going into, and it's best to use precaution."

"You're going in with the SEALs. What about your safety?"

"I used to be a SEAL. I know what the hell I'm doing."

"And are you willing to take the chance that something could happen to those girls because I wasn't there to decipher the glyphs immediately?"

He wrapped the towel around his waist and gave her a look she couldn't interpret. "Your brother and I agreed, and it's not up for discussion. You're staying here until we know what we're dealing with. We might not even find the glyphs, but there's sure as hell the possibility that Ramos still has men watching the area. We don't want one of them to see you."

"So you and my brother make all the decisions, and I'm just the puppet you pull out whenever you think I might be useful."

"It's not like that, Darcy." He dropped the towel and went to his suitcase, where he pulled out a black Speedo bathing suit and a neoprene dive suit.

"It certainly feels like that. What am I supposed to do if something happens to those girls when I know a matter of hours could mean their life or death? How can I live with that? How can you live with that?"

"In this business you have to learn to live with a lot of things," he said, the tone of his voice telling her he'd had more than his fair share. "And in the end you just have to make the best choice and move on. We need you alive and viable for the whole mission, not just part of it, and our goal is to take down Ramos and destroy his lab. We can't do that without you."

"I wish I could discard human lives as easily as you and my brothers seem to," she spat out. The words were meant to cut, and she immediately felt shame for even saying it aloud.

"Never easily," he finally said. "But sometimes necessary."

"I'm sorry," she said, biting her lip. "I shouldn't have said that. I didn't mean it." Brant and her brothers were heroes. She knew they did what they did because they loved their country and they wanted nothing more than to protect the innocent.

"It doesn't matter, Darcy. Just leave it alone." He used powder to pull on his wet suit, and then he packed a change of black clothing in his waterproof duffle. Guns and ammo went in the bag, and he strapped on his Ka-Bar around his ankle.

"I just think you're making a mistake," she said after a while. "I know how to protect myself, and I can keep up with you. Please, let me help."

Brant had his gun in his hand and pointed at the sliding glass doors of their villa without answering her. The glass door slid open, and the woman she'd seen at the bar when she'd first arrived at the resort slipped inside.

The woman had her own gun in her hand and a rifle slung over her shoulder, and she was dressed in black from head to toe.

"It's all clear," she said, her green eyes taking in the tension between Brant and Darcy with one look.

Brant nodded and slung his bag over his shoulder. "Darcy, this is Jade."

Darcy looked at the woman and nodded, but she didn't have it in her to smile like she was glad to see her.

"Jade," Brant said. "Don't be a bad influence. She doesn't need any help in that area."

Jade smiled and set her rifle down where she could reach it easily. "Maybe I'll teach her a couple of pressure points. You never know when you're going to need to bring a man to his knees."

"Very funny," he said, dryly. "I'll be back." He kissed Darcy once on the forehead and then slipped out the sliding door as silently as Jade had come in.

Darcy couldn't just sit there and not *do* anything. Jade did a quick walkthrough of the villa and then came back into the living area.

"I don't like those back windows being so open," she said. Jade's voice was as smooth as whiskey, and Darcy felt a quick dart of jealousy at the other woman—the woman the others treated as part of the team instead of an outsider.

But then the woman in question turned to her and smiled and said, "So how about you crack open that bottle of wine and tell me what Brant did to piss you off?"

"We don't have that many hours to kill," Darcy said. But the thought of getting a little drunk didn't sound like such a bad idea at the moment, so she grabbed a bottle of wine and two glasses from the bar.

"Make him pay, love. Sometimes it's the macho heroes that need a kick in the ass to make them remember that their relationship isn't a mission where they get to give orders all the time."

"That about sums it up," Darcy said, pouring the first glass to the rim.

"None of that for me," Jade said. "I wouldn't do you much good if I was piss-faced now, would I."

Darcy grunted and went over to the sofa, propping her feet on the table. "Let me ask you something." She didn't wait for Jade to give her the go ahead. "Does it piss you off that they stuck you here on babysitting duty while they're off doing the real work?"

Jade's brow raised, and her mouth quirked in a half smile. "Girl, this is a real job. I'm here because I'm a hell of a lot better shot than all of those muscle-men put together. And they know it. You're in good hands. Now, tell aunty Jade what Brant did to hurt your feelings, and I'll kick his ass for you."

"I can kick his ass myself," Darcy said, draining the glass.

"I think you probably can."

"The whole mess started four years ago—"

CHAPTER TWELVE

The city of Chiapa de Corzo was silent as a tomb at just shy of four o'clock in the morning. It had been thirteen years since he'd been an active SEAL, but the moves and thoughts of working as a well-oiled machine came back as naturally as breathing.

The five girls had been staying at the Palacio Concordia—a hotel reserved for dignitaries of state and other important guests. The security was top notch, and there never should have been any question of their safety. Which meant Ramos had the guards in his pocket. It was the only explanation.

The hotel resembled the palace of its name and was surrounded by a twelve-foot stone fence. It wasn't overly large, the hotel only having about a hundred rooms, but it had a large courtyard and two pool areas. According to Darcy, the men who'd kidnapped the girls would have left the new glyphs close to where they'd been taken—meaning somewhere inside the hotel or grounds itself.

"DEA is in position," Max's voice came through the earpiece. "Waiting for signal to move."

"Two guards down and wrapped," Dec said, meaning he'd immobilized the night guards and restrained them. "Cleanup can take them away for interrogation. We're clear for entry."

"That's our signal, boys and girls," Shane's voice said in his ear. "On my count."

Brant felt the adrenaline rush through his body as Shane counted down. The feeling was almost as good as sex. Almost. Shane hit zero and Brant moved from his position at a low run, tossing his rope to the top of the stone fence and pulling it slowly so the metal spikes would catch against the rock. He tested his weight once and then started the climb. His feet touched the ground silently on the other side, and he looked around as the other SEALs landed at the same time, their move well choreographed.

"Stick to the plan," Shane called out. "Find those glyphs and be ghosts."

There were seven men on Shane's team, eight counting Brant, and he'd paired each of them in groups of two to search different quadrants. They had a lot of ground to cover in very little time.

"I've got a surprise package outside of the gates," Dec said. "Keep your eyes open."

Brant and Shane shared a look of surprise, wondering if Ramos knew they were there, and they moved along the corridors, continuing their search for the glyphs. More than a half hour passed, and Brant knew they were getting near the end of their window of opportunity.

"Bingo," someone said in the earpiece. "I've got a target confirmation in quadrant four."

Brant didn't recognize the first voice, but he recognized the second voice as belonging to his brother, Brady. "Repeat. We've got the glyphs. Getting a visual confirmation before evacuation. Two minutes."

"You heard them," Shane said. "Two minutes. Evacuate."

Brant took out his earpiece and said to Shane, "I'm meeting up with Dec. I want to know what the surprise package is."

Shane took out his earpiece as well to answer. "I'm coming too. My brother always has the best secrets. And

SHADOWS AND SILK

I'm curious to see what Ramos might have left for us."

They climbed their way back over the fence, and Shane gave his team further instruction to do a solo evacuation back to their base. Brant opened the tracker he had on Dec and followed the glowing red signal two blocks away into a deserted alley filled with dumpsters and boxes. He and Shane both had their weapons out as they approached the small enclave into the side of a building.

Shane's surprise was as obvious as his own if his indrawn breath was anything to go by.

"Who the hell is this," Shane whispered, looking at Dec for an answer.

Brant could tell the woman was scared, but the way she tilted her chin in defiance reminded him a lot of Darcy, and he almost grinned as her black eyes spat fire in Shane's direction. She was a tiny thing, barely more than five feet tall, but she wasn't a kid. The loose black clothing she wore draped over womanly curves and her long black hair was pulled back severely from one of the most stunning faces he'd ever seen.

"She has yet to tell me her name," Dec answered, almost bored. "But I found her trying to sneak in past the guards before I disabled them and I found this," he said, pulling out a black pistol, "hidden in her waistband. I'm a little curious to know who she is too."

"One of Ramos's whores?" Shane asked, circling her, trying to throw her off balance.

None of them missed the way she stiffened at Shane's insult. It told them she understood English, and her silence wasn't a lack of communication. All three of them spoke Spanish, but that wouldn't tell them what they wanted to know.

"What's your name?" Shane asked her. "You might as well tell us. We'll find out if you're friend or enemy soon enough." His grin was wolfish, and he raked his eyes over her body insultingly.

Brant knew Shane would never do anything to hurt a

woman or leave her if she was in trouble. It just wasn't in his nature. He was a protector. And if it had been Shane who Vivian had gotten her claws into instead of Brant, Shane wouldn't have been able to pull the trigger in the end and he'd have died. He didn't know what it said about him that he *had* been able to pull the trigger. Nothing good, surely.

"You are American soldiers, yes?" she asked. Her accent was slight, and there was no quiver of fear in her voice even though she held her hands together tightly in front of her.

"Why would you ask that?" Declan asked in Spanish this time, throwing her off.

"The way you move," she answered back in kind. "The way you're dressed. I need your help. My name is Elena Nayal. And Alexander Ramos has taken my father. Or his men did I should say. I'm afraid they're going to kill him."

"Why would Ramos want your father?" Brant asked.

"Ramos is always looking for those who speak and write Maya. My father is a descendent. As am I, though I cannot read the glyphs well. Everyone for miles knows of Ramos and that he's always looking for those who can prove themselves useful to him."

"If your father is gone, why were you trying to get onto the hotel grounds?" Shane asked. He'd turned all business, crossing his arms over his chest and staring her down.

She copied his gesture and stared right back. "Because Ramos's men showed up at our home this morning. They just walked in and took my father from his breakfast. They struck my mother and left her crying on the floor. They didn't see me in the back room, but I waited until they left and then I followed them."

The savage curse Shane let out said it all. She would have been killed if she'd been caught. It had been a brave, but stupid, chance to take.

"They did not see me," she said quickly. "But I followed them to the Palacio Concordia, and they took my father inside. I waited for what seemed like hours until they came out again, but my father was taken by two men in a car and I wasn't able to follow. I thought I might be able to get a sense of where he was if I went onto the grounds. I know now that I had very little chance of finding him on my own. So I'm asking you for help."

"Shane," Declan said. "Take her with you. Show her photographs of some of Ramos's top men and see if she recognizes anyone. Then take her home, and I'll put Huxley and Smith on watch just in case Ramos decides to make another visit to her house."

"Brady sent the pictures of the glyphs to your computer," Shane said to Brant. "They'll be waiting for you when you get back. You know the rendezvous point. My boys will take you back when you're ready."

Brant and Shane fist bumped and he nodded to Declan before he walked out of the alley. He was ready to get home to Darcy. To see for himself that she'd spent the night safe and sound.

It was almost dawn when the Zodiac brought him to shore. Brant swam the last fifty feet as the boat disappeared into the fog and back to the waiting helicopter. It would be gone before there was light in the sky.

When Brant slipped inside the villa through the sliding glass doors, Jade met him much as he had her a few hours before—with a pistol pointed at his chest. He nodded to her and then looked for Darcy. His brow raised when he saw the empty wine bottle and Darcy sprawled out on the couch, snoring lightly.

"Nice, Jade," he said, bending down to pick up Darcy. She burrowed against his chest and let out a little hiccup.

"Hey, I didn't pour it in the glass," Jade said, laughing.

"Besides, she needed to get a few things off her chest. She'll feel better for it and maybe won't knee you in the balls as soon as she opens her eyes. Though from the things she told me, you probably deserve it."

"You can go now."

She laughed again and put her rifle over her shoulder as she headed toward the door. "Be thankful for what you have, my friend. You never know when it's going to be taken away. It only comes once." Her smile disappeared and he could see the sorrow in her eyes.

"You really believe that?" he couldn't help but ask.

"Sure. What's the point otherwise?" Jade saluted and disappeared, locking the door discretely behind her.

He held Darcy closer and headed into the bedroom, placing her gently beneath the covers. He was too tired to take another shower, but he did anyway, getting the paint off his face and getting rid of the saltwater. When he came out again, exhaustion was pulling him under, and he had just enough sense to close the curtains and enshroud them in darkness before he fell into bed beside Darcy. He gathered her in his arms and inhaled her scent before sleep took him under.

CHAPTER THIRTEEN

The room was still dark when he woke sometime later, but his internal alarm clock told him it was at least mid-morning. Darcy wasn't there, and panic set in before he remembered the team watching them from afar. If anything had gone wrong, they would have sent up a signal. But still, he was going to blister her behind for not waking him to tell him she was leaving. She'd probably just decided to go for a swim.

He scraped his hands over his face and rolled out of bed. And then an idea began brewing in his head, and he was very anxious to meet Darcy out on the beach. The trouble would be finding a place to carry out his plan without all of SEAL team 2 being a witness.

Brant pulled on a pair of swim trunks and realized Darcy had unpacked all their things and hung them neatly in the closet at some point. The sight of her clothes lined up next to his and her makeup on the counter next to his shaving supplies gave him a jolt, but it was one that filled him with warmth.

The sudden need for her was like a drug, and he wondered if that feeling would ever dissipate. Maybe that's what love was—an overwhelming need to just be with one person forever. It sounded possible to his way of thinking.

He loaded one of the wicker baskets in the kitchen with

supplies and a few extra goodies to sweeten the deal, and then headed out to the beach through the sliding glass door. The sun shone in a bright blue, cloudless sky, and there was just a hint of breeze carrying the smell of salt from the ocean.

Eyes were trained on him from afar. He could practically feel the crosshairs on his head, and he gave the team a signal so they'd know he needed some privacy.

It turned out Darcy had already thought of that when he reached the end of their stretch of the beach and her footsteps disappeared into the rocks. He set the basket on top of the nearest boulder and climbed on top, hefting the basket up and over to the little cove on the opposite side.

What he saw there made his mouth water and his cock harden to painful proportions. The little cove would be covered with water at high tide, but for now it was smooth white sand, shaded by two palm trees that jutted out of the rocks to provide a small amount of shade. Small bits of driftwood and debris were gathered at the base of the rocks, but for the most part, it was pristine.

And there Darcy lay in the middle of it—her large white towel spread beneath her and her body slicked with suntan oil. Her mostly *naked* body. Her white bikini top was draped across the rocks, and the matching bottom could hardly be called coverage. Brant scowled and looked out across the water, but the cove was pretty secluded, so the chance the SEALs had gotten a peek was minimal. At least she'd used some common sense for once.

Darcy sighed and stretched under the heat of the sun, her limbs lethargic and her eyelids heavy. The breeze whispered across her skin like butterfly kisses, and she moaned as the kisses turned to heated licks across her breasts. Her eyelids fluttered open and she smiled, still thinking herself in a dream, as Brant's heated gaze met hers.

"Oh, it's you," she said softly.

"Expecting someone else, were you?" he asked, rubbing his stubble across her sensitive skin and making her shiver.

"A handsome pirate to steal me away on his ship and treat me like a princess as we traveled the seas."

"You get seasick."

She made a face. It just figured that her subconscious had to be the voice of reason during her fantasy. "Or maybe I was waiting for a dashing sultan to rescue me from murderous marauding mummies."

"Are we going to Egypt then?" he asked, the amusement in his voice obvious. "You've been reading romances again."

"I like that they live happily-ever-after," she said on a sigh as his lips traced along her collarbone. "The hero always comes for her. In the end he can't live without her." Fingers trailed across her belly and up her ribs until they touched the undersides of her breasts. Just a skim of a calloused finger across her nipple had her gasping for air and her nipple beading in arousal.

"What about me?" he asked. "Couldn't I be your fantasy?" His voice was meant to seduce—to entice. "I would come for you. Always."

"But you wouldn't stay," she said sleepily, arching, searching for the hand that left her breast. "You used to be my fantasy. When I was a girl. I dreamed of you coming for me. Loving me. I like my new fantasies better. It hurts when you go away."

Darcy thought she heard her dream whisper something against her ear, and then those hot licks of flame trailed down her neck, suckling and nibbling until she was swollen and throbbing between her legs.

"Tell me you love me again," the fantasy voice whispered.

The haze of the dream began to lift at his demand—as if he really needed to hear her say it. But there was no time to question or deny. His lips slanted across hers, his mouth fitting against her so perfectly that she trembled. It was a kiss different than the ones they'd shared before, but she didn't know why or how. The heat of him overwhelmed her, and then his tongue rubbed against hers, devastating her senses, and when he broke away she was wide awake and realized her fantasy was reality.

His eyes were wide and dazed, and she realized he was already naked against her—his body hot and hard—slicking across her skin as the tanning oil she'd applied rubbed onto him. Her body was floating in some weightless dream, but her limbs were so heavy she didn't know if she had the strength to lift them.

"More," he said. "I need more."

She tried to shake her head. How much more could she give? He'd already taken everything from her. His mouth touched hers again and fireworks exploded behind her eyelids. His hands held her face tenderly, lovingly, as he savored the taste of her.

When he broke away this time they were both panting for breath, and she could feel his erection thick and full against her thigh.

"I want it all," he said, kissing his way down her body, massaging her with his hands, and then moving between her thighs.

His teeth scraped over her bikini bottoms, and he pulled them down, exposing her so the salty breeze kissed her nether lips. She wanted to squeeze her thighs together, to relieve the pressure building there, but he held her open, staring at her with hunger.

"You're so beautiful." He traced his finger down the edge of one sensitive fold, and her hips came off the towel. "Close your eyes, love. I want you to do nothing but feel me in every way."

Darcy's eyes fluttered closed and her other senses grew

stronger—the sound of the waves crashing against the rocks, the scent of salt and coconut oil, and the heat of the sun warming her skin even as the breeze cooled it. A cloth came over her eyes and startled her, and she jumped even as Brant soothed her with gentle touches. He tied it behind her head, and now not even the smallest peak of light could be seen.

"No cheating," he said, kissing the tip of her nose. "Are you hungry?"

"For you," she said, her imagination going wild as she heard him moving around her, a rustling sound, followed by the distinct popping of a champagne cork.

She gasped as cold liquid splashed across her breasts and belly, tickling trails running down the crease of her thighs and teasing her sensitized skin.

"I never could get the hang of opening one of those," he said. "Here, let me help you. You're all wet."

Darcy moaned as he started at her breasts, licking and sucking the liquid from her skin, his tongue wrapping around each nipple, heating them, arousing them to tight buds that ached for something more. But he didn't stay there long, and she gave a disgruntled huff when he continued down to her stomach and sipped away the rest of the champagne.

"There. All cleaned up."

She shook her head in denial. She didn't want to be cleaned up. And he'd missed the hidden trails of liquid that had slithered between her thighs. Her body shook with need as she heard more rustles, and then something cold and tart touched her lips. Her tongue darted out and tasted fresh pineapple, tangy and sweet, and she opened her mouth and took the fruit between her teeth.

Brant's lips followed, and he bit the other half of the fruit before taking her in kiss that left her head spinning and her heart racing. He repeated the process over and over again—with lush strawberries and juicy mango—drinking away the stickiness from her lips and chin before kissing her into oblivion.

"I want you," she said, her body so heavy with need she didn't know how she'd be able to stand it a moment longer. "I need you inside of me."

"I'm going to take my time." He gave her one more kiss and then said, "I'm going to touch and taste every inch of you. Now turn over. You're looking a little tense."

That was an understatement. She was as taut as a tightrope, and her body felt so fragile she thought she might crack into a million pieces. He helped her roll over, and she waited, her body coiled, to feel what he planned to do next.

"Relax, baby." Something warm and thick drizzled across her back, and she moaned as his hands pressed into her muscles and he began a slow massage. He was true to his word—he touched her everywhere—not leaving out a single place on her body, so she felt like a limp noodle afterward.

"Now lift your hips for me," he said. And when she did, he slid his head beneath her so her pussy rested just above his lips. Warm breath blew against her—teased—and she knew he'd be able to see how wet she was for him. There was no hiding that kind of desire.

The first lick into her was like an electric shock to the system. Her back bowed and she clamped her thighs around his head. And then his tongue became relentless, flicking and suckling, until she came to a blindingly fast orgasm that had her riding against his face.

Her arms collapsed and her damp face lay against the soft terrycloth towel, and she realized the only thing she could hear was the rush of her blood running through her ears. Tears came to her eyes and she almost cried out in protest when the licks started once more. She was too sensitive—too swollen to take much more.

"You taste so sweet," he said against her. "Like honey and rain."

His hands were still slick from the oil and he massaged

her ass as he continued the long, slow strokes. And then his fingers grew closer and closer to her pussy until two fingers dipped inside while his tongue wrapped around her clit.

"I can't take anymore," she pleaded. "It's too much."

"You can take as much as I give you."

The tears fell faster and were soaked away by the cloth around her eyes, and she shook her head as the tingles started again low in her body. His fingers dipped inside her again, and then they pulled back to the small star of her anus, massaging the entrance with her own lubrication.

A finger slipped inside and she caught her breath, unused to the sensations it caused. Nerve endings tingled and she rose up on her elbows so she could get better leverage. She pushed against him, trying to take more, and the sharp sting against her ass had her gasping in surprise. Her bottom was hot where he'd spanked her and she could imagine it turning a fiery red in the shape of his palm.

"Ah, a greedy wench," he said, adding a second finger to the first. "Don't be impatient, love."

He stretched her, scissoring his fingers, and gaining a deeper entrance all the while his tongue played havoc with her clit and his other hand laid well placed slaps against her ass. She was so close to coming she could scream, but he was keeping her just on the edge.

"Damn you, Brant. Finish it."

He chuckled against her swollen folds, and her eyes almost rolled back in her head at the new sensation. Her hips were thrusting against his face and fingers, and noises she didn't even know she was capable of making escaped from her throat.

The hand spanking her ass retreated, and then she felt more oil being dribbled over the tender area, his hand soothing where it had stung. And then he did it again, only this time the oil dripped between her buttocks and gathered where his fingers were piercing her, making it even easier for him to slide inside.

She tried to breathe, but even the simplest of requests her brain was making to her body weren't being heeded.

"Please, please—" she chanted over and over again.

"Whatever you want, baby," he crooned.

His fingers left her and he scooted out from underneath her, leaving her bereft and hanging on the precipice of pleasure. Her nipples grazed the terrycloth of the towel, and her hips searched for him. She was seconds away from ripping the blindfold from her eyes when she felt the tapered end of something unfamiliar.

"You asked what I had hidden away in my suitcase," he said, pressing the device inside of her without stopping to let her adjust. She was more than ready for it, but it grew wider and wider as he continued to push, until she felt stretched and flames of pleasure seared her to her very soul.

"I wish you could see yourself as I do," he whispered. "Just relax against it. Take it all, baby."

She bit the back of her hand as the toy grew impossibly big, and then the flared base popped in easily, so it was locked inside of her. Darcy cried out as the oxygen finally exploded from her lungs, and the electricity gathering in her womb crackled through her nerve endings and across her clit.

It was too much. She'd never take it and him too. Her hands clenched at the towel and she tucked her knees beneath her, huddling against the shivers that wracked her body.

"I can't—I can't," she cried out, rocking back and forth.

"Shh," Brant said. "I've got you, baby." He soothed her with a caress and a soft kiss, and then slowly turned her body so she lay on her back. He splayed her legs wide and then settled himself between them.

Darcy felt the head of his cock probe at her entrance, and she whimpered, her hands grasping at the taut muscles of his arms for an anchor. He settled over her, but didn't enter her, and before long the anticipation had her shuddering with what was to come.

And then the tie around her eyes loosened, and she saw reddish light through her closed lids.

"Look at me," he commanded.

His voice sounded strained, almost as if he were in pain, and Darcy's eyes fluttered open. The dark green of his eyes was all she could see—as if she were looking straight into his soul and to the man he wanted to be. It was a powerful connection, and she realized with a start that when he walked away at the end of their time that there would never be anyone else like this. It would have been a mockery of everything she'd ever believed in.

Her knees hitched higher around his hips, begging him to slide inside of her, while the toy stretching her ass made her burn with a dark desire she was almost ashamed of. He moved against her, slicking the head of his cock in her juices, but still not pushing home.

"Tell me what I want to hear, Darcy." He pushed against her just a little so she could feel the stretching at her pussy. "Tell me," he demanded.

She shook her head in denial, wanting to close her eyes to block out the pain she saw in his face, but she couldn't look away.

"I said tell me. You've told me before."

She bit her lip to stay silent and keep from giving in to his demands. He couldn't keep asking her to tear what was left of her pride and her heart to shreds. It wasn't fair.

"Damn you," he said, his eyes blazing now with a combination of need and anger. "Damn us both."

And then his lips came down on hers just as he pushed the full length of his cock inside of her with one stroke. He swallowed her scream at the invasion, and her legs clamped around him as he began to move as if hell itself were licking at his heels.

He was so thick and full inside of her, just a thin wall

separating his hot flesh from the toy in her anus, and the pleasure was indescribable. Fiery licks of sensation devoured her from the inside, so she was stretched between a fine line of pleasure and pain as he began to move with short, forceful thrusts.

Sweat dampened his skin and the thick cords of his neck muscles strained as he pounded inside of her. But the green of his eyes never wavered from hers.

"Fuck. You're so tight. It almost hurts."

She was incapable of speech. Even of breathing. Her back arched and her hips welcomed every thrust, and her pussy spasmed in uncontrollable surges that were beyond her control, milking him deeper inside of her.

Her nails dug into his arms as liquid flames erupted from the center of her body, and she heard him cry out her name as the world dissolved around her.

CHAPTER FOURTEEN

Brant wondered what the human body's threshold for pain was. And then he wondered how close he was to achieving it. Because he swore the hole where he thought his heart should have been was breaking right in two.

He pulled away from Darcy's still quivering body, and quickly removed the toy, storing it in a bag to be cleaned later. And then he rolled onto his back and threw his arm across his eyes in case the tears he felt building inside of him actually came. The breeze cooled the perspiration on their bodies, and he knew he should hold her right now, but to God's honest truth, he needed someone to hold him first.

"If I could love anyone it would be you," he said, his throat dry and the words barely audible.

But the sharp sob of breath told him she had heard, followed by a self-deprecating laugh that made him hate the man he'd become. She rolled away from him and curled into herself, but he didn't have the strength or the courage to pull her back.

"I was married before." He didn't know he was going to say the words until they were already out, and now he had no choice but to follow through. He owed her an explanation. She needed to know why. He felt her go still beside him, and knew she was listening, even though she stayed unusually silent.

"Her name was Vivian Rothschild, and we met in a Miami bar while I was working undercover doing surveillance. She caught my eye because I thought it was you at first, and I wondered what the hell you were doing in Miami and how I was supposed to keep my hands off you without your brothers around to run interference."

Brant kept his arm over his eyes, but he felt Darcy turn toward him and knew her eyes were watching.

"But she wasn't you, and I was almost grateful. It was an instant click for me, and I thought *This is it. She's the one.* I didn't find out until later that she'd studied you—how you moved and the expressions that crossed your face. Even that smart mouth. She knew you inside out, and reeled me in like a goddamned fish. We got married that weekend. I didn't need to wait. I knew she was the one.

"Your brothers didn't even find out about the wedding until later, and I could see the knowing disappointment in their eyes as they looked at her and thought of you. It's as pissed as Cade's ever been at me. He didn't talk to me for months. But I made them swear they wouldn't tell you. I figured I'd break the news when the time was right. Maybe you'd settle down yourself, and then it wouldn't be so hard."

"Am I so hard to love then?" she asked. The sadness in her voice was enough to break him.

"You were a fucking child. What kind of bastard would I have been to have pursued you that young?"

"I was eighteen. Not a child. And adult enough to recognize love when it slapped me in the face. Age doesn't put limits on things like that."

"Believe me, society and your brothers would have. You have no idea what it felt like to look at you at sixteen and know that everything about the way you made me feel was wrong. And the older you got, the harder it became to fight. But you still had a lot of growing up to do. I wanted you to come to me as a woman. But if Vivian hadn't come along when she did, I would have stolen what was left of your youth and dreams and taken you for myself."

"If that's what you thought then you knew nothing of my dreams," she said, the anger coming through. "I guess it's lucky Vivian came along. Maybe I should thank her."

"You'd have to take a one-way ticket to hell to find her. It turns out she was a Russian double agent, and I had just enough security clearance to make me a target. Political stirrings were rising in Russia, and DHS had moles everywhere over there. They have the largest supply of weapons of mass destruction, and things are volatile politically."

Brant sat up and scrubbed his hands through his hair. He still hadn't looked at her. It was hard enough to get this out without those witchy eyes on him. He watched the waves coming in closer and closer to where they sat, and he wondered briefly how long they'd been out in the sun.

"Like I said," he continued. "She studied you and spent months setting the stage. We were married for six months before the lust started to clear and my brain began picking up on small things it should have seen from the beginning. My security clearance had been raised again, and I was working my way up the ranks pretty quickly. I knew identities of agents we had undercover in Russia, and several of them reported to me directly. Declan help me set a trap for her." He laughed but there was no humor to be found. "I went to him with my suspicions, and Dec just gave me this look like, "What took you so long?'"

"Dec suspected her as a plant from the moment he met her, but he waited until I saw it for myself. If he'd had hard evidence he would have come to me of course, but some things a man just needs to realize on his own."

The breeze had picked up and clouds had begun to roll in. It looked like a late afternoon storm was brewing, and it fit comfortably with his mood. The waves grew larger and more violent the longer they sat.

"What happened?" she finally asked.

The frisson of fear gripped his belly as he thought of what he had to tell her. Of what could make her look at him with revulsion instead of the love she'd tried to hide.

"We laid the bait and waited. I can't tell you how eerie it was to look into her face and still see you. Even after six months of marriage the resemblance took me off guard on occasion. But I knew in my heart and my head you weren't the same, even though it was still you who clouded my mind."

"Should I be flattered?" she asked. "You think it does anything for my ego to know you couldn't stomach the thought of loving me, so you had to find the first substitute that crossed your path."

"No. I knew it would hurt you. But every time I looked at you, I felt the noose tighten a little more around my neck. I was scared. And I was afraid I wouldn't be the same man, be as effective as an agent, if I gave in."

"You have no idea how hard it is not to hate you because of that," she said.

"I can make it easier."

His stomach clenched in fear, and he wanted to punch something—anything. Darcy had every right to hate him, and he deserved it. He'd married another woman who reminded him of her and kept it from her. And then, years later, when he'd gotten tired of fighting the attraction, he'd taken her to his bed and then run away as fast as he could because one time with Darcy had made him feel like his fate was sealed. And the fear she could betray him as easily as Vivian had clouded his mind and his judgment.

"I know this hurts you," he said. "But I need to tell you all of it. Tell you the truth." He took her silence as agreement and forged ahead. "Vivian knew how to get to me. How to seduce me with little glimpses of you. And she used that any time she thought I might be watching her too closely. That's what happened on the afternoon she took the bait. I knew when she walked through the door that she meant to kill me, but I let the scene play out. I told myself I was in control, and I was already trying to separate the two of you in my mind at that point. It was difficult, because when I tried to think of your face it was hers I saw, and my loathing of her began to eat away at what I felt for you.

"She saw me waiting for her when she came home, and she gave me that look you sometimes give. The one that makes the dimple flutter in your cheek and your eyes sparkle like you have a secret. She stuck out her chin and propped a fist on her hip, and I just lost control. I was so angry that she could manipulate me that easily. That she could make me want her by pretending to be you. So I took her with every raging emotion that was left in my body, and I said to hell with the both of you. I couldn't see past the haze of anger, so I barely felt it at first when she slid the knife between the ribs in my back."

Darcy gasped, but he couldn't seem to stop talking, and he sure as hell couldn't face her.

"She was a trained agent, so she knew where to put the knife to kill me the easiest way. But I guess luck was on my side, because the knife didn't nick my heart. I had just enough strength left to roll off the bed and grab the gun from the nightstand. I didn't even blink when I shot her. I was just glad it was over, and I lay there just waiting to die. I figure I had a few minutes at the most. I tried thinking of you. To remember your face instead of hers, but it didn't work."

"My God, Brant."

Her breath hitched on a sob, but he forged ahead, ready to get it over once and for all. "Declan knew she'd taken the bait and was already on his way over, so he's the one who found me and got me to a hospital. I don't remember much after that. I just remember being angry. I've been angry for a long time. I threw myself in my work, and said to hell with you and any memories I had of her. They weren't real anyway. And I knew the whole time I was fighting a losing battle."

Her fingers lightly traced the scar on his back, and he dropped his head down when he felt her lips kiss it lightly.

"You told me I looked at you like I hated you that summer I came to stay with your family to recover." he said. He turned to look at her and saw she sat behind him, her knees up against her chest and her arms wrapped around them protectively. Fat tears slid down her cheeks, but he couldn't read the emotions in her eyes.

"And the truth is, part of me did hate you. If I hadn't wanted you so much I never would have ended up where I had. I was angry and bitter, and I realized I couldn't trust anyone, much less myself. That didn't stop me from wanting you, but wanting and loving aren't the same thing. I thought I'd loved Vivian at first. And now that I know what a fool I was, I just can't take that kind of a chance again."

The reasoning for the paths he'd chosen smacked him between the eyes with the force of a hammer. Vivian's betrayal had almost killed him literally. But if he ever broke down and vowed to Darcy that he'd love her forever, and then she betrayed him by leaving or deciding she didn't really love him, then he would truly be destroyed, heart and soul.

CHAPTER FIFTEEN

Darcy didn't know what to say. She couldn't possibly think of the right words after the story Brant had just told her. And the words still didn't come an hour later after they'd each showered in separate bathrooms and gotten dressed.

Brant had pulled up the photographs they'd taken of the glyphs the night before, and she was studying them on the computer and trying to ignore the way he was watching her. He'd closed in on himself as much as she had, and neither of them knew quite the next step to take.

A storm raged outside, much like the one raging inside of her, and rain slapped against the glass doors and shadows danced across the hardwood floor.

"These glyphs are different," she finally said, breaking the silence.

She took a drink of the cold juice at her elbow to wet her dry throat. They'd been out in the sun long enough for her to get a fairly dark tan. If she'd had a fair complexion, she'd have a hell of a sunburn. As it was, she just needed to hydrate.

Brant came around and sat on the bar stool next to her, but she edged away so not even their arms or thighs touched. She needed some distance to think. The corners of his mouth pinched at her slight, but he looked straight ahead at the computer screen.

"How is it different?"

"The other clues all had coordinates included. I'm assuming it's a backup system just in case whoever is reading the glyphs can't figure out the clues. Though they've been pretty straight forward up to this point. These glyphs have no coordinates. Only the clues."

"What do they say?"

"This group here," she said, pointing out the symbols that had been found inside a janitor's closet at the Palacio Concordia, "says, *The land of temples and Kings has turned to dust, and the fiery mountains protect their memory.*"

"Fiery mountains," Brant said. "Volcanoes?"

"That would be my guess."

"What does the other group of glyphs say?"

"*The jaguar king sits upon a broken throne, and the heads of the fallen rise.*"

"Hmm, not as straight forward as the whole fiery mountain thing."

Darcy's lips twitched at his wry tone. "The problem with volcanoes is that Mexico has something close to three thousand of them. We need to find a group of them together that has ruins in the valley below. The land of temples and Kings is somewhat vague, but it leads me to believe it was one of the major sites."

"What about that last part with the broken throne and the floating heads? Which is creepy as shit, by the way."

"You haven't even begun to scratch the surface of creepy with the Maya," she said, draining the rest of her juice.

Brant got up and refilled her glass and then put it back in front of her. He grabbed a beer for himself.

"Good to know. Though I guess they missed the mark with the whole end of the world thing."

Weren't they being polite and civilized, Darcy thought, somewhat amused. It might have been the first time in fifteen years where they were going out of their way to not ruffle each other's feathers. She was already missing the sparring.

"The second clue is a little harder to decipher," she said. "The jaguar king is pretty common. And broken throne could either be a literal or figurative reference if it's talking about a fallen kingdom. What you said about the floating heads might be a more accurate term than the actual heads rising. The problem is, I can't think of one single site in Mexico where all of these things add up."

"What about outside of Mexico?" he asked, watching her instead of the computer screen now.

"That's a little easier. The ruins of Kaminaljuyu are located in Guatemala. It's not far from Guatemala City, but it's surrounded by valleys and volcanoes. It's beginning is estimated to be from around 1500BC. And as far as the temples and kings turning to dust, then it would be accurate. Kaminaljuyu today is only a few mounds and remains of carvings. Though one of those carvings is of a jaguar king beheading captives with an axe while jaguar deities float above him. The carving is just a fragment from the larger piece."

"Guatemala," Brant said, rubbing his eyes. "Fuck. You're sure?"

"As sure as I can be. Nothing else in Mexico makes sense. Is it so outside the realm of possibility that Ramos has control in Guatemala as well."

"No, it's very much a possibility. But it makes our jobs a hell of a lot harder." He took the cell phone from his pocket and typed in a number that had way too many digits for a normal call, and Darcy listened as he relayed the information to who she assumed was Declan.

Brant gave her a long, steady look, and she raised her brow in question, knowing Declan must have been discussing her in some way.

"Fine," Brant said and hung up.

"What's he going to do?"

"He's suspected Ramos might have power in

Guatemala, but there hasn't been any hard proof. No deaths or deals. He's keeping the territory clean. Which makes us think we might have a match for our lab location. Declan is seeing if we can get an aerial shot of the area you described. He'll get back to us soon."

Darcy closed the laptop and moved away, wondering what she was supposed to do trapped inside the room with Brant. There were things she needed to say to him. Things she *had* to say to him. But she didn't have the courage, or even the right words.

She crossed her arms over her chest and turned back to face him. He was exactly where she'd left him and he was watching her closely, trying to use that cunning mind to dissect her every thought.

"Let's go get some dinner," he said, surprising her. "I'm starving, and it'll be at least a couple of hours before Dec gets back to us."

Darcy nodded, grateful for the reprieve, and then she escaped to the bathroom to change.

Darcy was thinking too hard about something, which in his opinion, always meant trouble was coming. She also looked as beautiful as he'd ever seen her, and something in his chest stalled as she stared at him with eyes that held too many secrets, and shadows of pain.

He knew he'd never forget the way she looked—the impression of her would be stamped on his mind when he was old and withered. She wore blue. And the dress gathered at one shoulder and fell in a straight column to her thighs. Her skin glowed, and the spiked heels on her feet made her legs look a mile long. Her hair flowed down her back in soft curls, just how he like it best, and he imagined the way they'd look spread across his pillow as he buried himself inside of her.

SHADOWS AND SILK

He shouldn't want her again. Not after the intensity of the lovemaking that had happened between them that afternoon. But it seemed like the wanting never really stopped.

Brant took her arm and covered them with an umbrella as they made their way from the villa to the main restaurant. They were shown to a table on the covered balcony so they could hear the wind and rain and waves. White candles flickered between them, making the shadows in her eyes even harder to read. It should have been a night for romance—for loving softly and lazily as the rain fell around them. To talk with each other easily as they once done, sharing common interests or funny stories about the members of their families. But that wasn't to be.

"What's wrong, Darcy?" he asked after they'd ordered and were sipping on chilled wine. She hadn't looked at him since they'd sat down. She'd just stared at the direction of the ocean, even though it was too dark to see the waves.

He watched as he inhaled deeply, gathering her courage. "I don't want to go through with our six month plan. I've changed my mind."

Her words were like a slap in the face—his biggest fear come to life. She wanted to leave. So her words of love must have been shallow at best. He kept his expression blank even though his hands fisted in his lap.

"I see," he said for lack of anything better. He cleared his throat and took a drink, trying to think of the right thing to say without doing more damage to their strained relationship.

She turned those big, sad eyes on him and tried to smile. "I just think it's time we stop playing a game no one is going to win. There's no reason to prolong it. You have everything to gain here, and I have everything to lose. And frankly, I'm tired of being on the losing end when it comes to you. It's just not fair—" her voice cracked on a sob before she took a deep breath and continued. "And I'm tired. I deserve better than you're willing to give me. I don't want your half-assed marriage proposals and the if I could love anyone it would be you speech. I love you, Brant Scott. I've always loved you. And it's time for you to either be man enough to love me back or to walk away for good. I'm not settling for anything else."

He exhaled a slow breath when she said the words he'd wanted too badly to hear. She still loved him. She was just giving up on him. Panic had a cold sweat snaking down his spine. It was the first time she'd said the words while looking him straight in the eye. She meant them, he could see that she did. But he couldn't give the words back, even though the thought of losing her forever made him want to break things with his own two hands.

He could say the words. And he knew if he said them he'd mean them. But he was terrified about what came after the words. If he opened himself like that to her, she had the power to hurt him more than even his wife had.

"And you think you'll be able to just walk away."

He was surprised at how smooth his voice was. How controlled. He didn't know how to convince her that he'd been relying on her to give him another chance. To see him through the darkness in his heart and show him that only their love would be enough in the end. He just knew he was out of chances.

"Yes," she said with a finality that chilled him to the bone. "It's over, Brant."

He ignored the tears that escaped her eyes, wishing he could shed a few himself. "Do you think I have nothing to lose by having feelings for you?" he asked.

"Since you've never said what those feelings are, then no. I think you have nothing to lose."

"Did it ever occur to you that Vivian spent months watching and learning you without you or your brothers being aware? Your brothers, Darcy, who are some of the finest damned agents I've ever met. She could have killed you and no one would have ever known. All because you were my obsession. The one thing I could never get out of my system. Any time you spent with me would be taking a chance on your life. I'd have *everything* to lose by loving you."

"Even after all this, *that* is the excuse you're going to use? You can't even be honest with yourself." Anger had brought color to her cheeks and her eyes lit with fire. "Considering what my brothers do for a living, those chances happen every day. I'm not going to live in a bubble for them or for you. I've lived my life the way I've wanted to, with many objections from the overbearing men in my life. But this time I'll be living it without the hope that I can spend it with you."

Frustration ate at him. He was being more than honest with himself. He no longer had blinders on about his feelings for Darcy. He loved her. All of her. But how could he tell her after all the misery he'd put her through.

Their food arrived by waiters who looked at them nervously. It wasn't difficult to feel the tension between them. But their appetites seemed to have disappeared since both of them did nothing more than push the food around on their plate.

The rain had stopped by the time they left to head back to their villa. The paths were well lit, and drops of water dripped from the palm trees. Brant heard the furious whispers before he saw anyone, and he put his hand on Darcy's arm to pull her back some as they made their way around the bend.

Darcy looked at him, and he inched forward slowly, his steps silent so he wouldn't alert whoever was there. This wasn't an argument between one of the other couples at a resort. It was the kind of argument that could go from bad to worse in a second.

What he saw once they rounded the corner was Marco Luna and his son squared off face to face. The elder Luna held his son by his shirt collar, and whatever threat he delivered made Enrique pale considerably. When Marco finished he let go of his son and stormed off in the opposite direction. Enrique stood there for a moment with his hands on his hips, the anger surrounding him like a live current. He kicked once at the pebbles on the path and let out a stream of Spanish vile enough to raise both his and Darcy's brows. It wasn't often one so young was that creative with language.

Brant started walking and pulled Darcy with him, and Enrique turned suddenly at the sound of their footsteps. The look in Enrique's eyes was enough to make Brant was glad he was armed. Enrique didn't bother to say anything or acknowledge them. He just took off in the opposite direction of his father.

"Well," Darcy said. "That was interesting. A kid that young shouldn't have eyes like that."

"Maybe it would be a good idea to look a little closer at the Lunas."

Darcy had told Brant the truth. What she felt for him was too strong—and it hurt too much to not have him feel the same way in return. There was a time to fight for the things that mattered in life, but there was also a time for self-preservation. And six more months of this would be the end of her. It was time to finish this once and for all and disappear for a while so she could lick her wounds in private. It would only be natural that the hurt would lessen over time.

Brant was quiet beside her, and she didn't know what to think of his silence. Whatever his feelings, he hadn't seemed all that upset with her declaration. Not that she'd be able to tell even if he was upset. He was like her brothers as far as keeping their feelings close to the vest. Maybe it was for the best if neither of them said anything for a while.

His phone buzzed in his pocket just as he unlocked the

door to the villa, and he ushered her inside and out of the way while he did a quick walkthrough to make sure they'd had no visitors. He held his gun in his right hand and answered the phone with his left.

The conversation was short and to the point with whoever was on the other end.

"That was your brother," Brant said. "It looks like you were on target with the ruins in Guatemala. Dec couldn't get an aerial shot because they've restricted flight access, and satellite imaging isn't helping much because of the dense coverage of the jungle. What satellite did pick up was about two square miles of military grade fencing, and soldiers on a guard rotation. Dec says it looks like a military operation instead of drug lord territory."

"So what's the plan?"

He gave her a steady look as he put away his weapon and tossed the phone on the bar. "Dec says we're all going in, but I'm still undecided on whether or not I should tie and gag you and have you shipped off to safety. How well do you know that area?"

"As well as anyone. I did my dissertation on that site. I spent six months living and breathing every hill and valley where the ruins used to be."

Brant rubbed the back of his neck in frustration. "That's what your brother said. You're coming with us this time. We can't afford to leave Jade behind to protect you. She's too important on a mission like this. And we can't afford any misinformation from what Dec has managed to glean in the last couple of hours. You're going to have to get us into that compound."

"I can do that," she said feeling the rush of excitement spread under her skin. They needed her. And she wasn't going to be left behind. "Like I said, I know the area well."

"*Goddammit*, Darcy," he said, pounding his fist against the counter. "This isn't going to be a walk in the park. We're dragging you into the lion's den, and I can fucking see the excitement in your eyes."

"Why the hell do you even care?" she shouted back, finally having enough of his pretending that she mattered. "I'm just a quick fuck. Don't stand there and pretend like you really give a shit. You know what you are? You're a coward."

She saw the vein throb at his temple and the way his eyes darkened so they were almost black with fury. She'd crossed the line, but she didn't care. At least she could tell he was angry this time. He couldn't be a robot all the time. Anger and hurt were one emotion now, and she couldn't seem to stop the rollercoaster she'd started on.

"You say I was your obsession for years? *Years!* And then you tried to push me out of your life by marrying the first stand-in you could find, someone who looked like me and acted like me."

She saw the wine glass on the bar next to her and grabbed one, throwing it at his head.

"What the hell?" he said, ducking so the glass shattered against the wall behind his head. His eyes narrowed in warning, but she didn't care and grabbed another glass.

"Don't give me some excuse about me being too young. I was yours. I've *always* been yours." Another glass left her hand and smashed against the wall to his right. "And you pissed that away because you're terrified of what loving me makes you feel after the wife—who you didn't love and who didn't love you by the way—stabbed you in the back and betrayed you." He moved again, and she could see he was trying to close in on her. She threw two more glasses in rapid succession and he took cover behind the couch.

"A wife that should have been me in the first place," she yelled. "So yeah. You're a coward, Brant Scott."

"Jesus, Darcy, get a grip."

"Get a grip?" She was running out of glasses, and glittering shards littered the floor. "After everything you've put me through you want me to get a grip?" She threw another glass, but her aim was fading along with her rage.

SHADOWS AND SILK

"I waited for you. For years I waited. And I kept loving you. But now you don't even have the courage to fight for me even though I know how much you want me. Well, you can go straight to hell."

She moved toward the kitchen since he was slowly circling the room, trying to trap her. Another glass left her hand, and she noticed the small trickle of blood running down the side of his face. Good, it served him right. The look in his eyes was dangerous, but she wasn't finished yet.

"And I'm going to tell every one of my brothers the things you've done to me," she said, throwing down her trump card. "There won't be a place in this universe where you can run and hide. I hope they cut your privates off and shove them down your throat."

He rushed her and she threw the final glass in her hand, but he swatted it away so it bounced against the soft rug and rolled under the coffee table. Darcy turned to run through the kitchen and out the front door, but he leaped over the bar that separated them and she knew she'd never make it. There was no escape. He swiped at the blood on his face, and she tried not to flinch as he backed her into a corner.

Her back hit the wall, and she had nowhere else to run, so she stuck out her chin and glared at him defiantly. She had nothing to lose. This was the end, and by God, she'd rather go out fighting than for him to remember the tears she'd shed at dinner.

"So you've always belonged to me?" he asked, his voice dark and dangerous. "It should have been you I married?"

He stood directly in front of her now, so close that every breath she took made their bodies touch. She tilted her chin even higher, the dare in her eyes, when she answered. "Yes."

"Maybe you're right. And if you were always mine, then I guess it's my right to take what belongs to me."

His mouth slammed down on hers in a kiss that was more anger and pain than lust, and she struggled against him, trying to hurt him as much as he'd hurt her. Teeth and tongues collided, and she tasted the coppery tang of blood in her mouth. She pulled at his hair and clawed at his face and neck, but he held her arms immobile even as his body slammed her against the wall.

Their breaths came in short pants, and Darcy felt the moisture pooling between her thighs. He could always make her want. That had never been the problem. He lifted her arms above her head and anchored them with one hand, and she gasped as he pulled the top of her dress down, tearing it as he exposed her breasts.

"This won't solve anything," she cried out as his mouth fastened over her nipple. Fire shot straight to her pussy and she arched away from the wall and toward him, seeking desperately what she'd decided to walk away from.

"Then think of it as a going away present. Because I swear to God you'll never feel what you have with me with any other man. Remember this was your choice to walk away. Not mine."

The anger and hurt in his voice were like lashes whipping against her skin, and he was right. No other man would ever make her feel this way.

"I won't settle for anything less than what I deserve from you. So take what you want and then leave me in peace."

He growled low in his throat, a primal, angry sound that had her flesh pebbling. His hand skimmed up her thigh, raising the ruined dress so it hung at her hips, and she gasped when he ripped the panties she wore and plunged his fingers inside of her.

"Ahh," she cried out, clenching around him and drenching his fingers with a hard, fast orgasm that left her limp and breathless.

Her head dropped and rested on his chest, and she was barely aware he'd released her arms. His fingers dug into her hips and he jerked her against him, so she could feel the hard ridge of his cock straining against his slacks. Her

SHADOWS AND SILK

legs lifted and wrapped around him, and Brant worked at his zipper and let his pants fall to his hips. And then he was inside her, rocking high into her, and she forgot everything except how right he always felt.

It was a fast and frantic race to the end. No finesse or soft words. Just the slap of flesh hitting flesh and the groans and grunts of good, sweaty sex. Her nails dug into his shoulders and her head flung back as she felt him swell inside of her. He thrust one final time and her world exploded.

CHAPTER SIXTEEN

Brant pulled out of her and let her legs fall to the ground, but he didn't let her move away as she started to straighten her clothes. He picked her up and carried her over the broken glass into the bedroom, and he sat her down next to the bed.

They were both subdued, and she didn't look at him as she removed the tatters of her dress. He looked at the clock and then began removing his own clothes, their time before they had to leave dwindling.

"We've got to meet the others soon," he finally said. He sat on the edge of the bed, suddenly exhausted and wishing he could just hold her for one more night. No sex. Just the feel of her in his arms. "You should go ahead and get dressed."

She nodded and then went to the closet, and he watched her closely every step of the way. She looked as defeated as he felt. Darcy startled in surprise when she opened the closet door, and he saw why when she pulled out a neoprene suit in her size and the black waterproof pack that matched his own.

"They'd have dropped it off while we were at dinner," he said, answering her silent question. "You'll need to go in like the rest of us. Have you ever worn a suit like that before?"

SHADOWS AND SILK

"I've done some diving," she said.

She moved around the room silently, gathering a bathing suit and then grabbing the powder from the bathroom so she could put on the diving suit. She seemed completely unselfconscious about her nudity, as if she'd stripped everything bare and had nothing to hide from him.

Brant knew what he needed to do to fix the mess he'd caused. Darcy had been right—he was a coward. He loved her with every breath in his body, and he wasn't going to be able to let her walk away. He'd let his experience with Vivian destroy what could have been made between him and Darcy, and it was no one's fault but his own. She was no longer a child, and he was no longer the man who'd try to escape her hold. But would she believe him if he told her how he felt now? Or would she just think he was trying to hold on a little longer?

Darcy pulled on another of those tiny bikinis she seemed to have in spades—this one in bright red—and she did a quick check through her emergency pack to make sure she had everything she needed. He was just about to tell her the words she longed to hear when his phone started buzzing and the panic alarm on his watch shrilled.

"Get down, get down!" he yelled, reaching for his gun and rolling towards Darcy.

The windows blew in and shards of glass rained down on top of them, and he shielded her to keep her from being cut. He felt the small slices of several shards against his own nakedness, and he hit the switch on his watch to silence the alarm. His ears were deafened by the concussion of whatever had blown the windows in, and he knew without looking the same thing had happened to the windows in the other rooms of the villa. They were surrounded.

The lights went out, and he kept Darcy beneath him. If the backup SEAL team didn't get to them within another couple of minutes they were going to be in big trouble. He waited for his eyes to adjust to the darkness, and he could see the outline of men as they searched the villa, weapons in their hand. Darcy lay still beneath him, but he could feel the panicked breaths she was taking. He squeezed her hand, trying to comfort her, and she squeezed it back to let him know she was okay.

They were hidden partially behind the bed, and they'd only have a few seconds before they were found. Boots crunched over glass and several men stood only a few feet from where they lay. He held his gun up at the ready, knowing if he took a shot they'd see their hiding place and likely return fire. And with Darcy only shielded by his body, he couldn't let that happen.

He lowered his weapon, and the lights flashed on as suddenly as they'd gone off. In the split second it took for his eyes to adjust, men grabbed his arms and lifted him off of Darcy. He struggled against them, bringing one of the men to his knees, and he fought harder as more men grabbed Darcy and pulled her away. She struggled against them, digging in her heels and clawing at their eyes, and he roared as one of them struck her in the face.

He had no way to overpower them all. They came at him from all directions, and he fought furiously as he tried to keep his eyes on Darcy. The snaps of broken bones and the grunts of those on the receiving end of his fists didn't slow them down. When he took one to the ground there was another ready to take his place. One of them had a knife, and he felt the sharp sting of a blade cut his arm before he broke the soldier's wrist and dropped him to his knees.

Darcy lay limp against one of the soldiers, her eyes dazed and a bruise already forming on her cheek. The soldier picked her up and tossed her over his shoulder, and her head jerked up so he could see the final look of fear in her eyes before she was taken away.

He was losing too much blood and his left arm was all but useless, so when a fresh group of soldiers came to restrain him, he didn't have the strength to fight back.

"Darcy!" he yelled, still struggling as they brought him to his knees. "I'll come for you."

He could only thank God she wouldn't be able to see them kill him. Enrique Luna's evil black eyes met his and he laughed. He heard Darcy's scream as they took her away, and then it was lights out. This time there was no seeing through the darkness.

Brant woke with a start, a dull ache roaring through his head and a pair of furious grey eyes staring at him from above. Nausea rolled through his stomach and he rolled to his hands and knees while sucking in deep breaths. He tried to stand and Declan grabbed him under the arms and pulled him to a standing position.

"Darcy?" Brant said, his mouth dry and his vision blurry. He couldn't have been out long, but he had to pull it together. Only one thing mattered now. Getting Darcy back. To hell with the rest of the mission.

"Gone, but we've got eyes on her."

"Where the *fuck* was backup?" he demanded.

"Dead," Declan said. "All of them. SEAL Team 2 was completely obliterated. Someone fed Ramos their location."

"We've got a mole?" Brant asked, his voice quiet and deadly. He could see the fine tremors of rage coursing through Declan's body, and it wasn't all because of Darcy.

"I'll take care of it. He's a dead man."

"They were on us too fast, and there were too many of them. I couldn't stop them from taking her."

Declan looked at the bodies that littered the floor of the bedroom, and Brant followed suit. He hadn't realized he'd taken out so many before they'd gotten her. The fact that they'd left him alive was a miracle.

"You're not Superman. Though you'd probably be dead right now if we hadn't shown up when we did. They scattered like rabbits. Some of Max's agents were able to pin a couple down. Can you hang or do we leave you behind?"

"Like hell you'll leave me behind," he said, getting in Declan's face. "She's mine. And I'll bring her back."

Dec nodded sharply. "Let's go then. I'll sew you up once we're in the air."

Brant looked down at the cut on his arm that was slowly oozing blood. Damn, Dec was right. A band aid wasn't going to be enough.

Declan tossed him some clothes and he dressed quickly, lacing his combat boots in record time and checking his weapons as they crunched over glass and through what was left of the villa.

He saw Max and Jade, as well as a few other agents he recognized from DHS and the DEA, looking for survivors to interrogate or clues that would give them identities. Smith and Huxley were doing a perimeter check of the house, and Shane's SEAL Team was also present. Though they'd have widened the safety net to keep the curious at bay until they could leave. The last thing any of them wanted to do was deal with local law enforcement. And if they didn't get out of here soon, that's exactly what they'd be doing. This group of men and one woman was the team Declan trusted the most, and it was up to them to bring Darcy back.

There was no need to protect their cover any longer, and two black helicopters sat on opposite ends of their private beach. Declan tossed him an earpiece and he slipped it in while they ran out the back door.

"Pull out," Dec said.

Shadows moved from the trees around him and Shane and the rest of his team appeared out of nowhere, heading for the chopper on the right side of the beach. Max, Jade, Smith and Huxley ran behind Brant and Declan to the one on the left. Brant had purposefully left his shirt off until he could be stitched back together, and he was glad he did once he'd settled in his seat because his arm was bleeding freely again.

Jade tossed him a bottle of water and he caught it with his good hand, taking off the cap and drink greedily before pouring the rest over his wound. He stared straight ahead as Dec sat beside him and pulled out the first aid kit, and he didn't even flinch as the sharp bite of the numbing antiseptic or the needle as it pierced his skin. The pain meant he was alive, and being alive meant he could save Darcy. He *had* to save her.

"Shane," Dec said. "Do you copy? I'd prefer to brief everyone at the same time."

Brant knew the SEALS would be on a different frequency. Their orders were given by their own commander, and sometimes their plans strayed from the norm if things went to shit.

"Copy," Shane said. "We're switching over now."

"Ramos knows we're all here," Dec said. "He knows your name, Brant. The reason he left you alive was so you'd have to search for her. It's the same as his other games. Our only hope is that he doesn't know we've found him yet. They left glyphs drawn on your shower door."

"How the hell did he find out Brant's name?" Shane asked furiously. "He's an undercover agent. That cover should have been protected."

Declan finished stitching up his arm, and he covered it with gauze before wrapping a bandage around it. Brant put on his shirt and caught the dark green tube of paint Dec handed him to camouflage his face.

"Ramos found the girl we questioned in the alley," Declan said. "Elena Nayal. They tortured her severely until she told them about the American soldiers."

"Son of a bitch," Shane said softly.

While they tortured her, they showed her pictures of Brant and Darcy when they went to the ruins the first day.

The ruins were closed because Ramos had set a trap, waiting to see if anyone might be interested in the glyphs besides his men. He had cameras everywhere. Elena recognized Brant from the photos because he was with us when we questioned her that night. From the things they did to her, there's no way she would have kept the information to herself."

"No one blames her for that," Brant said. Even the strongest agents could break under the right torture.

"Did they kill her?" Shane asked.

"They tried," Dec answered. "She was beaten severely and raped repeatedly. And then they left her in the middle of the street in front of her home. She was awake and able to speak when I saw her at the hospital—barely. She's a fighter. But it's going to take her some time to heal."

"I saw Enrique Luna right before they knocked me out," Brant said.

Dec nodded. "That's where our intel failed us. We were looking at Marco as being the one Ramos was training to step in as his second in command. The Luna money would have been a big help. But it was Enrique who'd become the protégé. He's barely eighteen years old, and his pockets are deep thanks to his trust fund. But his father has the other accounts blocked until he reaches a certain age."

Declan pulled out what Brant knew was one of the latest technology gadgets only a few agents and military commanders with high enough clearance had access to at the moment. It was a tablet a little larger than an iPad, but when Declan turned it on there was a complete 3D rendering of the ruin location. It gathered all information—topographical maps and satellite images—and meshed them together for a complete picture. At least as complete as they could get without seeing it in person. Brant knew Shane and his team were looking at an identical screen in the chopper in front of them.

"Here's what we're going to do," Declan said.

CHAPTER SEVENTEEN

Darcy moaned as she felt the bile rise up in the back of her throat. Her head felt like men were taking jackhammers to her skull, and her stomach was on a never ending rollercoaster ride. Her jaw ached where she'd been struck, and she spat out blood from the cut inside her mouth.

They'd given her something—not *Rabbit*, thank God—but some other kind of drug to knock her out. She'd fought them for as long as she could before one of the soldiers had backhanded her. Another had jabbed a hypodermic needle in her arm filled with the drug and it had been lights out.

Her head and limbs felt leaden, and she tried moving her arms, wondering why they'd gone numb. She lifted her head and the nausea rolled through her once more, but she gritted her teeth and breathed in and out through her nose. Once the room stopped spinning, she saw that her hands were cuffed above her head and attached to a long chain that was anchored to the ceiling.

She pulled and tugged, hoping the chains would loosen, but the cuffs rubbed her wrists raw the more they moved. Tears coursed down her cheeks and desperate sounds escaped her throat as she struggled. She finally gave up, her head dropping to her chest and her body shaking with sobs as she tried not to become hysterical.

The chains were raised high enough so she had to stand on the balls of her feet, and the muscles in her calves cramped and knotted as she tried to relieve the pressure. She still wore the red bikini she'd had on before they kidnapped her, but terror gripped her as she remembered what Ramos liked to do to his victims.

The room was numbingly cold. Chills broke out across her skin and her teeth chattered uncontrollably. She tried to get her wits about her, to start thinking instead of cowering with fear, but it was harder than she imagined.

She closed her eyes and pictured Brant as he'd been before they'd covered her eyes. He'd been fighting like the devil himself, and she prayed that he was all right. She had to keep hope that he'd come for her. It was the only thing she had left to keep her sane in this nightmare.

Darcy took in a deep, shuddering breath, and then she repeated it several times until the fog cleared from her mind and her fear was contained—at least for now. She looked around, wanting to have a plan in mind if they let her out of the chains.

The room she was in was perfectly square. The floor and walls were gray concrete, and it was obviously temperature controlled to stay cold. A gray metal door was the only way in or out, and there were no windows or natural light, only the bright fluorescents that hung overhead. Long sterile tables lined two of the walls, and she knew enough about chemistry and the equipment used to know she must be in one of the cartel cooking labs.

They'd taken her to Kaminaljuyu. In Guatemala. Though she had no idea how long ago that was. She could have been out hours or days. Darcy tried pulling at the cuffs once more, and she winced and cried out as her wrists became slicked with blood.

"You've damaged yourself," an accented voice called out. "Naughty girl."

Darcy gasped as she looked at the man who'd come

into the room like a wraith. She hadn't even heard the door open he'd been so silent. Or maybe her fear was just that loud. She didn't recognize him, but she recognized the evil in his ice cold eyes. He was average height and whipcord lean, and he wore gray trousers the same color as the walls and a white lab coat. His hair was so blond it was almost white, but it was thick and long enough to pull back in a tail. He looked like a painting she'd once seen of the angel of death.

She couldn't place his accent. Not German, but something similar. She had to pull it together. There was no way she'd ever be anyone's victim willingly. She just had to hope and pray she didn't lose her nerve.

"Who are you?" she asked.

"I'm Doctor Lindberg."

"Is that supposed to mean something special?" she asked, ignoring her fear and giving him an unimpressed stare. "Never heard of you."

"Tsk, tsk, Doctor MacKenzie. I've heard you can be quite—difficult to control," he said, giving her a smile that didn't help the shudders wracking her body. "You might as well save your energy. You're going to need it."

He turned back towards the door and flicked the heavy lock, the click deafening in her ears with finality.

"Tsk, tsk, yourself, Doctor Lindberg. I don't think Alexander Ramos would want you to lock him out of a room. He seems like the possessive type. And if I know Ramos, you're just one of the many people who take orders from him. Why have I been stuck with you and not the top dog?"

Darcy felt satisfaction as she saw the brief flash of rage cross Lindberg's face, but it was gone almost as soon as it began. He gave her a cold smile and walked toward her, his fingernails scraping along the edge of the metal tables.

"Alexander Ramos is a petty thief. He'd be nothing without me, and he knows it. This is my drug. And I can take it away just as easily as I make it. The power is in my hands. Not his."

"Sure, honey. Keep telling yourself that. I don't recall anyone ever referring to it as the Lindberg Cartel. You're just the hired help. I bet Ramos can find any number of scientists to cook for him. Now run along and get Mr. Ramos. I'd like to speak to him face to face."

He laughed and the sound slithered up her spine. "You're something else, Darcy MacKenzie. A pain in the ass for sure, but you're entertaining."

"So my brothers tell me often."

He reached in his pocket and pulled out a pair of latex gloves, snapping them in place with quick familiarity, and Darcy felt her blood run cold. He smiled at her when he saw her fear, and she stilled like a statue as he reached back into his coat pocket.

"Do you know what this is?" he asked, holding up a gold pillbox that fit in the palm of his hand.

"Compact powder? Believe me, you're pale enough without it. Maybe try getting a little sun instead."

"This is my creation," he said. "What these underground labs were built for, and why Ramos has paid me so much money he's almost bled himself dry. But let me tell you a little secret. This is the pure stuff. Not the mix I've been passing off on Ramos. We're going to have some fun, Doctor MacKenzie. I always did prefer my women to have some intellect. And I like it when they fight."

The promise of what was to come flashed in his eyes, and Lindberg opened the little round case in his hand. Darcy could see it was filled with a loose white powder, and sweat coated her frigid skin while her heart pounded against her chest. There was no way out of this. She was going to die. And she was going to die painfully.

Think Darcy, think!

He moved toward her and stuck the tip of his gloved finger into the powder, holding the case steadily in his hand. She'd only get one chance, but he had to get close enough. Just a couple of more steps.

He was just about to close the case when he made that last step, and she kicked up with her legs, ignoring the excruciating pain in her arms and wrists as all of her weight was put on them, and she kicked out at his hands so the case of powder flew up and into his face.

All it took was one small touch of *Rabbit* on the skin for the drug to take effect. Doctor Lindberg had just taken an entire face full. White coated his face and eyelashes, and his pale eyes looked up at her with disbelief and hatred.

"You bitch!" he yelled.

If he touched her she would be just as dead as he was, and she prayed the increased dose would work even faster than a small amount. He stumbled back, and his skin flushed red from the effects of the drug, even as perspiration dotted his skin. She wanted to look away as he began tearing at his clothes, trying to get them off to seek the release his body craved, but she couldn't take her eyes off the horrific sight in front of her.

She had to be ready to fight him if he came for her. Her mouth went dry with fear as he tore the last of his clothes away, and his erection stood angry and red away from his body. Madness gleamed in his eyes, even as he took himself in his hand and started working the shaft with impossible speed.

He took a step towards her and Darcy screamed and screamed, praying for Brant and a miracle. The monster took one more step and then his eyes rolled back in his head and he collapsed to the ground, his head hitting the concrete with a sickening thud. His nude body lay still next to her feet, and the scent of death filled the air.

Darcy couldn't control the nausea this time, and she turned away as her stomach heaved and her eyes flooded with tears.

CHAPTER EIGHTEEN

"I want communication every step of the way," Declan said. "Smith and Huxley take the north side. Max and Brant cover the southwest and I'll take the southeast. Jade will cover us from here. SEAL Team 6 and 4 are both here. Don't get in their way. Our mission is to get all of the hostages out alive if we can."

They were all dressed for battle—dark green camo and facepaint, and night vision goggles strapped to their heads. The SEALs would go in first and take down as many as they could to clear the path for the agents going inside the underground compound. It must have taken Ramos every bit of four years to build such a place.

The sound of gunshots echoed in the distance, and Declan gave the signal for them to move into position. They all split off in the directions they'd been told to go. Dec had been right about this looking like a military operation. And not just any military operation. The way Ramos had his soldiers set up around the perimeter, and the way they moved in coordinated fighting positions looked like it had been taken from the US military handbook.

There was no time to scout the area any more than had already been done. It was sink or swim now, and the longer they waited the less of a chance for survival Darcy had. Brant and Max cleared the chain link fence and then ran for cover as all hell seemed to be breaking loose around them.

The ruins were exactly like Darcy had said. No more than mounds and valleys of grass with the occasional broken tablet or carving scattered about. It was a large area square footage wise, but they headed away from the main ruins and towards the opposite end of the gated area. There were valleys and hills here as well that were apart of the original Mayan site, but it wasn't the main area where the temples and relics had once stood. And within the swells of the hills were doors that led to the underground tunnels of Ramos's organization.

"We're in position," Huxley called out. "Going in."

Brant and Max ran to their own entry door, taking care of the guards they'd caught from behind quickly, and rigging up the small explosion to blast through the heavy door.

"We're in," Brant called out, going low through the smoke and into the tunnels.

"In," Declan said.

"Both of your areas are clear," Jade said.

"Shit! Shit!" Huxley suddenly yelled. Rapid gunfire and the screams of the dying echoed in theirs ears.

"Report, goddammit," Declan said. "Huxley? Don't you fucking die on me. Sophia will be pissed."

A small exhale of a laugh could be heard through the earpiece and Brant knew the sound well. He looked at Max and saw the other man recognized it as well, and even as the sounds of death filled their ears, they started down the tunnels with their weapons ready. They had to keep going.

"She will be pissed," Huxley said softly. "Smith is down. And I'm—hit." A few seconds of labored breathing went by before he spoke again. "Take care of her for me, Dec. I know you will. I've always known about—"

"I'll take care of her," Declan answered before Huxley could tell whatever deathbed secret he'd been about to share. "She'll be safe. I swear it."

The line went silent, and Brant and Max traded off covering for each other, moving through the tunnels like death itself when they came across the cartel soldiers.

"Report," Declan ordered.

"All the rooms we've found so far are empty," Max said. "We're coming up on the last few in this sector."

"I've got one that looks promising," Dec said. "It's got very nice locks."

"SEALs are kicking butt and taking names," Jade said. "The party is still going on, but there aren't as many to tango. No sign of Alexander Ramos yet. Keep your eyes open down there."

There were several locked doors at the end of the hallway, and then another that tunnel led to the left. The underground area was huge, and they'd never find what they were looking for paired off this way.

"I'm splitting off," Max said, echoing his thoughts. "We've got another tunnel. I should be headed in your direction Dec."

"Copy that. I'm still working on this door. It's coded."

Brant nodded once at Max, and then Max split off and went quickly down the other tunnel. Brant went through process of unlocking and securing each of the rooms he came to, and if he'd only been giving them a cursory glance, he would have missed the secondary door inside the last room he opened.

It was a bunker of sorts, with two cots and a makeshift closet filled with blankets and extra clothes. But behind it was another metal door. This one smaller than the others, only coming to his shoulders. There were two different locks on the door, but the keys were hanging right there on a hook.

"I may have something here," he said. "Stand by."

The keys turned easily in each lock, telling him they were used often and well maintained because of it, and he held his weapon at the ready as he turned the knob. The smell of blood and dirt and fear hit him in the face as he pushed the makeshift closet out of the way and let the light filter in.

Pale, dirty faces stared back at him out of terrified eyes, and he counted quickly, noting that Darcy wasn't among them.

"I've found the girls. It looks like at least one of them is hurt. Darcy isn't with them."

"I'll find her," Max promised.

Brant had to put his trust in Max. He had no other option.

"Hi," he said, making slow movements and keeping his gun down as he approached the girls. He knelt down in front of them, but to the side so he could see the door. "I'm going to get you out of here, but you're going to have to help me. I can't carry all of you. Is everyone able to walk?"

"Except for Jenna," one of them said. She looked to be the oldest. "I think her leg is broken."

"Okay then. I'll take care of Jenna and the rest of you are going to stay behind me." He took out the gun from his ankle holster and held it out to the one who'd spoken. "Shoot if I tell you to and then run like hell."

She nodded and took the gun, and then Brant scooped Jenna up in his arms. She was unconscious and he didn't like her color, but there wasn't time to examine her now. They started out the door, but Declan's voice made him pause.

"We've got a little problem here," he said.

"What kind of a problem?" Max asked.

"That door I was telling you about? I finally got it open. Ramos has this place set on a timer to blow to hell and back once the exterior doors are breached. We've got about twenty-two minutes to get out and get clear."

"Jesus," Brant said, not sure if he were swearing or praying. "Find her. You've got to find her."

"Get the girls out," Dec said. "Jade, meet him at the

exterior and you can lead them to safety."

"On my way," she said.

"I think I've got something here," Max said. Brant could only listen with helplessness as Max cursed at the lock on the door. "Gotcha, you bastard," Max said. And then he said something that froze Brant's blood.

"Oh—shit. This is bad."

"Is she alive, goddammit?" Brant screamed.

"She's alive." Brant heard Dec's exhale of relief. "But, holy shit is this something I never want to see again."

"Just get her out of there," Dec growled.

"Roger that. I should be on the east side. I think. This place is a maze. She's manacled by some heavy duty chains. It might take me a minute to get her down."

"I'm headed your way," Dec said. "I can't disarm this bomb. I don't have enough time, and it's unstable as it is. This place is going to blow. Get those girls out."

Brant sighed with relief that they'd found Darcy, and he looked at the bedraggled girls in his care and said, "We've got to run. Help each other if you have to. I know you can do it. I need you all to be really strong right now."

They looked at him like with trust in their eyes and nodded, and then Brant started running for the nearest exit.

His heart pounded in his chest and his lungs burned as they ran, and he tried to lead the girls so they wouldn't fall over the bodies they'd left on the ground. He heard Dec say, "Holy shit," as he caught up with Max, and then he listened to both of them curse as they tried to free her from the chains. He didn't know what Darcy had faced in that room, but he prayed he could help her get through it.

"Declan?" the sweetest voice he ever heard came through the earpiece.

"Figures you'd give him the credit," Max said good-naturedly. "But I'm actually the one who saved you, sweetheart."

"My hero," Darcy said. And then a single gunshot

sounded through his earpiece followed by another—an insurance shot—and then everything went silent and his blood chilled. Sweat soaked his skin and clothes by the time he saw the hole where there had once been a door, and he saw the quick pinpoint of light against the ground—a signal from Jade.

"I'm in place," she said. "I'll take them from here. Go help them. Go. Go!"

He handed Jenna over to her waiting arms. Arms he knew were strong enough to bear the load. And then he turned around and headed back inside the tunnels, the temperature not nearly as cool as when they'd first entered.

"Max, Dec," he said softly, knowing the receiver would pick up his voice. But there was no answer from either of the other men. He took out his earpiece so he wouldn't be distracted by trying to hear something that wasn't really there as he took the opposite hallway from where he'd been. He knew he was heading toward the direction Max had gone, but he didn't know how far he'd made it or how long the tunnel was.

The lights flickered, and he hoped to hell the SEALs had secured the perimeter and weren't right on top of them when this thing blew. He could count on Jade to pass the word.

Brant's footsteps were silent as he slowed and listened for any signs of life. His hand was steady on his weapon and his focus complete. He'd been in similar situations more times than he could count—only this time it was the woman he loved and his friends whose lives hung in the balance. He couldn't let that affect him though. They'd all be dead if he did.

He calculated the time they had left before the bomb blew in his head, and knew he was fighting a losing battle. But just as he had the thought he heard the whisper of voices from not far away.

The tunnels came to a crossroads, and it was sheer luck that had Brant coming up to the side and slightly behind

Alexander Ramos instead of directly in front of him. Fear and rage ate at Brant from the inside out as he watched Ramos yank Darcy up by the hair and hold the gun to her head. Her small cry was like a knife to the heart, and he swore Ramos wouldn't survive, one way or the other.

He had to take a deep breath and assess the situation. Declan faced Ramos, and his weapon was on the floor in front of him and his hands were up, though Brant knew that didn't mean anything. There wasn't man or machine who could move faster than Declan. Max lay crumpled on the ground to Ramos's other side, and there was so much blood around his body he knew his friend couldn't have possibly survived.

"You won't stop me," Ramos said. "Even now your SEALs are dead and the drug is being transported to the first of many auction sites." He rubbed the gun down the side of Darcy's face, and laughed as she flinched. "But maybe I'll keep her. I watched on the surveillance tape what she did to my scientist. She is feisty, yes?"

"You know none of us are getting out of here," Declan said calmly. "That little insurance plan you've got cooking down the hall will make sure of that."

"Then I guess I should kill you now so I can make my escape."

Ramos lifted the gun and several things happened simultaneously. Darcy went limp in his arms, Declan dropped and went for his gun, and Brant took the shot he'd been waiting for.

He didn't even wait to watch Ramos fall. He ran to Darcy and scooped her up in his arms while Declan threw Max over his shoulder and they both ran like hell towards the exit. The lights continued to flicker and the hill they were inside of seemed to moan and stretch around them, shaking loose chunks of concrete and debris.

The pale light of morning could barely be seen as the lights went out all together, and Brant stretched his legs and pushed himself even harder as an unholy rumble shook the ground beneath them. They shot out of the underground tunnels and headed for the safety of the trees. Then the earth crumbled beneath their feet, and the hillside behind them dissolved like snow. The atmosphere charged around them as a heat like nothing he'd ever felt chased him like a demon out of the depths of hell.

CHAPTER NINETEEN

The only thing Brant knew was that he couldn't let go of Darcy. The shockwaves sent them flying through the air, and he tucked her tightly against his body and turned so he'd take the brunt of the fall.

He landed with the force of a thousand men, and he stared up as the sun began to trickle through the leaves above him, and he wondered if this was the white light everyone talked about. He couldn't breathe and he had no feeling in his limbs, so he figured this must be it.

And then his lungs started to work and he inhaled in a deep gasp of air, even as the feeling came back to his limbs in the form of pain. Not heaven. And then the woman he still held tightly in his arms moved and lifted her head so he could see those bright blue eyes, and he decided maybe it was heaven after all.

"Brant," she said. And then she burst into tears, burying her head against his chest as her tears soaked straight through what was left of his shirt.

"It's all right, sugar," he said, pulling her closer. "I've got you. I've got you." He buried his face against her hair and breathed her in. "And I'm never letting you go. I love you, Darcy."

Her head jerked up, and if he'd been a hair slower, she'd have headbutted him in the chin.

SHADOWS AND SILK

"What?" she asked. "What did you say?"

Chaos reigned around them as helicopters started circling overhead and shouts and orders were carried out with equal urgency. He should get up and help get things organized, but he only had one thing on his mind at the moment—holding on to Darcy as if his life depended on it. He was through running and making excuses. Love did exist, and it was right there in his arms.

He rolled her to her back, the ground a soft carpet of moss and leaves, and he leaned down so they were eye to eye. Tears continued to fall, and he wasn't so sure a few of them didn't belong to him.

"I said I love you. It's no illusion. And I can't live the rest of my life without you beside me. It's always been you," he said, repeating the words she'd once told him. And then his mouth found hers, and all the aches and pains disappeared as her touch soothed his body and soul. It was a kiss of longing and of new beginnings, filled with sweetness and the promise of things to come.

Something nudged him in the side, and he barely noticed, so focused on the heat of Darcy's mouth and the way she felt beneath him. And then something a little sharper kicked him in the side, and he grunted as he looked up to see two disgruntled MacKenzies standing over them.

Darcy buried her face against his neck, and he could feel her silent laughter, but he wasn't the least bit amused.

"What the hell do you two want? Go away." He moved to ignore them and start kissing Darcy again, but Shane decided to speak.

"I'm assuming there's a wedding in our future?"

Brant felt Darcy still beneath him, and he leaned back so he could see her face. She looked at her brothers, her annoyance plain for them both to see, and then she looked at him and her gaze softened. He almost gave in and kissed her swollen lips again, but he wanted to know how she was going to answer Shane.

"We've decided to elope," she said, giving him a heart-stopping grin. "We'll send you a postcard."

"You heard her," Brant said, wondering what he'd done to ever deserve her. "Now get lost. I was in the middle of something."

Shane and Declan both grunted and walked away, leaving them alone.

"You're mine, Darcy MacKenzie. From now to eternity. No more running." He leaned down and touched his lips softly to hers, whispering the words he'd been so afraid to say against them.

He felt her smile and then she finally said the words he'd been waiting to hear again.

"I love you too, sugar."

EPILOGUE

Six Weeks Later

"Congratulations, Mrs. Scott," the nurse said, handing Darcy a sample packet of pre-natal vitamins and the DVD they'd taken of the sonogram.

She was still in shock, so she only nodded dumbly at the nurse and put the items in her purse. The nurse left her alone to dress, and Darcy felt the sudden urge to burst into tears and start laughing hysterically all at one time.

A baby, she thought, pressing her hand over her flat stomach. She was already six weeks along. It looked like Brant had been right. The broken condom had been fate lending a hand.

They both wanted a family, not to mention they'd been trying pretty regularly since they'd said their wedding vows. Brant loved her to distraction. He cherished her. And he never let a day go by without telling her how he felt. They talked and made love for hours on end, and she knew he and her brothers were cooking up some kind of business venture that would keep him closer to home.

Darcy grinned to herself in excitement. She couldn't wait to tell him and see the reaction on his face. It would be the ultimate surprise. And it's not like she could keep it a secret for very long.

Her doctor's office was inside John Hopkins Hospital, which was where Max Devlin had been in ICU for the last six weeks, and where the girls who'd been kidnapped had also been treated and released. Smith and Huxley's bodies were never recovered and assumed destroyed in the explosion, but she'd attended his funeral and watched his wife sit on the front pew next to Declan, stoic and pale, as man after man eulogized him with honor. But she'd seen something in the way her brother watched the widow that made her worry, and she hoped he knew what he was doing.

Max hadn't been doing so well. He'd taken a shot to the leg and another to the head, and amazingly he'd survived both of them. His doctor said Max's head must have been like granite, because the bullet bounced right off. Unfortunately, Max was still in a coma, and there hadn't even been the smallest sign that he was closer to regaining consciousness.

Darcy gathered her things and went to the desk so she could pay and schedule her next appointment. She waved goodbye and then decided while she was here she might as well check on Max. She'd developed a soft spot for her husband's friend during their time in Mexico. He might look like a CFO, and he had a bawdy sense of humor that reminded her of her brother Shane, but he was a damned good agent and a good friend.

She headed to the elevators that would take her up to the ICU level. They'd all taken turns coming to talk to him, hoping he could hear them, and she decided she could practice telling Brant about the baby on Max. That way she wouldn't be so nervous when it came time for the real thing.

Butterflies bounced around in her stomach the more she thought about it, and she started to feel a little queasy, which was ridiculous because she hadn't had even a little

SHADOWS AND SILK

bit of morning sickness over the last weeks.

"Buck up, Darcy. Women do this every day."

Except when the elevator doors opened on the eleventh floor and she stepped out into the hallway, she wasn't expecting to see her brother and her husband in deep conversation across from Max's room.

They both looked up when she got close, and she got lost in the way Brant looked at her, all the love he had shining right there in his eyes.

"It's like I'm invisible," Declan said.

"I'm sorry," Darcy said, her mouth quirking in a smile as she finally looked at Dec. "Did you say something?"

"Brat," he said, affectionately.

"What were you guys talking about so seriously?"

"Christmas," Dec said. She could tell he was lying, but she let it pass. They'd been having a lot of secret meetings lately, and not even her best tries as seduction had gotten Brant to crack under pressure. She narrowed her eyes at him and decided against asking more questions. She was in too good of a mood to let her brother annoy her.

"Everyone will be there," Darcy said instead. "Mom's ecstatic. It's been a long time since everyone was home for Christmas."

"If she mentions the damned firecrackers in the fireplace again I'm going to start looking for another family to adopt."

"Serves you right," she said, laughing. "I hope someday you have children who are as dangerously creative as you were."

Dec smiled at her, but she could see something in his eyes that made her a little sad. She didn't know much about her brother's personal life, but she knew he wasn't completely happy either.

"Stay out of trouble," he said, kissing her on the cheek. He and Brant shook hands and then Dec disappeared down the hallway and got on the elevator.

"What are you doing here?" Brant asked, putting his

arm around her and pulling her close. He nuzzled his lips against her neck and said, "This isn't the day you normally come."

She pulled back and looked at his chin as she felt the heat flush over her cheeks. "I was here anyway for a doctor's appointment. I figured I'd stop by and see how Max was doing."

"Oh, yeah?" he asked curiously. "And what did the doctor have to say?"

The way he asked had her examining him a little closer. She narrowed her eyes, curious about the hint of laughter she saw gleaming in his and then she gasped. "You already know. You dirty rat. How could you possibly know? I just found out."

He laughed and pulled her closer, and Darcy sucked in a breath as she felt his hand cup her breasts like he was weighing them.

"I should say I suspected. I've made it a point to become an expert on your body, so I notice even the smallest change. And you've definitely changed—here," he said. His thumb rasped over her nipple and she felt it bead, even as she felt the throbbing need of arousal begin between her legs.

"We're in public," she said, moaning as his nail scraped across the sensitive bud.

"Mmm," he said. "Then maybe we should go home and celebrate the good news. I've heard expectant mothers need to be pampered. Preferably on your back. With your legs over my shoulders."

Darcy gasped at the image and then nipped at his bottom lip before dancing out of his grasp.

"First one home gets to be on top," she said, laughing as she ran for the elevator. There was no doubt in her mind he'd be right behind her.

SHADOWS AND SILK

Inside the hospital room, the sound of beeping machines and the scent of disinfectant were driving Jade crazy. She sat next to Max, holding onto his hand, as she carried on a one-way conversation with him.

"Don't die on me, Max," she said, rubbing soothing circles in his palm with her thumb. "You're the best partner I've ever had. Though I wouldn't admit it to Donovan if he were still alive. You know how he liked to try and protect me instead of letting me do my job."

She let out a sad sigh, thinking of the good times she had with her husband that always equaled out the bad. She'd loved him. And then he'd pulled some macho stunt and had gotten himself killed. And Max had been there for her through it all. He'd let her grieve, and then he'd kept her busy so she wouldn't get lost in the grief. And now he was a step away from death too.

"You're going to miss out on the fun stuff if you stay in here too long. Declan has big plans for all of us. There are changes coming."

She stood up and brushed his hair out of his eyes. "Just—just don't die on me. I don't think I can go through it again. I'm not strong enough."

Jade squeezed his hand and then left the private room, the door shutting softly behind her. So she didn't see the small bump in his heart rate on his monitor or the way the corner of his mouth kicked up in a smile.

SECRETS AND SATIN

A MACKENZIE FAMILY NOVEL

NEW YORK TIMES BESTSELLING AUTHOR

LILIANA HART

SECRETS AND SATIN

PROLOGUE

Two Years Ago…

"I'm pregnant."

Jade Jax stared at herself in the mirror—wide green eyes tinged with a hint of shock and panic. She knew if she didn't practice saying the words aloud, she'd never get them out when it was time to do it for real. So much for birth control.

Nausea rolled through her and she gritted her teeth and breathed out slowly, trying to delay the inevitable. Her face was pale and clammy, and she'd become good friends with the end stall in the ladies' room in the Department of Justice building over the past three weeks.

"Dammit." She raced into the stall and emptied what was left in her stomach. It was only vaguely annoying she'd been in there often enough to notice one of the floor tiles was cracked in the shape of the Virgin Mary. Mostly it just reminded her she needed to pray. Then maybe she could put something in her stomach without it reappearing again.

She stumbled back to the sink and splashed cold water onto her face, and then she wetted a few paper towels and let the cold trickle down the middle of her breasts. She had to pull herself together. There were less than two hours until go time. The next mission was an important one, and Max wouldn't let her go if he thought she was sick—even if it was her husband they were going to be extracting.

Donovan had been in deep cover inside Alexander Ramos's organization for the last eighteen months. It was a dangerous job—a job she'd begged him not to take. They'd fought over it for weeks, but in the end she'd lost the battle. Donovan felt he was the right man for the job—the only person who could infiltrate the organization and pass on vital information to the DEA. And the hard part was accepting he was right. He was a good man, a good agent, and justice would always be more important than his safety. Falling in love with a hero was hell.

Their time together over the last year and a half had been sparse—stolen weekends in remote locations where they hadn't wasted time talking and instead fallen straight into bed. When you added it up, they'd actually been apart longer than they'd been married. It had been four weeks since she'd seen him last—four weeks since they'd made love. And made a baby.

Her hand went to her stomach protectively. Maybe this baby was a sign. She and the rest of the team were flying down to extract Donovan from Mexico. The assignment had gotten too dangerous, and Ramos was beginning to suspect some of his top men of betraying him. More than one body of his known lieutenants had been found—at least what had been left of them.

Don't think about it. He's coming home.

The DEA had enough information to begin the process of ending Ramos's reign forever. Donovan would come home, and they could be a family without threats or danger hanging over their heads at every turn. In fact, maybe it was time to turn in her badge and her weapon. The past ten years felt more like fifty, and the weight of the world was getting awfully heavy—not to mention the rifle she had to use much too frequently.

The more she thought about it, the more she knew it was the right decision. Max would throw a fit, but he could find another agent to replace her. The child growing inside of her couldn't grow up without a mother if anything happened to her.

Jade patted her face dry with a towel and slapped her cheeks for a little color. She had a mission to prepare for, and it was the most important mission of her life. Donovan was coming home.

"I'm pregnant," she said one last time to the mirror. This time she couldn't help but smile.

The DEA offices were on the fifth floor of the Department of Justice building, and she headed down the long gray corridor to her small office. They were supposed to meet at 14:30 for a briefing before the plane took off. She had just enough time to change clothes and check her weapons one final time.

Her office was a small square dominated by a metal desk. The floors were gray industrial grade carpet and the walls were stark white. A bookshelf stood in the corner, and the shelves bowed under the weight of books—anything from non-fiction to thrillers to the romances she kept on the bottom shelf so the guys wouldn't give her a hard time. She spent more time at work than home anyway, so it made sense to have the things she enjoyed close by. A green plant flourished on the corner of her desk, and pictures sat on every free surface. It was a cramped and overflowing space, but she wouldn't trade it for anything. It was hers. And having things that belonged solely to her was something she'd learned to treasure.

Jade pulled her pack from the bottom drawer of her desk and changed into black cargo pants and a long sleeved black T-shirt. She pulled the pins from her hair and let it fall around her shoulders, brushing it out quickly before pulling it back in a ponytail. Maybe it was time to cut it short. She wouldn't want to deal with the hassle of long hair when the baby was born.

Jade checked the magazine in her Sig and pocketed another two, but her pride and joy was in the long black case under her desk. She pulled it out and set it on top of her desk, flicking open the locks with her thumbs and pushing back the lid. The M-40A3 rifle gleamed back at her—the black so smooth and polished she could see her reflection in it.

The knock on her door had her yelling out, "Enter," and she closed the lid on the case with a snap.

She knew something was wrong the moment Max stepped inside and closed the door behind him. Max was a good boss and a great agent, and she knew his responsibility weighed heavily on him. He truly cared about his agents, and he'd flip his middle finger to the bureaucrats and politicians if it meant those under his command were going to get screwed. There weren't many she'd trust to watch her back if things went to shit, but he was one of them.

But the Max she'd worked with the last few years was almost unrecognizable in the man who stood before her. His face was drawn and his eyes shadowed with grief. His hair was disheveled as if he'd been running his fingers through it, and his normally impeccable clothes were wrinkled—his tie shoved in his pocket and the collar of his shirt unbuttoned.

"What's wrong?" Her voice was foreign to her ears. Her palms slicked with sweat and her lungs felt as if they were bursting in her chest. Somewhere deep inside she knew—knew that whatever Max had to say would break her.

She wiped her palms on her pants and shook her head, coming around the desk to face him head on.

SECRETS AND SATIN

"Jade," he said. And she knew. She knew Donovan was dead, as if someone had flicked a switch off inside of her.

"No, you're wrong." Her soul was splintering into pieces and he expected her to just believe him, without proof. "You'll see. We can leave early and go get him. We'll do the extraction and you'll see he's okay. We'll bring him home." Her voice rose higher and higher as panic took over. She was trained to never panic—to breathe deep and keep her focus. But she couldn't do it this time. She just couldn't.

"I'm sorry, Jade." Max reached out for her, but she moved back, knocking the picture frame from her desk to the floor. Glass crunched beneath her feet, and she bent down to salvage what was left of her wedding photo.

Glass sliced at her finger and blood welled instantly, but she pulled the picture from the shards and held it against her breast.

"No," she said again. "No, no, no. It's just a misunderstanding. I want to talk to our contacts in Mexico. I want someone to go in and bring him out now. If he's in danger, then we don't need to waste a minute."

Max knelt down beside her and held her trembling hands. The blood from the cut on her finger welled faster, soaking into the white cuff of his shirt.

"He's gone, Jade." His voice cracked, and he had to swallow a couple of times before he could go on. "I've spent the last three hours trying to cut through red tape and lies to get the answers I needed. Let me get this out," he said. "You know I have to say the words."

She shook her head, but it didn't stop him from speaking. "I'm sorry for your loss. Donovan Jax was killed in the line of duty."

"I said no!" she screamed. Her fist connected with the side of his face before she could control it, as if someone else had taken over her body. She scrambled away, knocking over one of the folding chairs she had against the wall. Her hip hit the corner of her desk, but the pain didn't penetrate.

"Get out, get out!" Tears clouded her vision, but she grabbed the first thing she saw—the plant in the ceramic pot—and threw it at his head. Max dodged and got to his feet, but he didn't try to stop the storm brewing inside of her. The look of sympathy on his face only made the tears fall faster. God, she never cried. Not when she'd been shuffled from one foster home to the next and not when a bullet had pierced her flesh.

The door to her office opened and worried faces peeked in.

"Get out," Max said, and they closed the door with a snap.

Blood trickled from the corner of his mouth, but he was still and silent, letting her rage around him until there was nothing left inside of her but despair. Her breath heaved in and out of her lungs and she let her arms hang down at her side as a sudden weakness seemed to overtake her. Her head dropped down and a chill settled over her skin, making her shiver uncontrollably.

"I want to see him," she said, her voice breaking. "I need to see him."

"Oh, baby," Max said, coming toward her. She let him gather her close, so her head rested on his shoulder. He was grieving too. She could feel the fine tremors coursing through his body. Max and Donovan had been close—as close as most brothers. "You know I can't do that."

"Don't play games with me, Max. I don't care about the red tape or expense reports. I want his body brought back here. I need to see him."

His arms wrapped tight around her and he buried his head against her shoulder. She felt the heat of his tears against her neck, and she tightened her own hold around him, trying to comfort the both of them.

"I can't, Jade." He paused for a few seconds. "There's nothing left of him to bring home."

Something broke inside of her—an agony that started

in her womb and ripped and clawed its way through her body. She would have doubled over if Max hadn't been holding her upright. Liquid rushed between her thighs and the coppery scent of blood filled the air.

She tried to scream, but the pain had taken control of her body, rendering her useless.

"Jade!" Max cried out, catching her as her knees gave out and she crumpled to the floor.

She'd lived through unspeakable tragedy in her life—the death of her parents when she was a child, the loss of friends she'd worked and served with, wounds, betrayal, and the loss of her husband—a man she'd loved with everything she'd had to give. But she'd never wanted to die before—not until she lost the only piece of Donovan she had left—the child she'd already imagined to have Donovan's wide grin and her green eyes.

Now there was nothing but blackness as the pain lessened and a cold numbness filled her body. In the back of her mind she thought she heard Max yelling something, calling her name, but she ignored it and embraced the cold. A smile touched her lips when she saw Donovan's face—one last time.

Six Months Later...

His body hurt. Everywhere.

It felt like his brain was caught in quicksand—his every thought disappearing into darkness just when he thought he finally had a good hold. He remembered being in Mexico with the team, on the search and rescue for Darcy MacKenzie. And he remembered looking into the black eyes of Alexander Ramos just before Ramos pulled the trigger and hit Max in the leg as he dived to the side. The bullet had burned like fire, and he'd felt the crack of bone as the bullet lodged in his thigh. The last thing Max remembered was Ramos's arm around Darcy's throat and the gun in his hand pointed right at Max's head. He hadn't even had time to pray before everything went dark.

But, God, had there been pain. Pain that pulsed and tore inside his body and sat heavy on his chest like cinder blocks so he could only scream in his head. His arms and legs were mired in the quicksand and the pain built and burned inside him until he wondered if he was in hell.

He didn't know how long he spent there—days—weeks—eternity. But he yearned for the one person who soothed his pain like a balm. When she came, her voice cut through the fire in his head, and her touch eased the confusion and fear that crept up on him when the darkness came again. He'd latch onto her words, though he couldn't always understand her, and he'd hold out hope that he'd one day get to see her again.

It was foolish, really. Jade Jax didn't belong to him. She'd never belonged to him. But a man who'd experienced death could be nothing if not honest with himself. He'd wanted her from the first moment she and Donovan had been transferred to his team, and he'd been envious of the obvious love between the two of them. He would have hated Donovan just on principle if he hadn't been such a good guy. So he'd been a friend to them both and kept his feelings to himself.

And then when Donovan died, he hadn't given the job of breaking the news to Jade to someone else. To another female agent or to a doctor or the chaplain. He'd felt he'd needed to do it himself, and his need to be the one to comfort her had cost her everything. She had every right to hate him. But she kept coming back to soothe his pain just when he started to lose hope again.

Then one day the quicksand around his limbs wasn't so heavy and the fire in his head died down to a simmer. And she was there again. Only this time her words were clear.

"Don't die on me, Max," she said, rubbing soothing

circles in his palm with her thumb. "You're the best partner I've ever had. Though I wouldn't admit it to Donovan if he were still alive. You know how he liked to try and protect me instead of letting me do my job."

He couldn't say he blamed Donovan for being overly protective. He'd do the same thing in Donovan's position. Warmth covered him like a blanket at the sincerity in her words. She didn't hate him. She wanted him to live. He wanted to squeeze her hand, but his hand wasn't obeying what his mind was telling it. But it was close—so close.

"You're going to miss out on the fun stuff if you stay in here too long. Declan has big plans for all of us. There are changes coming."

Interesting. And cryptic. Did that mean Declan had gotten the backing he'd petitioned for? Only a select few of them knew of Declan MacKenzie's plan to open a separate agency and fulfill off-the-books government contracts.

Her hand brushed his hair back from his face, and he wanted to nuzzle against her, to soak in the warmth she brought everywhere she went.

"Just—just don't die on me," she said. "I don't think I could go through it again. I'm not strong enough."

She squeezed his hand and then he knew she was gone because the emptiness made him cold once more. But he didn't return to the blackness he'd been mired in. His thoughts were clear and tingles pricked at his fingers and toes.

He believed in a higher power, and if this wasn't a sign he didn't know what was. Jade was his light. The person who'd brought him back from the brink of death. And she belonged to him. It could take months or years. He didn't care. He'd wait patiently and bide his time. A gift like her wasn't meant to be rushed.

Max felt the heaviness of sleep weigh down on him, but he didn't fear it this time. It was only sleep. And just before he dropped off, he thanked God for giving him a

LILIANA HART

second chance to love Jade.

Three months later...

"Come on, Devlin," Jade said. "Ten more reps."

"I'm going to kick your ass if you don't get out of my face," Max said. Sweat soaked his skin and his leg was on fire. He was in a pisser of a mood, but nothing he could say or do would budge Jade.

"You can certainly try. But that old guy over there looks like he could take you. You've really let yourself go. Too many Cheetos and General Hospital marathons. Eight more reps."

"I know how many more fucking reps I have. I can count."

He hated this. Hated that his leg felt as new and uncoordinated as a newborn's. He hated that he had to use a walker or crutches just to go anywhere. At least he was out of the godforsaken wheelchair, but he wasn't much better off. He couldn't drive or go back to work. He was useless.

"I know that look," she said, getting right into his face. "You're feeling sorry for yourself again."

Max hadn't expected Jade to dedicate herself to seeing him through rehab. They were friends—they'd always been friends—but Donovan had been the glue between them. Or that's what he'd always thought. Maybe he'd tried to keep that barrier between them because she was definitely in the "off limits" category. But loyalty meant something to Jade, and she'd picked him up from his house and driven him to rehab three days a week for the last two months, and she'd stood in front of him yelling encouragement and taunts in equal measures.

Spending so much time with her was heaven—and hell.

SECRETS AND SATIN

She'd slimmed down since Donovan's death—her tall frame was lean and muscular—and she had an edge to her that looked dangerous. Her dark skin had lost its healthy glow and she'd cut off all of her beautiful dark hair, so it was short as a boy's and wisped around her face, making her cheekbones more prominent and her face more angular. And her eyes—he'd always been a sucker for those eyes. Brilliant green and a little too lost—a little too sad.

He wanted to hold her—to hug her and take care of her. She'd had much too little of that in her life growing up, and he knew that's why Donovan had been so protective of her. But she didn't need anyone to take care of her. And wouldn't welcome it.

"You're slacking on me, Devlin. If you've got time to daydream then you're not working hard enough."

He leaned forward and took her mouth in a hard kiss before she could say another word. When he pulled back, her eyes had that deer in the headlights stare and her mouth had opened on a gasp.

"Good," he nodded. "Looks like I figured out a way to shut you up."

"Why'd you do that?" she asked. Her face paled and she took a step back, running her hand through her short hair with trembling fingers. He felt like a total cad.

"Sorry. It was self-preservation. I thought you'd prefer a kiss instead of my hands around your throat."

Her breath shuddered out with a laugh and she relaxed. "I guess I have been pushing you pretty hard. Maybe we should call it a day."

"I'll finish the damn reps, woman. I'm not an invalid."

Jade rolled her eyes and Max gritted his teeth. He struggled through the last two reps and let the leg weights drop back to the machine with a clank. He felt a little sick and a lot exhausted. "Finished. Kiss my ass, Jax."

"It's a good thing I know you so well. Someone else might take offense."

She wrapped her arm around his waist and helped him stand and stretch a little. He squeezed her shoulder, silently apologizing for his behavior, and said, "Yeah. I guess it's a good thing. Sorry about the kiss."

"Your technique needs work, Devlin, but I guess it beats the hell out of being strangled to death."

Max stopped her before she could drag him out to the car. His limbs were shaking with exhaustion and he just wanted to lie down, but he needed to get the words out. "I haven't thanked you for being here for me." What he didn't say was that she'd been there for him when even his own family had been absent over the last months.

"That's what family does, babe."

He couldn't have said it better himself. There was the family a person couldn't choose, those that shared blood and were obligated to love you because of it. And there was the family that didn't share blood but chose to love you anyway. He much preferred the latter.

Six months later…

"Jesus, Devlin," Jade said, clapping her hands over her eyes. "Your neighbors must love you."

It was just past eight in the morning and she'd only planned to drop off the little going away gift and leave. She hadn't been prepared for Max to answer the door stark naked and angry as a bear. His morning beard was scruffy and glinted with hints of red in the sunlight, and his arm was thrown across his eyes. His chest was broad and ridged with muscle, his waist trim, and a light smattering of white blond hairs trailed down his flat stomach and to the very impressive inches of flesh below.

She'd taken in the full sight of him before slamming her eyes closed. Not that having her eyes closed would erase what she'd seen. Her mouth went dry, and something like fear clutched in her belly. She never thought of Max as a man—well, maybe she had a little, but that was only because he'd kissed her and she remembered the heat of his lips against hers and the tingles that had awakened inside her dormant body. He was her friend and he stayed nicely tucked away in that "friend" box.

He grunted something unintelligible at her and went back into the house, leaving the door wide open. Jade followed him in, admiring the back view as only a woman could, and closed the door behind her. She'd have to be dead not to notice, and that was something that had become increasingly clear over the last few months—she wasn't dead. Shame ate at her as thoughts of her husband came to mind and she averted her gaze.

Max's house had always been a little stark, even though it was about ten times the size of her apartment. It was all white walls and neutral colors, light hardwood floors and stainless steel appliances. A few photographs of the team sat about here and there, but he wasn't one for plants or dust catching knickknacks other than a signed football that sat in a glass case on his mantel. Boxes were stacked and labeled, and it looked like he was all but ready for the moving company to come load his things.

"I take it the boys decided to send you out in style," she said, breaking the silence.

Max ignored her and walked into the kitchen. It was a big open space, and the only thing that divided it from the living room was the long island counter and the barstools that sat in front of it. He dunked his head into the sink, dousing himself with cold water. He'd let his hair grow longer since the accident, and when he came back up for air it dripped into his face and onto the counter.

Beads of water snaked down his naked chest, and Jade licked her lips, following the trails with her gaze until they disappeared below his waist. Her skin flushed hot and her nipples beaded beneath the thin tank top she wore. Her mind fought against what her body seemed to want—screamed that she wasn't ready for this—while the throbbing bud between her legs argued that it wouldn't mean anything. It would be a mindless release, and just because her heart was dead didn't mean her body needed to suffer needlessly.

Max dug around blindly in the drawer next to the sink and pulled out a dishtowel, drying his face and giving her a look that would have had her shaking in her skin if she'd been anyone else. She crossed her arms over her chest and arched a brow.

"Why the hell do you always have to be so damned chipper at the crack of dawn? It's an unforgivable personality trait."

"That's funny, because I've always thought the fact you can't hold your liquor better than a college freshman was pretty unforgivable."

"I'm sure that's supposed to be funny."

"Maybe you'll feel better if you put on some pants. It's probably not a good thing for every housewife on the street to know you're circumcised." Please put on some pants, she prayed. Her control was slipping by the second.

A piratical smile slashed across his face. "It's nice to see you're looking out for me, but no. I'm pretty sure nothing will make me feel better. Not even pants. Though a couple of aspirin couldn't hurt. You could always come back later—when I'm wearing pants—if I'm making you uncomfortable. Or maybe you just like what you see a little too much."

Her lips pressed in a thin line, and she felt her blood surge at the challenge. She knew he was kidding. She was used to banter. Hell, she worked with a team of men, almost all of them ex-military, and she would have left long ago if she hadn't been able to take their colorful vocabulary and trash talk. But this time the banter was too close to the truth. Moisture pooled between her thighs and she was swollen and throbbing with need.

SECRETS AND SATIN

Wasn't she allowed to need? Donovan was dead, dammit. And no matter how angry she was or how many times she'd gotten down on her knees and begged for his death to be a lie, he wasn't coming back. She was tired of being alone. She was tired of rolling over in a cold bed with no one there beside her. And she was tired of the constant ache inside her soul.

Her emotions warred inside her until she finally found the courage to say to hell with her brain. She wasn't dead. She wasn't dead. And Max was safe. She wasn't interested in hooking up with a stranger. It just wasn't part of her makeup to do that. But Max knew her better than anyone, and she knew him.

Max was a sexual creature by nature. He never seemed to be without female attention, and she figured with as many women who had shared his bed that he probably knew what the hell he was doing at this point. She wanted someone who knew how to give her what her body craved and then the ability to walk away with no hard feelings later. It should've been an easy enough task because Max wasn't the type of man to get attached to any woman.

"Maybe you're right," she said.

From the look on Max's face, she could have knocked him over with a feather. Jade stalked her way around the counter and smiled when he took a few steps back. Her gaze raked down his body and her eyes widened at the sight of him fully aroused. His cock was thick and heavy and ridged, the head flushed dark purple and his testicles drawn tight against his body.

"I guess it's nice to know it's not one sided," she purred.

"Listen, Jade—" he backed away again when she took another step closer.

"You're the one that made the challenge. I'm just calling you on it."

His jaw clamped shut and she could see the pulse pounding at the side of his neck. His eyes were hooded and the blue of his irises had darkened to the color of a lake in the evening. Jade grabbed the hem of her tank top and slowly lifted it over the top of her head. She hadn't bothered with a bra. Her breasts weren't large, but they were high and taut, and she smiled a woman's smile when Max sucked in a startled breath and his cock flexed against his stomach.

"You're making this really difficult," he choked out.

"No." Jade took another step closer, and then another, and Max was effectively trapped with his back to the island. "I'm making this very, very easy." She was just a hairsbreadth away, so the hair on his chest touched her sensitive nipples.

Her hand reached out and she pressed her palm against his chest. His warmth seeped into her skin and she was suddenly ravenous for more. She was five-foot-ten in her bare feet, so there was only a few inches difference in their height. His heart pounded beneath her hand and she leaned up to nip at his chin before fusing her mouth and body to his.

He stood still as a statue for a minute while she kissed him, while she gave him all the pent-up longing and frustration and desire she'd just started to feel again over the last months. And then he was kissing her back and she wanted to shout in triumph.

Max's brain deserted him the moment her soft lips had touched his, and all his thoughts rested in the several inches of flesh that was pressed into her stomach. He'd wanted this, dreamed of this for five long years, but even though his dreams seemed to be coming true, he knew this wasn't the way it was supposed to be.

But she was relentless in her pursuit. There was a hunger and desperation inside of her he wanted to soothe.

SECRETS AND SATIN

A wildness built inside of him he'd never felt before. She was his mate, and his body recognized her as such, and all he wanted was to possess, to take.

Her lips parted and her tongue licked into his mouth, and the flavor of her exploded through his system. She was sweet to the taste, like sweet cream and melted sugar, and he'd never in his life experienced anything that felt as good as touching her.

"You taste so good," she moaned. "Touch me."

His hands came around her, cupping the rounded globes of her rear, and he pulled her against him so she could feel how much he wanted her. She groaned into his mouth and he drank in the sound. His tongue dueled with hers and he growled as her fingers threaded through his hair and tugged him closer.

Her legs came around his waist and clamped tight around him, and she moved against his cock, searching for release. He'd forgotten how strong she was—long legs and lean muscles—and when she leaned back in his arms, his mouth found the tight bud of her nipple.

"Please, please," she chanted, and he was helpless to deny her.

He spun her around and settled her on the island. His knees were weak and he couldn't seem to find his balance. She was going too fast—racing too hard to the end—and he wanted to take his time now that he finally had her where he wanted her. Their rhythm was off, and he tried to pull back and shake some sense into his head, but her hot hand found his cock and began to stroke.

"Christ, Jade," he panted. "I won't last ten seconds if you keep doing that."

Her laugh was low and sultry, and a little wild. "Touch me," she begged again.

His fingers found the snap of her jeans, jerking it open and then pulling down the zipper. She lifted her hips so he could pull them down, but just the sight of her in the little white panties had him desperate for more. The cotton was damp and his fingers traced along the outer edge before slipping beneath to the soft curls.

She moaned as his finger whispered against the taut bud of her clit and she cried out when he moved lower and his finger slipped just inside of her. Max gritted his teeth as she clamped around his finger. She was snug and wet, and when he pushed farther inside, her velvety pussy rippled around his finger.

"So hot, baby." He was barely able to form a coherent thought. "You're so tight. You're going to fit like a glove around my cock."

Sweet syrup trickled over his fingers at the picture he painted, and her hips thrust against him, taking more of his finger inside. He kissed her stomach and then moved higher so his mouth latched on to her nipple. They were small and dark brown and they tasted like heaven. His teeth scraped one lightly and he felt her flex around him.

He was getting past the point of no return, and he knew he needed to get control of the situation because she clearly wasn't. He withdrew his finger and flicked it gently over her clit. It was swollen and so primed she probably could have come from the whisper of his breath. He placed several kisses along her collarbone and then kissed his way up her neck to the lush mouth that had tempted him from the first time he'd seen her. Her top lip was fuller than the bottom and utterly bitable.

"Look at me, baby," he said. Her nails dug into his arms and it was the sweetest pain he'd ever felt.

Her eyes opened and he had to kiss her again. She was stunning. Her face was flushed with arousal and there was a glow about her he hadn't seen in much too long. The green of her eyes was vibrant, and she looked like a woman ripe for loving. But he knew her like he knew his own soul, and this wasn't how he'd dreamed of their first time together.

"Don't stop, Max," she cried. "Don't you dare stop."

"I won't be a substitute for anyone else." His breath

was labored with his restraint, but he made sure he got his point across. "I've wanted you too long. And if you're coming to my bed it's because you want to be there. Because you want me."

She shook her head in confusion and tears filled her eyes. His heart broke at the sight of her tears and all she'd had to endure, but he couldn't do this. He wouldn't do this. He'd waited too long for her to see him as a man. As something other than a friend.

"It's okay if you don't want me," she said, pushing at his chest. "But maybe you could have told me before we got to this point. Now I'll just have to find someone else."

She struggled against him harder as the tears fell, and she swiped at them viciously, but it was like a dam had broken inside of her and nothing was going to stop them from falling.

"Don't make threats, baby. We're past that now."

"It's none of your business, Max. If you don't want it, no big deal. Someone else will."

He clamped a hand on her leg to keep her from running, but she wouldn't look at him. "It is my business. I've wanted you from the first moment I laid eyes on you, but you weren't mine to have. And I haven't waited this long to be some itch you can scratch because you're still grieving for someone else. When you come to my bed, there won't be anyone between us."

A choked sob came from deep inside of her as she struggled to get up. He released her leg and she jumped down from the counter, fastening her pants and scooping up her shirt from the floor.

"This is your fault, Max," she said, pulling the shirt over her head. She turned and headed for the door as fast as she could. "You're the one who made me feel again, and now you're not man enough to follow through with what you started. Well, fuck you. Have a nice life in Texas."

He waited until she got to the door and jerked it open before he called out to her. His body throbbed with unfulfilled desire, and his heart felt as if it had been stomped into the ground. But she didn't mean what she said. She wasn't the kind of woman to sleep with just anyone. He knew a part of her had to trust and care for him deeply for her to go as far as she did. But he wanted more. He wanted all of her and he'd meant what he said. He wasn't going to be a substitute for Donovan.

"I've made you feel again," he said. "Remember that it was me when you're alone in that cold apartment. And when you're ready to live for real, you know where to find me."

She didn't look back as she stepped out of his house and his life, and when the door closed with a quiet click, he felt the emptiness of not having her near like a punch to the solar plexus.

"Well, hell," he said. He punched the wall with enough force to leave a dent and then headed to the shower. He could take care of the ache in his balls now. He'd have to take care of Jade later.

CHAPTER ONE

Present Day

"I'm on the roof," Max said. "You've got to be my eyes."

"I've got you in my sights," Elena Nayal said through the tiny bud in his ear. "You've got about a minute-and-a-half until the two Secret Service agents make their way back around the house next door. Otherwise you're clear."

"Plenty of time."

His rubber-soled shoes helped him keep traction as he slid down the sharply pitched roof to the small window on the top floor. Black gloves kept his fingers from being torn to shreds, and the black mask over his face and the matching clothes helped him blend in with the night.

The climb up the side of the Dallas mansion had been the hardest part—not to mention a former president lived in the house next door, and on a night like this, where unfamiliar cars and people lined the street, security was at a peak.

The climb had tested his strength and endurance ten fold, and he was glad he'd pushed himself so hard through rehab. Even now, his leg was aching and he'd had to stop for a few seconds to catch his breath once he'd reached the top.

His feet touched on the tiny lip that jutted from the edge of the roof, and he lowered himself down until his hands had a good grasp on the ledge. His muscles bunched and strained and sweat dripped from his temple from the relentless summer heat. He lowered himself inches at a time and then dropped the rest of the way to the balcony. He landed silently and then took the tools from the zippered pocket of his pants.

"Forty-five seconds," Elena said. "I've deactivated the alarms for the top two floors."

"I've got a visual on the senator," Cade MacKenzie said. "He's dancing with a woman who has a face like a hatchet and a diamond the size of a quail egg on her finger."

Cade was the oldest MacKenzie—there being five in all—and once upon a time, Cade had been one of Max's best DEA agents. At least before the del Fuego cartel had killed Cade's lover right in front of him. Cade had left the DEA and moved to Texas, which was where he'd met the love of his life and settled down to a nice, normal life, where they had a house in a busy neighborhood, a toddler, and another baby on the way. Or at least it was normal if you ignored Cade's highly trained intuition and his ability to protect and defend—no matter what it took.

He and Cade had slipped back into their old routine as if they'd never been separated, and the change he'd made in his life over the past year had felt good. Damned good.

"That would be Martha Sandusky," Max said, taking a slim tool and using it to unlatch the window. "She's the wife of one of Senator Henry's biggest donors." The latch gave and Max slid the window up and slipped inside. "I'm in," he said.

"Just in time," Elena said, her voice soft and slightly accented.

Elena had been adopted by the MacKenzie clan over

the past year—much like Max and Jade and a few other team members. Once the MacKenzies decided to bring you into the family fold, there was no point in fighting it. Family was everything. You could always trust family and you knew they'd always have your back. Max had often wished he'd been born a MacKenzie instead of one of the Boston Devlins.

They'd met Elena in Mexico when their team had gone to wipe out the del Fuego cartel once and for all. Elena had been caught in the crosshairs and she'd been kidnapped, beaten and raped repeatedly before Alexander Ramos's men tossed her aside like garbage. She'd survived, and every day was a struggle, but she was a fighter.

Declan MacKenzie had talked her into coming to America and taking the job with Max and Cade in the Texas office of MacKenzie Security. Dec had promised her they'd train her how to fight—how to protect herself no matter what the cost—and he'd promised they'd hunt down every last member of the cartel that had touched her. It had been enough to convince her. And Dec had come through on his promises. There was nothing left of the del Fuego cartel.

Elena had been quiet at first—wary of the men she worked with—and she had a look in her eye that all but broke your heart. But Cade's wife, Bayleigh, had befriended her and had done a lot to help her heal. Therapy and the training she was promised had done more, though she still had a long way to go. Now it felt like Elena had always been there, keeping the office running smoothly and doing the occasional field work when they needed her.

He looked around the small guest bedroom and noticed a few items of clothing and a jewelry case open on the dresser. One of the guests from the party must be staying overnight.

Max stripped off his gloves, pants and shirt, revealing his tuxedo below, and then he peeled off the thick rubber soles on the bottom of his dress shoes. He carried everything into the bathroom and dumped them in the clothes hamper, knowing a maid would think they belonged to whoever was staying in the room and take them to be laundered. He remembered the ski mask and tossed it in as well.

He checked himself in the mirror, making sure the putty he'd used to disguise himself was still in place. His nose was a little longer and his jaw softer. Dark brown contacts covered his normal blue. He straightened his tie and smoothed back the dark wig. He'd let his own hair grow out since the accident, so it was just long enough to pull into a tail at the nape of his neck, and it covered the ridge of scar tissue in the side of his head quite nicely. But for now it was all tucked under the protective cap. Not even his own family would recognize him.

"The senator is moving to the game room," Cade said. "Looks like he's settling in for a round of poker. Bayleigh's going to be mad she missed this. There are almost as many celebrities here as politicians."

Max grunted and opened the bedroom door, looking out into the hallway. Music and the muted sounds of laughter could be heard from the first floor, and he quickly left the bedroom and headed towards the back stairway that was reserved for family.

The halls were deserted and he walked boldly through the second floor family wing towards the senator's office. He tested the doorknob and found it locked, so he used the lock pick tools he'd placed in the inside pockets of his jacket.

"Man, I'm good," he said as the lock snicked and the doorknob turned beneath his hand.

"That's not what I've heard." Cade said. "There was a lovely story about you in the Enquirer last week. Something about Agent Danger and how he should be called Minute Max instead."

"Fuck off, MacKenzie. I'm going to tell your wife

you're reading tabloids instead of building those shelves she wants for the baby's room."

As far as the public knew, Max was an ex-DEA agent who was disgruntled with the government after receiving a life threatening injury, and he'd gone back to his wealthy roots like the prodigal son, though his family had been less than happy to welcome him into the fold. No one but a select few knew he'd taken a job with MacKenzie Security—a government funded private firm that was so top secret only a few in power knew of its existence.

It had been Declan MacKenzie's brainchild for the past several years, and he'd been the one with the connections to make it happen. Declan was an interesting man—a secretive man—and whatever he'd done for the CIA had garnered him respect from everyone who'd ever heard his name. Max had worked with him on occasion, and he knew he was a brilliant strategist and an agent who could get the job done. It hadn't taken a lot of convincing for Max to resign as Special Agent in Charge of the Washington D.C. DEA and go to work for MacKenzie Security.

Being shot in the head by Alexander Ramos was the best thing that could have happened to him—though it hadn't seemed like it at the time. Society thought Max was spending his days as a playboy, living off his trust fund and spending as much of his family money as possible on anything from cars to real estate to questionable investments. Even his family thought that's what he spent his time doing.

And yes, the tabloids had started calling him Agent Danger—which gave those he worked with unending amusement and ammunition. It didn't matter that he'd never slept with any of the women they'd interviewed or done half the things he'd been accused of. The important thing was that people believed the illusion he presented.

"What kind of language is that?" Cade said. "You're famous now, Agent Danger—like a superhero. You've got to set a good example. Maybe you need a mask. Or some little tights."

"Or maybe I need to kick your ass. It's been a while since you and I stepped into the ring. I think it's time for a rematch."

"Hell, no," Cade said. "Last time I sparred with you, Bayleigh made me sleep on the couch because she couldn't sleep with all the groans. You have an unfair advantage. I still think you cracked one of my ribs."

"Nah, you're just a pussy."

Max did have an unfair advantage in the ring since he'd had MMA training, but Cade made up for the lack of training by fighting dirty. Max had almost as many bruises as Cade, but it had been fun.

He locked the office door behind him and went over to the thin laptop on the desk.

"There's a closed laptop on the desk," he said. "You read me, Elena?"

"I'm here," she said. "I didn't want to interfere with your male bonding time. Go ahead and open it. You'll need to put the device in the USB port, and then I can run it from here."

Max opened up the laptop and watched the screen flicker on. It was password protected, but Elena could get around that. It hadn't taken them very long at all to notice she excelled in technology, and Dec had made sure she'd gotten the extra training she needed for situations just like this one.

Davis Henry was a member of the Senate Defense Committee, and there were enough leaks coming from that office to sink a ship. Too many of America's enemies knew more than they should, and it couldn't be a coincidence any longer. It was a mess the government didn't want to dirty their hands with because Henry held a lot of power, and where there was power, there was money. Always the bottom line when it came to the government. And when the government didn't want to

SECRETS AND SATIN

dirty their hands, they called MacKenzie Security.

Their mission was to get into the Senator's personal files where they suspected he kept records of what he was selling and to whom. As of yet, they hadn't found a money trail, but it would only be a matter of time.

"This champagne is terrible," Cade said. "You'd think they could bring out the good stuff for five thousand dollars a plate."

"It must be terrible to rub elbows with the rich and famous while some of us are sweating our asses off in the car," Elena said, her accent thickening with irritation.

"Well, when you put it that way—"

"Could we pretend we're on a mission here?" Max interrupted. "The device is in the USB. Get me the password, Elena."

Numbers scrambled across the screen before he finished the sentence, and one by one the numbers turned into letters until the password was revealed. The screen went black and then the computer flickered on.

"Go ahead and put the flash drive into the other USB port," Elena said. "We're just going to download his entire hard drive, and then I can sort it all out back at the office on our own computers. He's got several encrypted files that are going to take some time."

"Uh, oh," Cade said. "Looks like the senator had a shitty hand. He's headed out of the game room and making his way towards the center stairs."

Max looked up at the door to make sure it was locked and he willed the computer to hurry. He got up and looked around the office. It was bigger than most people's living rooms. Floor to ceiling bookshelves were lined up across the wall at his back and a small sitting area sat directly across the room from his massive oak desk. An ugly painting hung on the wall over the sitting area, and it was so obviously a wall safe Max wondered why the senator even bothered to hide it. If he had more time he'd look inside and see if the senator kept hard copies of his records or a journal.

"He's heading up the stairs," Cade said.

Max went back to the computer to check the progress and did a quick search through the desk drawers while he was waiting. His hands were steady and his search methodical.

"Can you stall him?" Max asked.

"Not without jumping over all these people and making a fool out of myself. My other options are to shoot him in the arm or throw a glass of champagne at his head."

"Maybe you should just stay where you are," Max said dryly. He quickly flipped through a stack of loose papers in the top drawer but didn't find anything of consequence. He closed it softly and opened the next drawer. There was still two minutes until the download was complete.

"Wait a minute," Cade said. "It looks like the governor has a bone to pick with Senator Henry. Neither of them looks very happy."

"Not surprising. They hate each other's guts. The governor is a moron but he has impeccable timing. I just need one more minute."

Max finished looking through the drawers and started on the bookshelves. More than one person had the thought that the best hiding places were those in plain sight.

"It looks like the Secretary of Defense needs an urgent word with Henry as well," Cade said. "The governor has walked off in a huff, and now Henry and the Secretary are headed back down the stairs in a hurry. Something must be wrong."

"Not our problem," Max said.

"It's clear," Elena said. "You can remove the device and shut down."

"Something's going on down here, Max," Cade said. "You should probably hurry. Some kind of political powwow is happening in one of the alcoves."

"Elena," Max said. "There's no chance our signal was

picked up?"

"No, I would have gotten an alert if there was someone else monitoring the system."

Max grunted and shut down the computer, closing the lid and placing it exactly how he'd found it on the senator's desk. He pocketed the flash drive and the nifty device Elena had given him, wiped down the surfaces he'd touched, and headed back to the door.

He listened carefully for anyone out in the hallway and then slowly cracked the door open. The hall was clear and he stepped out of the office and made sure the door locked behind him. He straightened his bowtie and then headed for the stairs.

He almost made it.

"Hey! You there," a man's voice called from behind him. "Stop where you are."

Max turned and gave the guard a superior look. Another guard joined him, and Max swore silently as he saw the guard was already talking into his headset to alert security. Max shoved his hands in his pockets casually and adopted a bored expression, not looking like a man who'd just stolen national security files from the senator's computer.

"Are you talking to me?" he asked.

The guard came closer until he was standing just in front of Max. The stairs leading down to the party on the first floor were more than a dozen feet away.

"The senator's office is off limits to guests."

"I wasn't in the senator's office." Max picked at invisible lint on his sleeve and then gave the guard a sheepish look. "I was in that room right there," he said, pointing to the door next to the office. "A lady friend and I had a—meeting. She's familiar with the house and told me where to meet her. But I'd prefer that not get out. Her husband might not like it."

"You're going to need to come with us, sir," the guard said, pointing towards the way Max had originally come—

back to the family wing. "Do you have your invitation?"

Max let out an audible sigh and started walking. He stayed relaxed when the other guard flanked him. "I don't think you know who I am," he said indignantly. "I'm not going to be treated like a common criminal in the senator's home."

Max heard footsteps pounding up the back stairway and knew he had to make his move quickly. His foot lashed out and kicked the guard on his right at the side of the knee. A sickening crack sounded and Max covered the guard's mouth with his hand so his scream couldn't be heard over the party below. Max touched the pressure point in the guard's neck and let him fall unconscious to the ground.

The other guard reached for his weapon, and Max grabbed his wrist, twisting it so the bone broke and the gun fell from his useless grasp. He gave him a short punch to the jaw, and the guard crumpled on top of the other one.

"I need a distraction," he said, running towards the stairs at the front of the house.

"I'm on it," Cade said.

An enormous crash sounded below, and Max heard a few screams from the women in the crowd as champagne glasses filled to the rims crashed to the marble floor and splashed their dresses. Cade had come through, and Senator Henry was apologizing to his guests while berating the poor server Cade had tripped.

Max walked at a sedate pace down the wide center stairs at the front of the house, pushing past the crowd of people that had converged there while they waited for the mess to be cleaned up. He ignored the shouts from upstairs where he'd left the guards and kept moving forward, getting closer to freedom. He reached the bottom of the stairs and Cade bumped against him, giving him the opportunity to slip the flash drive into Cade's pocket. The front door was only steps away and people were starting to panic from the unknown shouts and the sudden swarm of security everywhere.

"There he is!" Someone yelled from behind him. "Stop him!" He didn't turn around to see who had said it. His training kicked in, and the only thing he worried about was blending. Making himself invisible. None of the people around him could tell who the guards were pointing to.

"I've got an alternative pick up en route," Elena said. "I just got word from Declan about half an hour ago that he's in town and we have extra men. I'm trapped behind a limo. Head east towards the next cross street and they'll meet you there."

Indignant shouts of partygoers echoed in his ears as guards shoved their way through the crowd, and Max slipped out the front door and down the garden path. The front gardens were lush and the fragrant scent of roses reminded him of his grandmother—overpowering and slightly stifling. Each of the estates in the exclusive neighborhood sat on a couple of acres that were tree lined and picturesque. Only people with a lot of money could force their lawns to be that green in a Texas summer.

The air was stagnant and smothering and the humidity so thick it felt like breathing water, so the only people outdoors were parking attendants. Max was halfway down the arched driveway before security guards swarmed from each side of the house. He couldn't fight all of them, and he didn't want to kill anyone. They were only doing their jobs. But he knew they wouldn't have any compunction about using their weapons on him, and damned if he felt like taking another bullet anytime soon.

He ran. It was all he could do, and he hoped to God the pick up team was waiting where Elena had said it would be. Yells came from behind him, but he focused on the trees to the east and to the street he knew would be on the opposite side.

The loud crack of a gunshot sounded like it was right next to his ear, and the bark on the tree in front of him exploded, sending tiny shards of wood into his face and neck. Blood ran into his eye and his leg ached as he pushed himself harder and harder. He weaved in and out of the trees, in no particular pattern, making himself a smaller target, but the gunshots didn't stop and if anything, they sounded closer.

He ran out of the cover of trees and straight into the open residential street in front of him. If his driver wasn't there, he was screwed. He heard the squeal of tires before he saw the tiny silver car turn the corner and drive straight toward him. He kept running as the driver's side window opened and a slim hand appeared, holding a semiautomatic handgun.

The driver laid down cover for him, firing shots steadily, and he heard a couple of grunts from too close behind him as the bullets found their target. The driver turned the wheel at the last possible second and the passenger door flung open. Max jumped inside, and the car was speeding back down the street from the direction it had come from before he was able to get the door closed.

"Thanks for the ride," he said.

Jade looked at him out of unreadable green eyes. "It just so happened I was in the neighborhood."

CHAPTER TWO

Max shrugged out of his coat and used it to wipe the blood from his face. None of the cuts were deep, but they were bleeding like a bastard.

"Dec's going to be pissed. You know he doesn't like bodies left behind."

"I just winged a couple of them in the leg to slow them down. Everyone's still breathing."

Max winced in sympathy, his own leg aching. He rubbed it absentmindedly to loosen the tight muscle. "They'll be looking for us. We've got to ditch the car."

"Already on it," Jade said.

And weren't they being fucking polite with each other, Max thought.

She got onto the highway, weaving in and out of light traffic, and finally swerved into the far right lane to take the exit towards the Galleria. Jade's driving had always made him a little lightheaded, but with the pounding headache on top of it, he was hoping he could keep the contents of his stomach down instead of on the floorboard of the car. The mall parking garage was massive and overflowing, and she followed the road as it spiraled upward until they were almost to the top.

Max pushed his hand against the roof so he wouldn't end up in her lap as she took the corners with a squeal of tires. He jerked against the seatbelt with an oomph as she zipped into a small parking space between two large SUVs.

"You're looking a little pale, Max," she said, her grin letting him know how much she'd enjoyed herself. Her eyes sparkled and there was a flush to her cheeks. This was the Jade he knew. The one he'd met so many years ago who loved what she did and had a zest for life.

"You did that on purpose."

"Of course I did. My driving is the only time I ever get to see you with that look of panic on your face."

"Yeah, well you should have seen me a few months ago when Brant was here helping us on a job. He brought Darcy and the baby with him because she was restless and wanted to get out of the house for a while. She'd been complaining of going stir crazy since she was pregnant again and also taking care of a one-year-old, and Brant wasn't about to deny her anything, even though she probably shouldn't have been travelling as far along as she was. Then she ended up going into labor right in the office."

"You're kidding." Her laugh was like music to his ears, and he couldn't remember when he'd heard it last. "Declan never said a word."

"Because he was just as traumatized as I was. It's the only time since I've known him where he went completely pale at the sight of blood. It probably didn't help that Darcy threw a coffee mug at his head. She's got a hell of an arm. It bounced right off that thick skull of his. But Brant stayed completely calm and ended up delivering his son. The whole thing scared the hell out of me. I could go a lifetime without seeing all of that again."

Jade's smile softened. "Well, it's not every day a man gets to deliver his own child. Brant knows how lucky he is."

Max could have kicked himself for bringing it up. She hadn't gotten that opportunity with her own husband and child, and he could tell by looking at her that she was remembering that day as he was. But the look of sadness and desperation was no longer so heavy in her expression, and instead there seemed to be a peace that hadn't been there before.

"I've got an extra weapon and ammo in the glove box. We'll need to call in and have someone retrieve the car. It should be fine here for a couple of days though."

Max opened her glove box and removed the extra weapon and magazines she had there, and Jade popped the trunk. He was pretty conspicuous in a bloody tuxedo, and he waited until she'd gathered all of her things before getting out to join her.

"Which one do you want?" he asked, pointing to the line of cars on the opposite side.

"Get the red one."

"How did I know you'd say that?" he sighed.

"Some things never change."

Jade pulled license plates and an electric screwdriver from her bag and went to work while he pulled his iPhone from his pocket. The team had an app specifically designed to override the computers in modern vehicles. The door locks popped open with a click of a button and he slid inside the new model Camaro.

The push button ignition wouldn't start without a key fob or at least a key fob simulator. He switched apps on his phone and let it scan the computer inside the vehicle they'd picked. It only took a couple of minutes before the phone made the car think it had the right electronic device to start the car. He put his foot on the brake and punched the start button, and the car roared to life. Jade got in the passenger side and he put the car in reverse.

Adrenaline pumped through his body, and he knew when the crash came it would come hard. It had been almost two years since he'd come close to death, and it had been the hardest two years of his life. He'd changed—inside and out—and even though he was in better shape than he was before his injuries, he still had to deal with the horrific headaches that made him as weak as a baby.

"How's your head?" Jade asked.

"It's fine." Blood dripped into his eye and he swiped at it with his hand as he maneuvered his way out of the garage and back onto the highway.

"Liar. I'm more than happy to drive."

Max just grunted and pressed his foot down on the accelerator. It hadn't really sunk in that she was here sitting beside him. They'd fallen into their old habits and camaraderie as if they'd never been separated, and he felt as if the part of himself that had been missing was finally in place.

It had been nine months since he'd seen her. Nine months since the day she'd walked out his door and he'd moved halfway across the country. She hadn't answered her phone when he'd called, and she'd only answered emails when it had pertained to business. And it was all his fault.

"What are you doing here, Jade?" he asked, more harshly than he normally would have.

He couldn't help it. It hurt that she'd cut him from her life so easily, so completely. And a day didn't go by where he didn't wish he'd somehow handled the situation differently. He could have taken her that day. Given her what her body had needed even though her mind wasn't there yet. He could have pushed into that soft warmth and let her pretend it was someone else, all the while hating himself for giving in.

He heard the soft exhalation of her breath and his cock came to full alert. It didn't matter that it felt like jackhammers were pounding away at his skull. That one breath had whispered across his skin until it was everything he could do not to pull over to the side of the road and pull her into his arms.

"I'm here for a couple of reasons," she said. "A problem with your current mission has come to light, and Dec needs us to try to contain the situation. I'll fill you in once you do something about that headache."

"I told you I'm fine."

"I thought the doctors said the headaches would go away."

"Forgive me for wondering why the hell you care all of a sudden." He guessed he was angrier than he'd thought.

"I guess I deserve that," she said, looking out her window.

"We were friends, Jade. We are friends. That above all else. Running away was never the answer."

"I owe you an apology."

"Bullshit," he said. "You've never owed me a damned thing. Did you think I couldn't see you were hurting? That you had needs you'd been ignoring?"

"To tell you the truth, I was embarrassed. I'm still embarrassed. You always seem to be the one to witness my weak moments, and part of me hates that. I don't want you to think I'm not strong enough to handle whatever comes up."

"Baby, you're one of the strongest people I know. It doesn't make you weak to lean on someone every now and then."

"You deserved better than what I did to you, and all I can say is I'm sorry." She tapped her hand anxiously against her knee and kept checking the side mirror to make sure no one was following them. "If it helps, I've missed seeing your face."

"Yeah, it helps," he said, swiping to clear the blood from his eye again.

Max pulled into the underground parking garage next to the high rise where the MacKenzie Security offices were located and parked near the elevators. The gold plaque inside the front of the building said that floors 9-11 belonged to Reliance Financial Group. It was the same company Dec used in a similar building in his offices in Washington—a legitimate front for what was really going on behind the doors of MacKenzie Security.

His leg buckled when he got out of the car, and he bit off an oath as he had to wait for the muscles to stop seizing before he could walk. Jade kept silent and looked around the parking garage to make sure they were alone, but he could tell she was watching him from the corner of her eye to make sure he was okay.

Max wiped his thumb on his trousers to get the blood off before he could press it to the glowing blue plate next to the electronic keypad by the elevators. His thumb was scanned and the elevator doors opened with a soft whoosh. He could feel Jade's eyes on him while he went through the same procedure to go up to their private floors.

"Tell me about the headaches," she said. "I thought they were supposed to go away after a while."

"They have for the most part." His stomach lurched as the elevator went up, and the pain in his head was so intense blurry spots were appearing in front of his eyes. "It's the adrenaline. The headache is just part of the crash. It's why Dec hasn't sent me on any missions that will take an extensive period of time. He doesn't want me to be incapacitated in a dangerous situation and have to rely on a team member to get me out. They come on strong and hurt like a son of a bitch, but I'm usually fine if I take something before it gets too bad."

The elevator stopped on the floor to his apartment—just one level above where the offices were located. The floor of the entryway was dark gray marble streaked with white veins, and the walls were painted a dark burgundy. His door was oak, but it was reinforced with a steel core that would stop bullets or anything else short of a rocket launcher. He typed in his key code and said his name for the benefit of the voice recognition program. The door snicked open on silent hinges.

"My apartment is similar to this," Jade said as he flipped on the lights.

He watched as she looked around the open space with

approval. The walls were painted a soft ivory and the furniture was leather and overstuffed. Colorful rugs were scattered on the hardwood floor. He wasn't much for decorating, so his walls were bare and his shelves empty except for the worn paperbacks he enjoyed. But it was the view of the city that took her breath away. The windows were tinted so they could see out, but those in the building across the way couldn't see in.

"I didn't realize you'd moved," he said.

"I decided it would be best to move out of the apartment Donovan and I shared. So the memories wouldn't be quite so strong. It was the right thing to do."

He didn't know what to say, so he stood there and simply watched her as her hand trailed over the back of the couch. She was beautiful. She'd always been beautiful, but she was one of those women whose looks improved with age. What she'd been five years ago was nothing compared to what stood before him.

Black cargo pants fit her like a second skin, emphasizing the length of her legs, and a black T-shirt was tucked into them. She preferred a thigh holster for her weapon because it fit her better, and for some reason every time she strapped it on he got hard as a rock. He was hard now.

"Why are you here?" he asked again.

Max moved into the kitchen, hunting through the cabinet for the bottle of pain pills the doctor had given him for his headaches. He poured out two in his hand and then grabbed a soda from the fridge to wash it down with. He tossed one to Jade and she caught it one-handed.

She shrugged and popped the top on her soda. "I told you. I'm here because those were my orders."

Max couldn't read the expression on her face. Jade had gotten good at that over the years. She'd been trained as a sniper—to have patience in all things and to think through the best possible outcome. She was quiet in nature and often too serious, but he thought that might have more to do with her upbringing as an orphan more than anything. And at the moment, she was closed up tight and nothing he could do or say would get her to tell him the truth until she was damned good and ready.

"The whole team is here and Declan will explain everything all at one time. We've got a mess on our hands."

Max's brows raised and then he winced as the movement pulled at the cut by his eye. "So it took direct orders for you to finally face me?"

"It just sped up the process." She gave a secret half-smile that had his cock jumping in response. "I would have gotten here eventually. Now go take your shower and I'll tend to the cuts on your face before everyone shows up."

"At some point, Jade, we're going to have a long conversation. I hope to God you're ready for it."

He stalked toward his bedroom, his body trembling with the fading adrenaline and his head pounding so hard he could barely see. He needed her with a ferocity that he'd never experienced before, and it had only grown stronger and wilder since their time apart. She was going to have to tell him exactly what she wanted, without other agendas or needs clouding the issue, because his control was hanging by a thread.

CHAPTER THREE

Jade let out a slow breath when Max headed out of the room. The way he'd been looking at her had been so full of hunger and lust she'd felt the tingles of attraction sliding across her skin. Anyone would be shaking in her boots after seeing a look that hot and full of desire.

She was glad to see Max was a creature of habit when it came to how he lived. The apartment reflected him—solid and comfortable and a little bit dominating. The first aid kit was under the kitchen sink where he always kept it, and she got everything out and ready on the kitchen table.

She started a pot of coffee for Max—he practically lived on the stuff—and she grabbed another soda for herself. She unstrapped her holster from her thigh and laid it on the countertop—the backup weapon she kept at the small of her back went next to it. More than half an hour had passed before she heard the water shut off.

Feet finally padded against the floor behind her and she smiled as familiarity settled over her. "You've got too much gourmet food in your fridge to fulfill the single man living alone cliché," she said, turning around to tease. But the words died on her lips as she got a good look at him. Her mouth became dry and her heart thudded in her chest.

If his body had been a sculpture when she'd seen it nine months ago, it was a masterpiece now. Sweatpants rode low on his hips and a towel was draped around his neck to catch the droplets of water from his hair. He had to have been pushing himself in his workouts because his chest and shoulders were broader, the muscles more defined. And that was saying something, because they'd been pretty spectacular before.

"What can I say? I'm a man who likes to eat."

The predatory look in his eyes when he said those words had her imagination going wild, and the thought of becoming his main course had her squeezing her thighs together to relieve some of the pressure there.

"Let me look at those cuts." She somehow managed to get the words past her frozen vocal cords. He sat in one of the hardback chairs, and she could tell by the little half smile on his face he was more than enjoying her reaction to him.

He spread his knees so she could get in close and get a better look at the cuts. The heat of his body felt like a warm blanket and the space between them was so charged with energy it was like she could feel him sliding his hands across her body.

This didn't feel like the last time—when she'd been so desperate—so full of hurt and rage and longing. This time the chemistry wasn't a figment of her imagination. And she had a decision to make. It was obvious he wanted her. He'd said he'd wanted her for years, and she'd never even realized.

He wouldn't have said or done anything while Donovan was still alive because Max was an honorable man, but it amazed her she'd never noticed. Usually a woman could sense when a man was attracted to her, but Max had marked himself as friend and had never once crossed the line. She knew this mission was about to change that.

The question was: Would they be able to go back to how things were when it ended? Because there was no doubt in her mind it would end. Max didn't exactly have the best track record when it came to his relationships. Not to mention with his background and who his family was, he'd eventually need someone who could continue the Devlin legacy and uphold the name. And that person wasn't her.

She'd already made the promise to herself that she would never marry again—never give her heart and soul to one person the way she had with Donovan. That kind of love hurt too much, and she wasn't strong enough to take it again.

"How's your headache?" she asked.

"The medication is kicking in. Though I've found something better than drugs to ease the pain."

Even she couldn't miss the innuendo there. She'd spent months wondering if he'd really wanted her as he'd said. Wondering if he'd turned her down because he didn't want to hurt her feelings. Her experience with men wasn't vast. Donovan had been her first and only lover. She wasn't good at reading subtleties or playing the dating game. She was blunt and preferred when others were the same because it was what she understood.

If he'd been so overcome by the sight and feel of her, then he wouldn't have been able to stop. Would he? But she couldn't be imagining the interest she saw in his eyes now. And there was nothing in the world that could've hidden the erection tenting the front of his sweatpants. She could go into an affair with her eyes open this time, without the guilt plaguing her or the anger making her do things she normally wouldn't. This would be a healthy coupling between two people who knew what they were getting into, and when the mission was over, they could go back to the way things were before she'd screwed them up.

Jade couldn't, and wouldn't, expect anything more from him than a casual affair. Max deserved to have a woman who was whole, who could give him a home and children and hold up the traditions of the Devlin name. She could no longer offer that to any man. Not to mention his grandparents would probably go into apoplexy if he brought home a mixed-race orphan girl from Louisiana. Her future was in her work, and that would have to be enough to fulfill her.

"You've still got some splinters embedded in the skin," she said, touching around the deepest cut near his eye.

She grabbed the tweezers and got to work, taking out the thin slivers of wood as the wounds bled sluggishly. He didn't flinch and he stayed perfectly still, but his gaze never left her face. His eyes were heavy lidded, and the brown contacts were gone so the brilliant blue blazed with hunger.

Her breasts grew heavy and her nipples spiked against the thin material of her bra. Warmth spread through her body and it felt as if some invisible thread was binding them closer, though their bodies weren't touching. She stood between his open thighs, basking in his heat and enjoying the feel of him beneath her fingers.

"You said you were here for a couple of reasons." His voice was seductive and low, and she finally found the courage to meet that endless blue gaze. "The first is the mission. But you haven't told me what the second reason was."

"That was careless of me," she whispered.

They stared into each other's eyes, completely lost to anything else around them. It was a stare that lasted too long and saw too much. A stare that heightened the senses and changed how each breath was drawn, so they were completely in sync with one another. It was like being caught in a spell, so body and mind were no longer theirs to command.

Jade drew in a shuddering breath and glanced down at his sensual lips, ripe and full and so tempting she could have spent hours there, but then she remembered he was waiting patiently for her to see to his cuts and heat rushed to her face at how easily she'd been distracted. Only he could do this to her—only when he was near was her ability to focus on the job at hand sorely tested.

The splinters were gone and she wiped the cuts with an antiseptic pad before placing a couple of butterfly bandages over the deeper ones. She froze when she felt his hands on either side of her knees. His touch was molten through the fabric of her pants, and he squeezed once before gliding his hands higher up her thighs and around so they rested just below her rear.

"You didn't answer me, Jade. What was the other reason for coming here?"

She couldn't keep herself from touching him, from feeling the coarseness of his stubble beneath her hand. Her thumb skimmed across his bottom lip and his nostrils flared at the boldness of her touch.

"Answer me, dammit."

Impatience simmered inside him, and his fingers flexed against her backside. He reminded her of a big golden tiger locked in a cage, waiting for the opportunity to pounce on whoever opened the door.

"You told me before—" she licked her lips and ran her fingers through his damp hair, massaging the back of his skull. "You told me to come find you when I was ready to live for real."

"And?" he asked.

"It looks like I found you. Now what are you going to do about it?"

CHAPTER FOUR

Jade could see the surprise in his eyes, and the way her challenge affected him. His hands cupped her ass and he pulled her closer, so her breasts were only a whisper away from his mouth. She leaned down boldly and took his bottom lip between her teeth, sucking it into her mouth before letting it go with an audible pop.

"You're under my skin, Max Devlin. All these months of separation, and I still couldn't get you out of my head. There are no ghosts between us now. Memories—yes. But no ghosts. We're just a man and a woman, and I know what I'm asking for. Give me this one time. Just to make the ache go away."

She kissed him in earnest then, lips and tongues melding. His hand clasped against the back of her head, holding her in place as he took control. If he hadn't been holding her steady, her knees would have buckled because kissing Max was like sending an electrical current through her system.

"You think just once is going to do it?" he asked, pulling away. "You'd better be damned sure what you're asking me because I promise, the kind of living I have in mind is like nothing you've ever experienced."

"I need to be touched," she moaned. "I've missed it so much. I'm yours for the taking."

SECRETS AND SATIN

He pulled her hips down so she straddled his leg and she groaned as pressure was applied against her pussy. A wicked hunger rose inside of her, daring her to push him for more.

"I love your ass," he said, palming the globes in his hands. "It's definitely my favorite body part, and yours is grade A, baby. My dick goes rock hard every time I see you bend over. Your ass is going to be mine, baby."

"God, Max—"

His teeth nipped at the sensitive flesh of her neck while his hands massaged her ass. "Be damned sure this is what you want," he whispered. "Because there will come a time when we're past the point of no return. I've waited too long for you. Do you have any idea the things I've dreamed of doing to that sweet body?"

How could she answer? She gasped as his head dipped down and he took one of her nipples between his teeth through the barrier of her shirt, biting down gently. Her pussy became hotter and she began to writhe against his leg, looking for relief from the pressure building inside of her. She'd been married and widowed, but never in her life had she felt anything like what was happening to her now.

"I'm going to be demanding," he said. "And there won't be anything you'll deny me when you're in my bed. Have you thought about the consequences of that?"

"It's all I've been able to think about," she panted. "I want you. Just you, Max."

"You're going to get me, sugar. But you don't have any idea who you've set yourself up against. I know you, Jade Jax. And you coming to me is the perfect excuse for you to get what you want and not have to face the consequences. Yes, you're ready to live for real. I can see it when I look at you now. But you're still feeling your way back into the world, and you think I'm a safe choice for testing your wings."

She froze against him as his words mirrored her thoughts. She shook her head to deny him, but the fire burning between them wouldn't be doused so easily.

"Don't push this, Max," she said, her hand putting against his chest. "I want you. My body comes alive for you. Let it be enough." She didn't bother to add he'd probably lose interest before long anyway. She knew exactly what she was getting into. They'd use each other for as long as it lasted and move on.

His fingers gripped her hips and he held her against his muscled thigh. "I'm not safe, baby. I've waited for this too long, and once you give yourself to me, you're mine."

She shook her head, denying him the one thing she couldn't give.

"You'll give me everything you have without question. If I tell you to bend over so I can watch my dick slide into that sweet ass, then that's what you'll do." His voice was dark and sinful and she shivered at the image he described. "There won't be any hiding when you're with me. Is that something you'll be able to live with?"

Jade's mind was cloudy with the promises he made, and there was no turning back now—not after she'd come so close to satisfaction.

"Only if you can live with the things I want to do to you," she managed to get out. "I won't be a bystander in this affair." She nipped at his ear and felt the growl rumble in his chest. "I may not have as much experience as you when it comes to certain things, but I'm a fast learner and I can hold my own. You may dominate me in the bedroom, but we'll stand side by side when it comes to the job. One has nothing to do with the other. I want your promise on that or I walk out the door right now. Are we clear?"

"Crystal." Max smiled as he tugged her shirt from her pants and pulled it over her head. "And don't threaten to walk out my door, or I'll have you bent over my knee with my palm prints on your ass."

Her ass clenched and her eyes widened at the suggestion, and he laughed, a caress that touched every

SECRETS AND SATIN

nerve ending in her body.

"So you like the idea of being spanked, do you?" he asked. "Maybe I'll surprise you."

Jade didn't know what she'd expected from Max, but these dark promises weren't it. She was way out of her league, and as passionate and daring as she'd thought sex with Donovan had been, she realized now how sheltered her experience had been. Not that Donovan hadn't made her blood race or had been unable to give her orgasms, because he had, but the sheer chemistry she felt with Max made her realize how wide the spectrum of pleasure was. And he hadn't even been inside her yet.

She wished she was the kind of woman who owned sexy lingerie, or had the kind of breasts to fill that lingerie out. But she'd never taken the time to learn to be a girl. Her whole life had been about survival, from the time she'd been a child in the orphanage to adulthood when she'd sworn to serve and protect.

But the way Max was looking at her in that moment made her feel very feminine. It didn't matter that she wore a plain white cotton bra. His eyes were dark with arousal and took in every inch of her, as if he were committing the sight of her to his memory.

"Do you know how good it's going to feel to finally be inside you?" he asked. "I've dreamed of it often, but then I'd wake up alone and so hard I had no choice but to jack off or live with the pain in my balls."

Jade moaned and shifted her weight against his thigh, undulating her hips and feeling the flickers of electricity gathering in her clit. His words brought a clear picture to mind, and the thought of him masturbating while thinking of fucking her was its own aphrodisiac, even if it was a lie. If he woke up hard, probably all he had to do was roll over and slide into whoever was laying next to him.

His hands skimmed up her flat stomach and cupped her breasts, his thumbs flicking across her cloth covered nipples before moving to her back to open the clasp of her bra. Jade trailed her fingers down the hard planes of his chest and across the ridges of his defined abs, and gasped as her gaze went below his waist. His cock was hard and huge, and his erection was so impressive the waistband of his sweatpants couldn't contain it.

Her fingers moved lower and she was just about to take it in her hand when a sharp knock pounded against the door.

"Fuck." Max's jaw clenched as he quickly pulled her shirt back over her head. "That'll be the team. Sometimes MacKenzies are a pain in the ass."

Jade snickered and moved on unsteady legs to lean against the counter and put herself back together. Max looked rakishly disheveled, his hair mussed and his lips swollen from her kisses. Not to mention his sweatpants left very little to the imagination.

"All I know is you'd better put that hard-on away or they'll call you something a lot worse than Agent Danger," she said, laughing again. "You know Cade never passes up the opportunity to get his jabs in."

He looked down to where her gaze was riveted and grunted. "I figure they're used to it by now. I've had a perpetual hard-on since you walked through my door five years ago, but I'll go put a shirt on since Elena is probably with them." He grinned wolfishly. "You can answer the door and deal with Declan. He's probably not going to be happy about the way things went tonight. Maybe you can soften him up some."

Jade snorted. "Not likely. There's only one woman that man is ever soft around, and it sure as hell isn't me."

Max slipped into the bedroom and she grabbed her weapon from the counter and went to the door—you could never be too careful. She checked the camera and opened the door to a group of men who towered over her substantial height, and Elena, who stood behind them hugging her computer.

"Sorry to interrupt your party," Declan said, moving

past her and straight to the kitchen. "Some of us would like to get some work done around here."

"Don't mind him," Cade said, following close behind. "You know how pissy he gets when he has to fly. I've never met a man who hates to fly as much as he does, yet has to do it so often."

"I'm not afraid to fly," Dec said, grabbing a couple of beers from the fridge and tossing one to Cade. "And if you keep poking at me, I'm going to tell Bayleigh."

Brant Scott, Dec and Cade's brother-in-law, laughed from the corner and took the beer Dec handed him, leaning against the counter to watch the show.

"I'm tired of everyone threatening to tell my wife on me," Cade scowled. "I'm not afraid of her."

"Yes you are—" several voices said at once.

"I just don't like sleeping on the couch," he said. "My feet hang over the end. Not that I know what sleep is. I swear my child must be half vampire. She thinks nighttime is playtime."

"I think that's called poetic justice," Brant said. "Because Darcy and I have perfect children. Both of them were sleeping through the night at two weeks old. Your mom said you get what you deserve. You must deserve an awful lot."

"You have no idea," Dec said. "He enjoyed his power as the oldest immensely. I'm surprised Shane wasn't scarred for life after some of the things Cade did to him."

"You're not completely innocent in this, you know," Cade said. His arms were crossed over his chest, his posture defensive and his scowl black. "You're the one who wrote that poem about him under the bleachers. I don't think he had a girlfriend his entire freshman year."

Dec grinned, stretching the white scar along his jawline, and tapped his beer bottle against Cade's. "Well, now that I think back on it, he probably deserved it."

"Speaking of," Max said, coming into the fray. "Where is Shane? I haven't seen him in a while."

"He's back in the world," Dec said, referring to Shane coming home after a long mission overseas. "It's haying season, so he's helping Mom up at the house for the next few weeks, but he and the team are on call if we need them."

Jade took a seat next to Elena and watched the byplay continue for a few minutes. She had been brought into the MacKenzie family so seamlessly over the past couple of years that it seemed like she'd always been there. The MacKenzies were special—they were hard-headed and tough and could be scary as hell if the occasion called for it—but underneath it all was a deep caring and respect for each other and for their jobs. They believed in justice and that right should always win, and they were loyal—to each other and their wives. She trusted every person in the room, and she realized how rare that was.

"They are always like children," Elena whispered, her lips twitching at an insult Max tossed off to Cade.

"That's because they're men," Jade said.

"And proud of it," Max said.

Jade's body went hot when she met his gaze over the top of Elena's head. The look he gave her reminded her exactly how male he was. The banter and voices around them became muted as she remembered what Max's hands had felt like against her skin, but reality came crashing back when Cade nudged her in the shoulder.

"You falling asleep on us?" he asked.

The spell was broken and she turned to elbow Cade in the ribs.

Max let out a slow breath and ignored the long look Declan gave him. Dec was protective of Jade, just like all of the guys were, but Max didn't need the subtle warning he saw in Dec's gaze. Jade was going to be his. And he'd fight anyone who tried to tell him differently.

He headed to the coffeepot, poured himself a steaming cup, and didn't bother to add cream or sugar. He needed the kick, and he was hoping the caffeine would take the edge off the pain in his head. The pills he'd taken had eased the headache, but the dull throb was still there. At least it was manageable.

"I'm assuming there's a reason Dec has come down from his mountain on high and is now drinking beer at my kitchen table?" Max asked.

"Sometimes I like to mingle with the commoners," Dec answered dryly.

Dec took a seat at the head of the table and everyone else grabbed a chair to pull up. He passed out a manila file folder to everyone and the joking expression he'd had earlier was completely gone. This was Dec in business mode.

"Senator Henry is screaming from the rooftops about the breach of his security tonight," Dec said. "Henry doesn't know who broke into his office and tampered with his computer, but he suspects Martin Vassin."

Cade let out a long whistle and Max leaned forward in his chair. "I thought Martin Vassin was killed in that explosion at the Kremlin last year," Max said.

"Martin needed a little time to regroup after he found himself short of liquid assets when an arms deal went bad with a Turkish terrorist cell," Dec said. "The weapons were intercepted by the authorities and the Turks were screaming for Martin to make good on his promise by sending someone to enforce the deal. Martin took the easy way out and chose to die for a little while instead of facing the iron crowbar of the Turkish enforcer."

"So now Vassin is alive and well and his coffers are full?" Max asked. "What's the connection with Senator Henry?"

Dec leaned back in his chair and steepled his hands across his stomach. Max knew he'd already committed to memory every piece of information that was in the closed file in front of him. Dec's mind was like a machine.

"Vassin is one of the more intelligent arms and information brokers. And he's tapped into Senator Henry. He's got deep pockets and his position on the defense committee is well placed."

"I don't like where I think you're going with this," Max said.

"Wherever you think I'm going just took a hundred and eighty degree turn," Dec said. "It's a sticky situation. We knew Henry was involved in the high-level security leaks, and this all started about six months ago. Since then we can blame the loss of the Iranian military convoy last month and the bombing at the US Consulate in London that killed Senator Ryan at Vassin's feet. Gabe Brennan and his team of agents are investigating and hunting the parties responsible since Vassin didn't do the dirty work himself. Vassin is just the facilitator."

Max raised his brows at the mention of Gabe Brennan. Gabe made Declan look like an altar boy. He was a scary son of a bitch, but Dec trusted him implicitly, which was saying something because Dec didn't trust many people.

Max had never had any direct dealings with Gabe, but he'd heard the rumors that his wife had left him and had turned mercenary because of something terrible he'd done. Now there was a price on her head, and nobody knew if Gabe was going to let her go free or if he'd try to bring her in and collect the bounty.

"Then Henry's a traitor, plain and simple," Brant said. "And he should pay just like Vassin is going to pay."

"Not so simple." Dec shook his head. "That's what we found on the flash drive from Henry's personal computer. His nineteen year old daughter is a sophomore at Harvard and was studying late one night at the library when Vassin and his men kidnapped her."

"Damn," Max said.

"I started the ball rolling as soon as Elena gave me the

information. We don't know where Vassin is keeping her, but he has homes all over the world. My gut says she'll be close though."

"God," Jade said. "And the senator would do anything to protect his daughter. Even betray his country."

"Bingo," Dec said.

Max watched Elena go very still and shudder at the mention of what had happened to the senator's daughter, and she seemed to draw in on herself even more. But Jade placed her hand on the other woman's shoulder and squeezed it reassuringly.

"Am I to assume you're going to need the Devlin name for this mission?" Max asked.

Dec's lips twitched. "Why do you think we keep you around? That blue blood comes in handy on occasion. And your cover as the disenchanted agent doesn't hurt either. The word has been put out that you've got sensitive information from your days at the DEA, and that you're willing to part with it for a price."

"Wow, I'm a real asshole," Max said, deadpan.

"This time more than normal," Cade said, making everyone laugh.

"Your mission is to lure Vassin into the open. He never negotiates deals one on one. It's how he's stayed alive so long. He'll want to send someone in his stead to make the transaction. You've got to convince him that you'll only work with him directly. We need to take out Vassin and we need to find the Senator's daughter. I've called all agents in on this and Shane's SEAL team is willing to act as unofficial backup."

"What kind of information am I supposed to have that Vassin will want?" Max asked. "I don't have security clearance anymore."

"No, but you have the drop and destroy locations for all of the confiscated weapons. We have to make it real or Vassin will know it's a setup."

Max raised his brows and ran his hand over the top of

his head in agitation. The DEA confiscated ridiculous amounts of contraband weapons in its day-to-day activities. Weapons that not even the military had access to. Arms dealers were more prevalent in the United States than one might think, and the successful ones had a network set up so they could ship contraband weapons all over the world.

Once the DEA got word of a deal and confiscated the shipment, the weapons were taken to a warehouse on one of the military bases where they were highly guarded until the warehouse was full. Then the weapons were taken by convoy to a secured location where they were melted down to scrap. Once the weapons made it to the meltdown location, there was no danger, but the convoy transporting the weapons to the base was vulnerable, even though they were carefully guarded.

"Are you sure?" Max asked. "It could backfire on us if Vassin did happen to get the routes." What Max really meant was that if Vassin somehow captured Max, there was a possibility the location could be tortured from him anyway.

"It'll be fine," Dec said. "You'll have your bodyguard there as backup. Max Devlin never goes anywhere without a bodyguard. Even the newspapers have remarked on that more than once."

Dec had started building him a solid cover while he'd been lying unconscious in the hospital, and he'd kept layering on top of it for the two years after. He was a reckless playboy. A man who skated the line between former hero and current criminal. His friends, associates and morals were considered questionable. Max was the bad boy everyone in polite society was too afraid of offending. They wouldn't dare turn their backs on him because he wielded to much power over the companies and stock holders that were part of the Devlin fortune.

"And who gets the privilege of standing in the line of fire for me?" Max asked.

SECRETS AND SATIN

"That would be me," Jade said, her lips quirking in a smile. "I am the best shot after all."

"You know, if that wasn't completely true, I'd resent that statement," Cade said.

"I think your ego can take it, big boy," she said, grinning.

Cade nodded soberly. "My wife says my ego is very—healthy."

"I believe she had something to say about your ego and its size the last time she was in labor too," Declan said. "We all learned more than we wanted to know about your anatomy, or lack thereof."

Everyone at the table broke into loud guffaws, and Cade's lips quirked, acknowledging that round to Declan. Except for Max. He was motionless in his chair, his eyes drilling holes into the side of her head. She'd seen the way his gaze shuttered at the mention of her going in as his bodyguard, and she tried not to let it bother her. But dammit—it did. She was tired of the men in her life trying to stand in front of her all the time. Max had relied on her before this thing between them became personal.

"Max, you and Jade will head down to your place tonight," Dec said. "It won't be long before Vassin gets in contact with you. The rest of us are going to stay here for the time being and keep going through Senator Henry's passcoded files to see if we can find anything else that could lead us to where his daughter is being kept."

Dec scooted back his chair and stood, tossing his beer bottle in the recycler before heading toward the door. The others all followed suit, and Jade went with them to the door while Max leaned back in the chair on two legs and watched them all.

"Take what you need out of the weapons room with you," Dec said. "And take the black Explorer in the garage. We'll dispose of the one you lifted earlier. Both of you stay on your guard. Vassin likes to play dirty."

Jade closed the door behind them and turned to face

Max, her arms crossing over her chest. "I can tell you right now you're not going to say one word about my assignment," she said. "I saw the look on your face the minute it left Declan's mouth. This is my job. And I may sleep with you, but that doesn't give you the right to act like a Neanderthal and make me stand two steps behind you. I mean it, Max. The minute you try to stand in front of me, I walk. Period."

Max's lips thinned in a straight line and he stalked toward her until he stood so close they were almost touching. His arms came up on each side of her shoulders and trapped her against the door. She narrowed her eyes in warning.

"Stop threatening to walk out on me, or your ass is going to be so red you can't sit for a week. I know better than anyone how capable you are on the job. But that doesn't mean I can help the natural instincts to try and protect what's mine. I'm a man. I think the Neanderthal is in our genes."

"Some more than others," she said sweetly. "Do you trust me to have your back?"

"Always," he said, with no hesitation. "But that doesn't mean I have to like it. Especially since you are going to be sleeping with me. There are certain allowances that have to be made for people you're intimate with."

"Clearly you've been reading Emily Post again."

"Don't be a smartass." He leaned down and gave her a hard kiss, and Jade couldn't help but twine her arms around his neck and kiss him back with everything she had. When he broke away they were both panting and she wondered if they had time to disobey orders and take the edge off before they headed out.

"We'd better not chance it," he whispered against her lips. "Declan will be down here pounding on the door if we're not out of here in the next five minutes. And once I get you naked, nothing is going to stop me until I'm coming so hard inside of you that you feel me for a week."

SECRETS AND SATIN

Jade's mouth went dry and her fingers tightened at the nape of his neck. "Promises, promises," she said. "Or maybe it'll be the other way, Agent Devlin. Maybe I'll ride you so hard you'll be feeling me for a week."

Jade pushed him back and gave him a saucy wink, and Max let out a startled laugh. She felt good. Free. And she realized it had been a long time since it hadn't felt like something was strangling her from the inside. She wasn't weak. And she didn't need to be coddled. Donovan would always have a special place in her heart. He was her first love and the man she hadn't gotten to spend nearly enough time with. The memories would always be there, and time had softened the grief—whether she'd wanted it to or not.

She realized Donovan would've been happy she'd chosen Max. They'd been close as brothers. The last of the guilt that had been wrapped around her heart broke free and a peace settled over her she couldn't explain—as if Donovan were laying a hand on her shoulder and telling her it was okay.

Jade turned away from Max and headed out the door so he wouldn't see the tears in her eyes. She could no longer feel Donovan imprinted on every part of her life. He was no longer her first thought when she woke in the mornings or her last when she went to bed at night. Moving on had happened whether she'd wanted it to or not.

CHAPTER FIVE

It was past dawn by the time they got close to Max's home, just north of San Antonio in the hill country. The sun was already a bright orange ball rising over the hills in the distance, burning off the thin layer of fog that had settled low across the ground.

The grass along the narrow two-lane road was brown and dead, and the cedar trees were sparse and so dry, Jade hoped no one lit a match anywhere in the vicinity. The whole state was liable to go up in flames.

There was a rugged beauty about the whole area—the rolling hills and miles of pastureland—and she could see why Max had been drawn to the area. It was a far cry from his DuPont Circle brownstone. That posh area of wealth and prestige had belonged to the old Max—the Max that had been more carefree and easy to laugh before his injury.

She looked at the man sleeping in the passenger seat, taking in the longer length of his hair and the growth of beard on his cheeks. He overwhelmed the space beside her, and even in sleep, he looked a little bit dangerous—a little bit rough around the edges. This wasn't the same Max who had grown up surrounded by wealth and every want at his fingertips. This was a man who'd worked his way up the ranks the hard way and paid the consequences. There was an edge of danger to him now that hadn't been there before, and she wasn't afraid to admit that she found it attractive.

She slowed the Explorer as they came to a steep turn and then navigated across a slatted wooden bridge that ran over a creek that was more mud than water.

"We're almost there," he said, eyes still closed.

"I thought you were asleep."

"I woke up when you started muttering to yourself about the skunk smell. You'll get used to it, city girl."

Jade snorted out a laugh. "So speaks the boy with the silver spoons in both fists."

Max grinned and stretched, putting his seat back in the upright position. "Yeah, well, it took me a little while to get adjusted. It's really quiet. There are no honking horns or sirens. Just crickets and the occasional coyote howling."

"How's the headache?"

"It's gone. They never last more than a few hours and sleep seems to be the cure more so than the pills. It's mostly an annoyance. Watch the turn here," he said. "The road drops straight off into the ditch."

"I guess you don't get much company out here."

"That's the point. There's no one around for miles and I've got sensors in the road to alert me if someone's coming. I originally put them around the perimeter of the property, but there are so many wild animals they kept setting the sensors off."

Jade took the corner slowly, holding her breath as she kept the Explorer on the narrow road. Max hadn't exaggerated—there was a ten-foot drop off on each side and the tires came almost to the edge of the pavement. The curve straightened out and she had to squint her eyes against the sudden darkness. Tree branches gnarled over the road and hung low so they almost scraped the top of the car, and limbs scratched against the side windows.

"Jesus, Max. This is a little overboard, don't you think?"

"I like my privacy," he said, shrugging. "And this place

is off the books. No one but Declan and now you knows where it is. You're sworn to secrecy."

"So you're saying I shouldn't have posted the picture of the exit I took on my Facebook page?" She widened her eyes playfully. "Oops."

"You're getting a little cheeky, Jax." His eyes darkened and he reached across the console to trail his finger along her jawline, and her flesh pebbled at his touch. Things had gone from playful to seduction in a matter of seconds and she was still trying to keep up. "We're going to be pulling into my driveway in about forty-five seconds. I'm going to be inside you in about fifty."

"Why are you waiting so long?"

Max sucked in a breath and she licked her lips, pressing her foot to the accelerator. She shot out of the tree-lined tunnel and back into the glaring sunlight. Dust kicked up around the tires and at the top of a small rise, Max's house came into view. It was a long, one-story ranch house built with rough timbers and a slate roof, with a wide porch wrapped around all sides. It wasn't anything like she'd been expecting.

She was about to comment on the fact when she caught what Max was doing out of the corner of her eye. He'd unbuckled his seatbelt and pulled his shirt up, and he was unbuckling his belt with deliberate movements. The Explorer veered into the grass and she swerved it back onto the long stretch of Max's driveway.

His erection was prominent behind the zipper of his jeans, and he popped the top button open. Her breath came faster and her foot pressed to the floor, shooting them forward. He worked at the zipper next, pulling it down slowly and she licked her lips at the sight of him bare beneath the denim.

"You lick your lips like that every time you see my cock," he rasped. "It's the sexiest damned thing I've ever seen, and every time you do it I can't help but imagine you taking me between those sweet lips."

SECRETS AND SATIN

Jade slammed on the brakes and the SUV skidded to a halt just in front of the house. She released her seatbelt and Max hit the lever at the side of his seat so it leaned all the way back, and he was pulling her across the console almost before she had it in park.

Their mouths fused together, lips and tongues clashing, and he lifted her so she straddled his hips and the hard length of him pressed against the very heat of her. It was out of control—wicked sensations and fiery licks of pleasure that skated across her skin and gathered in her womb.

His hands wound into her hair and he held her head still as he took control of the kiss, as he licked into her and tasted every whimper that escaped her lips while her hips mimicked his tongue. A startled cry broke free as a little electrical current pulsed in her clit and a tiny orgasm ripped through her. She tore her mouth away from him and pressed her head against his chest as the small shudders rocked her body.

"Let go, baby," he whispered against her ear, licking at the sensitive shell and making her shudder again. "That's just the first one. I can't wait to taste that sweet pussy and have you come against my lips. And then the feel of your muscles clamping around my cock as you come again."

Jade could barely catch her breath. The sensations were overwhelming and the eroticism of his words electric. She felt the dampness of her desire between her legs, and she was suddenly unsure of herself. She wanted this more than she realized, but there were nerves fluttering in her belly and a sense of the unknown.

Max jerked her shirt over her head, tossing it in the backseat, and baring her aching breast. He flicked the clasp of her bra and it followed in the direction of the shirt.

"Christ, look at you," he said, a flush mantling across his cheeks. His gaze was hooded and he exhaled slowly as his hands came up and cupped her breasts, his thumbs rasping against the sensitive tips of her nipples. "So pretty and full, just waiting for my mouth."

Max leaned forward and took a straining bud between his lips. She'd never been able to come more than once when she made love, but she could feel the low hum of desire building inside of her once more.

"Wait—God, Max," she pushed against his chest, but he grasped her hips and rolled her pussy against him. Her eyes rolled back in her head and her lashes fluttered closed at the sensation. It was all too fast. Too much. She didn't know what to do with this much pleasure. He lifted his head to move his attention to her other breast and she took advantage of the space between them.

"Wait," she said again.

He sucked in a breath and seemed to shake himself out of the lustful daze he'd been in, and he finally met her gaze, a question in his eyes.

"I need to say something." She licked her lips nervously, and bit at her bottom lip, and his eyes followed the movement.

"Say it quick, baby, because I'm losing control fast here."

"I just wanted to say that it's been awhile since I've done this."

He froze completely against her and the unreadable mask he used when he was working shuttered over his face. She felt the blood rush to her cheeks, and almost rolled her eyes at the words that had actually come out of her mouth.

Of course he knows you haven't done this in a while. Idiot.

"That's not what I mean," she hurried on. "Not exactly. It's not a big deal. I just want to make sure you tell me if I do something—" She paused for a second, searching for the word. "Wrong," she blurted out. "Or something you don't like. I'm just out of practice." The words left her in a rush and she wondered if there was a rock big enough to crawl under.

CHAPTER SIX

Max's senses came back to him in a hurry after her confession. He could only blame his ineptness on the need to be inside her so badly. As it was, his balls were drawn so close to his body that he could practically feel the come ready to spurt from his cock.

He was insane. That was his only excuse. He didn't know what he'd been thinking. No, he hadn't been thinking. That was the problem. But he was about to rectify that. She deserved more than a fast fuck in the front seat of a car.

He knew she wasn't experienced. Donovan had shared in confidence on a mission once that he had been Jade's first and only lover, and he'd loved the fact that she'd only belonged to him. She was giving herself to him, despite her anxiety and her inexperience, and he would cherish the gift as much as Donovan had.

"Jade," he breathed out, taking her flushed cheeks between his palms. He leaned forward and kissed her once—softly—and then lifted her so he could sit up and reach the door handle. He thanked God he lived in the middle of such remoteness because otherwise they were sure to be arrested.

He opened the car door and she immediately covered her breasts, struggling to get off his lap. Confusion flittered across her face and he kissed the underside of her jaw before wrapping his arms around her and lifting her physically from the vehicle. Jade was almost as tall as he was, but once his feet were steady on the ground he swept her up in his arms and watched the surprise light across her features.

"What—"

"Ssh, baby. I'll take care of you. I'll make this right."

"There was nothing wrong before," she protested. "Have you changed your mind?"

"Far from it," he said, kicking the car door shut with the bottom of his foot. "I just remembered the best things are worth doing right. But just a warning, I probably won't get it right until the second time. I'm pretty sure I won't last long once I finally get inside you." Her mouth opened in surprise and he leaned down to nip at her bottom lip. "But I'll make it up to you," he said. "I promise."

He carried her easily up the porch steps and to the front door and called out his name for the voice recognition program he had installed, and then he said the code aloud to override the system. The front door opened silently and he carried her into the cool darkness of his home. The door locked automatically behind him and he carried her straight to the back of the house, to the bedroom he rarely had time to sleep in.

The shutters were pulled over the windows, but he didn't need the light to see his way. He felt her flesh pebble and a shiver rush through her body as the cold breeze from the air conditioner blew across her skin. His bedroom was large and the oversized bed dominated the middle of the room. The sheets and down comforter were white because he hadn't had time to mess with anything but the basics.

Max set her on her feet and then pushed her back so she sat on the side of the bed, and then he turned the dial above his nightstand so a light glowed just over the bed, casting them in a soft wash of light. He kneeled in front of her, unlacing her boots and pulling them from her feet. He pulled off her socks next and then rubbed the arch of each foot, moving his thumb in slow circles as she moaned at the unexpected pleasure.

Her gaze was wide and curious, the insane passion they'd shared before banked, but still burning in her emerald eyes.

"You don't have to do this," she said, touching the side of his face with her hand. "I'm not glass. I won't break."

"I know. But I'm bigger than you. I can do what I want," he said, grinning.

He was so hard he hurt, and he wanted her more than he had the first time he saw her, but he relaxed as he saw the fire light in her eyes at his words. He realized this was the first time he'd ever been completely comfortable with a lover. Jade was his friend first—he knew all her quirks and faults and strengths—and he knew they'd find their way with each other in bed just as they'd found their way outside of it.

He helped her to her feet and then quickly stripped off her pants so she was left in nothing but a pair of black boyshort panties. He looked up her body from where he knelt and watched as her head dropped back on her shoulders, almost in surrender. He kissed the top of her thigh and then higher, just above her hip bone, before slipping his fingers beneath the edge of her panties and pulling them down.

"God, Jade," he said, the words choked at the sight of her womanly flesh. "So pretty."

A small patch of soft black curls sat just above the swollen nubbin of her clit and the completely bare folds beneath. He touched one of the creamy folds gently, delicately spreading her juices around the entrance of her pussy. His finger barely slid inside her and he groaned as she clamped and shuddered around him.

"Max—"

"Ssh, baby. Let me see all of you." He guided her back

to the edge of the bed and pushed her down gently. Her skin was dark against the stark white of the comforter and she watched him out of hungry eyes. That look made it hard for him to remember that he was going to go slow and take his time.

He quickly unlaced his boots and tossed them aside, and then stood and pushed his jeans down, stepping out of them, while he watched her eyes get bigger and bigger at the sight of him. She licked her lips again while she stared at his cock, and he almost came then and there. He clamped his fist around the base of his cock and then took a deep breath to get himself back under control.

"Don't take this the wrong way, but that looks painful," she said. "For me, I mean. Holy shit, Max."

He laughed, but the sound was strained. "We're going to fit like we were made for each other. Put your heels on the edge of the bed." His voice rasped the words and his mouth went dry as she did as he asked. "See, already I can see how ready you are for me. Your pussy is glistening for me, your clit swollen. Oh, yeah, we'll fit like hand and glove. I'm going to sink right in."

She whimpered, her hips shifting greedily as she waited for him to take his place between her thighs. His fingers touched lightly up her leg, swirling over her knee, and then higher until he pressed against her thighs and had them splaying open wider. He leaned forward and kissed her taut belly, licking and nipping his way up until his lips opened and he suckled at her nipple. She jumped beneath him and her hands came up and grasped his upper arms, her nails biting into his flesh.

"No, don't stop," she cried as he released her nipple with an audible pop and kissed his way back down to the sweet folds of her pussy.

"Do you know how long I've waited to taste you here?" he asked, kissing just above her pubic bone.

He looked up her body from where he knelt between her legs and her eyes burned with the fire of his touch. His gaze stayed steady on hers as his tongue slid up the syrupy seam of her pussy until he found the swollen bud of her clit. And then his eyes shuttered closed and he was lost in the taste of her.

Jade thought she knew what to expect—what it would feel like to have Max's mouth on her there—but the heat of his tongue and the way he seemed to know exactly where to lick and suck had her going wild almost as soon as he touched her.

His tongue rasped across the sensitive bud, over and over, until she was straining against his mouth. If he'd only press a little harder, move a little faster, she'd be able to reach that pinnacle.

"Please, Max—don't tease," she said, her head moving back and forth against the sheets. He spread her legs wider, opened her further, and his tongue moved lower, kissing the weeping entrance of her vagina.

"God, Jade. You taste so sweet. Better than I imagined. And look how wet you are for me." His finger probed at the entrance of her pussy, dipping inside once before he added another finger.

She felt stretched to the limit, even with only his fingers, and she sucked in a breath as he worked them slowly inside, preparing her for more. Her body arched and her breasts ached as his mouth joined his fingers, and she reached for his head, her fingers tangling in his hair as she pulled him closer. She felt the orgasm building, her body tightening and straining against every lash of his tongue. And then his fingers curled inside of her, finding the sensitive flesh that was sure to drive her mad.

"Max!" she screamed as his tongue moved faster and faster. Perspiration sheened on her skin and her body went molten as little electric shocks pulsed in her clit and shot through her body. Her hips bucked against his face and mewling cries grew louder and louder as she spun into oblivion and exploded against his lips.

"Fuck, you are so beautiful," he said, pulling away.

"No, don't leave me," she begged. "More—more."

"I'm not going anywhere, sweetheart."

He scooted her farther into the center of the bed and crawled between her open thighs.

"Shit." He closed his eyes and gritted his teeth. "Condoms. I don't have any here. Please tell me you're on the pill."

"I'm protected," she finally managed to say.

"Thank God, because otherwise you and I were about to make a baby. I'm going to shoot so deep and far inside of you, that would be the only outcome."

Jade froze as emotional pain overwhelmed her, but he didn't seem to notice the change in her. She could do this. She wanted him, and her body was throbbing with need. All she had to do was turn off her mind and just feel.

He hooked her knees over his shoulders and held open the lips of her pussy with his fingers, watching her from dark hooded eyes. Just that small touch was enough to get her back in the game. He grasped his cock in his hand and rubbed the thick head against the opening of her slit.

"Watch, baby. Watch me take you."

Jade couldn't tear her eyes away. He pushed the head in slowly, splitting her in two as he worked his way inside of her. She sucked in a startled breath and her vaginal muscles flexed around him as he kept pushing. Her tissues were swollen and his fingers hadn't been preparation enough for the size of him, no matter what he'd said about them fitting like hand and glove. She whimpered as his thumb began to rub her clit in circles, and he had to pull out and push in several times before he was finally buried to the hilt.

She took a deep breath once he was seated fully inside of her, and even that tiny movement made little electric shocks sizzle across her skin and gather in her womb. She relaxed around him and tried to focus on breathing.

"Fuck. I'm not going to last. It's been too long." Sweat glistened on his skin at the effort it took to hold back, and he closed his eyes and clamped his jaw shut so the cords in his neck stood out at the effort.

He pulled all the way out again, so just the head was still buried inside of her, and the sight of her juices coating his cock was enough to have her hips rising and searching for him. The discomfort quickly turned to pleasure as he pushed back in to the hilt. She flexed her muscles around him again and he gritted his teeth even harder.

"God, don't move."

"Look at me, Max," she said, waiting until his eyes opened and settled on her.

His eyes glowed brilliant blue and she could see the control he was fighting to maintain. Her hands reached out and touched his chest and she drew them down his body until they reached where they were intimately joined. She licked her lips and tightened her vaginal muscles once more, loving the way his gaze darkened and became even hungrier for her. And then she trailed her hands over her stomach and up higher until she cupped her breasts and tweaked her nipples between her finger and thumb.

"What are you waiting for?" she asked. "Fuck me. Hard."

Wildness entered his eyes a second before he came down on top of her, and she screamed out his name as he gave her exactly what she'd asked for. His thrusts were hard and deep, and his long fought control shattered as he gave in to the beast inside of him. Her heels dug into his flanks and her nails bit into the skin of his back as her hips raised to meet him.

"Yes, yes," she cried as she felt the pressure building inside of her, spreading from her womb and through her whole body. Their eyes locked and held as she tightened around him.

"That's it, baby. Come for me. Milk my cock."

Her eyes fluttered closed and she let go as the orgasm overtook her and sent her spiraling and shuddering out of control. He stiffened above her and shouted her name as he erupted inside of her, each spurt of hot come felt straight to her soul.

They collapsed in each other's arms, a sweaty, tangled heap, and Jade felt a single tear escape from her closed lids. What she and Max had just shared had been more than she'd expected—more than she'd hoped for—and she felt the memory of her husband slip further away as she began this new chapter of her life. It wasn't a tear of sadness—or maybe just a little—but a realization that there was no turning back.

Being with Max had shaken her to the core. He'd been her friend first, and she'd loved him as a friend. But that love had shifted now that he was actually her lover. Despair filled her soul as she realized that she could love again—that it did happen twice. But she could never keep hold of the man in her arms. The clarity of it hit her in the face like a slap. It would be best if this mission and their affair ended quickly, and then she could go back to her life and Max could move on to the next woman.

CHAPTER SEVEN

Max felt her try to draw away, and he somehow found the strength to lift himself so he could see her face. Her eyes were closed and a single tear coursed down her cheek, and he wondered if she regretted what they'd just done.

He knew without a doubt nothing in his life would ever be the same. Nothing had ever felt as right as being connected with Jade mind, body and soul, and he knew he was thirty-six years old and could say he hadn't realized what making love was until just now. It made a difference when you actually loved the person you were inside of.

He wiped the tear away with his thumb. "Did I hurt you?"

Her tear-drenched eyes opened and she shook her head. "No. You didn't hurt me. I'm just a little overwhelmed. I wasn't expecting it to be so—powerful."

"I'd never ask for you to forget him," he said softly. "He was a good man, and he loved you."

"I know that. I wasn't thinking about him. Not really." She licked her lips and he leaned down to kiss her before he pulled out of her and rolled to the side. He gathered her in his arms and brought her close, so they were face to face. "It's just—I feel like I've broken away from that part of my life. Almost as if it never happened."

"Shh—" he said, touching the side of her face. "Of course it happened. And no one, least of all me, would ever want you to forget what you had with Donovan. But you need to know that I think he'd be proud of the woman you are now. The strength you've shown over the last couple of years. And I think he'd give his blessing that you chose me." The tears she'd been fighting fell down her cheeks, and he kissed each one away. "And I think if he were talking to me, he'd slap me on the back—God, he had giant hands, didn't he?" he said, making her smile. "Then he'd warn me that I'd better love you the way you deserved or he'd make me sorry."

Her smile froze and panic shone in her eyes, but he put his finger over her lips when she opened her mouth to speak, halting the denial he knew would come out of them.

"And I'd tell him he didn't need to worry. Because I've always loved you the way you deserved. Even when you belonged to someone else."

Her breath hitched on a sob and she rolled out of his arms until she lay flat on her back. Something felt like it was ripping inside of him. It was obvious she wasn't comfortable with his confession, and he tried to tell himself it was okay. That she probably just needed time. But part of him wondered if she had no deep feelings for him—wondered if he was just someone she felt comfortable with to move onto this next stage in her life.

She scrubbed her hands over her face and then sat up on the side of the bed, so her back was to him. "You think maybe we could grab something to eat?" she asked. "I'm starving."

He stayed silent for only a second, reminding himself to be patient. "Sure. I'll grab the groceries out of the car and you can grab a shower. Then you can cook while I get my own shower."

"What if I can't cook?" she asked, finally turning to face him, a smile tugging at her mouth.

"I figure if you can calculate the wind and distance

when you're firing that rifle of yours, then you can probably follow a simple recipe."

Her laugh was low and husky as she pushed off the bed and made her way into the bathroom. "You're taking a hell of a chance," she called back. "I hope you like burnt toast."

He was pretty sure she was kidding.

"We've got the ingredients for oatmeal or omelets," Max said half an hour later after she'd gotten out of the shower. They'd stopped at a corner store at the last town and stocked up, and it was a good thing because there'd been nothing more than a few cans of soup in the pantry.

Her travel bag had been sitting on the bed and she pulled out a pair of loose sweats and a tank top. She looked to the door where he stood and saw his own hair was wet and droplets of water still rested on his shoulders. She figured he'd made use of another shower somewhere in the house. He wore jeans and nothing else, and it was a distracting sight.

"I'll make omelets," she said. "You couldn't pay me any amount of money to eat oatmeal." At his confused look she explained. "It's the breakfast staple of orphanages everywhere. Seven days a week, summer, winter or fall, there'd be a bowl of oatmeal sitting on the table."

"Omelets it is," he agreed and she followed him into the kitchen.

They worked in companionable silence, her whisking the eggs while Max set out ingredients on the counter for her to easily reach. The savory smells of onions and butter and melted cheese filled the air.

"I didn't realize you had a pool," she said, looking out the wide kitchen window into the backyard. A large arbor shaded the porch and the blue water gleamed crystal clear and looked welcoming against the already warm temperatures.

"I didn't get around to giving you a tour." His smile was sheepish as he set the table. "The house has three bedrooms, two baths, a game room and a living room. Hopefully you'll get to see the ceilings of all of them over the next couple of days," he said, wagging his brows.

She couldn't help but laugh at his obviously cheerful mood. Max went over to the stereo and flipped on the switch, turning it down low so the music was only background noise.

"Was it all bad?" he asked.

Jade didn't have to ask what he was referring to, though she tried not to dwell on her childhood much. "It wasn't great." She slid the omelets onto plates and then sat them on the knotty-pine kitchen table, taking the chair across from him. "It was the little things that made it difficult. Never having any privacy. Making friends but never getting to keep them. Nothing belonged to you—not the clothes on your back or the battered schoolbooks that had been donated. It was harder for me because I was almost ten when I went into the system, and I knew what it felt like to be wanted. And then all of a sudden I wasn't."

"I read your file when you joined my unit," Max said. "Your parents were killed just outside of New Orleans?"

"Mmm," she murmured, pushing the food around on her plate. She'd never been comfortable talking about her past. Not even with Donovan, but Max just sat there patiently and waited her out. "It's just one of those stupid, senseless things. We were eating lunch at a little restaurant one Sunday afternoon, and some asshole drives his pickup truck straight through the plate glass window in front and opens fire. My dad shoved me down and behind the table so I was hidden, otherwise I probably would have been killed too."

"And you didn't have any other family to take you in?" he asked.

SECRETS AND SATIN

She snorted out a laugh and shook her head. "My mother was the only daughter of one of the wealthiest men in New Orleans. Imagine their surprise when she eloped with a poor black law student who was on full scholarship to Tulane. They cut her off without a cent and told her she was as good as dead to them. They didn't even come to her funeral. So they sure as hell didn't offer to save me from the system. And my daddy didn't have any family, so I wasn't left with a lot of choice."

"You turned out to be good people, Jax." Max smiled and took their plates to the kitchen sink. "Your parents would be proud of what you've become."

"I wonder sometimes," she said. "I wonder if I would have ended up in the same place, doing the same things if they'd lived."

Max held out his hand and she placed hers on top of it, and then he pulled her to her feet and placed his hands on her hips.

"I like to think you would've ended up exactly where you are." He leaned down and kissed the corner of her mouth. "That no matter where you'd gone or what you'd experienced before, that you'd still end up naked in my kitchen."

"I'm not naked," she whispered.

"Well—" A smile quirked at the corner of his mouth. It was a smile she'd seen frequently from the old Max—the teasing grin and laughing eyes. "My bad."

Before she could respond, he'd pulled loose the drawstring of her pants and jerked them down so they fell to her ankles, and then her arms were tangled in her shirt as he pulled it over her head.

"There we go," he said. "I wouldn't want you to make a liar out of me."

"No, we wouldn't want that." Jade walked her fingers down his chest and she felt her nipples harden as he sucked in a shaky breath the lower she went, until she traced just above the edge of his jeans. The folds of her sex creamed at the thought of what she wanted to do to him. "It's no fun being naked alone." She kissed the hard planes of his chest as her fingers toyed with the snap.

"Maybe you should do something about that," he said, his voice hoarse.

She smiled against his warm flesh as she began kissing her way down his torso and his hands slid into her hair, pushing her down until she knelt in front of him. Her fingers flicked open the button of his jeans, and she carefully drew down the zipper over his erection and then tugged at the denim until it was pulled down to his knees. He held her head steady as he stepped out of his jeans.

"I want your mouth on me," he rasped.

She nuzzled against the taut muscles of his thigh, inhaling the musky scent of him before letting her gaze travel back up his body to meet his eyes. The blue of his eyes almost glowed with carnal heat and she could see the wildness there—waiting to break free. She loved that she could bring him to the edge of his control.

Her hand gripped the base of his cock and a harsh male groan echoed from above her. It was thick and ridged, and she couldn't get her thumb and fingers to touch. Clear liquid seeped from the flared head and she flicked her tongue out, catching the drops on her tongue and tasting the salty essence of him.

"Don't tease, baby." His hands tightened on her head and he tried to move her head so her mouth was perfectly aligned with his dick. "Give me what I want or payback is going to be a bitch."

Jade moaned as her lips stretched over the glistening crest and the flat of her tongue rubbed against the sensitive underside. She didn't take him down farther—not yet. Her fist kept a tight hold of him and pumped slowly while she savored his taste, and her nails scraped down his thigh, causing him to shudder and groan.

His body was tense and straining against her, and she could tell he was fighting the urge to thrust inside her open mouth. A light sheen of sweat glistened on his torso, and his head was thrown back in ecstasy.

"Enough playing," he growled. "Take it all."

Jade pulled back with one last lick and blew a soft breath across the flushed and swollen head, making his cock jump in anticipation. Bringing him pleasure like this heightened her own arousal and her pussy was drenched with need for him.

"Now, Jade. Suck me. Open that sweet mouth."

He pushed his cock against her lips, nudging for her to open and take him in. Her eyes met his as she let him inside—as she sucked down the hot, thick stalk of flesh. She relaxed her throat and flattened her tongue against the underside, and when he reached as far as she could take him, she began to swallow so the undulations were just another added pleasure.

"God, baby," he groaned.

Jade loved seeing him like this—past the point of control and so caught up in need for her that nothing else seemed to exist. His fingers tightened on her scalp and he began to move with slow, deep thrusts, pulling all the way out so she could flick her tongue across the tip of him and then pushing back in to the base of her throat.

But it wasn't long before the slow thrusts became short and hurried. She tightened her lips around him and continued to rasp her tongue against the sensitive underside of his cock. His flesh was hot, and the taste salty and male, a deep rich flavor that had her pussy creaming and her mouth suckling harder to taste all of him. Her hand reached up to cup the taut sac between his thighs and his groans became louder, his thrusts more erratic.

"Fuck—"

Before she could protest he pulled out of her mouth and jerked her up by the arm, spinning her around so she was bent over the kitchen table.

"No—" she gasped. "I wanted to finish—"

"Not this time, baby." His hands clamped over hers

and moved them so she gripped each side of the table, and he pushed her forward so she was standing on her tiptoes, her legs spread wide. She barely had time to gasp before he was pushing inside of her.

"Max!" she cried out. Her pussy wept for him, but the fit was still snug as he stretched her to accommodate his size, and she was still a little sore from their time before. But it was a glorious pain and pleasure all rolled into one. A kaleidoscope of colors burst behind her eyelids as he seemed to penetrate her very soul.

"So tight," he groaned, pushing inside her with a steady pressure that had her whimpering with the need for something more. His hand palmed her ass and she let out a sharp cry as his hand came down on her cheek, leaving a hot, burning sensation. "Oh, fuck!" he rasped out. "Do you know how wet you just got?"

His palm came down again on the other cheek, and she rose up on her toes, feeling the burn all the way through her body. Her clit and nipples ached and she lifted her hips and pushed back against him.

He leaned over her, his breath coming in shallow pants, and he placed small kisses up her spine to the base of her neck. And then he bit down gently and her vaginal walls clamped around him. She shuddered at the primal feel of him taking her this way.

"Please, please—" she begged.

And then she screamed.

Max stood up straight and gripped her hips in an iron grasp before pulling out so only the flared head remained inside of her. And then he thrust hard and deep and her senses imploded. Her body quivered with every animalistic thrust and her cries and his groans melded together so they were only a distant echo in her ears.

Her hips moved back against him and flesh slapped against flesh in a steady rhythm. She pushed herself up and tossed her head back as he hit somewhere far deep inside of her—a place that had her womb convulsing and her clit throbbing for release. Her shrieks filled the air and Max brought his hands around to cup her breasts. He pinched her nipples between his finger and thumb and her legs tensed and her back arched as she shook and shuddered around him. Brilliant pinpricks of light danced behind her eyes as every nerve ending she had exploded into fractals of shape and color. Her pussy spasmed, tightening around his cock as her orgasm reached its pinnacle.

"God, Max!"

"That's it, baby. Come all over my cock."

The eroticism of his words sent sizzling pulses shooting to her clit, and the maelstrom of wicked pleasure spiraling through her body made her tongue less cautious. She knew the words were forming on her lips before she could stop herself, and she shook her head, almost as if that would be enough to keep them inside. But it wasn't, and the words came out in a rush.

"I love you. God—I love you." She could only pray he didn't hear them over the thudding of her heart.

His thrusts became faster, harder, and he pushed inside her one last time before she felt the hot spurts of semen filling her. His body stiffened and his groans echoed in her ears as they both fell limp to the table.

Their breaths were erratic and Jade closed her eyes, enjoying the feel of him against her back and the kiss he placed on her shoulder. And then she stiffened, remembering the words that had escaped her lips. It wasn't fair to let him think there could be more than what they had, but she hadn't been able to keep her feelings contained.

"That's what I wanted to do to you nine months ago when we were in my kitchen and you were wrapped around me like my every fantasy come to life." His fingers trailed up her hip and he pulled out of her slowly, making her moan at the absence of him. "You have no idea how hard it was for me to send you away that day. I didn't want to."

"But it was the right thing to do," she said softly. "I didn't realize it then. You're a good man, Max."

"I can be even better." His hand smoothed over the sting in her bottom and then he pulled her limp body off the table, swinging her into his arms and heading to the bedroom. "We've got a lot of time to make up for."

"As long as you don't try to make it all up in one day. I'm practically half-dead here."

He laughed and tossed her on the bed and her eyes widened as she saw he was already hard for her—again. And then he was inside her and she didn't think for a very long time.

CHAPTER EIGHT

Almost a week passed with nothing more to do than wait, talk or make love. And Max wasn't afraid to admit a certain amount of frustration where Jade was concerned. He knew he'd heard her tell him she loved him. That's not something he'd have imagined. But she acted as if she'd never uttered the words, and any attempts to bring it up or talk about possibilities for their future were met with a change of subject or her distracting him with sex.

It was almost as if she didn't believe him when he tried to tell her he loved her and wanted to spend the rest of his life with her. And he knew she was keeping something from him, something that made her afraid of taking the next step, but damned if he could figure out what it was.

Even now, after another attempt, her satiated body lay limp over his in one of the lounge chairs by the pool, perspiration dotting their skin and their breaths returning to normal. The sun was an orange ball of flame high in the sky and temperatures had reached well over a hundred degrees that day. They'd fallen into easy companionship and regular habits through the week—going for a run just before dawn, followed by showers then breakfast. Jade had set up small targets and they'd gotten into a friendly, if very spirited, shooting competition. It stung his pride a little to know she was ahead in points.

Their afternoons had consisted of long, lazy swims and their lovemaking had gotten so creative he was considering taking out extra health insurance. She was a generous and attentive lover, and she was willing to try anything he demanded of her. As long as he didn't try to push the emotional aspect. He almost laughed. He never would have thought he'd be in the position where he was the one who wanted more. He was living every man's fantasy—a dream woman in his bed and no strings attached. It was any man's fantasy but his.

"Any word from Declan?" she asked lazily, circling her fingers on his chest.

"Mmm," he said, his hands skimming down her spine in a long, languid motion. "Dec said he's starting to hear rumblings from Vassin's camp. They've been digging deep into both of our files, trying to find something that isn't there. He also said Vassin is putting feelers out, trying to find out how to locate me. This property isn't listed with my other holdings, but it's not impossible to trace. I wanted him to have to work to find me."

"You've never said how your family feels about what you do."

He snorted out a laugh. "I was never their favorite person to begin with. I've always been a bit of a disappointment to them."

Max rubbed the back of his neck, trying to relieve the sudden tension there. He didn't like to talk about his family. The wounds were still deep from the loss of his parents in a plane crash, even though he'd been very young when it had happened, and there'd been a void in that part of his life that his grandparents hadn't been able to fill once they took over his care. He would have gotten more love and affection from strangers.

"Grandfather liked me the most once I joined the Marines. It gave him a better standing with his constituents to have a grandson in active combat. He also thought it would be good for my record when I was discharged and decided to take my place in politics."

She lifted her head and a smile quirked at the corner of her mouth. "I must have missed that phase of your life."

"Yeah, I missed it too." He felt the tension he carried whenever he talked about his family lighten and was able to laugh a little. "I took up the MMA training while I was overseas, and it became addictive. So you can imagine his surprise when I signed up to fight in the ring and chose to ignore the family summons home so he could throw a big party in my honor and introduce me to all of his campaign contributors. And then the DEA recruited me and I never looked back."

He'd made a lot of detours in his life, searching for something to give him purpose and support as his family never had. Carrying a badge had given him that purpose, and he was grateful for it.

"Like you, I often wonder if I'd have taken a different path if my parents had lived. It's hard for me to remember them other than what I see from pictures. I remember my mother's laugh and the way dad looked when he tied his tie in front of the mirror. I remember they loved me and reminded me how important it was to bring honor to the Devlin name. To always remember where I came from and be grateful to those before me who'd made sure we never had to worry about where we'd get our next meal."

"They'd be proud of your service," she said. "You've more than brought honor to the Devlin name."

"Not according to my grandparents. They sent flowers when I was shot, and my grandfather tried to get power of attorney over all my holdings and my trust, using the argument that I'd never be of sound mind again. He's still trying to get control last time I talked to my attorneys."

Jade raised her brows. "On what grounds?"

"Of consorting with nefarious criminals, squandering Devlin money, and blackening the family name. In their eyes, there's nothing in what I've become to be proud of.

And I have to let them continue to think that way."

She propped herself up on crossed arms and looked angry on his behalf. That was enough to wash away his own anger at the people who'd raised him. He'd come to realize they didn't have the ability to love or nurture as they should have, and it wasn't worth wasting the time or effort on them any longer, though that didn't make the hurt go away.

His body was still joined with Jade's, and he smoothed a hand down her back and rested his hand on her rear, loving the feel of her. She was so soft and smooth compared to his own body, though the strength beneath that softness was obvious.

"To show you what a good friend I am," she said, grinning, "The next time you're invited home for dinner, I'm going to let you take me as your date. We'll see what the Senator has to say about that."

"I'd take you anywhere and be proud of it," he said seriously, watching as the laughter faded from her eyes. "The deficiency is in them, not either of us. Just like it was with your mother's family. Two lost souls, babe." His hand squeezed at her hip and he laid his other over her hand on his chest. "And we turned out just fine."

A high-pitched alarm sounded on his phone and Jade rolled off of him and grabbed the pistol she'd put under the chair. He grabbed his own weapon and the phone and they ran back into the house.

"Someone's on the main road to the house," he said. He pulled on a pair of jeans and a white shirt and then shoved his feet into his boots. Jade did the same thing and then pulled the black bag she'd stashed from under the bed. Max flipped on the flat screen TV and watched as the surveillance cameras gave faces to their visitors. The road leading to the house made them have to slow down enough that the cameras could see inside the car.

"It's not Vassin," Jade remarked, loading a magazine in her weapon and then putting it at the small of her back.

SECRETS AND SATIN

"But there are only two. How do you want to handle it?"

Max picked up his own weapon and then he picked up the familiar thumping sound in the distance.

"Shit," he said.

"They've got a chopper. That could be bad." Nothing much ever fazed Jade. That's why he'd always liked working with her.

Max hit the security panic button and metal shutters closed over all the windows. Damned if he wanted to have to replace a bunch of broken windows if they came out of this alive.

"They'll try to take me," he said. "Vassin wants the information too bad. And these men aren't likely to see you as a threat. Let's let them keep believing that."

He looked her over from head to toe and couldn't help the rush of desire that thrummed just below the skin and had his dick spiking beneath his cargos. Her skin had darkened and glowed from the time in the sun, and her cheeks held a flush that any red-blooded male would recognize on a woman who'd just been satisfied. The green of her eyes was vibrant and sharp as she opened the front door to see which direction the chopper was coming in from.

"ETA two minutes," she said.

He pulled her back and closed the door with a snap, pressing her against it with his body, his cock pressed between the juncture of her thighs as his mouth slanted over hers in a scorching kiss. It never seemed to matter that he'd just had her. He'd always want her. His tongue pushed into her mouth, tasting the dark pleasure and drinking in her moans as she rocked back against him. He broke free and they stood staring at each other, panting for breath.

"It's good to know you're locked and loaded," she said.

He grinned and shoved away from the door, opening it so they could meet trouble head on. "Have I told you I'm crazy about that mouth of yours?"

"That's not what you said the time we got stuck during that hurricane and went three days without electricity."

"That's because I wanted you so bad I could hardly breathe. The close quarters weren't helping."

"Then let's finish this quick and we'll do a replay. Only this time you can do whatever you want to me. We'll make our own storm." She winked at him and then chambered a bullet in her gun, taking her place just to the side of one of the thick cedar posts on the porch.

Max took a seat on the front steps and propped his arms on his knees in a casual pose so no one would get too jumpy, and he watched as a cloud of dust plumed from the bottom of his driveway. A sleek black sedan shot out of the tunnel and sped toward them even as the whoomp, whoomp, whoomp from the chopper became louder and the blades kicked up red dust and dead grass.

The helicopter was bullet-shaped and black, and it touched down in the wide expanse of his lawn just as the car pulled to a stop. Max slowly got to his feet and walked out to meet the new arrivals halfway. He kept his hands loose at his sides as two men got out of the car.

Dressed in worn jeans and T-shirts, they could have been any average Joe walking down the street. Except for the fact that they just looked like thugs. Slicked back hair and big, meaty hands that would do serious damage if they made contact. One of them had a ragged scar on the side of his eye and the other had a tattoo of a snake wrapped around his neck.

Both of them were armed. Max counted at least 3 weapons hidden under their clothes. These guys were the muscle—probably hired out locally and too dumb to do any research other than what Vassin spoon-fed them.

It was the two men coming from the helicopter that would have to be watched. They were dressed in black cargos and T-shirts, reflective black sunglasses covering their eyes and their guns visible in the shoulder holsters they wore. They moved with an easy balance that only someone who'd been trained could carry off. They looked ex-military or government, and that just pissed him off.

"You Max Devlin?" one of the thugs from the car asked.

Max ignored him and watched as the two from the helicopter moved in closer. They'd all positioned themselves neatly around him so he stood in the center of their little circle.

"Hey, I'm talking to you," the same guy said.

He could have sworn he saw one of Vassin's personal men grin when he continued not to respond to the overgrown bully. Max kept his gaze on the two in the sunglasses, knowing where the real threat was.

"Martin Vassin requests your presence, Mr. Devlin," Sunglasses #1 said.

"I don't know a Martin Vassin. And I don't have time in my schedule at the moment. You can contact my personal secretary if he's looking for a donation. As you can see, I'm on vacation."

He moved slightly back and to the side, repositioning his body so Sunglasses #2 wasn't at his back, and he nodded to Jade up on the porch. She looked sexy as hell leaning against the porch railing, and the two thugs couldn't seem to take their eyes off her. The two in the sunglasses barely spared her a glance, dismissing her as non-threatening. Their first mistake.

"I'm afraid we're going to have to insist," Sunglasses said. "You've put out the word that you have something for sale. We'd like to buy."

"Like I said, I don't know Martin Vassin. I'm picky about my customers and I have a reputation, which you'd know if you bothered to look into my background. Now if you'll excuse me, gentlemen. This is private property."

The guy with the snake tattoo reached out and grabbed his arm and Max gave him a chilling look that had him dropping it in a hurry, though he tried to bluster his way through by taking another step closer.

"You don't want to touch me again," Max said. "It makes my bodyguard unhappy."

"I don't see no bodyguard," Tattoo said. "Just your cunt whore and you, pretty boy."

"What Mr. Evans means," Sunglasses #1 broke in smoothly, "is that Mr. Vassin has given you the option of coming with us the easy or the hard way."

"No," Max said.

No one moved as they waited for him to say something more. But there was nothing else to say. He'd made his position clear.

Tattoo snorted out a laugh. "You can't just say no. He just told you you could come the easy or the hard way."

"Yes, Mr. Evans, I can hear. My answer is still no."

A red flush worked its way up Tattoo's face, either in embarrassment or anger; Max didn't know, but probably a little of both. He was the weak link, the one whose anger would get out of control and make him do something stupid.

They all spread out a little around him, widening the circle, and Max smiled, recognizing the brawler in each of them.

"You've fucked up, Devlin," Tattoo said, cracking his knuckles. "Looks like you're going to get the hard way. And maybe when we're done with you, Jimmy and I will show your whore what a real man feels like. Maybe we'll let you watch so you can pick up some pointers."

"That's the second time you've insulted my woman," Max said. "You're going to pay for that. And if you do it again, I'll kill you."

"How you plan on doin' that?" the one called Jimmy asked. "It's four against one, asshole."

"Well, Jimmy—" Max paused and raised a brow. "You don't mind if I call you Jimmy, do you?" The tension rose higher than the heat and they began to shift, waiting for the opportunity to strike. "The first thing I'm going to do is take out Mr. Evans. I'm going to kick in his knee and then deliver a second kick to the stomach, while using him as a shield so I can take out Sunglasses over here." Max pointed at the man in question. "I'll probably break his arm, but I haven't quite decided yet. I like to keep my options open."

No one moved a muscle as he continued on. "And then I'm going to get to you, Jimmy. You'll want to put some ice on the headache you're going to have. And then that'll leave Sunglasses number two. If he's smart he won't try to throw a punch and I'll let him deliver my message back to Martin Vassin without any damaged body parts."

"You're a crazy-assed motherfucker, is what I think," Jimmy said.

"I've been called worse," Max said. And then he put his words into action. His foot struck out and hit Tattoo's knee, bones and cartilage crunching with a sickening sound, and his high-pitched scream was cut off by the second kick in the stomach.

Max caught him on the way down and used the momentum to push him into Sunglasses #1, throwing him off balance so Max could grab the other man's arm and twist. He felt the shoulder slip out of socket and then he kneed him in the kidney and tossed Tattoo and Sunglasses in a heap on the ground together.

His blood pumped and his muscles sang as he dodged a blow from Jimmy's meaty fist, and the sting in Max's knuckles was sweet satisfaction as he gave Jimmy a quick jab in the stomach followed by an uppercut to the jaw.

The sound of a gunshot had everyone looking up to the porch in surprise. Jade stood much like she had been before, completely relaxed against the thick post, only this time her gun was pointed in their direction, obviously having just been fired.

"No one said knives were allowed in this fight," she said.

Max gave Jimmy another shot to the jaw, taking him down for the count, before he turned his attention to the last man standing. The man's hand was covered in blood and he held his wrist tight where the bullet had gone through. She'd made a hell of a shot—a small target that had been in motion—but he knew she'd hit exactly what she'd aimed for.

A Ka-Bar lay in the dirt at his feet, and Max looked down at his arm, where a long slash oozed blood down his tricep. He hadn't felt the sting with his adrenaline pumping so high, but he was sure he'd feel it soon. At least it wouldn't need stitches.

"I guess you don't get to go back to Mr. Vassin unharmed after all," Max said coolly. Groans came from the men who littered the ground as two of them tried to make their way back to standing positions. Jimmy still lay unconscious. He'd probably be that way for a while.

"Tell Mr. Vassin I expect him to get in touch soon. I won't make deals unless I meet face to face. And you can tell him my price has doubled." Max headed back up the porch stairs while Jade kept her weapon trained on the men. "Now get off my lawn."

The two who'd arrived in the helicopter limped their way back and took off for destinations unknown. It took Tattoo a little longer to disappear because he had trouble getting Jimmy into the car with his knee not working properly, but he eventually managed it.

Max didn't slump over and grab his head until they were both out of sight. It never paid for the enemy to see your weakness.

"Come on, tough guy," Jade said, tugging his arm so it wrapped around her shoulder. "Let's get you a couple of those magic pain pills."

"I guess I should thank you for saving my ass." His words slurred through the debilitating pain.

"It's just another day at the office," she said. "Besides, I've gotten pretty fond of your ass."

CHAPTER NINE

It took less than twenty-four hours for Martin Vassin to make contact and apologize for the "miscommunication" between Max and his men, and then invite Max to Las Vegas to be a guest in his hotel so they could meet face to face without the added hostility of other parties. Max had told him he'd need twenty-four hours to decide and had hung up the phone on a very surprised Martin Vassin.

In reality, he'd needed an extra twenty-four hours so Declan could start putting his backup plans in motion—because Declan always had backup plans—and so they could gather the necessary equipment and supplies for their trip. Max's plane had to be flown in to Austin and refueled, and he and Jade had taken off and were almost to Las Vegas before Max called Vassin back and told him they'd be landing in the next ten minutes. He wanted Vassin scrambling and as flustered as he could get him. And Jade was going to help him do that.

"This dress is ridiculous," she said, smoothing down the short black linen dress she wore. "No bodyguard would wear something this stupid. And how am I supposed to run in these heels? I feel like a giant. We're the same height."

Max's mouth quirked at the continued complaints, and

he put his hand possessively on her lower back as they left the plane and made their way to the waiting limo.

"And I've got no place to put my gun."

"I'm sure you'll find some place—creative," he suggested and then helped her into the limo as she struggled to keep her skirt from riding above her waist.

Damn, he thought, his cock hardening in an instant. The long expanse of her legs and the valley between them enticed him like nothing else ever could as she maneuvered across the seat. Already ideas were forming in his head on how they should spend their drive to the hotel, and she gave him an arched look as her gaze landed below his waist.

The driver closed the door behind them and they were silent while the luggage was loaded into the trunk. The vehicle finally started moving, and Max waited until they'd turned from the airport onto Wayne Newton Boulevard before he took a device out of his pocket to scan for bugs. He wasn't surprised to find one under each of their seats.

Jade opened her handbag where he knew she'd stashed her weapon, and probably a few other goodies, and she came out with the small rectangular device that would emit the frequencies needed to make the bugs unusable.

"I guess ten minutes wasn't enough time to take him off guard if he's already got listening devices in his limo."

"What do you want to bet they're permanent?" Max said. "He's the type of man who wouldn't trust friends any more than enemies. But you're probably right—I bet they're scrambling to get our room outfitted as we speak."

"What did Declan have to say? I was putting on this ridiculous getup while you were talking."

It never ceased to amaze Max that the only time he ever saw Jade really uncomfortable was when she had to play a traditional feminine role. She was naturally one of the most beautiful women he'd ever seen—her skin flawless and the bone structure of a queen—but she tried to downplay her looks. She never wore makeup and it was rare he saw her in something other than jeans and T-shirts.

"You're beautiful."

"What?" she asked, flustered by the compliment, and then she tried to joke her way around it. "Declan called to say I'm beautiful? That doesn't sound like him."

"I just wanted you to know that," he said, ignoring her discomfort. A flush tinged her cheeks and she looked out the window at the passing traffic. "But I think you're beautiful whether you wear something like this or that old ratty robe with the hole in the pocket. Though neither of those are my favorite thing for you to wear."

"Let me guess," she said. "Garter belts and black lace?"

"Not even close."

His voice lowered so it was a seductive caress, whispering across her skin. He watched as her nipples hardened beneath the thin fabric of her dress. She shifted in her seat and crossed her legs and he couldn't help but smile. He took her hand and kissed the tip of her finger before nipping it slightly and moving on to the next, watching the green of her eyes darken as his tongue swirled around the tip.

"No, my favorite thing for you to wear—" he whispered —"is me."

He smiled with satisfaction as a small whimper escaped her lips and wished he had time to lay her down on the leather seat and put words into action.

"And you need to learn to accept a compliment," he said, settling back against the seat and adjusting his cock, though there was really no comfortable position other than balls deep inside of her. "Just because I tell you you're beautiful doesn't diminish how you do your job. There's no one else I'd rather have at my back. Now say, thank you, Max."

Her lips quirked in a half smile. "I don't think so. But if you play your cards right I'll be thanking you profusely later. Now what did Dec say?"

"They've still got no leads on the girl. He's gone ahead

and activated Shane and the rest of the team because he doesn't want to leave us without backup if we need it. We've got to keep things rolling with Vassin until they can at least get an idea of where she's being held. Dec said Vassin hasn't been in touch with Senator Henry in more than two weeks, and the Senator is frantic."

Jade bit down on her bottom lip while she thought it out. "It's not good for him to stop communication. It could mean Vassin has reached the end of his use for the Senator and his daughter."

"That's what Dec thought as well. We need to find her fast. Vassin has a home here in Las Vegas. We need to try and get an invitation. Maybe we'll get lucky."

The limo turned onto Sands and then made the slow drive to the massive front entrance of the hotel. It took up the entire block, and towers speared into the sky at each corner while huge angels that had been carved into the sides trumpeted over the street. There was nothing subtle about the elegant veneer—the electric excitement and the undercurrents of desperation could still be felt even in the finest establishments. Max glanced at Jade and caught her surprise as she saw where they were.

"I didn't realize Vassin had done so well for himself. I was expecting a dive off The Strip."

"Illegal arms dealing is a profitable business. And Vassin only owns about thirty percent of the hotel. But word is he's got the capital to snap up more shares when they come available."

He looked Jade over again slowly, and if he didn't know exactly how dangerous she was, he wouldn't be able to tell by looking at her now. She looked softer, and the touch of makeup made her eyes bigger and more alluring. Most of Vassin's men still wouldn't believe she was capable of being a bodyguard, even though the four men who attacked them knew the truth. It wouldn't be long before Vassin learned just how deadly she was.

SECRETS AND SATIN

Jade turned off the white noise device and put it back in her purse as the limo stopped in front of the hotel, and she pulled down her skirt and wondered how the hell she was supposed to get out gracefully. It was a hell of a lot easier in her opinion to run through the jungle in BDUs than to brave an hour of wearing high heels in polite society. She felt like a fraud any time she had to play the part of sophisticated lover. What the hell did she know? She was an orphan from Nowhere, Louisiana, though she'd worked damned hard over the years to get rid of any accent that might give her away.

The door opened and she waited until Max got out of the car before she scooted over, and she breathed a sigh of relief that he was thoughtful enough to block the view as he held his hand out to help her.

He didn't try to keep her hand as they followed the bellman into the lobby. Max knew her habits better than anyone, and he'd never tie up her hands in case she needed to get her weapon free. Just like she knew to always stay to his left in case he needed to get to his.

Max broke away as someone in an expensive charcoal suit and red tie met him with an outstretched hand, and she kept watch, looking for signs of Vassin or any of his men in the crowded lobby. The hotel was too big to see all of the possible hiding places, but she spotted two men in the main lobby who had the look of professionals, though they were both dressed as tourists. She spotted another at the restaurant across the way, sitting at one of the outdoor café-style tables, eating lunch and drinking coffee. He was better at the façade than the others, but the way his eyes kept skimming across them gave him away. That and the bulge she spotted beneath his sport coat.

Jade kept her eyes sharp as the man in the suit led them through a door marked Private and then to a wood-paneled elevator that opened with a key card. The suit handed Max an envelope with two identical cards and then they were all rising to the top fast enough to have the bottom drop out of her stomach.

"A lovely room," she said to fill the silence once they were left alone in the penthouse.

The main area was wall-to-wall white carpet so thick the heels she wore sank deep into the pile. A long glass dining table that sat ten was on one side of the room and a cardinal red circular couch like none she'd never seen before sat on the other end. The entire back wall was nothing but glass and looked out over the Strip, but she could see for miles out into the desert beyond.

"I have to say, I prefer the penthouse in my own hotel," Max said, taking the bug sweeper from his pocket and moving from room to room. "This one seems a bit obvious for my tastes. Vassin seems like a man who would overcompensate for certain things in his decorating." He let out a low whistle when he came out of the bedroom. "That bedroom is the perfect example. We'll have fun in there later," he said, waggling his eyebrows.

Jade stopped her task of gathering the two tiny listening devices she'd just found in the living area and looked up to see if Max was serious.

"I didn't realize you had a hotel," she said, taking the devices to the table to join the others they'd found.

"Of course I do, love. Seven of them. What kind of self-respecting billionaire doesn't have hotels to diversify his holdings?"

He looked completely serious, and it was sometimes hard to remember that behind the gutter fighter was an honest to God businessman. He'd never talked about it while they were at the DEA and most of the other agents they worked with had no idea about his background or that his family was one of the wealthiest in the world. He was just so normal and down to Earth, and she knew he'd be doing this same job whether or not the money was there.

But thoughts of what he'd told her earlier, about how he should always remember where he came from and what the Devlin name stood for, only cemented the idea that she and Max would never work out. She was so out of her league she could only shake her head at the absurdity of it all.

"In fact," he said. "We should take a couple of weeks off and head to Australia. We just opened a new hotel there and I need to check to make sure everything is running smoothly."

Jade watched as Max shook his head at the collection of bugs they'd found throughout the penthouse. More than a dozen sat lined up on the little bar that divided the kitchen and dining room, and she took the neutralizer out of her purse and set it next to them, wondering what to say. Max set the bugs on the floor and then systematically crushed each one beneath his heel before dumping them all in the garbage.

"Why don't we focus on the job here before we start making other plans," she said, nerves prickling along her skin. "One day at a time. I figure you more than anyone else would know that's the best way to live."

"Yes, except for the fact that I happen to love you, even though every time I say it you get that look right there on your face. Is the thought of me loving you that repulsive, or are your feelings for me that non-existent?"

The words were angry, and the blue of his eyes seemed to become brighter, sharper, as he stared her down and waited for an answer. She'd known this was coming. He'd tried to bring it up on several occasions, and she'd always changed the subject and ignored the hurt she saw in his eyes.

"And how many women have you said those words to?" she asked. "You know what, never mind. I don't want to know. It's none of my business." Her own anger and ineptitude made her lash back at him. "Why can't we just leave things as they are?" She turned away and paced back and forth in front of the bar, while Max stayed completely still. That was never a good sign. Max was always in constant motion.

"I've never said those words to any woman, and it pisses me off that even now you don't believe me. I understand if you need time to adjust to what's happening between us, though to tell you the truth it feels like we've been adjusting for the last two years. Yes, I want a future with you and all the things that go with it, but that can wait until you're ready. What I can't understand is that you don't seem to want me to love you at all. Explain that one to me."

"Why the hell aren't you happy that you're getting every man's fantasy? You get to fuck me without any of the other bullshit."

His mouth tightened in a straight line and his nostrils flared at how casually she'd debased what had happened between them, and guilt ate at her insides for deceiving him. But she couldn't tell him the truth. Not yet. Though she knew the time would come soon. No one but her and her doctor knew she'd never be able to conceive again. Jade had made sure that secret hadn't gone into any files or reports to Declan or Max. She didn't need any more of their pity.

And as much as he'd like her to believe that he really did love her, part of her was skeptical. She was a nobody with no background or pedigree, and she had nothing to offer him. Once he got past the sex he'd realize his version of love and hers were two completely different things.

Max's muscles were tense with anger. "So just to be clear." His voice cut like a knife and she would have flinched if she hadn't been holding herself so rigid. "Everything between us up to this point has been about nothing but sex. We shouldn't try to cloud the issue with emotions or attachments or talk of the future in general. It's just fucking." His voice got softer the more he spoke, which she knew was a dangerous sign. "Just like it would be with any other warm body."

"You're overreacting," she said. "I'm just saying we should enjoy it while it lasts and not dwell on anything else. You're the one trying to make things more complicated."

"Why, because I like to have feelings for the person I'm inside? I'm not a fucking robot. And we've been through too much together for you to tell me to my face that you don't have feelings for me. Which means there's some other reason for your resistance and whatever it is is going to piss me off."

She felt the blood drain from her face and fear made her words harsh and regretful. "Or maybe you don't know me as well as you like to think you do. Take what you can get, Max. Or you can take nothing. It's your choice."

A knock sounded at the door, but neither of them moved to answer it as they measured each other and where they stood. Jade couldn't take the waves of hurt she felt coming from him, and she finally turned on her heel and headed to the door that led out onto the balcony while Max went to deal with whoever was at the door.

The wind was hot and arid and slapped across her face as she made her way to the half wall that separated her and the three hundred feet to the pavement below. Jade watched the lights and traffic of the city, the movement and flashes of color dizzying at such extreme heights. Despite the heat, her skin was chilled and she wrapped her arms around her torso to ward off the cold.

She heard the patio door open behind her and felt Max's stare.

"That was a messenger delivering an envelope from Martin Vassin. We've got tickets to the Heavyweight Championship tonight. Front row seats. We're supposed to meet to discuss our options."

"Do you think he'll show?"

"Doubtful. He's playing the watching game for now.

He needs time to evaluate what he sees and determine the best way to manipulate us. It's what he's best at." She felt him come up directly behind her, though he didn't touch. But the heat between them was as scorching as ever and her body tightened, waiting to see what he'd do with the anger she could still feel lashing at her skin.

"Wear the gold sequined dress tonight. We don't need to be subtle, and it's best if he doesn't take you seriously."

"Maybe we'll hear from Dec that they've found the girl and we can take him down without having to jump through his hoops."

"What's the problem, baby? You've already scratched your itch and now you're ready to run back home?" His hands touched her waist and scalded straight through the fabric to her skin. "Surely you haven't reached your quota of fucking in the short time we've been together. Or will any cock do since there's no emotion involved?" She tried to jerk away from him at the harshness of his words, but he put his hand in her back, keeping her in place and faced away from him. "That's all it is. Right, Jade?"

His hands smoothed down over her ass and hips to the bottom of the hem of her skirt, and his fingers skimmed along the bare flesh of her leg. "I guess I should have just given in to you nine months ago when you wanted me then. It would've been the same either way. Or maybe I just don't make you wet anymore. Is that the problem?"

His breath was hot on the back of her neck and already her pulse was pounding and need was rising inside of her. All he had to do was touch her and she was ready for anything, even though she could feel every ounce of his anger vibrating through the tips of his fingers.

He pushed her skirt above her waist and his fingers were suddenly there between her thighs, probing at the moist flesh.

"No, that's not the problem," he said, nipping at her shoulder. "Feel how wet you are for me. Fucking drenching my fingers."

SECRETS AND SATIN

He withdrew his fingers and she whimpered as his hand fisted in the black thong she wore, ripping it from her body. She tried to shake him off so she could turn around, but he held her there with teeth and his hips like a stallion pinning a mare. She wanted to face his anger with her own—anger at him and herself and the world because she couldn't have her happily ever after. Tears were pointless, and wishing for something she couldn't have only made the pain worse. It was best to put it all away, to compartmentalize her emotions so she didn't give too much—or at least give more than she could handle.

Two fingers plunged into her without warning and she cried out as her body adjusted to the invasion. She felt the liquid rush over his fingers, making the entry easier with every push and pull of his hand and her hands reached in front of her to grab on to the railing. His beard rasped against her neck and she spread her legs wider to take more of him.

"Please, Max—"

"What do you want, baby?" he asked. "My cock? Or will anyone's do?"

"Stop it," she panted, pushing her hips back against him. "Don't be this way. You know it's only you."

"No, I don't know that. That would be something discussed between a couple in a monogamous relationship. One that meant something besides the occasional fuck." He pressed against her hip and she felt his cock, rigid beneath his slacks, grinding against her.

His fingers worked in and out of her while the heel of his hand pressed against her clit. She was going to come, and she shook her head as she felt her muscles tighten around him. She wanted him inside her when she came. Tingles gathered in her clit and her legs shook with tremors. She was almost there.

And then suddenly there was nothing but aching, empty space behind her.

"I'm not here to scratch your itch. You know where to

find me if you want something more."

Her breath sucked in on a sob, and she stood completely still as she tried to grasp what he was doing. Her skirt was still rucked around her waist and her hands had an iron grip on the top of the railing. But her spine was stiff in her humiliation as she stared straight ahead.

The patio door opened behind her. "We need to leave in twenty minutes. Be ready." And then he was gone and she wondered how things had gotten so complicated. Because the only time she'd ever hurt as badly as she did now was when her husband had died.

CHAPTER TEN

Jade kept her head held high and her expression serene as she and Max were shown to the seats marked VIP. They hadn't spoken since what had happened between them on the balcony, and he was doing his best to ignore her, despite his eyes going dark and the obvious bulge behind the zipper of his tuxedo slacks once he saw her in the excuse for a dress he'd asked her to wear.

Gold and sequined, the dress was strapless and fit like a bandage, stopping just below her ass and giving her the illusion of curves where she knew there were none. Matching stilettos made her legs look a mile long, and she'd actually bothered to put on makeup, so the green of her eyes was vibrant against the smoky shadow and thick eyeliner.

They were close enough to the ring to be spattered with sweat or blood, and she affected a slightly bored expression while she tried to catch sight of Martin Vassin. The arena was packed and the hairs on the back of her neck were standing up.

"I don't have a good feeling," she said, leaning into Max so she could be heard over the noise of the crowd.

"Because you're not an idiot," he said. "We're being watched. I feel like I have a target on the back of my head."

The announcer came on, his deep voice accelerating and growing louder and louder as he introduced the first boxer. The crowd went wild, jumping and screaming, and the whole arena vibrated from the stomps and shouts.

Max stiffened beside her and she looked over to see what was wrong.

"Hey, sugar." Jade arched a brow as a scantily clad ring girl latched onto Max. She read the woman's lips more than hearing the actual words, but the intent was plain as day.

"What do you say you and I get to know each other a little better?" She practically had to yell the words to be heard over the crowd, but Jade saw red as her hand trailed down Max's chest toward his belt. He caught her hand before it could go too low and then quickly let go.

The woman's skirt was white and short and her bikini top barely contained her generous breasts. Her body was tanned and slicked with oil and her dark hair hung in loosed curls down her back. Red lips pouted seductively as she moved in closer to Max and slid something into his hand. It was the only thing that kept Jade from knocking her back on her well-padded ass.

There was no doubt she was a beautiful woman, and jealousy reared its ugly head as she wondered again what Max was doing with her. She'd seen some of the women he'd dated over the last few years and she didn't come anywhere close. Jade grabbed the woman's hand before she could rub Max's chest again.

"Don't touch—sugar," Jade said, her smile sharp.

The woman's dark brown eyes flashed once and then she ignored Jade, turning back to Max while he read the note she'd delivered to him.

"What do you say?" the woman asked, rubbing her breast against his arm. "I've been watching the two of you since you came in. You can't tell me you're together." Her eyes cut to Jade and she smiled cruelly. "Why would you want her when you could have someone like me?"

SECRETS AND SATIN

The question so mirrored Jade's own thoughts she could only stop and wait to see what happened. The woman's fingers walked up Max's chest, and it was Max who grabbed her wandering hand this time.

"She asked you not to touch," he said, his voice dark and dangerous.

Jade saw the arousal in the woman's eyes and the way she shuddered when he squeezed her hand.

"But I promise it'll be worth it," she purred. "Lose the baggage and I'll show you just how much."

Max folded the note and put it in his jacket pocket, and then pulled Jade close so she was snuggled against him. His arm was warm and tight around her, and she let out a breath she hadn't known she'd been holding. She'd missed his touch, and it was only then she realized how distant he'd been.

"Tell Mr. Vassin I'll agree to meet him tomorrow, but if he tries to fuck me over again things aren't going to end well." His scowl darkened and the girl took a step back. "Now if you'll excuse us, my companion and I have better things to do. It looks like we were given the cheap seats from where I'm standing."

The girl gasped in outrage at the insult, and Jade couldn't help the twitch of her lips and the small laugh that escaped. Max led her back down the aisle and out of the arena and the crowd. The feeling that someone was still watching them didn't dissipate, and she found herself looking at every face in the crowd as they made their way to the private entrance that led to the penthouse. As soon as they were in the elevator, Max had her pressed against the wall, his mouth ravaging hers as her stomach flipped from the speedy rise to the top.

His tongue invaded, stroked, and she moaned as the taste of him exploded on her tongue. The heels she wore made them the same height, and she felt the hard length of his cock pressing against her mound. She widened her legs, the dress rising up to her hips, as she pushed against him.

The zipper of his slacks bit into her pubic bone, but she welcomed the pain.

"God, Jade. I can't stay away from you." His lips trailed down to her neck, sucking and biting as his hands skimmed up her legs. "You're like a drug. No matter how much I know I need to keep my distance just to preserve my own sanity, you tempt me back."

Jade tore away from him with a cry, shocked at the pain she heard just beneath the arousal. She pulled her skirt down and pressed her hand against the elevator wall to get her balance.

"What?" he asked. "Isn't this what you wanted? You've gotten your way. I don't seem to be able to go longer than hours without being inside you."

"You're angry with me." Her chest was tight, her breathing labored as she tried not to flinch at the coldness in his eyes. "That's not what I wanted. Not how I want things to be between us. You're not thinking about this clearly. Once the haze of sex clears you'll see things differently."

"Do you really think so little of me? That I don't know my own mind and heart well enough to understand what I feel for you?"

"If you do," she said quietly, "then it's the biggest mistake you'll ever make."

"Only because you're hiding something from me." His anger washed over her and she looked away, willing the elevator to get to the top. "Once you trust me enough to tell me what the hell is going on in your mind, we'll be able to move forward instead of dancing around the real issue. Whatever it is."

The elevator doors opened silently and Max put his hand on her lower back, leading them to the room. He was clouding her mind, making her question her judgment at keeping such a secret from him, and she knew once she told him, the love he spoke of now would cease to exist.

Max held the keycard to the door and waited for the

green light to come on before they went inside and did another scan. They found two more bugs, neither of which were hidden very well, and Max destroyed them just like he had the first ones. She pulled out the white noise device and set it on the bar while Max pulled out his phone and made a call.

"Vassin wants to meet at noon tomorrow," he said as soon as Dec answered the phone. "I need maps for the coordinates he gave me and any possibilities for traps in the surrounding area. Just send them through email." He listed off the coordinates and waited as silence filled the line.

"That's the middle of the fucking desert," Dec said. "There's nothing around for miles."

"Perfect," Max said, his smile grim. "I've got a plan. Send over whatever you've got on the location. How's the search for the girl?"

"It's like she doesn't exist," the frustration in Dec's voice obvious. "Elena was able to trace back the locations of the last emails sent to the senator. We have it narrowed down to a tri-state area, though my gut is going with Vassin's property in northern California. It's a remote area on the cliffs overlooking the water and it's heavily guarded. I've gone ahead and activated Shane's team. They should be en route by this time tomorrow."

"And where are you?" Max asked.

"In the room directly below yours," he said, making Max smile. "We'll have your back tomorrow."

"Vassin's instructions are for me to go in alone." He caught Jade's eye as he related the information to Declan, and he saw the worry there. "Vassin will be there, but he won't be alone. He'll try to double cross me."

"What do you have in mind?"

"Let's meet at 0800. We'll slip down to your room since ours is being monitored so closely. And if things go right no one will die tomorrow."

"Always a good plan," Dec said and hung up.

Silence and tension filled the room as soon as he put the phone away, and he sighed as exhaustion seeped into his bones.

"Let's go to bed." He held out his hand and waited as she stared at it like it was a trick of some sort. "Just to sleep, Jade. We can table our discussion for another time."

She licked her lips once, the indecision clear on her face, and he dropped his hand. "I actually thought I'd go ahead and look at the maps Declan is sending through email. I think I know what you have in mind, and it'll help to get as much information as possible. The good thing about this place is that the weather is consistent."

"Goodnight then," he said, turning toward the bedroom. He stopped when he reached the door and looked back at her. "You know, Jade, I never thought you for a coward."

He didn't wait to see how his words sliced at her. He just stripped out of his tuxedo and hung it in the closet before crawling between the cool sheets of the bed and willing himself to go to sleep. For the first time since his accident he wondered why God had allowed him to survive. He'd thought when he'd first woken in the hospital it was because she'd given him a reason to live. Now he wasn't so sure.

Max never slept deep. He'd spent too much time in the dark abyss of it during his stay at the hospital to ever want to go there again. But when he felt Jade's body flow over him and her mouth surround him like liquid silk, his mind snapped to full alert, right along with his cock.

"Jade—"

"Ssh. Just let me touch you. Just this once. This is all that matters."

"This won't fix the problems."

SECRETS AND SATIN

"Just because there are problems doesn't mean the want will stop. At least not yet."

"Not ever," he insisted.

"Let me make love to you. You always try to take control. It's my turn."

The bed was a lake, plenty of room so they could have slept on their separate sides without touching, but he'd felt her the moment she'd slid beneath the cool sheets. Shadow and light danced across the bed from the neon signs and flashing lights of The Strip, and he watched out of half-closed eyes as she slid down his body and drove him crazy with hands and mouth.

His muscles bunched from the strain to hold back, to not take control as she'd accused him of doing. Instead he raised his hands and took hold of the headboard, vowing to keep them there if it killed him. If she wanted his body then he'd give it to her, but damned if he'd give her anything else until she started giving something back. He wouldn't touch or taste in return. He'd just lie there and try to hold onto his sanity.

Her sharp nails briefly dug into his thighs before her hand smoothed up and grabbed the base of his cock. He sucked in a breath as he felt her hot little tongue on his balls, drawing each one into her mouth and rolling it around on her tongue. He could have come from that alone.

"Jesus—" he panted.

Her laugh was seduction itself, and her tongue licked up his shaft in one long stroke until she got to the flared head. He'd never been so hard, and he watched down his body as his dick disappeared between her lips.

"Yeah, baby. That feels so good. Take more of me. How far can you swallow me down?"

Her eyes met his just as her tongue flicked the sensitive skin on the underside of his head, and then she rose up on hands and knees and her mouth opened wider before she began the slow descent on his cock, taking in every bit of the straining flesh until he felt the back of her throat.

"Fuck!" he yelled. "I'm going to come. I'm going to shoot everything I have into that sweet mouth."

She moaned around him, sending vibrations up his spine and frying what was left of his brain. His hands fisted into the headboard and he heard the crack as it snapped under the pressure. His head fell back and his hips moved with short, controlled thrusts as the pressure of her lips tightened and her tongue swirled.

His balls drew tight and he felt the imminent explosion gathering at the base of his spine and then shooting up his cock. She moaned as semen hit the back of her throat and the added vibrations only made the sensation that much wilder. Spurt after spurt shot from his cock until his body lay limp, his breathing ragged, and he raised his brows in surprise as she crawled up his body and straddled his waist.

"Touch me, Max. I want your hands on me."

God, she didn't ask for much, he thought.

"This is your show, sugar. Or maybe you just don't know what to do with me? I can see how wet you are from here. Your pussy is slick with cream for me."

Her thighs tightened around his hips, but she held herself above him, watching him out of dark eyes filled with curiosity and trepidation. He couldn't get a hold on his anger, and he knew she felt it rising inside of him like a tempest.

"My cock is still hard for you," he whispered. "I can't seem to control it where you're concerned, so do what you want with me. My body is yours."

"You're trying to punish me for not being capable of giving you what you want." Her words were soft and soothing despite the tension in the air.

"Who says you're not capable, Jade? Or have you made up your mind that only one man could ever have your love? Is there just nothing left inside of you?"

"There's more inside of me than you could ever understand."

SECRETS AND SATIN

Something in her expression had him almost giving in and taking her in his arms. Whatever her demons were, she didn't want to share them with him, and he watched as determination flashed into her eyes before she set out to drive him crazy.

Her hands cupped her breasts, tweaking at her nipples before trailing down her stomach and into the creamy folds below. Her eyes fluttered closed as her fingers played with the swollen flesh, and he swore he'd never seen anything so erotic in his entire life. His cock jumped between her thighs, but she held herself still, lost in the pleasure she was giving herself.

She parted her folds and dipped her finger into her pussy and then she pulled it back so he could see the glistening juices. She leaned forward and touched his bottom lip, painting it with her desire. The scent of her went to his head, and his tongue flicked out to taste before drawing it into his mouth.

Her lips came down on his and she moaned as she tasted herself, and then she was gone again just as he was about to break his promise to himself and touch her how she wanted to be touched.

"Max," she moaned as she leaned back and sat poised over the head of his cock.

Her hand wrapped around it and sweat broke out on his brow at the torture from anticipation. Already he could feel the need to come again. She sat down slowly, so he was able to watch with rapt fascination as the flared head parted her slick folds. The snug, wet heat of her had him gritting his teeth, and every pulse of her inner walls sent electric shocks straight to his balls.

"I need you so much." The sob caught them both by surprise, and he looked up to see the tortured expression on her face. "Don't punish me for being something I can't. For not being able to give you what you deserve." She lifted up again, slicking his shaft with her syrup before lowering herself again. "Now is all that matters."

He groaned as she finally seated herself to the hilt, and his hands released from the headboard and grasped onto her hips, keeping her impaled before she started to move. A war raged within him as he saw the dreams he'd had of them together fade away and reality take its place. He'd been selfish in his own wants, thinking that because she'd finally come to him that she was ready to move on in all ways. To him it felt like he'd been waiting for her forever, but this was still new to her, and maybe—just maybe—he could convince her that she deserved to be loved as much as he did.

"It's okay, baby," he said. "It's okay. I've got you." She shuddered around him as the words seemed to release something inside of her and she collapsed onto his chest. He rolled with her across the large expanse of bed without separating their bodies, and then he began to move.

He didn't try to hold back his feelings. He couldn't have if he tried. They'd be there whether she felt the same way or not, and he wanted her to feel them all in every kiss and touch and thrust. He hooked her legs over his arms and she cried out as he went deeper, deeper, until he felt like more than their bodies were joined.

It didn't take long for either of them to find their pleasure, and his release exploded inside of her. He groaned and jerked over her body as her muscles clamped around him and her orgasm rippled along his sensitive cock.

And when their breaths slowed and their bodies cooled, he pulled out of her slowly and lay behind her, gathering her in his arms. "It's all right," he said again. "I've got you." He felt her body relax as she fell into a peaceful sleep.

CHAPTER ELEVEN

"I think you're out of your damned mind," Cade said the next morning. "You can't think to actually meet Vassin without any backup."

"Tell me how you really feel, MacKenzie. I don't think the rest of the people on this floor heard you."

Elena had manipulated the security feed in the hallway and elevator so he and Jade could sneak down to Dec's room. The team was already gathered around the breakfast table downing gallons of coffee and looking at the maps he and Jade had already studied until he felt like his eyes would start bleeding. And it seemed like Cade was in a pisser of a mood.

"Call me crazy, but it just seems like a bad idea to go waltzing into enemy territory alone and expect to walk away again."

"There's no other way," Max said patiently. "We're between a rock and hard place until the senator's daughter is located. We have to play out this farce and hope Vassin stays on the hook. As long as he thinks I've got a product to sell, he'll be willing to bite. If we scare him away, he'll probably kill the girl and leave the country. At least for a while. This is the only way we have a chance of getting them both."

Cade paced back and forth in front of the window, his

scowl black as irritation came off him in waves.

"What's with him?" Max asked Brant. "He's usually an asshole, but he seems to be in fine form this morning." Max's brows raised in surprise as Cade growled at him.

"He talked to Bayleigh this morning," Brant answered. "She said she's been getting pains every once in a while, but she thinks it'll be a few days yet until the baby comes."

"Damned woman said she was going into work," Cade said, turning to face them. "Can you believe that? I told her no one would want to buy lingerie if she was giving birth in the middle of the floor."

"It'd be a hell of a statement for birth control," Brant said, smiling.

Cade shot him a scowl and continued his pacing.

"I told you to take the next flight out," Dec said patiently.

It was obvious to Max they'd been having this discussion long before he and Jade showed up.

"She told me not to come home." Cade was so clearly insulted by this Max had to bite the inside of his cheek to keep from laughing. "She said I had to stay because the family needed me and that the baby would be ready by the time I got back. Apparently, she can see into the future now. Doesn't she know babies come when they want to?"

Max felt some unknown emotion swell inside of him. Cade might bitch and moan and worry, but he would stay and do this mission because they needed him. When Bayleigh called to tell him the time was near, he'd be out the door and on the next plane in a hurry, but he'd stay as long as he could. Max knew the MacKenzies considered him part of the family and that any one of them would be there to back him up if needed.

"I swear this is the last time we're doing this," Cade went on. "Pregnancy takes a perfectly sane and intelligent woman and turns her into something not even I would want to face in the dark."

"You said you weren't going to do this again the last

time she was pregnant too," Declan said. "Clearly her vow to make you sleep outside for the rest of your life didn't take."

Cade stopped his pacing and grinned. "It turns out she changed her mind. I'm hard to resist."

Jade and Elena snorted out a laugh, and Max felt a pang of jealousy at what Cade and Brant both had. They knew their love with their wives was secure and would never be thrown back in their faces. They'd found women who complemented them in every way—women who would stand by them no matter what.

"Maybe if we got back to work, it wouldn't worry you so much," Dec said. He pointed to the area of the map where Vassin had designated as the meeting spot. "There's nothing out here but desert." He looked over at Max, his brows drawn in thought. "We're not going to do you much good if you need fast backup unless we came in by air." Dec scratched at the scar along his jaw and gave him a steely look out of eerie gray eyes. "The closest cover is more than a mile away in this mountain area, but there aren't any easy roads to get there."

"No," Max said, shaking his head. "You're better off continuing the search for the girl and waiting it out here. Vassin's more than likely going to be pissed after our meeting. If your gut's telling you she's in northern California, then you and the team should head in that direction."

"Yes, because I always leave my agents high and dry without backup in the middle of a mission."

"That sounded surprisingly like sarcasm," Jade said. "I think he's starting to mellow."

"Ha, are you kidding me?" Cade asked. "I've never known anyone who needs to get laid so bad."

"Max met a very nice prostitute last night at the boxing match," Jade said, tongue in cheek. "I'm sure he'd be glad to introduce you."

Dec growled and said, "If you guys could step off my

balls for a minute I'd like to get this hashed out. I can read between the lines as to why you don't want backup from us," he said to Max. "But have you considered all the variables for what you have planned?" Dec turned his attention to Jade. "What do you think? The sun could be a problem, depending on where you have to set up."

"The sun will be directly overhead. It'll be fine."

"You know, sometimes it'd be nice for you to actually say whatever the hell you're thinking so the rest of us know what you're talking about," Cade said irritably. "That cryptic bullshit gets old."

"Amen to that," Brant said, lounging back in the chair.

"The plan is simple," Dec said, his smile not at all comforting. "Max is going to meet with Martin Vassin. Alone."

Red sand kicked up from beneath the tires of the Jeep as Max navigated off the main road, following the coordinates that had been mapped out for him. The sun was directly overhead, a red ball of flame that reflected off the sand and made the eyes water with its intensity.

Dec hadn't been kidding when he'd said there was nothing for miles around. Desert stretched out in all directions, except for the range of mountains directly in front of him. It took him more than half an hour to reach the designated area, and he wasn't at all surprised to see two black Jeeps similar to his own and another helicopter. Men lounged against the sides of the vehicles, their weapons visible and dark sunglasses covering their eyes.

Max stopped the Jeep and watched as a man got out of the back seat of one of the vehicles. Martin Vassin wasn't a big man, but he carried himself with an air that only a man who thought he was important could manage to pull off. Despite the hundred degree temperature, his suit was dark and crisp, and he adjusted his tie before his men gathered at his sides. His hair was dark and silvered at the temples and his complexion was pitted with scars. He was a gangster in a three-thousand dollar suit. Nothing more, no matter what title he tried to give himself to pretty it up.

Max pulled on his baseball cap and opened the door of the Jeep, letting his feet sink into the sand. His eyes stung, even through the protection of his sunglasses, and already he could feel the grittiness in his teeth.

Vassin's guards took a protective stance as he came closer, and Max almost smiled at their confusion. They wanted him to be afraid, to know who was running the show, and Max wasn't giving them the satisfaction.

Impressions were important to a man like Martin Vassin, and he knew exactly what they saw when they looked at him. They saw a man carelessly dressed in old jeans and a T-shirt with a baseball cap pulled low over his shaggy hair. It didn't matter that Max could've bought and sold Martin Vassin a hundred times. Appearance mattered to him and it was part of his power trip to look more sophisticated, more powerful than his enemy. Max knew exactly how to play him.

"I don't see a suitcase full of money," Max called out as he stopped about fifteen feet away, drawing his line in the sand.

Vassin's smile was sharp and cruel. "I was under the impression a man such as yourself didn't need my money." His gaze raked Max from head to toe. "Perhaps I was mistaken. Perhaps the rumors are true and you are no longer the one to control the Devlin fortune."

"My fortune is fine. Much larger than yours the last time I checked. This is a business transaction. If you don't have the money, then I don't have the information. It's simple enough." Max turned his back to head back to the Jeep and he felt the movement behind him.

"Just a minute, Mr. Devlin. You don't expect to leave here so easily, do you? I want that information. And I plan to get it."

Hands grabbed the back of his shoulders, and he was spun around to face Vassin again. His men had spread out, and the two restraining him checked him over for weapons before taking a step back.

"He's clean," one of the guards called out.

Vassin's brows rose in surprise. "You're either very brave or very stupid, Mr. Devlin."

"I've been called worse," he said, shrugging.

Vassin chuckled, his eyes filled with curiosity. "This is what we're going to do. You and I are going to get in the helicopter and go to my home. You're going to give me the locations for the weapons convoy, and once you do and the information has been verified, you'll be free to leave. Without my money."

"And if I choose not to go with you?"

"Then I'm going to put a bullet in each of your knees and leave you lying here in the desert. You won't die right away, but the buzzards will still feed off your flesh. I'll come back again tomorrow and see if you've changed your mind about giving me the information."

"Huh," Max said, taking off his cap and running his fingers through his hair. "That's pretty creative of you. But I think I have a better idea."

Vassin's smile grew bigger. "I can't wait to be enlightened. You're an entertaining man, Mr. Devlin."

Max held up the hat in his hand seconds before a shot rang out and a bullet flew right through the center of it. Vassin's men had their weapons up, pointing at Max, but Vassin was smart enough to wave them back.

"The next one is centered to go right through your forehead," Max said. "Your toy soldiers might take me out, but not before you join me. Are we clear?"

Vassin nodded and waved a hand for his men to put their weapons away, and they all did as he asked.

"Now let me tell you what we're going to do. I'm going to walk back to my Jeep and drive away. My price has just doubled again. I expect to see half of the money delivered to a place of my choosing within the next six hours. You'll call me in exactly five hours and fifty minutes for the location. If it's not in my hands in six hours, I'm going to get on a plane and fly to London, where I'm supposed to meet Jarron Sikes. He's very interested in the information I have to offer. And he knows better than to try and fuck me over."

Vassin's expression turned deadly at the mention of his closest competitor.

"Once you show your good faith with the first half of the payment, you and I will meet again at a time and place of my choosing, where you'll give the second payment to my associate and I'll relay the information you've purchased."

Max wadded the ball cap in his hands and smiled at Vassin. "Six hours," he repeated. And then he turned around and walked back to the Jeep just like he said he would. He didn't let out the breath he'd been holding until he was back on the main road, speeding toward the city of sin.

CHAPTER TWELVE

It took almost two hours to drive back into the city, and by then Max was starting to get a bad feeling in the pit of his stomach. He hadn't liked the calculating look that had come into Vassin's eyes just before he'd left, and he knew without a doubt Vassin would be thinking of a way he could double cross Max. Again.

His phone vibrated against the passenger seat, and he picked it up, expecting to hear Jade's voice on the other end of the line.

"I've got a confirmation from Shane," Dec said instead. "The girl has been spotted at Vassin's California residence, but we're going to wait to coordinate the rescue with your next meeting. We don't want to take the chance of them killing her."

"He's got less than four hours until the first delivery has to be made, but my gut isn't feeling all that great about the transaction. He's going to try to screw me over."

"Have him make the first drop in a public place. The casino should work nicely for what you have in mind, and the rest of us can spread out to watch for any tricks. We'll already be in place long before he contacts you."

Max's anxiety eased some after he hung up the phone. The ball was in his hands, and it was his show to run. He only wished that one small nagging piece of doubt wasn't

SECRETS AND SATIN

eating away at him.

Jade took the mountain pass instead of the desert road that Max had to take, so she was back to the hotel long before he was. She changed out of her dusty clothes and got in the shower, scrubbing away the sweat and grime of the afternoon. That hadn't been an easy shot to make, and the conditions up in the mountain where she'd set up had been less than ideal.

She didn't even feel his presence until the cool breeze wafted across her skin as the shower door opened. It had always amazed her how quiet he could be for a man of his size. He moved with lethal and predatory grace, and he knew how to get the job done efficiently. When his hands came around and cupped her breasts and his hard cock probed between the crease of her rear, she knew it to be truer than ever.

"If my lover catches you in here, he'll kill you," she whispered.

She felt him pause just before his hands tightened on her breasts. "He'll never know I was here. I'll be in and out before he gets back."

Jade's hands pressed against the cold tile of the shower as he pushed his way inside of her. There was no foreplay, no preparation, and the fit was snug and uneasy, the penetration almost painful. The muscles of his thighs strained against her, and she went up on her toes and started to push back.

"Mmm, that's it, baby. I can feel you starting to cream for me." He pinched her nipples, bringing them to a standing peak, and she could feel the tug and pull in her clit. "This is going to be fast and hard. You'd better hang on for the ride."

"All I've heard so far is a lot of dirty talk and no follow

through—" She gasped as he thrust deep and hard, the snug tissues of her vagina grasping at him as she tried to adjust. He was right. All she could do was hold on for the ride.

Her hands slid down the tile until she was grasping the small built-in bench, and Max's grasp on her hips only grew tighter as he pounded harder and harder. She felt like a rag doll as he controlled her body, and she felt him grow impossibly large inside of her. Her hand slipped down between the wet folds of her pussy and she found the tight knot of nerves there, swollen and ready to explode. Every time he pushed inside her fingers glanced over where their bodies joined.

"Come on, baby. Come for me. Play with that sweet pussy."

She flicked her fingers expertly and felt the spasms deep inside as she felt the first spurt of come shoot from his cock. It had been a hard and fast ride, just like he'd promised.

"Wow," she panted a few minutes later. "I'm lucky I didn't drown. I don't think my legs work anymore."

He laughed and pulled out of her and they both groaned at the sensation. "Tell your lover he'll be hard pressed to beat that. Though I'm not sure my heart could take another round."

He helped her stand and then grabbed the washrag folded on the little shelf in the corner. "Why don't we grab some dinner and have some fun before Vassin calls? We've still got a couple of hours to kill."

He lathered the rag and scrubbed her from head to toe before repeating the process with himself. Jade was still trying to catch her breath, whereas he seemed to be full of energy all of a sudden.

"I could probably eat," she said.

They dried off quickly and she walked naked into the bedroom where her clothes and underwear were. She still wasn't used to the clothes that had been selected for the trip, and she stood staring into the closet, wondering what the hell she should wear and why the dresses couldn't leave any room for her weapons.

"Wear the red one," Max said, toweling his hair.

Jade rolled her eyes and then pulled the red strapless dress from the hangar. It had enough elastic in it so she wouldn't have to pull it up every five seconds, but there wasn't a lot of room for error if she bent or sat the wrong way. And no way in hell would she be able to wear a bra.

She grabbed a red lacy thong from the drawer and stepped into it, shimmying it up her legs with quick efficiency, and she was just about to pull the dress on in the same manner when she caught Max's stare. Her eyes widened and she had to stifle a laugh at his quick recovery. His dick was already hard again.

"Geez, Max. I thought you said your heart wouldn't be able to stand another round."

"Apparently my body thinks it'd be worthwhile to die trying. Christ, you're beautiful. You take my breath away."

She shook her head and went back to dressing, never comfortable with the compliments he seemed to be able to give so freely. "With that kind of talk I'm going to let you buy me a steak dinner." Her hair was mostly dry and she combed it down with her fingers so it wasn't sticking up every which way, and she slipped on a pair of flat gold sandals.

It wasn't often she just got to sit and watch Max, but she took advantage of the opportunity while he finished dressing. He'd changed so much since his injury. The suave and debonair playboy was still there somewhere. You could see it in the way he easily pulled on the expensive slacks and shirt, the way his demeanor became almost haughty with the change of his clothes. But there was a roughness to him now—a wildness that wasn't easily contained—and she wondered if he'd have been the same kind of lover two years ago as he was now.

"Max," she said, waiting until he finished slipping on

his shoes. "I want you to know that whatever happens I don't regret anything." She saw his lips tighten and knew she wasn't getting the words out right. "I just mean that I'm glad it was you. And that you wanted me."

He came up to where she was sitting and held out his hand, waiting for her to take it, and he pulled her to her feet. "I want you like I want to breathe. Never doubt that for a second."

For as long as it lasted, she thought to herself.

CHAPTER THIRTEEN

It always amazed her how easily she and Max fell into a rhythm outside of work. They knew each other better than most spouses did—quirks and likes and dislikes—because you had to know the person who was guarding your back, and you had to trust that they were doing it right.

Dinner was a relaxed affair, and Max delivered on the steak—medium and juicy for both of them. They talked about books, because that was one of the biggest things they had in common. It was a love she hadn't been able to share with Donovan because he'd pick a movie any day over a book.

They also talked about their childhoods and how similar Max's was to her own—the disinterest and lack of love his grandparents showed—even though he'd grown up in a house with everything at his fingertips. It just went to show that you could be neglected inside the home as much as outside, and from what she could tell, he had no desire to try and mend the rift between them. He'd told her some people just weren't capable of love, and then he'd changed the subject.

Jade could admit she was grateful he didn't try to talk about their future again, or bring up their fight from the day before. He hadn't questioned her again or tried to convince her that he loved her, and she wondered if maybe he regretted the words now, because he was acting like they'd never been said to begin with. She told herself that was a good thing. That the sooner he moved on, the better it would be for both of them, because it was getting harder and harder to convince herself they shouldn't be together—that she shouldn't come clean and take her chances.

Max wasn't a man who would go long without a woman. He was too—sexual. Even now, sitting in a public restaurant and obviously with his current lover, he drew the attention of other women like moths to a flame. They gave him long looks and flirtatious smiles, but he acted as if there was no other woman in the room but her. She still didn't understand why he wanted her, but it was very easy for her to understand his appeal, because even now she wanted to lure him back to the room and have her way with him. He was turning her into a sex maniac. She smiled at the thought.

"Do you think he'll call?" she asked after the dessert dishes had been cleared. It was five minutes until the first delivery was supposed to be made.

"He'll call. He's trying to gain the upper hand again by manipulating my instructions."

They stood and left the restaurant, passing by the expensive shops and the tunnel where an aquarium of sea life swam overhead. The hotel was loud and boisterous, richly gaudy with bright colors and hanging crystal chandeliers. Everyone moved at a frantic pace, as if they'd never get to experience all the delights one hotel could offer them.

Max's hand was a warm comfort on her back as they headed into the casino. The carpets and walls were rich and red, trimmed with gold and the flashing lights of the machines. The clanging of bells, the rush of voices, and the sound of coins hitting metal made her head throb with the need for quiet. She definitely wasn't a Vegas kind of girl.

SECRETS AND SATIN

She liked the quiet, the solitude of her life. Her circle of friends wasn't large, mostly those that worked at the agency, because no one outside understood what it was like to take a life to save countless others. But she was okay with the path she'd chosen because she knew it was a job that had to be done for everyone's sake. And she was good at it.

She caught sight of Brant dressed in cargo shorts and a T-shirt sitting at one of the machines nearby, a bottle of beer at his side as he fed coins into the slot. Max led her over to one of the high stakes blackjack tables and put down enough cash to have paid all of her bills for an entire year. They were the only ones at the table besides the dealer, and she caught sight of Declan at one of the poker tables on the opposite side of the room with a big stack of chips in front of him. He was dressed in a tuxedo with the top button unbuttoned and his tie draped around the collar like he'd been on an all night bender.

She didn't see Cade but she knew he was around somewhere. He and Declan looked so much alike they couldn't stand too close together without drawing attention to themselves. God hadn't made men like that to go unnoticed.

At one minute until the deadline, Max's phone vibrated against the green felt of the table. He placed his bet and asked for a hit before he picked it up.

"You're late," he said into the phone. "You've got one minute to find me in the casino. Otherwise I'm on the next plane out of here to go meet Jarron Sikes."

He hung up the phone without waiting for a reply and finished his hand of cards. Jade watched the second hand click on Max's watch as the minute passed, and then another, and then twenty more. He handed her a stack of chips so she could play too, and he was relaxed beside her, making jokes as her pile grew smaller and his grew larger, but she could tell he was worried that Vassin hadn't taken the bait.

"I'm out of chips," she said almost an hour after Vassin had called.

"Don't worry, you can have more of mine." He gave her one of those slow, lazy smiles that made her heart flip in her chest, and he pushed his chips toward the dealer to cash in. "I guess we should go find something else to occupy our time."

She saw the smirk from the dealer out of the corner of her eye, and she took the hand Max offered her. Dec and Brant had moved around over the last hour, and she finally caught sight of Cade at the sports bar, watching a baseball game with seemingly rapt attention. She knew he was highly aware that they were leaving though, and she felt Dec start to circle in closer.

"Stay close," Max whispered in her ear. "Something isn't right."

The problem was going to be when they reached the elevator. Because they were in the penthouse suite their entrance was restricted to regular guests, but Vassin and his men had access to the whole hotel. She caught Dec's worried gaze and then took a step away and to the left of Max just in case he needed room to maneuver. She had her own instincts, and the only thing she knew was that she had to protect Max, no matter what the cost.

Max opened the door that led to the private elevator and saw the long hallway was clear. There wasn't any sound or any sign that someone waited for them, and he and Jade moved quickly to the elevator, their footsteps silenced by the plush carpet. He swiped the keycard and the elevator doors whooshed open immediately. He looked inside and saw it was empty before they stepped inside.

Just before the doors closed a man slipped through and had a knife at Jade's throat before Max could move to intercept. He must have been waiting, lurking behind one of the closed doors that lined the hallway. That quickly, things were out of control, and he had no way to get to the man without harming Jade too.

Max's blood turned to ice as he saw the man's hands on her. Her pulse beat rapidly just above where the knife was held, but she was completely still, completely calm. The air felt as if it had been sucked out of the elevator, and Max and the man stared at each other, taking each other's measure.

"You've made a very dangerous enemy, Mr. Devlin," the man said. He was the same height as Jade and he used her body effectively to protect his own. His dark hair was shaved close to the scalp and his beard was the same length. Brown, soulless eyes stared at him, and Max knew he'd slice Jade's throat in a heartbeat and show no remorse if Max didn't tread very carefully.

"I can easily say it's mutual, Mr.—?"

"Smith."

"Yes, very clever. You can tell Mr. Vassin that if she dies then he won't find a corner of the world far enough away to hide in."

The man's eyes narrowed and he tightened his hold around her neck so the blade bit into the skin. A single drop of red welled and Max felt his whole body go still. This fucker was a dead man.

"If he wanted to disappear, you would never find him, but that is not why I am here. We are all businessmen, and Mr. Vassin decided he didn't like the terms you set forth earlier. He felt it was a little one sided. After all, if he gives you half the money, what's to keep you from taking it and leaving him high and dry? Here you go, sweetheart." The man kept his eyes on Max as he put a black briefcase in Jade's hands. "Hand this over to your boyfriend very slowly. I wouldn't want my hand to slip and slice that pretty neck."

Max reached out and took the briefcase from Jade,

keeping his eyes on her attacker. He couldn't look at her, afraid of what he'd see in her eyes. Or maybe more afraid of what she'd see in his.

"Be careful, Mr. Smith." He set the briefcase by his feet so his hands would be free. "Good bodyguards are hard to find."

"You seem to be rather careless when it comes to her wellbeing. Do you toss your lovers away so easily then?"

"Well, lovers are easier to find than bodyguards." His casual attitude flustered the man, and he hoped the lack of concentration would be enough for him to make a mistake so Max could strike out. But this man was a professional, and he knew exactly how to hold her, how to position the knife so she'd be dead before Max could ever make a move. "Why don't you deliver your message so we can get things rolling? I'm a busy man. And I've got a plane to catch. I think I've decided I'd rather do business with Jarron Sikes after all."

"Unfortunately, that is no longer an option. Mr. Vassin doesn't want you to think that he's not an honorable businessman, so the first half of the payment you demanded is in that briefcase. But we're going to take your lover as our own insurance. Once you've given Mr. Vassin the information he wants, you can have her back. An easy transaction."

"And how am I supposed to give Mr. Vassin this information, and where do I reclaim my property?"

"He's extending an invitation to his home here in the valley. Come alone and unarmed.

Now hit the button to take you to your room."

Max stared at him out of glacial eyes, and the man must have seen the promise of his death there because he tightened his grip around Jade and took a step back. Max hit the elevator button for the penthouse level and stood impotent while Mr. Smith maintained control.

The man pulled Jade out of the elevator and the doors started to close. "Tonight, Mr. Devlin."

SECRETS AND SATIN

The last thing he saw before the doors closed in his face was Jade staring back at him, the complete trust there in her eyes that he'd come for her. And by God, he wasn't going to let her down.

CHAPTER FOURTEEN

He had his phone in his hand dialing Dec's number as soon as the doors closed.

"What's going on? The staff here watches that private door like hawks. I couldn't get anywhere near it without drawing attention to myself."

"Vassin's man took Jade as collateral and left the first half of the payment with me." Max paused as Dec swore viciously. "I can meet with Vassin at his home tonight and give him the convoy locations, and then he says I can take Jade and leave."

"They'll try to kill you."

"That's what I'm planning on."

"Give Elena a few minutes to mess with the cameras and then head down to our suite. I've already got blueprints for Vassin's home here. We'll get her back."

"Damned right we will," he said and hung up. His fist punched against the elevator wall and he shook out the sting as he rode to the top.

Once the elevator doors opened on his floor he let himself into his room, and waited for the signal that Elena had overtaken the cameras. He changed into sand colored cargos and a white shirt, and he laced up his combat boots, much preferring their familiar weight over the expensive loafers he'd been wearing.

SECRETS AND SATIN

He didn't have to wait long for Elena's signal, and he took the stairs down to the floor below his. Declan was there waiting with the door cracked when he approached their room.

"Vassin lives in northern Las Vegas," Dec said, heading to the table where the maps were spread out. "His home is gated and sits on more than twelve acres of land. We've got an hour until sunset. The darkness will be in our favor. I've got some new toys I've been wanting to try out."

"If he hurts one hair on her head, he's a dead man," Max said, a vicious fury riding just beneath his skin. "I mean it, Dec. I don't care what kind of red tape or government promises have been made to hand over Martin Vassin. He will die if she's hurt."

"I'll help you bury the body if it comes to that," Dec said, nodding. "We're in this together. And you know as well as I do that accidents can happen on a mission. We'll worry about covering our asses when we need to. And if we can't cover our asses then Gabe Brennan sure as hell can. He owes me a favor."

Max nodded in gratitude and then leaned over the table, staring at the blueprints of Vassin's home. He was so caught up in his plans he didn't realize the phone ringing was his until the sixth ring.

"Devlin," he said, answering the phone.

"So now we are on an even playing field, my friend. This is much better."

Max signaled to Dec that it was Vassin on the phone, and he and Elena got to work trying to track his signal.

"Put Jade on the phone," he demanded.

"She's tied up at the moment and unable to talk. I'm sure you can speak to her once you arrive."

"How do I know she's alive?"

"I guess you'll just have to take my word for it," Vassin said, chuckling. "She is quite a handful. Such spirit she has. And her eyes are like green fire shooting sparks at me. It's very—arousing."

Max's hand gripped the phone tighter and he had to remind himself not to let anger take control. He needed to keep a clear head for Jade's sake.

"I'm assuming there was a point to this call," Max said.

"Ah, yes. Our business transaction. I've decided to play your little time game and see if you're as good as playing by my rules as I was at playing by your rules."

"I hate to break it to you, Martin, but you were pretty shitty at following the rules."

He laughed again and Max caught Dec's eye, telling him to keep him talking while Elena tracked his cell phone. Once she was locked onto it, it would be like a homing beacon once they started looking for him. And once they found Vassin, they'd more than likely find Jade with him.

"Yes, I called your bluff quite handily. Let me tell you my rules. It is a two-hour drive from the hotel to my home if there's no traffic. You have an hour and fifty-five minutes to get here."

Max paced the floor and kicked at the edge of the sofa. "Or what?" he asked.

"You remember our mutual friend Mr. Smith?" Vassin asked. "He is very good with a knife. You could even say he loves his work. For every minute you're late in getting here, Mr. Smith will start removing body parts. The timer starts now, Mr. Devlin."

The line went dead and he carefully put the phone in his pocket instead of throwing it across the room like he wanted.

"We've got his phone," Dec said. "He's still en route himself." Dec handed him an earpiece for communication, and he flicked the tiny sensor to turn it on and then slipped it into his ear. It fit neatly into the canal so it wasn't visible.

Max grabbed the keys to the Jeep and was already halfway out the door. He didn't have even seconds to spare.

"We'll be right behind you," Dec called out as the rest

of the team started gathering their gear. "Try not to piss anyone off too bad before we get there."

Max let the door slam behind him and took the elevator all the way to the garage floor level where the Jeep was parked. Dusk had already started to fall, and it made the lights of The Strip seem sadder somehow, the people walking the streets with greed in their eyes more pathetic.

He tried not to look at the clock as he sped through downtown and toward the long stretch of highway that would take him to Vassin's home. Night closed in and his foot pressed farther to the floor, taking the Jeep as fast as it could go while he kept an eye out for cops. He heard the occasional conversation in his earpiece, but he blocked it out once he heard that the team was en route. Dec always had a little bit of magic up his sleeve. He was always prepared for every eventuality.

He saw the barricade just after he took the last exit off the highway. A car blocked the driveway, and two men leaned against it, waiting for his arrival. He slammed on the brakes and got out of the Jeep almost before it had stopped rolling.

"Not bad," one of the men said, looking at his watch. "You might be able to keep her all in one piece after all. Put your hands on the car and spread your legs."

Max did as he was told, anxious to get a move on. The timer was still ticking. The men patted him down and took the Glock at the small of his back and the Ka-Bar that was in his boot. They cuffed his hands behind his back and then shoved him in the back seat of the black Lincoln they'd been driving, leaving Max's Jeep in the middle of the road.

He didn't fidget in his seat or try to make his position more comfortable since his hands were behind his back. He just stared into the rearview mirror until the driver kept glancing back at him nervously, and then he finally flicked the mirror up so he couldn't be seen. Max smiled and looked out the window. They had reason to be nervous.

The car pulled to a stop in front of black iron gates, and they opened slowly, letting the car pass through. Max looked around the grounds for alternate escape routes and then looked at the mansion in front of him. It was three stuccoed stories with white balconies on the top two floors and an orange tile roof. Palm trees flanked the front walkway and the corners of the house, and a long rectangular pool complete with fountains was the centerpiece of the front yard.

The men pulled him out of the backseat of the car and unlocked his cuffs, and Max flexed his wrists, trying to get the blood circulating again.

"You've got three minutes until they start cutting," the driver said. "But you've got to find them first. Better run."

Max took off through the front door and he heard Dec in his ear. "The phone signal is on the third floor. West corridor. Last room on the left."

He wasn't expecting it to be easy, so when he took the stairs two at a time to the second floor and met with two of Vassin's goons, he barely paused when they came at him. He was a machine, and his feet and fists were all the weapons he needed. He made short work of the men—a kick to the solar plexus for one and a punch to the jaw for the other—rendering them both unconscious.

He continued up the third flight of stairs and followed Declan's instructions to where the phone signal had been coming from. He heard footsteps from behind him from the guards who'd just stumbled over their friends, and he took out two more who tried to block his way to Vassin.

When Max burst through the door and into the spacious office, his blood ran cold at the sight that greeted him. Jade was standing against one of the bookshelves, a gag tied around her mouth and her wrists tied in front of her. An apple was precariously balanced on top of her head.

"Ahh, you're just in time for the fun, Mr. Devlin," Vassin said from his place behind his desk. He was leaned back in his chair, his eyes giddy with delight at the upcoming festivities. Mr. Smith stood at the opposite end of the room, tossing a knife in his hand.

Max didn't stop to think. He saw Smith toss the knife one last time and get into position to throw it, and he flung his body at him, taking him down just as the knife left his hand. The rage building inside of him made him feel inhuman, more monster than man, but he didn't hesitate to deliver a killing blow to the throat, crushing his trachea.

He was up on his feet again in only seconds, but killing Mr. Smith had wasted precious time. He looked to where Jade had been standing, and his heart almost stopped at the sight of the knife buried in the bookshelf where she'd been standing. She'd dropped to the floor the second Max had moved to attack.

"I'm a gun man myself," Vassin said, pointing the weapon at Jade as she worked at the restraints around her wrists. She'd managed to spit out the gag, and she was working quickly and efficiently to get free.

"You owe me a transaction, Mr. Devlin. I'll take the convoy routes now if you please. And if you even think about lying to me I'll put a bullet through her brain."

Max could hear the commands from Declan as the team stormed the house. He shouldn't have been surprised that Dec had brought in extra agents for the job. By their code names he knew that it was Cal Colter and Duncan Stirling who had landed whatever aircraft Declan had managed to get a hold of. Whatever it was, it was stealth and something that had the agents sounding giddy with excitement.

"You're going to kill me anyway," Max said. "Why should I give you that location?"

Vassin smiled like he was dealing with a bright student. "You're very astute. It only seems fitting that I kill you since you killed Mr. Smith. I believe you told him that good bodyguards are hard to find. Unfortunately, that's true, and he was mine. Maybe I'll take yours instead. I wouldn't mind a bodyguard that gives bed service. It would certainly simplify things."

Max watched from the corner of his eye as Jade got her hands free, and he moved closer to Vassin, hoping he could get close enough to disarm him. The sounds of fighting echoed in his ear, and he knew if wouldn't be long before Vassin realized something was wrong. And then he'd start taking out whoever was closest.

Even as he had the thought the lights went out and they were thrown into complete darkness. A piercing alarm sounded, and Max immediately hit the ground and began rolling as Vassin started firing into the darkness. His only thought was to get to Jade. He'd pinpointed Vassin's location and was about to pounce when the lights came back on as suddenly as they'd gone off.

It took a second for his eyes to adjust, and that second almost cost him his life. He heard Jade's scream of warning from his left just as Vassin brought the gun up, and he swore the time between when the gunshot sounded and when a hundred and thirty pound dynamo smacked into his side, taking him to the ground with her momentum, was almost simultaneous.

His arms came around her as they hit the ground, and his biggest fear was that she'd just taken the bullet that had been meant for him. He rolled with her and put her body protectively beneath him as the door was kicked open and more shots were fired. Max didn't bother to watch the red bloom on the front of Vassin's shirt, and he didn't bother to watch as Declan followed up on his shot with another for insurance.

His hands immediately went to the woman beneath him, checking her body for the bullet hole he knew he'd find. Panic ripped at him, and the rush of blood in his ears drowned out all other noise. But finally he realized she was speaking to him, and that there was no blood.

"This seems like a bad time to cop a feel," she said. "I've never been much of an exhibitionist."

SECRETS AND SATIN

Max dropped his forehead to hers and tried to slow his racing heart. "Don't you ever do that again. You scared the hell out of me."

"Hey," she said, taking his face between her hands and forcing him to look into her eyes. "I was watching your back. That's what partners do. You're one of the good guys. I couldn't let anything happen to you."

"You're one of the good guys too, Jade Jax. But if you ever pull a stunt like that again those spankings you got before are going to seem like child's play."

"There you go making promises again," she said.

He was laughing as he kissed her.

"Should we leave?" Cade asked. "I could be wrong, but I don't remember make out sessions being part of the ops, though I wouldn't mind hearing more about the spankings. That sounds intriguing."

"I believe you had plenty of make out sessions with your wife during that del Fuego mission," Dec said. "But I can see how this could give a bad name to my agency. Maybe if you two are finished we can get the hell out of here and call this in for cleanup. Shane just radioed in and said the senator's daughter is secure. We can debrief later."

"Much later," Max said.

CHAPTER FIFTEEN

Jade wasn't surprised to see a very irritated Max standing on her doorstep two days later. They'd flown back to Texas together, but as soon as Declan had debriefed the team, she'd snuck away like a thief in the night and flown back to D.C. with Declan. She'd been trying to make it a clean break. End of mission. End of their affair.

They didn't have a future together. He needed someone who could pass on the Devlin name, someone who could give him more than she ever could. And she needed—no, it was best not to think about what she needed. Those answers hurt too badly. She was doing what was best in the long run. Now she just had to make Max understand it.

But him standing in front of her looking rumpled and sexy was more than she could resist.

"You couldn't possibly think I'd just let you go," he said, pushing past her into the apartment.

She let out a little sigh and wondered what to say. What to do. "No, but I had hoped maybe you would. For both our sakes. You're making this too hard, Max. Why do you have to be so damned stubborn?"

His smile was a vicious slash of white, and she swallowed at the determination she saw there. No, he wasn't going to make this easy.

SECRETS AND SATIN

"I guess you're just lucky that way." She didn't try to move away from him as he came closer, his body heat enveloping her like a caress. He touched the side of her face and lowered his head so their foreheads touched. "I thought I'd lost you. Nothing in my life has ever been that terrifying."

She closed her eyes and soaked up the comfort he was offering, touching her hands to his chest to offer her own. "It scared me too," she admitted. "I thought of you. It's what made me fight to get there in time. I wanted to be able to touch you again. To taste you just one more time."

"And yet you ran away," he whispered against her cheek.

"Yes," she said. "Because I had to see if I was strong enough."

"And what did you discover?"

"That when it comes to resisting you I'm very, very weak. Touch me, Max. Make me feel alive."

His mouth devoured hers in a kiss meant to show them both that they were still living—still breathing. Her hands clasped around his neck and he encircled her in his arms, his hands grasping just beneath her rear so he could pull her against his raging arousal. It was a slow dance of lips and tongue, a seduction as they circled towards the back of her apartment to the bedrooms. She was almost dizzy with the need to have him fill her, to make her feel whole.

"Which door?" he asked.

"The one at the very end. God, Max, kiss me again. I never get tired of it."

Her room was dark and cool and they moved into the shadows. She hardly felt his fingers working at the buttons on her shirt. She only knew he couldn't stop kissing her or she'd die. Cool air hit her skin as her shirt slithered from her shoulders to the floor, and she found the edge of the T-shirt he wore, her hands pushing beneath it and splaying across his taut abdomen. He was so hard, his skin so hot.

Their lips barely separated as she pulled the shirt from

his body, and her hands immediately went to the buckle of his belt. She wanted him naked, wanted them both naked so she could feel how perfectly they fit together. And then all of a sudden her wish came true and she grasped the iron rod of his cock in her hand even as her pussy wept for it.

His hands clasped at her rear and he lifted her onto the bed, coming down over her so the fine hairs on his chest tickled across her skin. He pressed a knee between her thighs and she opened for him gladly, her nails biting into his shoulders in anticipation.

"Don't ever take a chance like that again," he said, kissing his way down her neck to her breasts. "Not for me. I don't know what I'd do if anything happened to you."

If she'd been capable of speech she would have made him promise the same thing. She knew they had no future together. Knew that he'd eventually go on with his life and settle down to happiness. But she knew she'd feel the exact same way if anything ever happened to him, whether he belonged to someone else or not.

"Please, Max—" she begged, her fingers fisting in his hair as his lips trailed lower. "Lick me. Take me in your mouth."

She felt the vibrations of his growl across her clit and she almost came then and there, but then his face was between her thighs and he was pushing her legs up so her knees rested on her chest.

"God, look at you." His breath feathered across her folds and she creamed more at the eroticism of how she was displayed. "You're so wet for me."

His tongue licked along the seam of her pussy and she almost came off the bed, the sensation was so great.

"And you taste like the sweetest sugar. I'm going to eat you all up."

And then he delivered his promise and his mouth was everywhere at once—his tongue spearing inside of her and then licking up to swirl around the sensitive bundle of nerves in her clit. He'd flick his tongue rapidly, only to slow to long, easy licks just as she felt the beginning spasms of release. It was torture and pleasure all rolled into one.

His fingers probed, gathering her juices and spreading them around before he finally slid two fingers inside her vagina. Her muscles spasmed and he kept his tongue swirling and licking just to the side of her clit, holding her on the precipice of satisfaction.

"Max!" she screamed.

And then his fingers and his tongue moved in tandem and she was flying high as the first orgasm ripped through her body. She shuddered against him and whimpered as he went back to the long, slow licks. Perspiration gathered on her body as she felt the heat start to rise inside of her once more. Then the heat turned to something darker, more dangerous, as his fingers left her pussy and moved down to the forbidden rosebud of her anus.

She whimpered as his finger circled the entrance, lubricating it with her own juices, and she sucked in a startled breath as one finger penetrated. The nerves inside sizzled at the new touch, and her clit throbbed as he worked himself farther inside, only to pull out and gather more lubrication before pushing in again. And then a second finger was added and she was panting with the vicious need that had built up so quickly.

Two fingers scissored inside of her, stretching her as his mouth found her clit again. Guttural cries tore from her throat at the unfamiliar sensation. She didn't know what was happening to her body, only that she was holding on to the ledge and in danger of falling into the abyss.

"I'm going to fuck you here," he said. "I'm going to make you mine in every way possible. Turn over for me, baby."

Jade moaned as he withdrew his fingers and she was able to relax her legs. He sat on his knees in the middle of the bed, his cock rigid and standing straight out from his body. The flared head of the crown was flushed dark red and she could see the moisture gathered at the tip. She licked her lips at the sight and watched as his cock flexed.

She turned over on her hands and knees, the anticipation building inside of her. His hand pressed at the middle of her back and she went down on her elbows so her face was pressed against the cool sheets and her ass was in the air.

His hand clamped against her hip and he moved in behind her, holding his dick with his other hand, and she tried to relax as he dragged his cock through the seam of her pussy, smearing her juices on the head. He pushed inside of her a little before pulling out, and she couldn't help but turn her head and look. Her cream glistened on his cock and every time he swiped it through her folds she trembled a little harder.

"Stop teasing," she said between gritted teeth.

His laugh was harsh as he pressed the head of his cock again her rear passage. "I just want to make sure you're ready for me, baby. Relax for me now. That's it."

She did as he asked and sucked in a breath as he pushed into her. Pleasure and pain like she'd never experienced assaulted her sensitive nerve endings and her nails dug into the mattress.

"So tight." Max's voice was strained, barely a whisper as he pushed past the tight ring of muscle. His hands tightened on her hips and she felt the sudden urge to move, to push back against him and find the relief she needed.

"Do you have any idea how fucking sexy this looks? I love your ass." He palmed the globes with each hand before spreading her cheeks wider. "Fucking beautiful. My cock stretching you, feeling you pulse around me."

He withdrew almost all the way out and then pushed in again, going a little farther this time. And he kept pushing and pushing until she felt his balls slap against the folds of her pussy. He groaned as he felt her contract around him, and he fell forward on his arms, his breath hot against her back.

"I'm not going to last. It's too good."

Jade couldn't remember how to breath, much less speak, and when his hand curved around her stomach and then delved into the slick folds of her pussy she was completely lost to sensation. His hips began to thrust as his fingers moved faster. His grunts and her whimpers of pleasure drowned out the sound of flesh slapping against flesh as their movements became more hurried, more frantic.

"More, more," she begged. "Please, Max. I love you so much. Please."

Sweat dripped from his face onto her back and his fingers plunged into the depths of her pussy and that was all it took to send her over the edge. She screamed and exploded around his fingers and cock, and then he stiffened behind her and she felt the hot spurts of semen shooting into her ass.

"Jade!" he shouted as every last drop was wrung from his body. He collapsed on top of her, and she was too weak to do more than lie there.

"Tell me again," he said against her neck. "I need to hear the words from you."

She stiffened as her mind began to clear, and she scrambled to move out from under him. He lifted himself off her and rolled to the side, and she curled into herself, cursing her lack of control.

"Let's start this again," he said. "I love you. And I heard you say the words. I need to hear them again."

"It's just something people say in the heat of the moment." Her voice caught on a sob, and she wondered if she'd ever be able to forgive herself for lying to him.

"Dammit, Jade. Give me something." Frustration edged in his voice and he ran his fingers through his hair. "You can't tell me you didn't feel anything just now. That what just happened was only sex."

"You don't understand!" she cried out, pulling one of the pillows in front of her and hugging it close.

"Then explain it to me! You give your body to me in ways you've never given it to anyone before. You trust me with your life, but not your heart. And you say you love me when I'm buried deep inside you, but you can't look me in the eye and say it now. So yes, explain what the hell the problem is. Explain why I can't get down on my knees and ask you to spend the rest of your life with me. To grow old with me and have children with me."

"I can't have children!" she screamed and then clamped a hand over her mouth as a sob escaped.

Every last bit of air deflated from his lungs as the words penetrated. It felt as if the oxygen had been sucked out of the room. Sound ceased to exist—just an empty void as the blood rushed to his ears.

Reality came crashing back as her gut-wrenching cries broke through the fog surrounding his brain. She curled up in a ball in the center of the bed and her body shook with tremors. To see a woman so strong break down was almost more than he could bear, and he went to her, gathering her in his arms and rocking her back and forth like a child.

"I'm so sorry, baby," he whispered through her sobs. "I'm sorry." He waited until she was quiet in his arms. Until only the occasional tremor shook her body. "I won't ask you if you're sure, even though I didn't see any reports on it after your miscarriage."

She tried to move away from him, but he just shifted their positions so she sat cradled in his lap.

She turned her head away from him when she answered. "I had the doctor leave it out of the written report so I could go back on duty. The damage was too severe, they said. The bleeding too bad. So they had no choice but to give me a hysterectomy or I would have bled to death."

SECRETS AND SATIN

Max let out a slow breath and held her tighter. "I wish you would have told me. You didn't have to go through that alone."

"Maybe I just wanted to delay the inevitable," she said. "I couldn't tell you. At first because I was ashamed of the way I broke down when you told me about Donovan. I'd never lost control like that before." She sucked in a shuddering breath. "And then I lost—I lost the baby, and it was my fault because I lost control."

"No—" His heart ached for her, but she had to know she was wrong. "You can't blame yourself for what happened. It's just as easy to blame myself for the way I told you. But it wasn't anyone's fault, baby."

"Then time started passing and every day it seemed like that day faded a little bit more in my memories. And then you were there and I started seeing you as something I never had before. Only I wanted you too bad to tell you the truth." Her voice seemed to steady as she explained, and the light finally began to dawn. "You were right. I think I thought you'd be safe. That you could satisfy my body but not touch my heart because I didn't believe I'd ever be able to love again. And I didn't think that you could ever love me. I've watched the women go in and out of your life over the years, and I thought I'd be one of them. But then I realized that I was lying to myself and I loved you more than I thought I would ever be capable of loving."

"God, Jade—" He kissed her brow and pulled her closer. "You have no idea how much I needed to hear you say that. I love you too, sweetheart. I loved you when you belonged to someone else, and I love you even more now. And there will be no more women in and out of my life. In fact, there hasn't been any woman but you in my bed for more than two years. You're it for me."

"That's what I was afraid of," she said. The sadness in her voice had him lifting her chin with his finger so he could look into her eyes. "You deserve so much more than what I can give you, Max. You deserve to have a woman who's whole, so you can get down on your knees and ask her to spend her life with you. To have children with you."

"You're going to piss me off, love," he said, rubbing his thumb along her bottom lip. "Do you think you telling me you can't have children is going to make me stop loving you? Let me ask you something," he said before she could answer. "When you were stuck inside that orphanage, did you dream of a couple like us coming in to take you home? Do you think there's not someone exactly like you waiting for us right now? Or that there won't be two or five or ten years from now? You make me whole, Jade. Just you. Not anything else. As long as I have you then everything else will happen as it should."

"God, you make it sound so simple." She scrubbed her hands over her face, wiping away the tears.

"Because it is simple. Marry me. Love me. And let me love you back. Nothing else matters."

"Your family might have something to say about that," she said with a bitter laugh. "You can trace the Devlin name practically to the dawn of time. You have a legacy, Max. Something you can only pass down to a biological child. Why would you deny yourself that?"

"I can just as easily pass it to a child who needs a good home," he said with a shrug. "They're just things, Jade. It's just a name. It pales in comparison to spending the rest of my life without you."

Her arms wrapped around him and she buried her face against his chest. "I love you so much," she whispered.

"That's a step in the right direction for sure. I'm not on my knees, but I'm pretty damned close," he said, lifting her face once more and seeing the hope in her eyes. "Marry me, Jade. Spend your life with me. Love me."

"More than you know," she said. "Always."

EPILOGUE

Two Months Later...

The bride was beautiful. It was all Max could think as he watched her walk down the aisle, the white gown showing off the glow of her skin and the radiance in her eyes.

The MacKenzies had insisted they have the wedding at the family farm in Surrender, Montana. He stood with the preacher and his best man, Cade MacKenzie, under a canopy of trees burnished red and orange and gold as summer finally gave way to fall. Max looked out at those witnessing their special day with pride. All the family he needed was here to watch him take Jade as his wife.

The smile she gave him as she met him at the end of the aisle had his heart swelling in his chest. Love shone across her whole face and there was a joy inside her he hadn't seen in a long time. She took his outstretched hand, and it was easy to see their future in her eyes as they promised to love and cherish for a lifetime.

And at the end of the ceremony, Max closed his eyes and said a small prayer, thanking Donovan for being there to love her first. To love her how she deserved. And then he thanked him for giving Max the gift of being able to love her too.

Declan MacKenzie stood off to the side and watched Max and Jade make their promises to each other, and a bitter disappointment and jealousy filled him, though he wanted to be happy for them.

He was happy for them.

He knew better than anyone that his path had already been forged. There wasn't a happily-ever-after in his future. Not when the only woman he'd ever wanted had been married to a traitor. And especially not when that woman was a traitor herself.

No, his shot at happily-ever-after had long since passed. Because now it was his job to hunt down the love of his life and catch her in her own web of lies and deceit.

SINS AND SCARLET LACE

A MACKENZIE FAMILY NOVEL

NEW YORK TIMES BESTSELLING AUTHOR
LILIANA HART

LILIANA HART

PROLOGUE

Ten Years Ago...

"Mmm, is it morning already?"

Declan MacKenzie grabbed a stack of shirts from the drawer and put them in his duffel bag before turning to look at Sophia. Just the sound of that sexy, sleepy voice had his dick spiking behind his jeans and his heart hammering, even though he'd had her only a couple of hours before.

"It's still dark out," he said. "You can grab a couple more hours of sleep before you need to get up for class." He zipped up the bag and shoved his wallet in the back of his jeans.

"It's not working, you know."

His lips quirked in a smile, but he kept his back turned, going to the closet to grab his boots. She knew him better than he knew himself sometimes, and his head was a scary place to be. He thanked God he had her to help balance the shadows that plagued him.

"What's not working?"

"You can't possibly think you're hiding that hardon

from me," she teased. "It'll give all the other soldiers something to talk about. Unless you want to come over here and let me help you get rid of it?"

He dropped his boots on the floor and moved to sit down in the corner chair, but he made the mistake of looking at the bed and all thoughts of the new mission he'd just been assigned flew out the window.

"Jesus, Soph," he groaned, his hand going to his belt buckle.

She was a vision—tousled blond hair framed the face of an angel, kiss-swollen lips and that sexy mole just at the corner of her mouth. She pulled the sheet down slowly, revealing plump breasts and small pink nipples. He could see where his beard had abraded her skin from the night before, and he reminded himself he needed to be easier with her, but if anyone made him lose control it was her. He flexed his shoulder, the soreness from the bite of her nails a reminder that she wasn't always gentle with him either.

The sheet continued its downward journey until she was completely bare before him, the naked folds of her sex glistening and swollen with desire. She crawled to the center of the bed and moved to her knees, skimming her fingers up her thighs and belly until she cupped her breasts in her hands.

"You'll have to make it good," she purred. "This will have to last me until you get back."

"I'm only going to be gone a week. I think you'll survive."

"If you're not interested, I guess I just need to take care of it myself," she said, pouting those pretty lips. She'd been a virgin two years before when they'd started dating, but she was the best kind of lover—generous and curious in equal measure—willing to try anything until sometimes he felt like she was teaching him.

"Like hell you will," he growled. "But if you're not screaming in ten minutes I'm going to come and leave you hanging. I've got a flight to catch." He grinned as the light of challenge flared in her eyes and she crooked a finger at him.

"I've got faith in you," she whispered. "I bet you'll have me coming in five. Plenty of time to spare."

A laugh burst from his lips and he moved to the side of the bed. She grabbed at his belt buckle and unfastened it before moving to the button of his jeans.

"Time's ticking, hot shot. What are you going to do about it?"

Husky laughter escaped her throat as he grabbed both of her ankles and flipped her back onto the mattress.

"I guess I'm going to make you scream."

He pulled her to the edge of the bed and pushed his jeans down to his hips so his cock sprang free. He'd be lucky to last five minutes himself. Her feet rested on his shoulders and he gripped the base of his cock, sliding the head through her slick folds until he groaned from the torture. Someday he'd be able to take her without a condom, but not yet. He had plans for the future he wanted to implement very soon.

"Hurry, Dec," she panted. "I can't wait."

He leaned over and opened the nightstand drawer, grabbing a condom and ripping it open with his teeth before sliding the protection on. Her hands went to her breasts and squeezed and he filled her with one solid stroke.

"Fuck me hard," she screamed.

He bent over her and held her legs together so her feet stretched above her head. And then he did as she'd demanded.

His hips jerked against her in uncontrolled thrusts and his fingers burned against her flesh. He'd be feeling the grip of her sweet pussy wrapped around him for weeks. Her cries were loud and he had a feeling his neighbors would be getting an earful if they listened too closely, but it was like music to his ears.

SINS AND SCARLET LACE

He dropped her legs so they splayed open, and he came down on top of her as he felt the familiar tightening in his balls and up his spine. Her legs twined around his waist and he buried his head against her neck as he felt her tighten around him and the vise-like squeeze of her walls clamping around him.

"I love you, Sophia," he whispered in her ear. "Always." And then they followed each other into ecstasy.

Four Days Later…

Sophia wiped her brow with the back of her sleeve and picked up another box, carrying it into the bedroom she'd soon be sharing with Declan. Her parents were going to have kittens once she told them she was moving in with him. She still had a year of school left before she got her degree, not to mention her parents were both very traditional and wouldn't be happy about her decision to live in sin. Which was why they would keep thinking she was living in her dorm room until the semester ended. Maybe she'd find the courage to tell them by then.

But sin was just fine with her as long as she was sinning with Declan, and if she was lucky, he'd ask her to marry him sooner rather than later. They hadn't talked about it, but she could tell it was coming. They loved each other too much for there to be any other option for them.

She unpacked another box of her clothing and then fell back on the bed. It was sometimes overwhelming to think that life was so perfect. She'd been a small town girl, moving from a poor community in southern Virginia to the big city to attend Georgetown University on a full scholarship. She swore her eyes had nearly popped out of her head the first few months after she'd moved.

But then she'd met Declan and things had just clicked.

She knew immediately she'd found the other half of her soul. It felt stupid to say, and her friends had told her she was just too inexperienced to know any better, but she figured she knew her heart and her body recognized the man who was made just for her, so she ignored her friends and trusted her instincts. And she and Declan had been together for two full years without a hitch, with a lifetime in front of them.

She pulled herself off the bed and headed back into the living area of his apartment—no, their apartment—to grab another box and put things away when she heard a key rattle in the lock.

Excitement filled her and she ran to the door to undo the deadbolts and the chain. But when she opened the door it wasn't Declan there as she'd expected. It was his younger sister Darcy. She was a few years younger than Sophia, and she knew Declan and Darcy were close even though she'd only met the girl a couple of times. She was actually one of the few members of Declan's family she had met.

"Darcy?" Sophia got a good look at the girl's face and saw the streaks of drying tears down her cheeks. "What's wrong? Are you hurt?"

"I came to get some of Declan's things," she said. "Mama said he'd want his own things when they land and get him settled in a room."

Fear clutched at her belly and she grabbed Darcy's arm in a tight grasp. "What are you talking about? What's happened?"

"The attack—" her face crumpled again as she looked at Sophia. "One of the Black Hawks was shot down with a surface-to-air missile. All the SEALs on board were killed, but Declan was somehow thrown from the wreckage before it crashed. They said they didn't know if he was going to make it, but they've got him stabilized at a hospital in Germany and are flying him back here because there's a surgeon who knows how to fix him. Mama said he'd be just fine. He's too stubborn to die."

Darcy's breath hitched again, but Sophia was too numb to cry. She dropped her hand from Darcy's arm and backed up a few steps until her knees hit the back of the couch and she sat down hard.

"I didn't know," she said. "How—how long ago?"

"I'm sorry I didn't think to tell you, but I don't even have your number. I know you and Dec are close. From the looks of your things in here, it looks like you're closer than I thought." Darcy grabbed one of the empty boxes she'd left sitting around and headed into the bedroom. "Come on," she called out. "We'll get him a few things and then we'll head to the hospital. You'll want to be there when he arrives."

Three weeks later…

Declan knew Sophia was there—he'd heard her whispered words of encouragement through the fog in his mind and felt her lips brush across his forehead.

He couldn't seem to break free of the nightmares that plagued him. He felt as if he'd been swimming through a black, inky sea toward the light that shone at the top of the water, but just as his hand reached out to break through the surface, something grabbed hold of his ankle and pulled him down again until he was swimming through the faces of the soldiers he'd seen blown into oblivion.

He thought surely he must be dead too, because he remembered jumping into the Black Hawk with the SEALs he'd been working with, his hand grasping Lieutenant Jake Long's forearm, pulling him up as the copter went airborne. He remembered looking into Jake's face, pale green eyes staring back at him from a face smeared black with camo paint.

He'd still been holding onto Jake's arm when consciousness had briefly returned. It wasn't something he'd ever forget—the way he couldn't hear anything but his own heartbeat when the rescue squad came to search for survivors or how he'd seen everything in sharper colors for just a few minutes. And then he thought of Sophia because he wanted her face to be the last he saw.

So much blood on his hands. It had been his meet, his op, and eight men were dead because he hadn't been careful enough. He should have known, should've anticipated. The longer he worked within the covert ranks of the CIA the more his name was whispered by the men who would pay to see him dead.

It was too late to change who he was now. He was Declan MacKenzie. And he'd always be hunted. Which meant anyone tied to him would become hunted as well. He would gladly sacrifice his life for his country, but not Sophia's.

He loved her. So much that the thought of what he had to do clawed its way through his guts, sinking sharp talons into his heart and ripping it out of his chest. But it was the only way because they would never stop hunting him.

Her voice called out to him and it soothed the ache in his chest, and he let himself tell her he loved her in his dreams. One last time.

Sophia stretched her neck and back and got up from the uncomfortable chair she'd pulled up to the side of Declan's hospital bed. She had a class in another couple of hours and she needed to look over some notes.

He'd been in and out of consciousness the last couple of days. Finally. And it still brought tears to her eyes that he'd opened his eyes and looked directly at her before whispering he loved her. He'd woken again some hours later, but his mom and dad had been taking their turn sitting by his side. But every time he opened his eyes now she could see his strength and determination growing, and he spoke a little more, even though it was hard for him with the bandages on his face.

Parts of his chest had been badly burned and there were several deep gashes in his legs that worried the doctors. He was hooked up to so many machines she was afraid to touch him, and he moaned in his sleep when the pain medication started to wear off. But she had to be strong for him and keep up a brave face.

Declan had a lot of work and rehab ahead of him if he wanted to be back on his feet and back with his unit, not that she really even knew what he did. It was all very secret, though she knew he was in Special Forces of some kind, and he never went anywhere without his dog tags. He said they were his good luck charm.

She pulled the mangled tags from her pocket and stared at them, letting the sharp edge bite into her hand. The two tags were melded together from the fire, and part of his identification had disappeared. But they'd survived, if not whole, just like he would.

"They look like hell, huh?" he rasped from the bed.

Her head came up and she moved to the side of the bed, taking his hand. "Do you need any water?"

"Not yet." He swallowed once and stared at her from unreadable eyes, but she could see the pain he tried to keep hidden.

"Let me get the doctor. They wanted to check you the next time you were awake."

"Not yet, Soph. I need to say something. I need to tell you—"

"Ssh," she said. She didn't know where else to touch him. His hand was the only thing not wrapped in bandages. "It's okay. You told me already."

"No, you don't understand." The machines next to his bed beeped rhythmically, but there was no erratic movement in his heartbeat. He was steady and stable. "I've made a mistake."

She shook her head, not understanding what he meant.

"I realized something when I was flying out of that helicopter. When I looked over and saw friends dead on the ground beside me, their limbs torn from their bodies and some of their faces unrecognizable."

"God, Dec—I'm so sorry, baby."

"Just let me get it out, Soph." The bite in his voice stung, but she let it go. He was hurting and she had no idea what to do to make it better. She couldn't imagine losing her friends in such a way. She nodded and his lips tightened to a straight line, shifting the bandages that covered the wound on his face.

"What I'm trying to say is that when a man sees death staring him in the face, there are things he thinks about—regrets and wants and needs and mistakes."

He licked his lips again, but she didn't ask him if he wanted any water. Something tightened inside her and the air around her became heavy, closing in on her until she thought it would crush her.

"And I realized as I was waiting there getting ready to die that you were not the future I saw."

"This isn't the time or the place to talk about this, Dec," she said, trying to smile even though his words broke her heart. "You're in pain and you're distraught, and I won't hold it against you once you're on your feet again. You said you loved me, and I know you meant it. I've got to leave for class soon, but I'll be back later tonight."

"Don't come back, Soph," he said, gripping her hand before she could pull away. "I mean it. I'm going to tell the nurses you're not welcome here. I didn't mean it when I said I loved you. If anything, that was the delirium. I'm nothing but clearheaded now. I'm sorry if this hurts you, but it's for the best. You're young and you can't possibly know what you want for the rest of your life, but it's not me. It shouldn't be me. Because I don't and can't love you the way you want to be loved. You're a naïve kid who still has a lot of growing up to do when it comes to how relationships work."

"This isn't funny, Dec. Why are you trying to hurt me? It's cruel." She pulled out of his grasp and backed away from the bed. She didn't realize that tears fell down her cheeks, but he did, and it killed him inside.

"What's cruel is letting you think there could be any more between us than good sex and a few laughs. It's over, Soph. Go find someone else who can give you the attention you need. You can find love anywhere if you look for it hard enough."

"If I walk out the door, I won't be back." She grabbed her jacket and backpack off the floor as anger started to replace the hurt. "I'll hate you with every breath I take for as long as I live."

"Goodbye, Sophia." The words were definitive and she felt her heart snap in two at the coldness in his voice. This wasn't the same man who'd shared her dreams and her bed for the last two years. This man was someone else, and she'd be damned if she'd wait for him to come to his senses.

She didn't say anything as she opened the door to his room and closed it calmly behind her. She ignored the questions from his parents and the startled cry from Darcy as she pushed past the MacKenzie family to the stairs. She didn't want to wait for the elevator. She had to get out into the open now, before she broke down completely.

Cold slapped against her cheeks and icy pellets of rain stuck like needles into her skin as she ran through the parking lot to her car. She didn't know how she managed to start the car or drive back to the apartment—Declan's apartment—where she'd just finished unpacking the last of her things.

She didn't let the sobs break free until she'd unlocked the door and smelled the familiar scent of his cologne. She dropped to the floor where she stood and let the tears fall as the last of her innocence was finally shed.

And she didn't stop to think as she packed several boxes of the things most important in her life and loaded them into to the trunk of her car. He could burn the rest or sell it for all she cared. There was no way in hell she was coming back to get more.

She locked his apartment door behind her and tossed the key in a dumpster on the way out. She was through with Declan MacKenzie, and if she never saw him again it would be too soon.

CHAPTER ONE

Eight Years Later...
Mayan Ruins, Guatemala

Declan MacKenzie knew when an op was about to go to shit. He'd always had a sixth sense when it came to life or death situations—the way the skin at the back of his neck tingled or the way he could feel the crosshairs being centered between his eyes. The one and only time he'd gone against his gut, he almost hadn't made it back home alive, and the jagged scar on his face was a daily reminder that the only things he could trust were his own instincts.

His sister's life was on the line, and if they wanted to get Darcy back from the drug lord who'd kidnapped her, then the team he'd put together would have to be smarter and faster than the soldiers Alexander Ramos had hired to protect his compound. Dec's men were well trained, and his brother, Shane, was watching his back, along with Brant Scott and Kane Huxley. If he had to trust anyone, it would be those three.

Dec looked at the team gathered around him, waiting for their orders, and he knew someone was going to die. That feeling in the pit of his stomach just wouldn't go away. But Darcy was counting on them, and he was in charge because he knew how to make the hard decisions and had the spine to follow through with them. God knows he'd had to make some hard ones in his thirty-five years. Lives were lost every day in his line of work, but he'd never had to face that it might be one of his own family.

He stared into the eyes of each of his team members and knew he'd gladly sacrifice himself if he could save the lives of his brothers and sister. His good friend, Brant Scott, loved Darcy whether he wanted to admit it or not, and that made him family. The poor bastard. Smith had three children and Huxley had a wife. Everyone had someone at home counting on them. Except for him. He'd destroyed those dreams long ago.

Dec quickly strategized the best way to keep them all alive. "I want communication every step of the way," he commanded. "Smith and Huxley, take the north side. Max and Brant will cover the southwest, and I'll take the southeast. Jade will cover us from here. SEAL Team 6 and 4 are both on site. Don't get in their way. Our mission is to get all of the hostages out alive if we can."

They were all dressed for battle—dark green BDUs, face paint, and night vision goggles strapped to their heads. The SEALs would go in first and take down as many soldiers as they could to clear the path for the agents going inside the underground compound.

The sound of gunshots echoed in the distance, and Declan gave the signal for them to move into position. He watched his team disappear into the surrounding foliage and counted down the seconds in his head. He ran toward his own checkpoint, hoping he was right and the bulk of Ramos's men would be in his area.

He stayed to the shadows and watched Ramos's soldiers set up around the perimeter while the feeling in his gut intensified. The way they moved in coordinated fighting positions looked like it had been taken from the

SINS AND SCARLET LACE

US military handbook, which meant things were worse than he imagined. He knew there was a mole somewhere among the agents or politicians he worked with, but their identity was still elusive. Too many missions had been compromised for there not to be someone on the inside. Several of the agents under his command had been outed and brutally terminated, and he didn't believe in coincidences.

Hell broke loose about the time he reached the edge of the clearing where the southeast entrance to the compound was located. Soldiers swarmed and came at him from all directions. Fear never had a chance to take hold—fear was crippling—and he took out the two soldiers closest to him while Jade Jax shot a steady stream of fire from that magic rifle of hers and made it a more even playing field.

A bullet grazed his arm at the same time one of the soldiers dived at him and took him to the ground. Dec felt the air leave his body as the meaty flesh of his attacker slammed against him. He wasn't as big as his brothers—skimming right at six-feet, his muscles lean and sinewy—but his movements were fluid as he absorbed the hit. His left forearm slammed into the soldier's throat as he reached for the Ka-Bar stuck in his boot. Dec barely noticed the surprised look in his attacker's eyes as the knife sunk into flesh, and he pushed him aside and reached for his gun as others came at him.

Jade was consistent in her shots, and adrenaline pushed Dec to fight harder and faster until the ground was littered with bodies and he was finally in position next to the locked metal door that led into the compound.

"I'm in position and going in," Dec said through the com set. "Check in."

"We're in position," Huxley called out. "Going in."

"We're in," Brant said.

"Everyone is clear that I can see," Jade said. "But I've got blind spots to the north."

"Shit! Shit!" Huxley suddenly yelled.

Rapid gunfire and the screams of the dying echoed in Dec's ears, and his heart stopped beating as he waited for the inevitable. His blood turned cold and he fell back against the wall as he shook his head in denial. Smith and Huxley should have been fine. He'd calculated the risks and taken the biggest ones for himself. They should have been fine.

"Aww, God—Dec," Huxley said, his voice raspy with pain.

"Report, goddammit," he ordered. "Huxley? Don't you fucking die on me. Sophia will be pissed."

A small exhale of a laugh could be heard through the earpiece and Declan closed his eyes as another soul was added to the list of those he'd been responsible for and failed. Huxley was his closest friend—more like a brother—and they'd been there for each other through the tough times. Dec had stood by him at his wedding—when Hux had married the one woman Declan knew should've belonged to him—and he'd let it happen because Hux had been his friend.

"She will be pissed," Huxley said softly, his breath hitching again. "Smith is down. And I'm—hit." A few seconds of labored breathing went by before he spoke again. "Take care of her for me, Dec. I know you will. I've always known about—"

"I'll take care of her," Declan answered before the others could hear Huxley's deathbed confession. "She'll be safe. I swear it."

CHAPTER TWO

Three Weeks Later...

Sophia Huxley sat huddled in the corner of the small square room. The walls and floor were grey concrete and the fluorescent lights were harsh. The wooden chair beneath her wobbled, and she had to keep both feet pressed to the floor so she didn't slide forward. A small metal table sat bolted to the floor, scarred and dented from years of abuse. A long stretch of mirror reached across the opposite wall, and she knew they were watching her.

Her mouth was dry, and she wrapped her arms protectively around her roiling stomach. She couldn't remember the last time she'd had a full meal. Maybe a few weeks ago when she'd gotten the news of her husband's death. Things had been a blur since then.

She'd lost track of how long she'd been inside the interrogation room. She was in trouble and she didn't know how to fix it. She had no family, no close friends. Kane had made sure of that after they'd married. His jealousy had caused her to cut all ties.

Shame crawled up her spine and wrapped around her skin like it always did when she remembered what a fool she'd been. Dec hadn't wanted her enough, loved her enough, so she'd ended up with a man who'd reminded her of him—in the way he spoke and the way he'd charmed her with his teasing personality—only she hadn't known at the time it had all been an act.

It had taken her more than a year after Declan's cruel parting before she'd started dating again, but Kane Huxley had walked into her life and been relentless in his pursuit, and six weeks later she'd married him. Sophia hadn't known until she'd walked down the aisle that Declan and Kane had been friends—not until she'd seen the stone mask come down over Declan's face—the scars there still puckered and red—as she promised to love and cherish another man—a man who would never have her whole heart. It wasn't every day the bride spent time throwing up in the bathroom instead of enjoying her reception.

Another round of shudders wracked her body, the muscles of her arms and legs knotting into tight balls, and she bit her lips as she tried to massage the areas. They'd dropped the temperature in the room and her teeth chattered as she waited endlessly for someone to come in and speak with her. They called her a traitor. A terrorist. And a dry sob escaped at the thought of what might happen to her.

There was no one left she could turn to. No one who could find out why they were calling her such terrible things.

Thoughts of Declan came to mind—at least the way he'd been when he'd loved her. It hadn't been the first time she'd thought of him over the years, but it was the first time since the day he broke her heart that she actually wanted to see his face one more time. Maybe he'd been right when he told her when one was faced with moments of life or death, thoughts of the things or people who meant the most were what occupied the mind. Unfortunately for her, it seemed like it was still him. Leave it to her subconscious to enjoy being kicked while she was down. Declan had been Kane's friend and Kane had betrayed them all. There was no reason for him to come to his widow's rescue.

Her head snapped around as the grey metal door opened on silent hinges and a man stepped through. She didn't recognize him, but he was a hell of a lot scarier than the agents who had taken her from her home in handcuffs.

Sophia shuddered involuntarily at the humiliation being handcuffed had brought her—as her neighbors gathered on their lawns and the reporters swarmed around her and she was driven away.

"Mrs. Huxley," the agent said. "My name is Agent Brennan. And you're in a whole hell of a lot of trouble."

His size filled the doorway and the freshly creased slacks and blue dress shirt couldn't hide the savagery within. His hair was dark as night and swept rakishly across his forehead, and his eyes were the same piercing blue as his dress shirt. He held a large file in his hand and had a weapon at his hip.

Her fingernails bit into her palms and she tensed as he moved into the room and took the chair on the other side of the table. His chair either didn't wobble or he didn't care about the discomfort. He didn't look like the kind of man you'd want to cross.

The pain from squeezing her fists was only a reminder that the nightmare had become reality, and she stared past Agent Brennan into the long expanse of mirror, wondering what the men behind it saw when they looked at her.

"Mrs. Huxley?" Agent Brennan asked, the frown lines marring his forehead making him all the more menacing. "Are you all right?"

The laugh that escaped was harsh and filled with disbelief at his question. "Why am I here?" Her voice cracked and she swallowed once, trying to soothe the dryness.

"Let's not play games, Mrs. Huxley. Things will go much easier for you if you just tell us the truth."

"What truth?" she spat, heat rushing to her cheeks as

her temper unleashed. "I've been called a terrorist and a traitor without any explanations. I've been locked in a room for hours without food or water, and no one has read me my rights or asked if I'd like an attorney."

"Terrorists have no rights. Welcome to the United States of America."

"I'm not a terrorist," she said, but the words trembled past her lips and fear rooted in her belly. "I'm not. I haven't done anything."

"Your husband was a high ranking agent within the CIA who had top-secret security clearance. Do you know what his legacy is, Mrs. Huxley?" He didn't wait for her to answer. "He's the man who put a price on his agents' heads and sold them to the highest bidder. He's been responsible for the deaths of fourteen agents, and God knows how many more names he sold before he had the good sense to die."

Sophia shook her head in confusion. "This is a mistake. My husband was a contractor for a steel company. He never took government contracts because he said they didn't pay enough. I'll be the first to agree with you that he'd be capable of murder, but he wasn't an agent."

She watched in horrified fascination as the heavy file landed with a thud onto the table. He flipped it open and picked up the document that sat on top. Attached to it was a photograph of her husband. He pushed it towards her and her blood ran cold at the sight of him. Everything she'd never known about him was listed on that one sheet of paper—his security clearance, those under his command, his contacts, his family—her.

"My God," she said, meeting Agent Brennan's stone cold gaze. "This has to be some kind of a joke."

"I promise you, it's not. Your husband went to work every day and looked into the eyes of the people he was selling out. He was a murderer."

His eyes flashed with anger and she felt the blood drain from her face. The words he'd said earlier suddenly hit her.

She had no rights. No friends. No protection. She was locked in a room with a man who could do anything he wanted so long as she confessed what he thought was the truth, and those watching would do nothing to stop him.

"I want out of here," she said, pushing back her chair and coming to her feet. The muscles in her calves cramped and the pain almost brought her to her knees, but she stood her ground and gritted her teeth through the pain. "I want to know what you think I've done. I want an attorney. You can't keep me in here when I've done nothing wrong." Hysteria edged its way into her voice and she looked around the room, looking for some way to escape.

"Have a seat, Mrs. Huxley. Do you expect me to believe this act? That you could be married to a man like him and not have any idea the kind of hell he brought down on people's lives?" Agent Brennan's voice never rose, as if he was used to watching a woman approaching breakdown status.

Sophia stared at him in shock and answered before she could think better of it. "Of course I know the kind of hell he brought down on people. He was a master at manipulation, at mind games, until you no longer recognized yourself anymore and his truths became your reality. You see these two fingers?" she asked, holding up her right hand so the crooked appendages were easily seen. "He did this the day I told him I wanted a divorce. And then he held a knife to my throat and raped me while he told me he'd kill me if I ever tried to divorce him." She pulled down the collar of her shirt so he could see the faint scar where the knife had bit into her skin.

"As soon as I managed to crawl away and scramble to my feet I grabbed the rifle I kept by the door and held it on him until he left. But I never found the courage to file for divorce. And every day after I looked over my shoulder because I knew if I ever let my guard down he'd find some way to strike when I wasn't looking." She looked at her hand and flexed her fingers back into a fist. "I guess he found a way to strike back at me after all, because here I am. So you don't scare me, Agent Brennan. I've lived through the hell of Kane Huxley."

"It's an interesting story," he said. "And I have no doubt he would do something like that to his own wife. But it doesn't excuse the evidence that says you're as guilty as he was. Do you know how he died?"

Sophia just stared into the cold depths of Gabe Brennan's eyes and didn't answer. There didn't seem to be a point.

"Kane made a deal with the wrong man." He leaned back in his chair and steepled his hands across his stomach, as if they were just having a casual chat. "We'd deployed a team to Central America to destroy one of the largest drug labs in the world and disband the Ramos cartel. Huxley sold out the team so the soldiers were waiting for them, but the drug lord in charge decided to take Kane down with them instead of parting with the five-million dollar fee Kane had asked for."

"I don't know anything about this. About what he did," Sophia said again.

"You were married to the man. You shared his bed and his home. You can't tell me you didn't know what was going on." Gabe spread the file open and fanned the papers so they arced in front of her. "The evidence doesn't lie."

She barely glimpsed at the papers and kept her eyes steady on him. "Kane Huxley and I were married in name only," she said, feeling the humiliation creep up on her once again. Her eyes darted to the long expanse of glass—she could feel their gazes on her. "I barely saw him when we were married, and I only saw him twice in the three years after I told him to leave."

"Maybe so, but Kane has been an agent within the CIA for a dozen years. Surely you became suspicious of his behavior during that time."

SINS AND SCARLET LACE

Her fists pounded down on the table, sending some of the papers to the floor. "I was too busy trying to outguess his moods and keep my sanity," she screamed, her voice breaking again. "Do you know what it's like, Agent Brennan, to be young and confident and on top of the world, and then have that world shattered in the blink of an eye? Until you have no self-confidence or self-respect because someone is in your face day after day, listing your faults and implanting new ones in your mind just because they like to fuck with you?"

Tears coursed down her cheeks, but she ignored them, just as she ignored the brief glimpse of pity she saw in Gabe Brennan's eyes. She didn't need anyone's pity. She needed her freedom. It was all she'd wanted since she'd made the mistake of tying herself to Kane.

"You're an accountant at a very large and prestigious firm, Mrs. Huxley," Gabe went on, changing the subject abruptly. "The money your husband collected for selling out the agents had to go somewhere. Your firm moves millions of dollars all over the world every day. It wouldn't be hard for you to do the same for your husband."

"You wouldn't even suggest that if you had any clue what our marriage was like. Kane didn't talk business with me. He could barely stand to be in the same room with me."

"Beg your pardon, but why did he marry you in the first place?"

"I was a contest. Nothing more than a prize to be won. And I played easily into his hands. Let's just say I have bad judgment when it comes to men."

Gabe leaned forward and separated several documents from the pile, pushing them in front of her. Her eyes widened in horror as she recognized her signature neatly below her husband's.

"These are documents for six different bank accounts," Gabe said, spreading them out so she could see.

Sophia glanced at them quickly and felt the noose

tightening around her neck. She shook her head in denial. It looked like her signature, but she knew she'd never signed these documents.

"Where's the money, Mrs. Huxley?"

Her gaze shot up to meet his stone cold glare, but she didn't flinch.

"I don't have any money, Agent Brennan. I never did."

She could sense his frustration, but she could just as easily see the wheels turning in his head, looking for ways to trap her in a lie.

"The signature on those bank accounts tells me differently," he said. "I'm willing to bet your accounting background would make it next to impossible for you not to keep printed records somewhere of every transaction that came in and out of those accounts. Technology can't always be trusted, can it? Which is why agents are turning your house upside down as we speak. They're talking to friends and your employer. They'll be taking apart your office and the computer you use there. We'll find it, Mrs. Huxley."

Nausea roiled through her stomach as he so easily destroyed her life. She'd have nothing left once they were finished with her. Her firm would dismiss her at the first hint of scandal. She didn't have many friends left, mostly acquaintances, and her parents were no longer living. If she didn't have a job, she could kiss her house and everything she'd worked for goodbye.

"Whoever cleared the money from those accounts wiped all traces of where it came from. And if we can find out which terrorist cells funded you and your husband's very lucrative side business, then we can track them down and bring justice to all of the agents whose covers have been compromised, and we can hopefully save the lives of dozens of others. We have no idea how many identities have been sold, or who is in immediate danger."

Sophia didn't want to look at the condemnation in Gabe Brennan's face any longer. She didn't want to see his proof. She knew Kane had done this to her, had betrayed those agents and cost them their lives.

"You're going to want to help us here, Mrs. Huxley. Your husband is dead. There's no one left to take the fall except for you."

Sophia closed her eyes and didn't respond. They'd made up their minds. Tears leaked from the corners of her eyes and trailed down her cheeks. The last time she'd cried had been the day Declan had told her he no longer loved her, but she couldn't seem to stop the tears now. She was too tired and weariness had settled deep in her bones.

"There's nothing more I can tell you." The silence that followed was heavy with tension and she finally opened her eyes to face what was to come.

"Have it your way. You'll be taken to lockup until the teams have finished searching your home and office. You could be there days or weeks, it's anyone's guess, but I do know you'll be getting a visit from Doctor Renfro within twenty-four hours. He's got this nifty injectable serum that makes people want to talk. If I were you, I'd come clean before that visit. I hear it's not a pleasant treatment."

The scrape of his chair across the concrete floor was like nails across a chalkboard and sent shivers down her spine. She'd lived on fear for five years, looking over her shoulder for Kane to make good on his threats, but it was nothing compared to the fear she felt now.

Agent Brennan gathered the papers—the papers that proved her guilt—and put them back in the file folder.

"I didn't see any next of kin in your file," Gabe said as he walked to the door. "And your name has already been splashed across the media. One of your co-workers enjoyed his fifteen minutes of fame a little too much. Do you have anyone you want us to contact? Someone to attend to any personal matters while you're visiting us?"

"Declan MacKenzie."

Sophia had no idea why it was his name that came to mind first, or why she thought he could or would help her now. Kane had delighted in telling her how many women Dec had had over the years and how many they'd shared together. But she'd learned to recognize Kane's lies the longer he spouted them. Declan was a bastard for sure, but deep down he had an honor and character that Kane would never possess. And she believed if she called on him for help now he'd come just because his sense of right and wrong and his honor would let him do no less.

Agent Brennan stared at her with an unreadable look on his face, but she could have sworn she saw a glimmer of surprise in his eyes.

"Call Declan MacKenzie," she said again, her voice stronger this time. "He used to be military. Special Forces. I don't know if he still is, but he is—was—my friend. He's the only person I have left to call."

She had to believe that everything would be okay. The truth would come out and everyone would see that she was innocent. That Kane Huxley had been a monster to the core. Dec would believe her. He knew her too well to think she could ever become a traitor.

"That can be arranged, Mrs. Huxley." Agent Brennan stepped out of the room and closed the door quietly behind him, and for the first time since her wedding night she had hope that everything would be all right.

She waited several minutes for someone to come get her and take her to her cell, but the minutes dragged on and the lethargy in her muscles had her dozing. The door didn't make a sound when it opened again, but the hairs stood up on her arms and a feeling she hadn't felt in a long time settled low in her gut. She knew he'd be standing there before she lifted her head.

The sight of Declan MacKenzie sent emotions rioting through her body—relief, longing, embarrassment and sorrow. Her marriage to Kane had destroyed part of her, though she'd been scraping and fighting to repair it since she'd separated from him. Kane had taken every opportunity to play psychological games, until she'd started believing the things he'd said.

Dec looked the same at first glance. He was still an intimidating figure—it was just something about the way he carried himself. He moved like a big jungle cat and had the grace of a dancer. His dark hair was shorter than when she'd last seen him—buzzed close to the scalp—and his beard was the same length, though she could still see the jagged scar that followed the line of his jaw. The occasional strand of silver in his hair was new.

"Dec," she said, the chair tipping over as she got up hastily. Her legs shook and she felt the tears well in her eyes. She'd never seen anything that looked as good as him standing there, and she rushed toward him, throwing her arms around him.

"God, Dec. I'm so sorry." The tears finally let loose, but only because she wasn't alone any longer. "I didn't have anyone else to call. Thank you for coming. Thank you," she repeated again and again.

"Sophia." His lips glanced off her temple as he said her name and then he took a step back, so she was no longer touching him.

It was then she realized the obvious. Other than the brief glance of his mouth on her skin he hadn't touched her in any way. His hands were still in the pockets of grey dress slacks and the sleeves of his white dress shirt were rolled up to show his sinewy forearms. Tension coiled in the broad muscles of his chest and shoulders and the scar along his cheek turned white as he clenched his jaw.

Her eyes widened as she saw the weapon holstered at his side and she took a step back. And then another. Her gaze flew back to his and then she knew. He was one of them, and he'd never believe her over the evidence that was so damning. For the second time in her life, Declan was going to destroy her, and she had no one to blame but herself. The old saying was true—fool me once, shame on you... The only fool in the room was her.

"The only way I can help you is if you tell the truth."

His familiar voice slid across her skin like silk and she had to remind herself to breathe. This wasn't the same man who'd once loved her. Who'd used that same voice to tempt and seduce. This man was her enemy. And she'd brought him right to her door.

"Go to hell, Declan MacKenzie. And take your evidence with you."

CHAPTER THREE

Six Months Later...

Sophia stared at the empty house she'd once shared with her husband and realized she didn't have one good memory of the place in the five years she'd lived there.

She'd lived there mostly alone as Kane hadn't wanted much to do with her once he'd married her, but the times he had come home... she shuddered and reminded herself it was best not to go there. He'd only touched her twice during their marriage. The first time on their wedding night. The second time when she'd told him she wanted a divorce. Neither experience had been pleasant.

The boxes on the table still needed to be taped, so she found the roll and closed them up methodically, labeling each one as she went. She'd been lucky to find a buyer for the house, even if she'd had to take a lower offer. The important thing was that she had enough to pay off her debt and just enough to see her through until she found a new job.

If she found a new job. No one wanted to hire a criminal. And trying to explain to would-be employers that it had all been a misunderstanding got her nowhere.

It had been months since they'd cleared her of the charges of conspiring with her husband in treasonous acts, conspiracy to murder, and laundering half a billion dollars that was doused in the blood of some of America's finest.

The government had no proof and she'd passed their tests, so after weeks of being contained in one small room with nothing more than a bed and her own company, they'd finally had to let her go. But not before she'd lost her job and had most of her assets seized.

The bank had called the loan on her house so she'd had no choice but to sell. She could only be grateful her mother had left her the little house she'd owned up until her death a couple of years before. Her father had passed away the year after she and Kane had married, and she didn't have any other family. That house was her saving grace and the only place she had left to go. If she was lucky, she could find a job as a waitress or as a cashier somewhere. She couldn't afford to be picky.

The sound of a car pulling into her driveway had her grabbing for the rifle she habitually kept by the door. It had certainly worked at chasing off Kane, and it worked even better on nosy reporters. Someday she hoped they'd get the hint and leave her alone.

But when she stepped onto the front porch with the rifle in her hand, the last person she expected to see was Declan. He got out of the black Jeep and raised his brows when she pointed the rifle in his direction.

"Are you going to shoot me?" he asked.

"I'm undecided. Are you here to take me back in?"

He sighed and she realized he looked tired, but she knew looks could be deceiving. She'd lived with a consummate actor, and as far as she was concerned Declan and Kane had been cut from the same cloth. His gaze landed on the Sold sign that was staked in her front yard.

"I'm glad you were able to sell. I wish you'd let me help you."

"You had your chance. You'd be the last person I'd

take help from. What do you want, Dec?"

"I needed to see you," he said.

The gun wavered in her hands and she lowered it some so he wouldn't notice how the words affected her. There was nothing left between them but bitter memories and regret.

"You've seen me. Now leave."

"Soph, I need to explain why I was there. Why I had to be so hard on you."

"I don't want to hear explanations. I want you to leave. I can tell by looking at you that you feel guilty." Bitterness tinged her voice even though she tried not to let him see how betrayed she felt. "There's no reason to feel guilty. You had a job to do, and we're no longer the people we used to be. No harm, no foul. You only took part in destroying my life. Again."

"I was going to ask you to marry me when I came home from that last mission," he said.

She sobbed out a laugh and felt the hysteria bubbling inside of her. "Don't you dare say that, you bastard. Not after all this. The least you owe me is honesty. I suppose next you'll tell me you sent me away and told me you didn't love me anymore for my own good."

"I thought I was protecting you. The last thing I wanted was for you to be dragged into this kind of life, where someone will kill you just as easily as they blink. It's not what you deserved. I know you probably don't believe me."

Tears ran down her face freely now and he was just a blur in her vision. She leaned against the porch column as all her strength seemed to drain from her bones.

"No, I don't believe you. You killed me that day, Dec. The scars you left on me are just as permanent as the one on your face."

She meant to hurt him, to lash out, but he didn't even flinch at her words.

"I know, and it was too late to do anything about it by

the time I realized I'd made the biggest mistake of my life. You were already in love with Kane and I'd lost my chance."

"I was never in love with Kane," she screamed. "I was just a mark to him. Did you know he romanced me like you did? What did you tell him about us? He knew how to get to me. How to make me believe that there were other men like you out there. It didn't matter that the physical connection wasn't there. I told myself he was a good man and that's all I could really ask for. And I decided that if he was a good man then I could probably grow to love him one day."

She swiped at the tears on her face, clearing her vision, but Declan still stood in front of her as stoic as ever. She wasn't sure he was capable of emotion. He'd proven that when he'd relentlessly questioned her for weeks to try to prove her guilt.

"He hated you," she said. "Did you know that?"

Declan's voice was tight when he answered. "I got the idea once we started going through his personal belongings."

"I didn't realize how deep his jealousy went. Hell, I didn't even know the two of you were friends until I saw you at the wedding. Stupid me."

"Not you, Sophia. Never you. He fooled us all."

"He raped me on our wedding night." The words came out of nowhere, and she wasn't even sure she'd said them aloud, but the stiffening of Declan's posture and the barely restrained fury on his face assured her she had. "And the whole time he held me down—" She paused to gasp in a breath through her sobs. "The whole time he made me say your name. He made me think of you. So I'd remember the choice I'd made, and that I'd never have you again."

"Sophia—"

He took a step forward, but she lifted the gun again, her hand steadier this time. "No," she yelled. "Stay right where you are."

SINS AND SCARLET LACE

Declan moved back to where he was, but she could tell he wasn't happy about it.

"He liked to play games. To mess with my mind until I was jumping at shadows." Her laugh was bitter. "I guess it's what all of you super spies are good at. But I'm nobody's doormat. Not yours or Kane Huxley's. But God, it was a relief when they knocked on my door and told me he was dead. I thought everything would finally be okay."

"None of it matters now," she said. "What matters is that he was a monster and I'm going to be paying the consequences of marrying him for the rest of my life. You and Kane are the same person in my eyes. You manipulate and make decisions for people without care or thought to their feelings. Maybe it's your line of work, or maybe it's just your basic character. Who the hell knows? But I know I'm purging my life of the Kane Huxleys and Declan MacKenzies in my life. Now get off my property."

He stayed exactly where he was and kept his gaze steady on her. "You loved me once, Sophia. And no matter what I told you then, I loved you too. That never changed, and I hated myself for having to hurt you. But I thought it would keep you alive. You can try to tell yourself you hate me, and God knows I have a lot to answer for, but you know what we had was never a lie."

She pulled the trigger and felt the kick of the rifle in her hands. A plume of dust went up at Declan's feet, but he didn't try to dodge or duck out of the way.

"I said get off my property."

He nodded, but she could see the understanding and sorrow in his eyes, and she wanted nothing more than to run into his arms, just to be held and told everything would be okay. It had been so long since she'd been held. But she couldn't take a chance on him again. Not after he'd let her be taken to that cell.

"You've forgotten one thing, Soph. I know you didn't take the money, but that doesn't mean others think the same way. Until it's found, you'll always be a target for someone. Who's going to protect you if not me?"

"I can protect myself just like I am now."

"You're crazy if you think I'm going to let you deal with it alone. I'll be here if you need me. That's a promise."

"I needed you once, Declan. Those days are over."

He nodded again and smiled sadly. "I'm glad he didn't kill your spirit." He opened the door of the Jeep. "It was what I loved most about you."

Sophia waited until he backed out of the drive and rode out of her life before she went back inside and closed the door softly behind her. She dried her tears and went back to packing her things. It was her life, and it was time she started living it.

CHAPTER FOUR

Present Day...

The Virginia heat rolled in visible waves across the land and the humidity was thick enough to drink.

Declan stayed crouched in the gulley to the side of the small farmhouse Sophia had moved into more than a year before. White paint peeled from the wooden sides and the roof looked like it needed to be repaired in places. Sagging steps led up to a tiny front porch and the only sign of life was the wilting fern that hung from a hook.

He'd watched her struggle and try to put her life back together for the last year and a half, and he'd helped when and wherever he could, though he knew she wouldn't thank him for it if she ever found out he'd been behind the receptionist job she'd gotten at a local insurance agency. She was virtually unemployable anywhere else and everyone knew her name after it had been splashed across the national news. He'd left money anonymously and kept watch from afar, even though his first instinct was to pound down her door and make her listen to reason. He'd known she'd be in danger from the moment they'd discovered the money was missing, and he'd known this day was coming.

Dec ignored the bugs and the way his clothes stuck to his skin—he'd been in worse conditions—and he crept toward the house until he could see the back door. He was dressed for hunting—black BDUs and night vision goggles. The moon was barely a sliver in the night sky and the house was completely dark, inside and out, but he'd been trained to see danger in the shadows. He'd been doing it most of his life.

Sophia's time was limited. His gut had been screaming to get her out and to safety for a while now, but something had changed over the last couple of weeks and the danger had escalated. After months of waiting, someone was finally coming after the money and it was obvious they didn't care what happened to Sophia in the process. He had no idea why they'd waited so long. Maybe because they thought she'd relax her guard or the CIA would stop keeping tabs on her as time went on, but the fact was someone wanted that money and Sophia was in the line of fire.

It hadn't taken long for him to spot the men tailing her around town. They'd been good, but he was better. They didn't move like military or operatives—more like mercenaries—but they at least had the presence of mind to try and blend into the town Sophia had moved to. It hadn't taken him a second to see the weapons hidden under their clothes or the way they casually watched from the shadows as Sophia ran errands or went to and from work. From the number of weapons they were packing, it looked like their orders were to do whatever was necessary to get the information they needed, and that scared the hell out of him.

Sweat snaked from his temples into his beard, but he didn't move a muscle as he watched and listened to his surroundings. Sophia's house sat on a wide expanse of land filled with trees and overgrown brush, and she had no neighbors for miles. The house had belonged to her mother and it had been left to Sophia after her death. It was the perfect place for the solitude she craved. And the perfect place for an ambush.

There were more than half a dozen men he'd counted, rotating in shifts and changing their locations for surveillance. He'd found a couple of campsites less than a mile in each direction from the house, but Sophia had been clueless to the danger. He hadn't seen her watching over her shoulder or taking extra precautions at night, which meant she was finally beginning to feel safe. He hated that he had to destroy her illusion.

Dec blended with the trees as he made his way toward the back of the house. The back door was exposed, and he'd have to move quickly so he wasn't seen. He let the thin metal tool drop from his sleeve into his hand and then he moved like the ghost he was often compared to.

The pick was in the lock and the door was opening in only a matter of seconds, and he shook his head at the quality of her security. He slipped inside and crouched down low, closing the door and locking it behind him. He waited as the house adjusted around him, and he listened to make sure everything sounded as it should.

The house smelled of her—like lemons and honey and something a little darker, a little sexy. His body tightened instantly, his cock swelling behind his zipper as the familiar scent assaulted his senses and seemed to say, Oh, yeah. I remember her. Mine. She'd always had that effect on him, from the first moment he'd laid eyes on her, and he could no more control his body's reaction to her now than he could then.

The clock on the oven glowed eerily green, and he pushed the night vision goggles to the top of his head, letting his eyes adjust to the little bit of light given. It was enough, and he could easily see the layout of the house. It also helped that he'd walked through it several days before while she'd been at work.

The house wasn't large. One main living area that opened into a kitchen the size of a closet. One bathroom.

And one bedroom. The air was stifling inside the house, and he knew she wouldn't waste money she didn't have by running the air conditioner. The windows were cracked about an inch high, but it wasn't enough to let a cooling breeze through.

His steps were silent as he edged into the bedroom and saw her lying in the middle of the double bed—white sheets twisted beneath her lush and naked body—beads of perspiration coating her skin.

She'd been beautiful when he'd met her at nineteen. But at thirty, she had a woman's body that left him speechless. Her hips were softer, rounder, and her breasts fuller. The only thing she'd changed was that she'd let the soft golden curls grow back between her thighs.

Sophia had always reminded him of a woman born in the wrong decade. She had the looks of a 1940s movie star. Her hair was a pale golden blond that waved in soft curls around her face, and he remember the soft thatch between her thighs was a shade darker—the color of honey—and what it hid tasted just as sweet. Her brows were thick and arched and she had a tiny mole just above her lip that had once driven him crazy with lust.

He had every intention of rekindling their past and righting the wrongs he'd done. But first he had to keep her alive.

Dec sat on the side of the bed and quickly placed his hand over Sophia's mouth before she could scream. Her eyes snapped open and the whites of her eyes seemed bright in the darkness. She struggled against him, but he had her pinned, and he leaned down quickly to try and alleviate her fears.

"It's me, Soph. Calm down." His words were barely discernable. Less than a whisper in her ear. "You need to do what I say, and do it now. You're in danger. Do you understand?"

He felt a shudder of breath leave her body, and she relaxed against him as recognition took hold.

"Dec?" she said.

"Get up and get clothes on. No lights. We don't have much time."

He was just about to move from the bed when he heard the familiar sound of a revolver cocking and felt the circle of metal pressed against his chest. He stilled instantly, and watched as her eyes narrowed in anger.

"You're the only person I see here that's a danger to me. Get out of my house." Her words were just as quiet as his had been.

"I'm getting damned tired of you threatening to shoot me. This is no time for games. We can play cops and robbers later. I'll even let you use my cuffs."

"I'm going to enjoy killing you. I've certainly thought about it enough."

She pressed the barrel harder against his chest and he almost grinned. Sophia had always had a dynamite temper once she got riled. There was nothing that made him harder faster than seeing that fighting spark in her eyes.

"You won't have to worry about killing me if you waste any more time. The men circling your house will take care of it for you. Of course, they won't stop at killing me. They'll probably kill you too."

"How do I know you're here to help me instead of screwing me over again? It's not like you to slum with a traitor. I wouldn't want you to ruin that infamous MacKenzie reputation."

Dec felt his jaw clench and his temper burn on a slow boil. If she'd had any idea how difficult it had been for him to go into that interrogation room and face her like that then she wouldn't be near so quick to bust his balls.

They'd had to physically restrain him when they'd brought her in that day, and the only reason he'd been allowed to stay and observe was because he'd promised he would stay out of the way and try to use his connection to her to help the investigation. No one had known he'd been sick as a dog after they'd finally taken her away, or that he'd bribed everyone he could find to make her time there as comfortable as possible, including the doctor who was supposed to administer the drugs and get her confession. It had been a damn good thing Gabe Brennan had been on his side, otherwise things could have gone very, very badly.

His smile was sharp as a blade and he moved closer, forcing her to change the angle she was holding the weapon. He leaned down to her ear again and felt her sudden intake of breath.

"Now, sweetheart. You're going to hurt my feelings. The only plans I have that involve screwing you over have us both naked and me sliding hard and hot inside of you." He let his gaze roam down her body and watched her nipples harden into tight peaks. "It looks like we're halfway there."

He knew she was going to strike before she did, and his fingers were already pressing down on the pressure points in her wrist. She dropped the gun as her hand went numb and gasped as she tried to move out of his hold.

"Over my dead body."

"We could be closer to that than you think. We've already wasted too much time. This fight can wait for another day."

He moved away from the bed and went to her drawers, quickly tossing panties and a bra, shorts and a thin cotton tank top onto the bed.

They both heard the slightest scrape coming from the front of the house, and that's all it took to spur her into action. She quickly put on the clothes and Declan pulled the gun from the small of his back, moving to look out the window. The side of the house had good coverage from trees, and he didn't see any of the mercenaries lurking outside. That more than anything told him he wasn't dealing with professionals.

Sophia grabbed an old pair of tennis shoes from beneath the bed, slid them onto her feet, and then grabbed the cameo necklace that belonged to her grandmother, fastening it quickly around her neck. He'd never seen her without it, and he'd always thought it suited her.

He motioned her over and she came immediately, and he was glad she at least trusted him enough to get her out of this.

The window was already open about an inch, and he slid it the rest of the way up, thankful it was a metal frame instead of one of the old wooden ones that would be swollen from the humidity and hard to budge. The window was narrow and he had to twist his body to squeeze through, but he did so quickly and efficiently, dropping silently to the ground. He kept low, not wanting to make himself a target by standing next to the white of the house, and he motioned for Sophia to follow.

Her eyes were wide and frightened and her hand shook slightly as she grabbed the edge of the windowsill. He waited until she was perched on the edge and then reached out and lifted her the rest of the way down. He didn't bother setting her on her feet, but instead hugged her against him protectively and ran. His steps were light, never making a sound, and Sophia stiffened in his arms as muffled curses came from inside her home once they figured out she was gone.

"She's gone," a deep voice called out. "Find her."

Lights flipped on throughout the house, and Dec pulled up behind a tree before looking back at the house. He counted at least six men walking through, tossing her mattress to look under the bed and pulling out the clothes in her closet to make sure she wasn't hiding inside. The sounds of shattering glass had her flinching in his arms and he held her closer, wanting to make them pay for destroying what little she had left.

These guys definitely weren't professionals. If he'd been going in with a team in a similar situation he would've cut the breakers and they all would have been outfitted with night vision.

He started running again, one hand holding his gun and the other holding on to Sophia. Her nails bit into his shoulders as she held on for dear life, and he could feel the thud of her heart against his own.

The layout of the land was visible in his mind and he knew they were getting close to another gulley. It was more of a dried up riverbed, but there was a good deal of brush and trees sprouting from the banks, making it the ideal hiding place.

He slowed his steps when the ground beneath consisted more of dead leaves and sticks than damp grass, moving with care so no sounds could be heard. He pushed aside the foliage and set Sophia on her feet, pressing down on her shoulders so she'd know to get low.

He followed her down and leaned close. "Stay here," he whispered.

"Where are you going?" She grabbed at his shirt to keep him from pulling away.

"To find out who sent them and what they want."

"Don't be stupid. There are a lot of men in there, and only one of you. Let's just get out of here."

"If you keep talking like that, I'm going to start to think you care."

"If you die being a macho jerk then I won't have anyone to help me escape."

"You're all heart, baby."

"At least I'm not all asshole," she hissed.

Dec shook his head as his dick spiked at the snap in her whispered voice.

"Baby, these yahoos will be a walk in the park. I'm used to dealing with the worst of humanity on a daily basis. I know what I'm doing."

"Fine. If you're not back here in ten minutes then I'm running like hell and not looking back. I've learned the hard way that the only one looking out for me is me."

Dec stared hard at her as he heard the shout go out behind him to start searching the grounds. She was in a good location and they'd never find her in the dark. But he needed answers and the only way to do that was to go get them.

"Stay low and don't make any sound. Don't even rustle the branches around you. I'll be back in half an hour."

He unclenched her fingers from his shirt, and then before he could talk himself out of it, he pulled her closer. The sizzle of heat between them was electric, a pulsing energy, the same as it had been so many years before. She was his soul, the one woman put on this Earth for him, and it was time to reclaim what belonged to him.

"Don't kiss me," she said, reading his mind. "It'll only make things worse."

"Sweetheart, I've got to disagree with you there. But we can argue about it later."

He turned his back on her and ran towards the shadows. The need for the hunt pounded in his lungs and beat through his blood. The sooner he took care of the danger that threatened his woman, the sooner he could claim what was his.

CHAPTER FIVE

It didn't take Declan long to circle around and head off the men as they made their way across Sophia's property. It was a large area to cover, and they'd spread themselves too thin, each man taking a different direction.

He could've heard the first man coming from a mile away. He wasn't even trying to be quiet as he kicked leaves and branches out of the way. Dec moved in behind him and snapped his neck quickly, the familiar scent of death permeating the air as he laid the man gently on the ground and moved toward the next one.

He'd only counted half a dozen men, but there was always the chance more could've been waiting in the wings. He hunted with a single goal in mind—to terminate any threats to Sophia.

He dealt with each man the same way as the first, until he got to the last. The man in front of him must have had a bad feeling because he let out a low whistle, a signal to the others, and no one answered him back. He stopped in his tracks, his weapon held at the ready, and he listened for movement. He never heard Dec come up behind him.

Dec kicked out at the man's knees, and the sickening crunch of snapping bone and cartilage had him crying out in pain as he fell to the ground. Dec followed through with a series of hits that caused numbing in the arms, and the weapon that had been in the mercenary's hand dropped with a soft thud into the leaves.

"Who sent you?" Dec asked, gripping the man by the hair and forcing him to look into his face.

"Fuck you." The man glared daggers at Declan, already seeing his death, and he spat on the ground at his feet.

"I'll pass. You're in need of a bath." Dec's grip tightened on the man's hair and he pulled the Ka-Bar from his boot, watching the man's eyes widen at the sight of the sharp blade. "I'll ask you again. Who sent you?"

Dec brought the knife to the man's throat, nicking it just enough for the coppery scent of blood to fill the air. "Your friends are dead. It's just you and me now, so you might as well tell me what you know. I'm willing to let you live so you can take a message back to your boss."

"He'll kill me faster than you will," he spat. "You might as well make it quick."

"Oh, believe me when I tell you I can make you live for a long time with the things I'll do to you. You'll only be wishing for death."

Whatever the man saw in Dec's eyes must have convinced him of the truth because his lips trembled with fear and the sickly scent of urine surrounded them.

"I don't know his name," the man said.

Declan pressed harder with the knife and the man cried out in protest. "Honest, I don't. We get our orders though an encrypted email account and then when the job is done, money shows up in our accounts. It's all electronic."

"What were the instructions for the girl?"

"To find out where the money is and to do whatever it took to make her talk."

"And once she told you where the money was?"

"Elimination."

"You've been very helpful," Dec said, knowing the feeling would be coming back to the man's arms soon. He swiped the blade quickly across his throat and moved out of the way before the spray of blood reached him.

Eliminate all threats to Sophia. That was his mission, and he wasn't going to veer from that path.

He pressed the button on his watch so it glowed, and he winced as he saw his time was almost up to get back to Sophia before she took off. She'd do it too, the stubborn wench. Dec took off at a run and just made it back to where Sophia was hiding when he heard the sound of a vehicle pulling into the drive of her house.

"Time to go," he said, pulling her from her crouched position behind the brush. "We're not out of this yet. It looks like the backup team has arrived."

The glare of headlights cut through the darkness and he watched as a cargo van skidded to a stop. Two men jumped out, weapons at the ready, and headed straight into the house. Dec cursed silently at his miscalculations. These men hadn't been following Sophia through the week. He would have seen them. But they'd been somewhere close and had been assigned some other task.

"Can you run?" he asked.

"As far as it takes."

"Follow me. Take the steps I take. We can't afford for you to have a broken ankle."

She nodded and he pushed the rest of the way through the brush and out of the gulley until they were on flatter land. And then they ran.

It took less than twenty minutes for the glow of fire to reach above the treetops, and Sophia reached out and grabbed his arm, pulling him to a stop. Her breath was labored and she bent over so her hands rested on her knees and she sucked in great lungfuls of air.

Dec stood silent and watched as the sky glowed bright with the haze of orange flames. Black smoke roiled in heavy clouds and hung suspended, no breeze to move them along.

"Oh, God," Sophia said, her face wet with sweat and tears. "Oh my God. That's everything. It's all gone."

SINS AND SCARLET LACE

Her voice was barely a whisper, but every word sliced into him. She'd endured more than any woman should ever have to, and she had every reason to blame him. He'd been the one to send her away, to chase her into the arms of another man. But he'd had no choice. At least he thought he hadn't. And those choices were the reason she stood here now, devastation etched on her face.

But after watching men who'd become his friends get blown to hell and back, he knew he could never have a normal life. Never have a wife or children without bringing them into harm's way. Because those men—his friends—had died because of who Declan was. Even during his Special Forces days he was being trained for deep cover within the CIA, and he'd had to make a choice. But the thing about choices was they had a snowball effect, and Sophia had been the one to suffer.

"Soph," he said, putting his hand on her shoulder. "I'm sorry, baby."

She shrugged him off, her gaze never wavering from the glow. "I don't need your pity," she said, her voice husky with tears. "Just get me out of here and back into town so I can figure out how to put my life together again."

"That's easy enough," Dec said, narrowing his eyes at the stubborn tilt of her chin and the blaze of anger in her eyes. "Because if you think for one second I'm going to let you out of my sight while these bastards are after you then you're out of your mind."

"You've been the catalyst to everything that has ever gone wrong in my life, Declan. Quite frankly, I'd rather take my chances with these assholes on my own. I don't think I can survive any more of your help."

CHAPTER SIX

Sophia fought the tears as Declan's black Jeep sped out of Virginia toward D.C. She kept her gaze averted out the window and ignored the worried glances he kept sending her way.

God, what was she going to do? She literally had nothing but the clothes on her back—no I.D., or debit card, no car. And nothing left of her family except the cameo necklace that hung heavily around her neck. It was all gone.

If she didn't show up for work, she wouldn't have a job much longer either. Her tiny nest egg wasn't much of an egg at all, and she couldn't even put a deposit down on a new place to live. She was completely at the mercy of Declan MacKenzie. Until he decided it was time to push her away again.

The tension grew thicker between them the farther they drove, but she refused to answer his occasional questions. Curiosity did get the best of her though when Dec turned into the heart of D.C.

Her hand gripped at the door handle. She recognized the area well. It was where they'd taken her two years before to question her about her husband's activities, and she'd be damned if she'd go back there without a fight.

"Relax," Dec said. "I'm not with the CIA any longer."

SINS AND SCARLET LACE

"Excuse me if I don't give a shit. If you're not with the CIA, you're with someone else. You don't have it in you to get out of the game completely, and I can tell you right now I'll die before I go back into some concrete box. I want out of this car. Now."

His knuckles turned white on the steering wheel, but it was the only sign she could see of his own rising anger. He'd always been too good at hiding his emotions, to the point where she often wondered if he had any at all.

"That's not going to happen, sweetheart. If I'm going to keep that pretty ass alive, then you're going to follow my rules. And believe me, I have plans for that ass, so I want to take good care of it."

Heat rushed to her face and her nipples tightened, too sensitive as they rubbed against the thin fabric of her shirt. Liquid pooled between her thighs and she clamped her legs together to relieve the pressure. He'd always been able to make her body react, just with a look or the sound of his voice.

Damn him. She'd been fine before he'd shown up. Kane had damaged more than just her self-esteem during their marriage. He'd made her feel so sexually lacking and unappealing that she'd lost the ability to achieve climax—not with her fingers or the multitude of toys she'd tried. And she'd tried everything. The need for release was still there, and she could bring herself right to the edge of orgasm but never reach the pinnacle, and it would leave her dissatisfied and in pain for days. She guessed it was the female equivalent of blue balls.

She'd finally gotten to the point where she'd stopped trying, and eventually the need for sexual satisfaction had disappeared all together. But just being in the vicinity of Declan had nerve endings waking up she thought long dead, and already she felt the swollen slickness between her thighs and the painful ache in her breasts. And there would be no relief for it.

"You had your chance," she finally managed to say.

"It'll be a cold day in hell before you ever touch me again."

Dec checked the rearview mirror once and then slammed on the brakes, bringing the Jeep to a screeching halt in the middle of the highway. Traffic was light in the middle of the night, and the few cars on the road veered around them with a honk of the horn and the occasional rude gesture.

"What the—" before she could finish the sentence he had her seatbelt unbuckled and pulled her across the gearshift so she straddled his lap. There was no time to struggle or protest. His hand tangled in her hair and the other pressed at her hip. His body was hot and hard beneath her and his arousal pressed insistently against her mound.

She sucked in a sharp breath as his lips rose towards hers, and she knew there was no point in pushing him away. As much as she hated what he'd done to her, and as much as she hated herself for going liquid at his touch, she wanted this. Passion hadn't existed for her for more years than she cared to remember—not since the last time Declan had touched her.

"Don't do this, Dec," she panted even as her hands clutched his shoulders. "You're just trying to prove a point. It doesn't mean things will go back to what they once were."

"Whoever said I wanted things to be what they were?" he said, biting her bottom lip and absorbing her moan with the warmth of his tongue. "We're two very different people than we were then."

"Yeah, a traitor and a bastard," she sneered. "What the hell? Let's fuck. I don't know what I was thinking."

"You're going to piss me off if you keep calling yourself that."

"I notice you didn't dispute being called a bastard." Her laugh was harsh and she bit back at his own lips, tired of the direction the conversation was headed. "So what now? You've decided to believe me all of a sudden just so you can get in my pants? I've seen more effective pick-up moves."

"I always believed you."

"Sell it to somebody else, MacKenzie."

The low growl that rumbled in his chest tingled against her sensitive breasts, and she felt his anger and frustration as his hand tightened in her hair. He'd always had a thing about her hair—he liked to run his fingers through it and massage her scalp when they made love slow and easy, but he would wrap it around his fist and pull it tight while taking her hard and fast. She'd always liked that edge of pain, though she'd been too innocent and embarrassed at the time to ask him for more.

His mouth covered hers and reality faded. The occasional car speeding by and the blare of horns sounded distant in her ears. There was nothing but the familiar taste of the forbidden and the scent of her own desire. She was starved for him. Desperate to feel his own need powering over her.

He pushed his hips up, so the hard length behind his zipper pressed against the swollen flesh between her thighs, and she held onto his shoulders like a woman starved for touch and writhed against him.

Release was closer than it had been in a long time, and she searched for it. Yearned for it. But it was still just out of reach, and she screamed out in frustration as his erection pressed into her clit.

His hand skimmed up her ribs and wrapped around her breast, his thumb rubbing across the sensitive bud of her nipple. The sensations had gone past pleasure and rode the edge of pain. She knew she'd be feeling the heat for hours—days—and never find the fulfillment she craved. It seemed Kane's death hadn't released his hold over her.

"Enough," she said, pushing against his chest. Her face felt overheated and she was almost delirious with the need racing through her.

"It'll never be enough." His voice was raw with

unfulfilled desire, but he'd made his point. If they stayed together then this would happen again. And again.

She'd lost her damned mind. Before she could scramble out of his lap he plucked her up and back into her own seat, then reached over and buckled her seatbelt. He threw the Jeep in drive and pressed his foot to the accelerator and they rejoined the few cars on the highway. The whole event had only lasted a few minutes, but now her body was burning for something she knew she couldn't have. Damn Declan MacKenzie.

Declan cursed himself for his lack of control as he turned onto 7th Street. His control in high-tension situations was something he was known for, but if the former agents who'd been under his command could see him now, they'd probably die laughing.

No other woman had ever been able to get to him like Sophia could. Between her smart mouth and the paradise he knew waited between her thighs, as soon as she got near he started thinking with the head below his belt instead of the one above his neck.

He checked his rearview mirror one more time and made another circle around the block. He hadn't noticed anyone following them out of Virginia, but he wanted to make sure he didn't inadvertently lead anyone to the front doors of MacKenzie Security either.

Dec watched Sophia out of the corner of his eye. Her back was ramrod straight and her arms were crossed protectively across her chest. She gazed straight ahead through the windshield and he could all but hear the internal tirade that was producing the fierce scowls on her face. He knew she hadn't come, even thought she'd been damn close. Sophia had never been the kind of woman to hold back sexually, and it hadn't been at all uncommon for her to come multiple times in a variety of ways. He'd felt her frustration as she'd ridden that edge, and he knew it was another hurdle they'd have to deal with.

He hit a button in the dash and a black chain link gate at the side of his building slid open, revealing a parking garage of sorts. There was nothing special about the building other than it was prime real estate—a two-story square block of grey concrete and stone that advertised a by-appointment-only financial service, and dark tinted bulletproof windows. A armored door led into a spacious lobby where an armed security guard and receptionist sat to ward off interested parties.

He turned into the drive and started the descent into the underground parking area, following the curved road down two full levels. There were several cars parked in the bays, but he rolled his eyes at the sight of the black and silver Audi Spyder that sat in the corner. Things were about to get interesting.

"I meant what I said." Her voice was cold enough to give him frostbite. "I won't go back in a cell."

He sighed and opened the car door. "No one is putting you in a cell, Soph. We're here to help you. Just remember that when you go in."

"Why do I get the feeling you're trying to warn me at the same time you're reassuring me?"

"I always said you were perceptive."

He led her over to an elevator and typed in a code that had a panel popping out of the wall. He placed his hand over the screen and felt it warm as it scanned his palm print for verification. The elevator doors opened and he waited for her to precede him just in case she decided to run. She had that look about her.

"Paranoid much?" she asked as he typed in another code before the elevator doors closed and began to rise.

"If you knew some of the people I've encountered over the last fifteen years, you'd have a true appreciation for my paranoia."

The elevator stopped one floor up and opened into a large control room. There were no windows since they were still underground and all of the screens on the wall were running a multitude of computer searches for different cases his teams were involved in.

A large conference table and chairs sat in the middle of the room and computer stations of various neatness levels faced the screens on the walls. There was also a sitting area to the left—bright red chairs and a matching couch surrounding a coffee table—and Dec felt Sophia stiffen the moment she noticed the others in the room.

He put his hand to the small of her back and felt the fine tremors shaking her body as she watched Gabe Brennan unfold from the chair and come to a standing position. His piercing gaze took in her appearance and the defiant expression on her face and his lips quirked in a smile of amusement.

Declan shook his head in warning at his friend. Gabe was a troublemaker to the fullest. He could read people at a glance—know their strengths and their weaknesses and how to manipulate them for his own purposes. It's what had made him such a great agent. It was what made him an even better agent now that he'd gone private like Declan, though Gabe's agency was based in London and he took international cases instead of dealing with domestic like Dec had chosen to do.

"Mrs. Huxley," Gabe said, just as he had so many months before. "It's good to see you."

She turned her cold stare toward Declan and he swore he felt his balls shrivel before she turned her gaze back to Gabe. "It's a pity the feeling isn't mutual."

Declan barely grabbed hold of her wrist before she pulled the gun from the small of his back.

CHAPTER SEVEN

Sophia felt the blood rush to her ears and her heartbeat slow to a dull thud as she faced down Gabe Brennan. Thought ceased to exist and she didn't even feel her hand reaching for Declan's weapon. All she knew was she'd never be a caged animal again, and she'd go out fighting instead of cowering in the corner like she had the last time Declan betrayed her.

Her hand wrapped around the warmth of the butt of the gun, but before she could pull it free Dec had her wrists wrapped securely in his grasp and he'd pulled her into his body in a hold that left no room for movement.

"Bad idea, sweetheart. At least wait to shoot him until we find out what he learned about the men chasing after you."

"Who said I was going to shoot him? You're the first on my list."

"You're a lot more violent than you used to be. Maybe you should stop wiggling before we give our audience a show that could make them blush."

She felt the steel length of his erection against her back and she stopped struggling.

"Pervert," she hissed, turning her head so the others couldn't read her lips. Her life had been on display enough over the last few months. She didn't need to add exhibitionism to her list.

Dec's lips touched her ear and his hot breath sizzled across her skin and through her nerve endings. "You never used to complain."

"Ease off, Dec," a feminine voice said.

Sophia felt Dec groan and she looked up to see the youngest MacKenzie scowling at her brother. Darcy hadn't changed much over the years, and it looked like she was still giving her brothers hell and taking names.

Darcy and Declan could have been twins, their coloring was so similar. Long black hair waved around an exotic face with high, slashing cheekbones and full lips. Her eyes were an electric shade of blue and they sparkled with a mix of good humor, mischief, and understanding.

"You don't want to get in the middle of this, Darce."

"Of course I do. Someone has to look out for Sophia. The men in this family have a tendency to steamroll whatever is in their way and not check for collateral damage." Darcy smiled at Sophia. "It's good to see you again, Soph. Though I'm sure you feel differently. Men can be assholes, so we women have to stick together."

"Is this bring your wife to work day?" Dec asked, turning to the man lounging on the couch. He tightened his hold around her waist when she tried to move away. "I must have missed the memo."

Brant Scott grinned and steepled his fingers over his hard stomach as he looked at his wife adoringly. His blonde hair was cut short and his face was stubbled with a couple of days worth of beard. He wore a weapon at his hip like the others, but there was an easy-going expression on his face that made him seem more approachable than the other two men in the room.

"What can I say? She can't bear to leave my side." He turned piercing green eyes in Sophia's direction and she was struck by how handsome he was. "We were supposed to leave for vacation last week, but Declan pulled us all in to help work your case."

SINS AND SCARLET LACE

"And now your part of the work is done and we're leaving tonight," Darcy said, glaring at Declan. "I'm terrified Brant's parents are going to call any minute and tell us to come get the kids. We have a one and a two year old," she explained to Sophia. "This is the first time we've gotten the chance to get away by ourselves since the oldest was born, and I'm getting my vacation. I love my children, but it's like living with small hurricanes. I'm still amazed our house hasn't crumbled around our ears."

"You got exactly what you deserved," Declan said, relaxing his hold on Sophia and leading her farther into the sitting room. "You were a nightmare as a child."

Sophia felt like she was trapped in her own hurricane. She wasn't sure where she was or what was going on, but she could feel the threat of danger breathing down her neck, and she didn't think it was the best time for a family reunion. The words trembled on the edge of her lips, but she wasn't able to get them out before Darcy's eyes lit with the fire of battle.

"Oh, really. Because it wasn't me that put those garden snakes in my backpack."

"No, but it was you who put itching powder in my jock strap."

"Ouch," Brant said, shaking his head at his wife. "That's harsh."

"You can't prove it was me," Darcy grinned at her brother. "And that was the best football game you ever played. You threw for four touchdowns."

"Jesus," Gabe said. "Why didn't you just let Sophia shoot me? Every time I walk into this office I get mixed up in some kind of MacKenzie family squabble. I'd like to get on a plane and fly back to London at some point today. I haven't slept in thirty-six hours."

"Can we get back to the part about me shooting you?" Sophia asked Gabe, pulling out of Declan's grasp and separating herself from the rest of the group. "It's the least you can do after letting my house get burned down."

"Holy shit. They burned down your house?" Darcy asked, shooting Declan a worried look.

"Finally," Gabe said. "We can get down to business. Somebody grab the lights."

Declan went to the wall panel and pushed the light switch all the way to the left so the lights dimmed to darkness, and Sophia watched in surprise as the walls turned to giant computer screens.

"We knew it was only a matter of time before someone came after the money," Gabe said.

"And just like I told you the day you brought me in, I don't have any money. I never had any money."

"And I believe you," he said, surprising her. "But the fact of the matter is someone used your name, your signature, and accounts tied to both you and your husband to hide millions of dollars. We think your husband withdrew the money and put it somewhere safe, intending to retrieve it again, but then he died and we don't know where he put it. We also found partial proof that he'd been keeping bidding records whenever he put a new agent on the auction block. More than likely the money and the rest of the records are all together. Maybe in a safe deposit box or a home safe?"

"You asked me those questions before. We didn't have a safe deposit box that I know of, and the safe we had in our house was searched by the assholes you had go through every inch of my house. I told you I only saw Kane twice the last three years of our marriage. The first time I didn't even know he'd been at the house until I found some things moved around in different places. He'd gone through my drawers and my jewelry box, but I didn't notice anything missing. He sent me a text with a picture of myself sleeping." She shuddered at the memory of how helpless she'd felt in that moment. He'd proven to her he could have hurt her any time he wanted.

"The last time I saw him was a few months before he died. He didn't bother to be subtle that time. When I came home from work he'd trashed the house. He was looking for something but couldn't find it. I don't know what. I held a gun on him until he left. I never saw him again."

"I remember," Gabe said, nodding. "We did our job, Mrs. Huxley. You're guilty until proven innocent. I don't care what anyone tells you."

"I still don't understand what any of that has to do with me," Sophia said, unable to hide the anger in her voice. "Kane got the luxury of dying. I'm the one who lost my job, my security, and now my home. I want out of this mess."

"That's why we're here," Declan said softly. "We can protect you and help right the wrongs that bastard did."

"You call him a bastard now because he turned traitor, but you called him friend all the years before," Sophia sneered.

"He was no one's friend. Just like he was never the husband you deserved."

Sophia sucked in a breath and felt her lungs burn the longer she held it in. She let it out slowly and her gaze iced over as she stared at Declan. "Maybe so, but he was the one who wanted me and I was stupid enough to believe him. Some of us want to be loved and live normal lives. Not everyone is cut out to be James Bond. I've been nothing but a pawn for both men I've ever had a relationship with, and I told you before I'd rather take my chances on my own. I trust myself. Not you, your family, or your friends. My life would be different if I'd never met you."

"That may be, but you can't change the past, sweetheart." She could hear the anger in his voice, but she didn't care. "Someone believes you have that money, and the speculation is more than enough to put you in danger. I'm going to protect you whether you want me to or not."

"I'm sure my heart should be all a-flutter over the caveman routine, but you're going to have to beat your chest and swing your dick around some other time."

Darcy snickered from the corner and then quickly covered it with a cough, and Dec's eyes turned a deep and stormy grey as he stared her down. But Sophia had never cowered in a man's presence, not even during the worst times of her marriage, and she wasn't about to start now.

"How did you know about the men coming after me?" she asked.

"We've had your email and banking accounts under surveillance in the hopes that someone would go fishing for the money," Declan said, freely admitting they'd invaded her privacy. "We got a red flag a couple of weeks ago, and I immediately went down to check it out. It didn't take me long to spot the men following you."

"I knew I was being watched. I could feel it," she admitted. "But I thought it was more of your goons. I know you've all been watching since the day you let me go."

"You knew someone was watching you, yet you continued to go on with your daily routine without taking the necessary precautions?" Dec asked, his voice nothing more than a growl.

"I had all the necessary precaution I needed pressed against your chest when you broke into my house. We both know if I'd wanted to pull the trigger I could have."

"I know I could paddle your ass for taking such stupid chances. You should have called someone to help."

"Yes, because my address book is just filled with contacts," she said. She looked back at Gabe. "Could you get on with it please? I'd prefer to leave while it's still dark outside."

Gabe's lips quirked but he did as she asked. "Dec got the flag on your accounts a couple of weeks ago, and we immediately looked at satellite imaging to see how many we were dealing with."

"They were mercenaries," Dec said, taking over. "Hired guns that were more muscle than brain. The last one I talked to said he didn't know the name of the person who hired them. It was all done electronically. The assignment would come in and when it was completed the money would show up in their bank accounts."

"I got partial identification through the satellite images," Brant said, standing up and going to the wall. He slid his fingers across the screen and two images came up. "We have Jimmy Gaines and Robert Slade. They don't have the smarts to pull off something like this alone. Their rap sheet is longer than my arm, and they've never been very good about covering their tracks. Former military. Dishonorable discharge for both." Brant crossed his arms over his chest as they all stared at the screen. "They have trouble following orders, but whoever they're working under this time scares them enough that they've kept their noses clean."

"Who else?" Dec asked.

"We also have Walter Dale. He's got a couple of assault charges in his file early on, but he's been clean for the last dozen years. Above average intelligence and good with electronics."

Sophia stared at the image on the screen. The man had longish dark blonde hair and dark brown eyes. His face was square and his shoulders were broad and muscular. He had the kind of looks some women might find attractive, but if it was her she would've taken one look into those soulless eyes and run the other direction.

"I don't recognize him," she said.

"We wouldn't expect you to," Dec said. "More than likely none of them have any connection to you or Kane. They're guns for hire. The only reason I recognize him is because we had a short conversation tonight. He was definitely the leader of the bunch. His instincts were sharper."

"Were?" Sophia asked. She felt the blood drain from her face at the thought of Declan taking such a chance. There'd been six of them, for God's sake.

"It was them or us, Soph. That's the first rule of war.

And I needed information."

Declan hated the look that came across Sophia's face when he'd admitted to killing the men sent to kill her. He'd never wanted her to see him as that person—the person he had to be when necessity called for it. It was just another reason he'd felt he had to push her away, and now here she was seeing it up close and personal.

She seemed to withdraw into herself even more, her arms crossed over her chest as if she were trying to ward off the cold.

Gabe grunted and turned back to the screen. "Did you arrange for a cleanup team to sweep the area?"

"There wasn't time," he answered. "They sent in a secondary unit about twenty minutes after the first. The house fire would have drawn local attention, so you can bet there's already an investigation underway. The authorities will think Sophia is either dead or she's been abducted, so we're going to have to keep a low profile from them as well. Maybe if we can make whoever's behind this think she's dead we can buy ourselves a little time."

"It'll be tricky," Brant said. "No one is going to give up that easily, and as long as they think there's a chance of her being alive and that she knows where the money is, then she'll be in danger. You could be looking at a long stretch underground."

"I'm willing to take the chance."

Brant and Gabe both nodded at his decision. What Dec wasn't saying out loud but the others understood was that he was going underground with Sophia and staying there until she was safe. Brant would take control of the D.C. branch of MacKenzie Security, and his brother, Cade, was already in charge of the Dallas branch. He trusted his family to keep things going and get the jobs they'd already been hired for done.

"Cal Colter and Archer Ryan are both off on assignment, so you need to get in contact and update both of them," he said to Brant.

Cal and Archer were two of his top agents and he wanted everyone to take extra precautions. Whoever was behind this was sharp enough with computers that it was possible Declan and the security firm he'd created could be compromised. No computer or security system was infallible. Not even his, though it was close.

"Close down the offices while you're on vacation. There's nothing else that's pressing at the moment. Make sure you pass the word to keep an eye out for breaches in the system."

"We can postpone the vacation if you need us to, Dec," Darcy said, coming up to him and putting her arms around his waist in a tight hug. She was a pain in the ass sometimes, but when it came down to it no one was more loyal to family than she was. "You don't have to do everything on your own. We'd help if you'd let us."

"I know you would, but I'd feel better if we shut down for a week or two. I want to see the kind of reach the person behind this has, and if he's as good at manipulating the systems and hiding his tracks as I think he is, I don't want to inadvertently put anyone in this office in danger."

"I'll let Cal and Archer know what's going on, but they'll probably both be another couple of weeks at least on their assignments," Brant said. "What are you going to do about the Dallas office?"

"The whole office is already in Colorado working on freeing those cult members. Things are tricky there, and last I heard from Cade they're trying to prevent another Jonestown. Max and Jade are working undercover inside. I'll fill Cade in when I can. I don't want to add to his worries."

"You're going to need help," Brant said. "You can't do

this on your own."

"I know, which is why I'm taking Sophia home to Surrender. I'd rather settle this on my own turf where I'm familiar with the surroundings. I've got the land and the resources to put up a fight if we need to."

"That's what you want?" Brant said, raising his brows in question.

"No, but if he's as strong of a hacker as I think he is I want to be prepared in case he runs down our location. Shane and his team are on leave, and I can have a few of them for backup in a couple of the empty cabins on my property. My cousin is the sheriff, so he can be on the lookout for trouble in town."

"You've forgotten one thing," Sophia said.

Declan could tell by looking at her that she was spitting mad and trying to rein in her temper. Jesus, he had it bad. One look at those pouty full lips and stubborn chin and he was hard enough to drive nails. Suddenly the decisions that had seemed so important years ago seemed like a mistake now. But he couldn't bear to lose anyone else because of who and what he was, and here he was dragging Sophia into the middle of games she didn't know how to play. Only this time there was no option for failure. He couldn't lose her like he'd lost his friends and the agents he'd known through the years. What was left of his soul would be completely destroyed.

"What's that?" he asked, knowing exactly what she was about to say.

"You've forgotten to ask me if this is what I want to do. I'm not an idiot. I realize I'm in over my head with whatever is happening here, and I'll take whoever you have to spare to protect me while I'm in hiding until this bastard is caught. But I'll be damned if I go anywhere with you."

"Too bad, sweetheart. I'm all you've got. What are you afraid of? That you'll take up where we left off while we were stopped in the middle of the highway? Don't worry, honey. I'm game if you are."

SINS AND SCARLET LACE

Her jaw tightened and he heard the barely audible growl of frustration in the back of her throat.

"This seems like a good time for me to make an exit," Gabe said, heading to the door. "You owe me one, my friend."

"More than one," Dec said. "I'll be there whenever you need me. Brant and Darcy will see you down."

"I don't know, Dec," Darcy said, biting her bottom lip with worry. "It seems like someone needs to think about what Sophia wants. I love you and all, but if she doesn't want to go with you then we shouldn't make her. Why don't you let her come with us?"

Dec gave his brother-in-law a look and Brant took the cue. "Come on, love. Our time here is done. I'm ready to see you in a bikini." He wrapped his arm around his wife's shoulders and herded her towards the elevator and Gabe.

"Don't you try to handle me, Brant Scott. I want to make sure Sophia's taken care of."

"She will be," Brant assured her. And then he whispered something in Darcy's ear that had Declan's eyes narrowing and his sister relaxing.

"Darcy," he called out. "Sophia is going to need some clothes and personal items. Can you drop them off before you leave for your trip?"

"Absolutely," she said, giving him a grin over her shoulder, laughter in her eyes. "I've got a company credit card, and I'm not afraid to use it."

Declan groaned as the elevator doors shut and turned to face Sophia. Only she was no longer in the room. No wonder Darcy had been laughing.

CHAPTER EIGHT

Sophia wandered through the large expanse of office space, marveling at the electronics that seemed to cover every surface. It was like being caught in the middle of a movie—spies and gadgets and farfetched plots—only she didn't know her lines.

She knew Declan wouldn't let her roam for long, but she'd had to get away. Being with him again hurt too bad, and she didn't think she was strong enough to take the kind of emotional pain again he'd given to her when he'd told her he didn't want her anymore. Not to mention her body felt like it was being flayed alive with the torture of unfulfilled desire.

A full kitchen sat on the other side of what she'd started calling the control room. It had state of the art appliances and it was obvious it was used as there was fresh coffee sitting in the pot. She opened the fridge and saw it was well stocked and her stomach growled in a reminder that she hadn't eaten a good meal in a long while. The one thing about living within her current budget was that she'd easily lost the extra ten pounds that had always been the bane of her existence. Not eating right would do that to a person.

"Go ahead and make yourself something to eat," Declan said from behind her.

SINS AND SCARLET LACE

She'd known he was there, could feel his presence as if he were already touching her. It had always been that way between them, as if they were connected in some cosmic way.

"I'd rather have a shower," she said, closing the refrigerator door. She was hungry, but her stomach was in knots and the fact she would have died if Declan hadn't come for her was starting to sink in. Keeping anything down would have been impossible.

"Are you going to be stubborn about this, Soph? I need to be able to trust you're not going to run off on your own and endanger yourself. Let me protect you."

"I don't really have a choice, do I? You made the decision for me and now I'm at your mercy."

"As long as you understand I'm not going anywhere, then we won't have a problem. You can use the bathroom in my suite. Darcy will be back with clothes in a few hours, so after your shower you probably need to get some sleep."

"Have you always been this bossy, or was I just that young when I knew you before?"

"Both," he said, his mouth quirking in a smile. "Come on. I'll show you where to get your shower."

Sophia stayed a few steps behind him as he went past a dining area. All she could think was that he was familiar and different all at the same time. He was broader through the shoulders than he'd been, as if he'd spent more time working out. She'd once known every inch of his body, and she'd thought she'd known his mind. Now she realized she'd known nothing.

He pushed at a seamless panel in the wall that opened up to reveal another area, and held the door open for her so she could step through. The room was one large, open space and Sophia immediately knew it belonged to Declan.

A small sitting area and television sat off to the left and a desk was pushed against the other wall. But it was the large bed that dominated the back of the room that had her pussy throbbing in an intense ache that had her biting her lip to hold back a moan.

Fortunately, Dec stayed by the door and watched her patiently. "The bathroom is just through that door. There's a robe hanging on the back for you to wear until Darcy gets here with your clothes. I'll make a couple of sandwiches so you'll have something to eat when you get out."

Her eyes were still glued to the bed, but she nodded quickly and waited till he left. He hadn't shut the panel door so she could find her way out again, and she let out a long, slow breath when she was finally alone.

She hurried into the bath and stripped out of her clothes. The shorts had a tear in them—they must have gotten snagged on something while they were running—and the shirt had grass stains and mud smeared across it. She might as well throw them both away.

Scratches of red streaked across her arms and one of her thighs had gotten it bad enough that dried blood coated the area. She dug around in the medicine cabinet just over the sink until she found ointment she could put on after her shower.

The water rained hot and felt decadent against her sore muscles, not to mention the water pressure was glorious. If she wasn't out of the shower at home in less than five minutes it was a cold shower and nothing much more than a drizzle at that.

God, her body ached. Her skin was sensitive to the touch and sizzled with need, and her nipples tightened to hard peaks. Maybe this time would be different. Her hand trailed down her body and slid between the slick folds of her cunt. She knew where to touch, the right amount of pressure, and how fast or slow her fingers needed to move to take her to the edge.

Her breath came out in broken pants and she laid her forehead against the cold shower wall as she came closer and closer to achieving her goal. Her cry of frustration echoed off the tile and she dropped to her knees, letting the water rain down on her. Her fists pounded against the shower floor and her sobs were silent as she realized she would forever be stuck in this purgatory of half-pleasure.

She reached up and turned the water to cold and scrubbed her body furiously. By the time she got out of the shower her body was still screaming for relief and even the touch of the towel against her skin was too much. When she looked in the mirror she saw a woman whose face was flushed with need, whose breasts were swollen and heavy, and whose eyes were filled with wild desire.

A robe of black silk hung from the back of the door, and she pulled it around her and inhaled the scent of Declan. He surrounded her—got under her skin—like no one ever had, and she couldn't explain the draw of him any more than she could explain why she knew she'd been wrong in saying he was just like Kane. The differences were there—in the way he watched her and the way she felt the comfort of his protectiveness wrap around her. He just couldn't be trusted.

Sophia ran a brush through her wet hair, and since she couldn't find a hair dryer she let it curl naturally around her face.

Declan's bedroom was still empty when she left the bathroom, and she padded back toward the kitchen in search for food. She stopped in the doorway when she saw him sitting at the island counter, his fingers flying across the keyboard of the laptop in front of him.

"Come on in," he said without breaking stride. "You've got a sandwich if you're hungry."

She saw the thick sandwich and pile of chips and her mouth started watering. A soft drink and a glass of ice sat next to it. Declan never missed a detail.

She took the barstool across from him and pulled the plate closer, and it took every bit of self-control to keep from inhaling the sandwich.

"I keep thinking I missed something," he said once

she'd taken several bites.

"Missed what?"

"That I'm just overlooking something in regards to the money. Kane had the money directly wired to the accounts with your name on them, and then he had all the money transferred to a bank in Houston, Texas. But that bank account was only in his name, so he didn't need your approval to remove the money."

"We checked with the bank there and he came in six weeks before his death and withdrew the money in the form of a cashier's check. The check hasn't been cashed, so he stashed it somewhere."

"I understand why these men want to get their hands on the money," she said. "It's a lot of money. What I don't understand is why you guys want it so badly."

"First of all, the minute we have the money in our hands, your name gets taken off the table." Declan closed his laptop and moved it to the other counter as he got up to grab a drink from the fridge. "The second reason is wherever the money is, the list of terrorists who bid on our agents is probably close by. We need that list so we can bring the agents who were betrayed justice."

"It's hard for me to believe the government would go on a vigilante mission of vengeance."

"The government wouldn't," Dec said. "Which is why they have privately funded agencies like this one, and like the one Gabe Brennan runs in London, to see to the matter. There are wars fought against our enemies overseas every day, but we have just as many enemies to war with on our own soil. That's what we do here."

Dec took her empty plate to the sink and rinsed it out, and she thought about what he said. She was glad to be in the percentage of people who didn't really know how much danger humanity was in on a daily basis. She was just fine with being as oblivious as the next person.

"Let me ask you something, Soph," he said, drying his hands on a dishtowel before coming to stand just to the side of her. "When was the last time you felt pleasure? Just for yourself?"

She jumped slightly as the sound of his voice slid across her skin and her face heated in embarrassment. Had it been that obvious? He hadn't moved closer, but it felt as if the space around her was smaller, and it was sure as hell harder to breathe.

"I know what Kane did to you during your marriage, and if I could kill him again for that alone I would, but when was the last time you felt pleasure, any pleasure, during sex?"

Sophia stood abruptly from the stool, making it wobble slightly as she caught her balance on the edge of the table.

"Considering I haven't had sex in six years, I couldn't tell you."

"What Kane did to you wasn't sex. What he did was unconscionable, and you shouldn't confuse the two. Rape was his choice—his cruelty. I know you remember what sex can be between two people—how it should always be about mutual pleasure."

"It doesn't matter, Dec. Kane managed to ruin that for me too. The last time I had an orgasm was the day you left on that last mission. It doesn't matter how hard I try or that I can feel myself teetering right on the edge. I can't do it anymore. And the more you tempt and tease me the more painful it becomes."

"But what if I'm the one who can give you what you need? Would it be so bad to lay back and let me give you the pleasure you've been longing for? To be selfish for a change and take without having to give in return?"

"I can't." The words were barely a whisper and she closed her eyes to keep from seeing the pity she was sure would be in his gaze. "I've already tried."

"Then it shouldn't hurt to let me try."

"I can't let you touch me again. I need some sense of self-preservation. And your hands on me is not the way to protect myself against getting hurt."

"So I won't touch you with my hands. Only my mouth. You'll be in control."

"Ha. Have I ever been in control around you?"

"Let me give you pleasure, Soph. Let me try to give you what no one else can. There are no expectations here. Only your pleasure."

Her breasts grew heavy with need and her nipples tightened to hard points and rasped against the silk of the robe. Her arousal had only grown in the few hours they'd been in each others' company. She could feel the proof slick on the insides of her thighs.

Her breath caught as he reached out to tug at the knot of the robe, and not once did his fingers ever touch her skin or press against her. The robe fell open, the black silk a dark contrast to her pale skin.

"My God, Soph." She grabbed at the robe and started to pull it closed again. "No, don't cover yourself. A woman with a body like yours should never be covered. I'd take the body you have today every time over the body you had at nineteen."

She somehow found the courage to look him in the face, to see if he was really that good a liar, but all she saw was his eyes turn a dark and turbulent grey and a slight flush of desire mantle his cheekbones. Her gaze traveled down his chest and farther down until she saw his straining erection trapped behind the zipper of his jeans.

"Just my mouth," he said again. "Nothing else until you're ready."

"Declan—"

"You're thinking too hard, baby. It's just pleasure. Are you going to let me see the rest of that sexy body, or are you going to keep hiding behind the robe? It's your choice."

Sophia knew he was waiting for her to make a decision. Would she run away like a coward or would she rise to the challenge and see if he could give her what her body desired?

SINS AND SCARLET LACE

She wanted the pleasure. She quickly shrugged the robe off her shoulders before she could change her mind.

"Jesus," he whispered. "You're so fucking beautiful. Better than my dreams. And believe me, Soph, I had a lot of dreams in the last ten years."

"Talk about being honest," she said, anger whipping inside of her from nowhere, warring with the arousal of her body. "You're telling me you dreamed of me while you fucked all those other women? Kane made sure to tell me about the waitress you picked up in Shanghai and the others along the way."

"Kane and I were never in Shanghai together, but I won't lie and say there weren't other women. I didn't stop living during the last ten years. You belonged to someone else, and I thought you were happy. My body had needs, just like the ones you're denying yourself by trying to pick a fight right now. But my dreams were something I never had any control of, and I couldn't tell you how many nights I woke up in a sweaty tangle of sheets with my dick so hard it was painful to the touch."

He moved a step closer and Sophia took a step back so she stood flat against the island. Her hands gripped the edge behind her and she stood frozen as he drew closer.

"Just my mouth," he reminded her.

Sophia cried out in surprise as his head lowered and his mouth covered a sensitive nipple. He suckled it, his tongue rasping over the turgid peak, and wicked sensations flexed deep in her womb at every hard draw of his mouth. The folds between her thighs were swollen and the tiny bud of her clit pulsed harder and stronger with every flick of his tongue.

Her head fell back on her shoulders and her grip on the counter tightened as she tried to stay upright. Just the touch of his mouth on her breasts was more pleasure than she'd imagined possible, and her moan came out as a sob for more as he pulled away and switched to the other breast.

"I can't wait to touch you with my hands again, to feel the weight of your breasts against my palms. I've always loved touching your breasts. The way they plump up in my hands when you're turned on and the way they feel against my chest when I'm buried inside of you. But not tonight. Tonight is only for my mouth."

Declan ran his tongue between the valley of her breasts, licking and kissing the underside, before trailing lower to her stomach.

He was giving her a precious gift. There were no expectations. No pressure. And she realized she trusted him to keep his word when he said there'd be nothing more until she was ready. This moment was about her orgasm and nothing more. And it was incredibly freeing.

His teeth nipped at the slight swell of her belly before he soothed it with his tongue, and then he dropped completely to his knees in front of her and he kissed her once just above her pubic bone before he sat back on the heels of his feet.

"Spread your legs a little wider," he rasped. "I want to see all of you."

Breathing seemed impossible and her heart hammered inside her chest at the anticipation. She slowly widened her stance so she was completely bared to him, and her cheeks heated in embarrassment when she realized there was no hiding her desire.

"So fucking beautiful." The whisper of his breath teased against her swollen flesh and she shuddered as chills pebbled her skin. "You're going to have to be my hands. Touch yourself for me, baby. Hold yourself open so I can lick every inch of you."

She moaned at the image his words brought to mind. Declan had a power over her she couldn't explain. She should have been mortified at what he was asking her to do, but her body obeyed the command before her brain had processed the thought.

Her hands went to her breasts first, squeezing them,

tweaking both nipples as she massaged the sensitive mounds of flesh.

"Mmm, I could come just watching you. You know what I want, Soph. I'm ready to taste you."

Sophia was lost in herself. In her pleasure. And she took her time roaming and rediscovering her body. Her hands trailed over her stomach and into the golden thatch of curls between her thighs. Slickness met her fingers and electric fingers of pleasure streaked through her body as she touched the distended bud of nerves between her folds, her fingers spreading the syrup of her desire as she teased herself.

And then his mouth was there with her fingers and she cried out as the heat scorched straight to her soul. His tongue stroked slowly through the swollen folds of her pussy, lapping up the cream that gathered there before probing and sending light licks of torture over her clit. The edge of release was within her grasp, just that quickly, but he knew where to touch, where to tease, to keep her from reaching her goal. She growled in frustration as she felt it slip through her fingers again.

"Patience, my love." His words vibrated against her pussy and she moaned at the sensation. "The build up will only make it better."

"Or worse," she panted.

His tongue was like the softest velvet as it laved against her with hungry strokes. He circled around and around the underside of her clit before moving back to the weeping entrance of her pussy. Her hands gripped the back of his head and pulled him closer, and the groan of satisfaction that rumbled from his throat vibrated against her sensitized flesh.

Sophia fought to hold back her screams of more, but finally it was too much.

"God, Dec. Please. Please. Make me come. I need to come."

Her chest wound tight with excitement as he heeded

her wishes and his tongue moved faster. She gripped his head tighter and her hips began moving against him, undulating in time with his tongue.

"Declan!" She exploded into a million fragments of light and color. He drank in the flood of her release as a starburst of pleasure zinged through her body in an orgasm so intense that it weakened her legs. Her knees gave out and she crumpled to the ground beside him, her breathing erratic and perspiration coating her skin. The thought of moving seemed impossible and she wondered if Declan would bring her a pillow and a blanket so she could sleep where she lay.

"Is this the part where you say I told you so?" she asked.

Declan laughed and got to his feet, and she rolled her eyes up in time to see the grimace of pain on his face as he readjusted the hard length trapped behind his zipper.

"You should probably get a couple of hours sleep," he said, his voice gruff. "I've still got some work to do, so you're welcome to use the bed. I'll wake you up when Darcy gets here."

He stared down at her and she could see the triumph of satisfaction in his eyes amidst the pain of discomfort.

"Do you need help standing or can you make it?"

"I'm good," she finally managed to say. She took the robe he offered and wrapped it around her body before standing shakily.

Dec rubbed a hand over the top of his head and then headed toward the control room. She didn't know if she should thank him or call him back for more. In the end she just watched him walk away.

CHAPTER NINE

Declan refused to give in and let his body have the relief it needed, so a few hours later he was still rock hard and so sensitive that even the soft cotton of his briefs made him ache. He was determined that he wouldn't let himself come until he was buried inside Sophia. He could, and would, wait until she was ready for him. If it didn't kill him first.

"Soph, we need to get a move on," he called out as he packed up his laptop and filled another duffel bag with a few necessities, like extra ammunition and the box of condoms Darcy had jokingly left for him when she'd delivered the clothes for Sophia.

"I'm ready," she said from behind him.

He turned to look at her and his dick jerked painfully in his pants. Her hair was pulled back in a ponytail, showing off the classic lines of her face, and she wore little white shorts that had his mouth watering and a yellow halter top that made him realize she couldn't possibly be wearing a bra. He wanted to curse and thank Darcy all at the same time.

Sophia had a backpack slung over her shoulder and not a stitch of makeup on her face. Dark circles rested beneath her eyes and she was pale, but she was still the most beautiful sight he'd ever seen. He'd been away from her too long. He should have checked on her during her marriage to Kane. If he had, he would have caught Kane in his lies a long time ago, but he'd been too afraid to see her again—afraid to face the reality that she might be happy with another man, living the same life she was supposed to have with him. So he'd stayed away, and always turned down the dinner invitations Kane would occasionally throw out.

"How long will it take us to get to Surrender?"

"If we were flying it would take a few hours. But we're going to drive, and we're going to take the long way just in case, so it'll take a couple of days. I've already alerted my brother and his team, so that'll give them extra time to get there and set up a perimeter watch."

"Which brother is this and why does he have a team?"

Declan grinned and slung his own pack over his shoulder. "My youngest brother Shane. He's a Navy SEAL commander and his skills come in handy for our offices from time to time. I don't think you've ever met him before."

"No, he wasn't at the hospital. I believe he was out of the country when you were first flown in, and your mom said she didn't know how to get in contact with him."

"He knew what had happened. Word gets around when you're out on assignment like that, but he couldn't leave the mission he'd been sent to do. It's part of the job description."

"You have so much family it's hard to keep them all straight. I remember thinking at the time that it was odd that's the first time I'd ever met all of them, except for Darcy, and that's only because she showed up on your doorstep unannounced one day. And then I realized later I should have seen the writing on the wall when you didn't want me to meet your family. Hindsight is easy to see, I guess."

"It's not that I didn't want you to meet my family," he said. "But I've learned to live cautiously over the years. My family is something I'd never compromise, just like you are, and I knew at the time that it would be better to keep those worlds separated. There's a price on my head in sixteen countries, Soph, and I live with the shadow of that every day, wondering each morning if it'll finally be the time when my past catches up to me."

She stayed silent as they went down the elevator to the garage level, but he could practically hear the wheels turning in her head. He hit the remote start for the military upgraded black Hummer in the corner and waited a few seconds before they approached and loaded their bags in the back.

It wasn't until they were buckled in and pulling into the late morning D.C. traffic that she finally said what was on her mind.

"Why would you risk your family now after you've gone to such lengths to keep them safe?"

He checked his rearview mirror and noticed Gabe pull in a few cars back in a silver sedan. His friend was a cautious man, and the fact he hadn't gotten on the plane back to London and his own business meant he had a bad feeling.

"Haven't you figured it out yet?"

"What?"

"You're my family too, Soph. You always have been."

They'd been in the car almost sixteen hours by the time they crossed the Minnesota border. Tension crackled across Sophia's skin more with every mile they drove, driving her to the point of exhaustion. They'd stopped for food and bathroom breaks along the way, but hardly any conversation had been made after he'd dropped his bombshell.

She sure as hell hoped he hadn't treated his real family

as badly as he'd treated her. The declaration was almost laughable. It didn't matter that a part of her had softened after the statement. God, was she that needy for affection that she'd believe any lie to roll off his tongue? Had she not learned her lesson the first two times?

"We need to find a place to grab a few hours sleep," Dec said.

She didn't know if she'd been dozing or only in a half-sleep daze, but she rolled the stiffness out of her neck and pushed herself up in the seat. The clock on the dashboard said it was a minute after three in the morning.

"Too bad I didn't pack my tent," she said sarcastically. There were no buildings or signs of civilization that she could see. The road was only lighted by the headlights on the Hummer, and the black shadows of pastureland whirred past them in a blur as Declan sped along the vacant highway. At least she thought it was a highway.

As if reading her mind Declan answered her. "I took a back way. This road will lead to a little town in another few minutes or so. They've got a place I've stayed at before."

"Isn't that against some kind of spy code to stay at the same place twice?"

She saw the gleam of white teeth from the corner of her eye as he smiled. He controlled the car like he did everything else—with precision. She knew he hated to make mistakes, and he pushed himself with a ruthless determination that made it seem like moving mountains was possible as long as Declan MacKenzie was behind it.

"Only if you go twice as the same person. Believe me, no one will recognize me."

She didn't know what to say to that so she kept quiet, but eventually her curiosity got the best of her.

"What do you tell your family? I don't see how you lived this life for that long and no one knew what you were involved in. It doesn't seem right to keep that big a secret from the people you're supposed to love the most."

She felt his sigh more than heard it, and she fully

expected him to blow her off or answer with a non-answer.

"What you're really wondering is how you never suspected Kane was involved in the same kind of life."

Sophia opened her mouth to deny it, but she realized he was right. "Maybe I am."

"It's nothing you would or should have realized, Soph. It wouldn't have made any difference. Kane was trained, we were all trained, to be whoever we needed to be. Lies become the reality, and the adrenaline fuels the mysterious persona that some of the agents get off on—not all—but some."

"A different woman in every city, a different backstory, a different look. It becomes its own kind of addiction. Believe me, Kane knew everything about you from the moment he decided to make you his mark. He knew every aspect of our relationship and the fastest way to reel you in."

"That certainly makes me feel better," she said, rubbing her hands along her arms to ward off the chill. She watched a large billboard pass by that said the exit for the next town was only 2.1 miles away.

"Ninety-nine percent of agents I know and have worked with over the years are good men and women, just like when I was in the Marines ninety-nine percent of the soldiers were honorable and wanted to make a difference. I've watched their backs and they've watched mine. We don't live the lie because we enjoy hurting our families. We do it because we want to protect them. Most people aren't wired to handle the atrocities that take place on a day-to-day basis."

"But you are?" She turned in her seat to face him, but he didn't glance her way.

"Yeah, I guess I am. But I've also been fortunate to have the family I do. The MacKenzies come from a long line of lawmen in some capacity or another, all the way back to my however many times great-grandfather who was one of the first U.S. Marshals. And when wars were started the MacKenzies picked up their weapons and joined in the fight to protect what was theirs."

"Hell, I had two brothers and a cousin all enlisted at the same time I was before I was recruited by the CIA, so my family knew something was going on I couldn't talk about. I can't tell you how many times I came across my brothers while on a mission in some godforsaken part of the world. But they never asked me questions because they knew I would hate lying to them, and we managed to coexist until I left and opened MacKenzie Security. I've handpicked my men, and I'd trust them with my life. Even better, I'd trust them with my family's life."

"Would you have recruited Kane to work for you if he hadn't died and what he'd done hadn't been exposed?"

He was silent for a long while, and he slowed the car and took the exit when they came upon it. The town was still as a tomb at that time of the night, but they were at least back in civilization. Lights from a corner gas station glowed yellow onto the vacant streets and gleamed off the hoods of parked cars.

There were two stoplights in town, both of them hanging from a single wire that stretched across the road, and a smattering of small businesses lined each side of the street. The largest sign in town was just past the second light and it said The Lodge in neon orange letters. The registration office was an A-frame log cabin, and it was surrounded by smaller log cabins that looked like something a pre-schooler would make from Lincoln Logs. They all had flat roofs and they formed a U-shape around the main office.

The lot was full of cars, but Declan found one in the back row and pulled in next to an old pickup truck covered in bumper stickers. He turned off the ignition, and Sophia put her hand on the door to open it and escape the tension.

She froze when he finally spoke.

"No," he finally said. "I wouldn't have asked him to join the team." His gaze was steady on hers and she sat back in her seat, watching him closely.

"Why not?"

"Because he knew how I felt about you, even after all that time. I'd wondered once or twice if he did it on purpose. If he talked about you in such detail because he wondered how I'd react, but then I ignored the feeling, blaming my own jealousy for making it seem over the top. I told myself he was a man who loved his wife and I needed to do what I'd been trained to do to survive the torture. I needed to lie."

"God—"

"But a man can only take so much torture before they finally find his breaking point. And I just couldn't bear to hear about it anymore—about the way you looked when he woke up in the morning and you were still sleeping, or how devastated you were when you were trying to conceive and couldn't."

"Lies," she whispered. "All lies."

"He played the game too well, because I ignored every instinct I had and convinced myself it was me who had the problem, not him. And I had no one to blame but myself because I sent you away, thinking I could protect you by keeping my distance. Then he brought you right back into the thick of things, and for one brief moment, I wanted to kill him. Because I knew the moment you walked down the aisle that you should have been walking to me."

Sophia's breath hitched and she closed her eyes. "I can't talk about this. I can't—" She turned her head and looked out the window and stared hard at the old truck. "You're the one who said we can't change the past. What you thought or did or the choices I made don't matter now."

"They matter, Soph. But we'll make sure you're safe first before we deal with the past."

Declan got out of the Hummer and went to the back to

get his bags, barely giving her time to get her wits together before he was pulling her door open and waiting for her to get out.

She'd been watching him since they'd left D.C. His eyes never stopped moving, and she knew he could tell her the color of the car on the opposite side of the lot if she asked. He stayed close to her while they walked to the front office, his hand resting on the butt of the gun he carried at the small of his back. He never relaxed. And being in such close company with him was driving her insane. What he'd given her the night before had only increased the need. She had a lot of years to make up for.

Her mind and her body warred with different needs—her brain needed security—safety—while her body needed to be exhausted. She wasn't good at living the lie as Declan and Kane had been. There was no denying that every moment she spent in Declan's company was bringing her one step closer to loving him again. The best thing she could do for her own sanity was to figure out where the money was as fast as possible and escape before she was asking him to use more than just his mouth on her.

CHAPTER TEN

Declan knew Sophia was trying to figure out a way to shorten their time together. He could tell by the way she kept glancing at him from the corner of her eye, her cheeks flushing pink, while she bit her lip in contemplation. If he wasn't very careful, she'd start looking for a way to ditch him and try to go out on her own. And that wouldn't end well for anyone.

She wanted him. That kind of need wasn't something she could hide from him, and the little taste she'd gotten the night before was only the beginning of her rediscovering who she'd once been. He'd seen the surprise on her face when she'd climaxed, and he'd felt how hard she'd fought to keep from achieving it.

Kane had damaged her. But he hadn't broken her. The fact she'd had the guts to stand up to him and make him leave after he'd threatened her was testament to that. Kane's death had only made him realize what was important in the grand scheme of things. He loved what he did and he loved his country. But he loved Sophia more. And if his past ever caught up to him he'd deal with it with her by his side. The problem was getting her to trust him again—with her heart and her body. He'd had easier missions.

The lobby of the registration area was rustic and

smelled strongly of Pine Sol and fish. The lights were dimmed and there was a bell sitting on the counter, but no one was sitting behind it.

Declan went up to the counter and rang the bell once, but there was no answer. "Hello? Is anybody there?"

"I'm here, I'm here," a voice called out.

A whirring sound came from one of the back rooms and a cherry red motorized scooter sputtered down the long hall. The woman riding it had to be at least a hundred years old.

"Some folks like to sleep around here, eh?" she muttered.

"I know we could use a bed," Dec said. It didn't bother him when she stared at his scar. Everyone stared at his scar the first time.

"Two beds," Sophia piped in.

"One room, two beds," he told the lady.

"What are you crazy, girl? You got to be in the same bed for it to work right." The woman turned rheumy eyes back toward Declan. "Girls don't know anything when they're that young, eh? Men need older women to teach them what's what."

"Yes, ma'am." His mouth quirked in a smile and he would have laughed out loud if Sophia's face wasn't already as red as the woman's scooter.

"My name is Janice, but people around here call me Marge," she said, maneuvering her scooter behind the counter and opening the fat registry book. "And the problem we're going to have is that I don't have one room with two beds left. It's fishing season, and there's a tournament tomorrow morning at the lake. The only reason I've got the one room left is because Wally Scroggins died last night. He didn't even get to make a good cast before he keeled over from a heart attack." She took a key attached to a giant letter 5 off the hook on the back wall and laid it on the counter.

"I'm sorry to hear about Wally," Dec said,

remembering the woman's pension for conversation from the last time he was there. "But we'll take the room."

She clucked her tongue and pushed the registration book toward him. "It's sixty-two dollars a night with tax. Your lady looks like she's about to fall over."

Dec looked at Sophia and could see the exhaustion etched in her face, but he could tell she was just as uneasy about the thought of sharing a bed with him. She was wound tight, and her arousal was a palpable thing.

"She's tougher than she looks." He pulled out cash from his wallet and signed the registration book under a fake name, pushing them both toward her.

"Ayah. Maybe she is. But she still don't know anything about men. You look like a man with plans, eh? Ha! Two beds. Better watch out for this one, girlie."

Sophia looked at him and quirked a brow. "I think you're probably right, Marge. Maybe he should sleep outside with the fish."

Dec rolled his eyes and grabbed the key and their bags. "Thanks, Marge. Sorry to disturb your sleep," he called out as he opened the door to go back outside, but Marge had already motored back down the hallway.

"Maybe they've got a sofa," Sophia said as they made their way to number five.

He knew good and well there wasn't much room for anything inside these rooms but a bed and a bathroom the size of a closet, but she was wound taut as a bow, so he didn't disabuse her of the notion. She'd find out soon enough anyway.

He put in the key and turned the old fashioned doorknob of their cabin and then pushed the door open to reveal a room of knotty pine furniture and fish carved from wood up on the walls. It didn't take Sophia very long to glance from one side to the other and see there was nothing but an enormous king size bed in the middle of the room.

"Do you really want me to sleep somewhere else?

Because as turned on as you are I'd think you'd get a lot more benefit from sleeping next to me."

Sophia swallowed and stepped inside, and she jumped as the door closed behind her and the deadbolt clicked into place.

"This is probably going to be a mistake."

"Only if you don't come."

CHAPTER ELEVEN

"I guess if you put it that way," she said, biting her lip. "The only problem is this doesn't go well with my plans for self-preservation. I won't let you break my heart again."

Sophia's eyes widened as he stripped off his T-shirt, and her gaze automatically went to the myriad of old shrapnel and burn scars from the helicopter explosion.

"I have no plans to break your heart. Actually, I think you have the chance to break mine this go around."

She was about to dispute him, but he interrupted before she could get the words out.

"I have an idea that I think will help you on your quest for self-preservation if you want to hear it."

"I'm not sure that I do." She licked her lips again and he saw the hard outline of her nipples from beneath her shirt.

He unzipped the black bag and rummaged around inside until he found what he was looking for. He tossed the metal handcuffs on the table between them and watched her eyes grow even bigger.

"I definitely don't want to hear your idea. Why don't I go back down to the office and see if they've had any cancellations?"

"No deal, sweetheart. We stick together. But I figure

it'll set your mind at ease if you're the one in control of the handcuffs."

He put his boots by the door and worked at his belt, stripping it out of the loops slowly, before tossing it onto the table next to the cuffs. His erection was hot and hard behind his zipper, and he unbuttoned his jeans and pulled the tab down a bit to give himself some relief.

"What do you mean when you say I'm in control of the handcuffs?" Her voice was barely more than a whisper, but the curiosity was there. "I've been in handcuffs. I didn't especially like it."

"It means we're stuck in this hotel room for the night with one bed to share between us, and I figure your self-preservation rule is tied to how I touch you. So the only way for you to get what you need is for me to follow through with the mouth only rule and let you cuff me to the headboard. I trust you not to take advantage of me." He winked and watched the color darken her cheeks. "Believe me, I'm willing to make the sacrifice."

Dec grabbed the cuffs, the key and his gun and headed over to the bed, feeling the heat of her gaze following behind him. He ignored her as he lay the gun and key on the nightstand and stripped out of his jeans and briefs before tossing them in the corner chair.

"Jesus, Dec," she sputtered. "Whatever happened to modesty?"

"Sweetheart, you know better than anyone that's never been my strong suit. Surely you remember that time we toured the planetarium. Though I'm almost positive the lack of modesty was your idea that time."

Her blush grew deeper as erotic memories overwhelmed her already primed senses.

The cuff snapped around his wrist, and he adjusted the fit so it wasn't too tight. He could undo the restraint any time he needed to, but Sophia didn't need to know that. There might be a need to get to his gun in a hurry, and he'd never hamper his movements that way. He pulled the comforter back all the way to the end of the bed. As hot as his skin was the last thing he needed was extra warmth, and he slid onto the cool sheets.

Declan didn't bother to try to hide his erection. Hell, he couldn't have if he'd wanted to. It stood tall and proud against his stomach, the veins rigid and the bulbous head flushed dark with need.

She hadn't moved from the entryway, but she watched his every move like he was her prey. He didn't mind giving up his dominance so he could see that look on her face.

One handcuffed arm grabbed one of the cheap slats of the headboard, and his other hand took hold of the base of his cock and squeezed. Her breathing became slow and deep, the desire naked in her eyes, and she took a step forward, almost as if she couldn't help herself.

His fist tightened and he stroked himself languidly from shaft to tip, and then he did it again. And again.

"Are you going to fasten the other wrist?" he asked softly. "I'm likely to get into a whole lot of trouble if you leave me as I am."

Sophia took a few tentative steps closer to the bed, and he stayed completely still, waiting to see what she'd do. He kept stroking his cock, watching her as she tried to figure out what she should do.

"Put your hand up with the other." Her voice was husky, and she cleared her throat once before putting one knee on the bed beside him.

Declan released his cock and hoped to God his plan didn't backfire, otherwise he was in for a miserable night. He gripped the rail next to his other hand and waited to see what she'd do next.

Her ponytail had come loose and tendrils of hair drifted into her face as she leaned over him and tried to reach the handcuffs. A frustrated breath escaped her lips when she realized she'd have to get closer, much closer, before she could do the job properly.

The bed dipped as her other knee joined the first and

she crawled upward until her breasts hung just above his face. The cold metal of the other cuff clicked around his wrist, and he took the opportunity to lift his head up and take her silk covered nipple between his teeth and tug gently.

She moaned and her head dropped down so it rested against the headboard, just above where his hands were restrained.

"I've got another idea." He grinned when she snorted out a laugh and moved back out of the range of his mouth. "You've got me at your mercy. Maybe you should do something with me."

"Or maybe I should just roll over and get a good night's sleep." The devilment in her eyes reminded him of when they'd first met. Of how carefree she'd once been. And how he'd taken that from her.

"You could," he agreed. "Or you could use this to your advantage and touch every inch of me however you wanted. You used to love to touch." His muscles strained with the need to break free and take what he wanted. "You could take off your clothes and see what happens?"

She moved the rest of the way off the bed and moved back several steps, and her face was unreadable other than the desire he saw in the depths of her gaze. The tension grew heavy while he waited to see what she would do, and he didn't realize he'd been holding his breath until her hand rose to the tie at the back of her neck and pulled the string loose.

The halter straps fell and the top caught on the tips of her breasts, and the chain of her grandmother's necklace dangled between her breasts. He groaned at the sight of her there, standing lush and confident as she realized her power. Her hands went to her shorts and she undid the button, each movement slow and deliberate. Then she pulled down the tab of the zipper and he realized his hands were fisted so tight around the slats of the headboard that the wood was creaking beneath the pressure.

"Jesus, Soph. You drive me crazy."

The shorts dropped to her ankles so she was left in a pair of plain white cotton panties, and she might have well been wearing the sexiest lingerie in the world. She teased him with glimpses of flesh by pulling up the hem of her shirt to bare her belly and then the undersides of her breast. And he groaned when she finally pulled the material over her head and the plump mounds became visible once and for all. The sight of her in nothing but the cameo necklace hanging between her breasts and panties was almost more than he could bear.

"Take off the panties. I want to see all of you."

"You have a lot of demands for a man who's handcuffed to a bed," she said, quirking a brow.

"Take them off and then come here. I want to taste you again. Come ride my mouth."

When he'd first introduced Sophia to sex so many years ago she'd been eager to learn and please. She'd been adventurous to the point he knew he'd never find another woman who would sexually satisfy him like she had. And he'd proven himself right through the passing years. No one had ever come close.

But he could see the familiar flare of excitement in her eyes at his suggestion, and her fingers played at the waistband of her panties before she pushed them down to join the shorts at her feet.

"Come here," he said again, letting the hunger seep out through his tone. The golden curls between her thighs glistened with moisture, and he licked his lips in anticipation of tasting her again. Nothing was ever as sweet.

"I thought I was in charge," she said, taking off the necklace before crawling next to him on the bed, much as she had before.

"Oh, you are, baby. Every step of the way. I just want to feel your pleasure. I want to taste your release and feel you tighten around my tongue."

Her eyes dilated to almost completely black and she crawled up his body until her knees rested next to his face. He turned his head and kissed her knee, and her hands grasped the top of the headboard and her knees straddled his face, and Declan decided this moment was as close to heaven as he was likely to get.

Sophia froze as his tongue licked long and slow through the swollen folds of her pussy. Her breath caught and she cried out when he flicked once across the sensitive bud of her clitoris before moving to another spot. He tempted and tormented with every probe, every caress, and she realized this would be over much too soon if she let him continue on this path.

The power was hers. Just this once. And she wanted to take full advantage of what he'd given her. Touching and tasting him would bring her just as much pleasure as it did him. Before she could talk herself out of it, she moved away from his wicked mouth.

He groaned at her absence. "I'm not done with you yet. Get back up here."

"I'm in charge, remember?"

"If my hands were free, you'd be in a lot of trouble right now."

"I guess it's a good thing they're not free then. Besides, good things come to those who wait. You're much too impatient."

"You have no idea." His voice was all seriousness and her flesh pebbled at the desire she saw in his eyes, as if he were starving for her.

She changed positions quickly so she straddled his face from the other direction, and she moaned as his tongue easily found its target once again. But this time she was the one with the banquet laid out before her.

Her hands flexed on the rippling muscles of his stomach, and she laughed mischievously as he jerked beneath her touch. His cock flexed, rising before her, and she leaned forward, letting her breasts brush against his abdomen.

He was so hard, the engorged crest flushed and swollen, and a small amount of clear liquid gathered at the tip. She remembered exactly what it felt like to have him inside of her. The way his cock wasn't straight but curved upward slightly, and the way the large mushroom-shaped head made her gasp in surprise when he finally pushed inside of her.

Pleasure speared from between her thighs and her hips moved involuntarily against his mouth, and her hand gripped the base of his cock as hunger replaced reason. Her tongue licked once around the head, gathering his essence on her tongue, and then she was lost in the sensation of pleasing him as much as he was pleasing her.

She sucked him in, swirling her tongue around the head, before pulling back again, working her way down farther and farther each time as her tongue lubricated the path. He moaned against her pussy and she tasted the saltiness of his pre-cum. Her nails scraped along his thighs and then she cupped the tight sac of his scrotum in the palm of her hand and his back arched off the bed.

"Jesus, Soph. You're going to make me come."

"Ditto. Let's see who can win the race."

His tongue stiffened and pushed into her pussy, spearing her over and over again, and her legs trembled as release drew near. She massaged his balls with one hand and stroked him once with the other before taking him in her mouth again, loving the way he swelled within her the closer he got to orgasm.

She relaxed her throat and began the slow process of swallowing him down so her lips touched the very base of his cock. She breathed through her nose as she held her position there, and she felt him freeze between her thighs.

"Fuck," he groaned.

And then she began the swallowing motions in the back of her throat, the undulating pressure that was sure to drive him over the edge.

"Fuck, fuck," he said again.

This time it was she that screamed around him as his tongue moved faster, never giving her a reprieve to catch her breath. He was relentless in his pursuit, and her body throbbed, the pulse in her clit a rapid flutter. Her body tensed and shuddering sensation washed through her as her release came like a tidal wave.

Sounds of flesh and pleasure rose around them, and Sophia almost cried out in triumph as Declan's release ripped from his body, the thick, salty streams filling her mouth before she swallowed him down.

He called out her name and she prayed she didn't say anything she'd regret later.

CHAPTER TWELVE

Declan felt a sense of peace come over him as they passed the Welcome to Surrender, Montana sign just at the top of the last hill. They'd driven straight through the rest of the way, not stopping for another night of rest, even though he knew they both needed it.

Sophia had been subdued and quiet since they'd left Wisconsin, and he knew she was thinking too hard about everything that had happened between them. It had been powerful, more so than when they'd been together before, and they hadn't done more than pleasure each other with their mouths. He knew he was pulling her in, trying to make her remember the times they'd had before so she could remember that they had been happy together at one point. He knew what he was doing wasn't fair to her or her need to protect herself, but he couldn't let her get away this time, and if he had to fight dirty to keep her then so be it.

He stopped the car at the top of the hill and put on the emergency brake.

"Come on," he said, opening the door. "It's not everyday you get to see a view like this."

She unbuckled her seatbelt and followed his lead until they were both leaning against the front hood looking down on Surrender. She wore a pair of black capris, a tank top in pink, and casual black sandals. The cameo necklace was her only accessory and she'd foregone makeup, but she was one of those women who didn't need it. Her hair was piled up on top of her head, and loose curls broke free as the wind blew, gentle and hot.

The two-lane road went straight into the town that sat nestled at the base of the hill. Bricked buildings with low flat roofs lined each side of the street like soldiers, and black awnings covered the wooden sidewalks. A white tin building with open garage bays claiming it was Charlie's Automotive sat off to the side. Charlotte MacKenzie, or Charlie as most people called her, was his cousin Dane's wife, and she was the best mechanic in this part of the country, and apparently in high demand. The bays and parking lot were full, and it looked like she was doing a brisk business.

Miles and miles of scenery could be seen from where they stood, and he was almost positive there wasn't a better view anywhere else on Earth. Lush green hills of grass rolled like waves as the wind blew, and red barns and clapboard houses dotted the countryside. White fences lined the roads and kept cattle and horses contained.

"It's the most beautiful place I've ever seen," she said.

"It's easy to forget what it's like when you live here everyday. All you think about is the next haying season, or finding lost cattle when it floods, or weathering the next blizzard and trying not to go stir crazy as you're trapped indoors for days on end. But when you've been away awhile it's always a nice place to come home to."

"You seem like you miss it."

"I miss my family. I've been trying to work out a way to get everyone back together again. We're too spread out. Cade lives in Texas with his family and works at our office there. Darcy lives close to me, up in Cherry Hill in Pennsylvania, but she's teaching at Columbia two days a week and the kids keep her busy. Shane technically still lives here, but he's on assignment so often he's hardly ever home. My younger brother Grant is the only one who stayed. He's married and has a couple kids." He pointed to the small area of water several miles in the distance. "See the lake over there?"

"I see it."

"Grant and Annabeth's house is just on the other side of the lake, through all the trees. Then there's another larger lake just past the trees, right in the middle of about 150 acres. That's all MacKenzie land. I bought another hundred acres that sits adjacent to it several years back."

He'd bought it back when he'd been thinking of marriage and family. When he'd thought about bringing Sophia home just like this and watching the wonder fill her eyes as she saw what could be their future.

But then he'd been damaged and thoughts of a home and a family of his own deserted him only to be replaced with the best way to keep the family he had as safe as possible. So his brothers and sister and cousins all had a stake in their ancestral land, and he had the land next to it that had been under development for the last ten years just in case things turned to shit.

He'd cleared a good portion of the trees, only leaving a thick perimeter to surround the area. His one goal in mind had been to protect his family, so the twelve-foot concrete wall and iron entry gates were the first things that had been built. He'd done background checks on his workers and had overseen it from the ground up, including his own house and the command center that had been built toward the back of the property, and his security rivaled Fort Knox. Two other cabins had already been built, and Shane's team would be making themselves at home.

His hope was that his brothers and sister would build homes behind the walls just in case they ever needed a safe haven. And eventually MacKenzie Security would be run from one command center on location instead of two in different parts of the country.

"Why'd you buy it if you aren't going to live on it?" she asked.

"Someday." He realized that someday might be never. He was thirty-seven years old and he felt like he'd lived three lifetimes. "Things get busy. Especially when you're working for the government on occasion, and it irritates them if you can't be in some senator's office immediately to explain your actions if they want you to. It's why I set up the D.C. offices where they are. But I'd like to move both operations here eventually and have everyone under one roof. The longer we all work in this business, the more frequently our names are thrown out. It makes my neck itch for everyone to be so far apart."

"It's a good plan," she said softly. "Good that you want to take care of your family."

"I've been dying to kiss you," he said, surprising her with his bluntness. "I realized last night that I haven't really kissed you in ten years and a handful of months, and it didn't really count when I kissed you in the car. That kiss was partly from frustration and partly from anger and not the kind of kiss you deserved. Will you let me kiss you?"

She took a step closer and his heartbeat raced as her hands pressed against his chest. "I won't let you break my heart again, Dec. I don't know what's happening here between us or if either of us has the power to stop it, but the longer I stay with you the harder it's going to make things for me. I decided the day I asked Kane for a divorce that I was only going to do what was in my best interest in the future, and then I ended up not going through with it out of fear."

"I'm not afraid anymore. Not of whoever wants that money or that look in your eyes that tells me I'm not going to escape whatever's happening between us unscathed. I no longer have illusions of marriage or children. I just want to settle down in a normal life with a job, if I still have one after this. And when it comes down to it, I'm not sure that you're in my best interest."

"What about friends? Lovers? Will being alone make you happy?"

"I can't say as having friends or lovers has really made me very happy up till now. Maybe I'll meet a few friends along the way. Maybe I'll have lovers. But it'll be my choice either way. Choice is something I've had very little of over the years."

Declan brought his hands up slowly, giving her plenty of time to back away. He wanted to touch her so badly, to spend hours caressing every inch of her body before burying himself inside her. His hands rested on her hips and he brought her closer, so she had to move her hands to his shoulders as her breasts pressed against his chest.

"I guess as long as you choose me we won't have a problem," he said, the corner of his mouth tipping up in a smile. "I'm not going to let you go this time without a fight. And I know I've got a long way to go for you to trust me as you once did. Sending you away was the hardest thing I've ever done—and I've made a lot of hard decisions over the years—the kind of decisions that cost lives if I wasn't careful."

She sighed and he felt her regret whisper across his lips. Her mouth was just too tempting to ignore any longer, and his head dipped down. His mouth skimmed over hers, as soft as air. Even their first kiss hadn't been so gentle. Maybe it should have been.

Her lips trembled and he drank in her sigh just before his tongue slipped inside—a slow sinuous mating that had her nails biting into his shoulders. The pain had never felt so sweet. He didn't know how long they kissed or if anyone noticed they were there. He didn't care. He just knew he had to make this woman love him again. She'd done it before, so it was possible she could do it again.

When he backed away her eyes fluttered open, dazed, and she trembled beneath his fingers. He didn't know if the thudding in his chest was from her heart or his, and he didn't suppose it mattered. He hadn't realized until just now how meaningless his life had been without having her to share it with.

The crunch of tires over the gravel in the road had him reaching for the gun at his back and had him pushing Sophia behind him so she was protected. He held the weapon down at his side until the car came into view, and the he let out a groan as a black Bronco came into view and the sirens were flipped on in earsplitting woops.

The door opened and black boots stepped out onto the road, and Dec sighed and put his gun away, as the man stood and faced them with hands on hips and a scowl dark enough to frighten anyone who didn't know his bark was worse than his bite.

"Well, well, well," he said. "Looks like I've found a troublemaker. Do you know what the fine is for public indecency?"

"You should remember well enough," Dec said. "I believe that was you who got the ticket for that misdemeanor when you were nineteen and caught out by the lake skinny dipping with Jenny Johnson."

Cooper MacKenzie grinned rakishly and ran fingers through his black hair. "Don't tell my wife about that one. I don't think she's heard that story."

Dec let out an amused laugh. "Are you kidding me? You made the newspaper, of course she knows. But she somehow decided to marry you anyway."

"I have other qualities."

"I'm sure you really think that." Dec reached out for Sophia's hand and pulled her closer to his side. "Why are you here busting my balls instead of rescuing kittens from trees and helping old ladies cross the road?"

"I'm just thorough like that, I guess. But maybe you want to tell me why I have active duty Navy SEALS setting up a perimeter around my town?"

"Damn, I'm going to have to tell Shane he's losing his touch if you spotted them that easily."

Cooper narrowed his eyes. "I was a Ranger, asshole. I

can spot a SEAL trying to move in on my territory from a mile away. So why don't you follow me to the house and tell me what the hell is going on? You're probably just in time for dinner. It's Thomas and Cat's night to host, thank God, so you know you'll be getting an excellent meal."

Dec nodded and let go of Sophia's hand so she could go back to her side of the car. "If Cat is cooking then we accept the invitation. Will there be room at the table? If you guys don't stop having kids you're going to have to buy a cafeteria so everyone can sit down in one room."

"Don't blame me. I only have two, and that's more than enough to keep us busy." Cooper finally looked over at Sophia and smiled. "I'm glad to see my cousin has stopped being a dumbass. It's good to see you again, Sophia, though I don't know if you remember me. I'm Cooper MacKenzie."

"I remember now," she said, giving him a small smile back. "Your mother called you the troublemaker."

"It's because I'm her favorite," he laughed. "You should hear what she calls my brothers. See you two at the house. Try not to get sidetracked in each others' mouths on the way."

Declan flipped him the bird, but he was smiling as he drove the rest of the way down the hill into Surrender. It was good to be home.

CHAPTER THIRTEEN

Sophia felt as if she'd fallen into a rabbit hole as they made their way through the town. Declan waved at a few townspeople as they passed by.

"We won't stay long," he said, turning left on one of the one-lane roads just past the town. "I know you're tired, but this is a good chance to fill everyone in at the same time and let them know I want them to increase their own security."

"You don't need to drag them into this, Dec."

"That's the thing about this family, sweetheart. I don't have to drag them anywhere. They'll be there whether I want them to or not. And they'll do it for you too just because I love you."

"You shouldn't say things like that." She looked out the window as they drove past miles of white rail fences.

"I figure if I say it enough then you'll start to believe me again."

"Sometimes love isn't enough. We've both changed over ten years, and I need something a hell of a lot more than your love. I need to be able to trust you again. To count on you when the times get tough. And I just can't do that."

Dec turned onto another road that cut into the rail fence, and Sophia caught her breath as she realized it was a long driveway that went on for more than half a mile. Trees lined each side of the drive all the way down and a tire swing hung from one of them. Horses roamed freely in the pasture to the side and the sunlight glanced off the big lake at the back of the property.

The house itself was a mismatch of stone and wood, and it looked as if rooms had been added as the space was needed. It was long and stood a full two stories with a wide porch that surrounded it on all sides. It looked like they were adding on some more at one end of the house, and as they got closer she saw the sign that said Dr. MacKenzie's Office and a sign that pointed to patient parking.

"This house used to belong to my aunt and uncle—my dad's older brother," Dec said. "When they died my cousins were all still fairly young. Cooper had just gotten out of the military, and Dane and Riley were both in college, but Thomas, the youngest was still in high school. So they all lived here together until Thomas went away to medical school. He took over as the town doctor almost ten years ago and he uses one end of the house for his practice. As you can see by the size, business is booming."

"There are a lot of cars," she said, trying to count the haphazardly parked vehicles in front of the house. "How does he have time to see all the patients?"

Dec laughed and pulled in next to a bright red SUV that belonged to his cousin Dane. "All the patients are gone for the day. These cars all belong to MacKenzies. I told you there were a lot of us. Come on, I'll walk you around the lake a bit and show you the land before you have to face everyone. You're the only woman I've ever brought home, and everyone knows about you from before, so you can expect the ladies to be curious. And they won't be subtle about it. I'm not sure the word MacKenzie and subtle are two that go together."

Sophia let Declan take her hand and lead her past the house and down to the lake. She wasn't sure how she felt about being put under the microscope for all MacKenzies to see, but she could admit her own curiosity about his family. She'd never gotten to see Declan in that kind of environment when they were together before, how he interacted with his family and how they interacted with him.

"You see that house there?" he said, pointing directly across the lake. "That's my parents' house. My dad was the youngest, so this house we're at now is actually the original MacKenzie homestead. The main structure dates back to the early 1800s. And every generation has added something new as the family expanded. When my parents married they built that house across the lake. The design mirrors the original structure here exactly, and then they expanded it so it would hold five children and all their friends. My cousins have all stayed close. They each have homes on this property. My parents are gone on another of their world travels. They only spend time here now when they know the whole family is going to be around."

She didn't interrupt or ask questions as he talked about his family. He might not realize it yet, but he missed them more than he thought. The sadness in his voice was unmistakable, and she got the impression that he was tired of living the life he'd chosen. If he didn't slow down and find something to balance out the horror he dealt with on a daily basis he was going to crash and burn.

"Thomas is married to Cat," he continued. "And they live in this house with their four children, so you can see the need for that extra wing they're building. Cat has some useful skills from her former life, so she does the occasional contract work for MacKenzie Security, but only the jobs where I know she won't be in danger."

"You saw Charlie's Automotive on the way in, and that shop belongs to my cousin Dane's wife. She's about forty-two months pregnant right now with their fourth child though so she's not able to get under the hood, and she's cranky about it because Dane is making her stay home until the baby is born. I think he's probably sleeping on the couch a lot these days."

"I can't say I blame her. She's probably going crazy without anything to do." Though the thought of a hugely pregnant woman trying to maneuver her way under the hood was amusing.

"Hunh," he said. "I'm sure we'll get to hear all about it at dinner. There are so many pregnant women in this family at one time or another it's hard to keep track. We like big families."

"And sex, apparently," she said dryly.

His lips quirked and she realized how rare this playful side of Declan was. "That goes without saying. Then there's my other cousin Riley and his wife and their three kids. He's a professor at one of the private colleges a couple of hours from here. And you met Cooper already. His wife's name is Claire and she's the librarian here in Surrender. My brother Grant and his wife and kids will be here too."

"I remember meeting him before. He's the quiet one and has those serious brown eyes. You and Cooper look like you should be brothers instead."

"We get that a lot. Me and Cooper and Cade and Darcy all take after the MacKenzie side in coloring. We've got a picture in the house of my great-great grandfather who looks so much like Cade that it's eerie. Blood is a weird thing."

He changed their direction and led her back in the direction of the house. She hadn't realized how far they'd walked, and the smells coming from the house made her mouth water. It had been a long time since she'd had a home cooked family meal, not since before her mother had died.

"It's beautiful," she said. "What you've all made here. And you probably don't realize how lucky you are to have this to come home to, or to have that built in support system. I can't tell you how many times over the last several years I wished my parents were still alive or that I'd been lucky enough to have brothers and sisters to call once everything started spiraling."

"You called me," he said softly.

The laugh that escaped her lips was sardonic, and she looked out over the lake as the sun started to set. "I guess that should tell you just how desperate I was."

"I would've been there whether you'd called me or not," he said, taking her hand so she couldn't keep walking. "I bloodied more than one lip and blackened more than one eye when I found out they were bringing you in, and I did the only thing I could do to make sure they kept me in the loop and didn't push me out completely. You have to believe that, Soph. I would never leave you stranded that way, without someone in your corner to fight on your behalf."

She let out the breath she'd been holding slowly. "It didn't feel that way at the time, that's for sure. But you're still here trying to take over my life, so maybe you're being honest with me."

"There's another reason why you called me instead of an attorney or anyone else who might have been able to help you."

"Because I'm a glutton for punishment?"

"No," he said, bringing her hand to his lips and kissing the palm softly, making her heart turn over in her chest. "Because even though we've had our struggles and I was an idiot for doing what I thought was right by sending you away, you realized something when your back was against the wall." His gaze followed to her lips where she was biting down nervously. "You realized, that despite everything, I'm your family too."

And then she stopped breathing altogether as his lips came down on hers. Fire rushed beneath her skin and bombs exploded in her head. His hunger took her by surprise, and she realized just how much he'd been holding back during their exploits. There were no handcuffs strong enough to restrain this man when his need was so fierce.

She ached to the depths of her soul for this man—only for him. His arms circled her waist and he pulled her close, so his erection pressed against her belly, and his lips slanted over hers as his tongue invaded her mouth. Heat surrounded her, enflamed her, and she gave back as good as he was giving, sucking on his tongue until she felt his harsh growl rumble in his throat.

How had she ever thought she'd escape Declan MacKenzie with her whole heart? The games they'd been playing where she'd had the illusion of control weren't going to work anymore. She needed him hot and hard inside of her, dominating her and taking her the way he had so many years before. His mouth had satisfied her but it hadn't quenched the fire of her desire.

The consequences would have to be dealt with later, and she hoped spending another night in Declan's bed would make up for the heartbreak he was sure to give her again before their time together was through.

"Hey, Kissyface," Cooper called out from the back porch. "Dinner's ready."

Sophia didn't think she'd ever laughed during a kiss before, but when they pulled apart they were having trouble holding it together.

"Maybe you can get Darcy to put itching powder in his jock strap," she suggested.

"Oh, she did something much better to him than itching powder. Being the only girl and the youngest in a family of nine boys makes you more imaginative than the average eight year old girl."

"Maybe I need to get some tips from her on how to handle MacKenzie men."

"I shudder to think," he said, wrapping his arm around her waist. "Besides, I'll let you handle me any time you want to. All you have to do is ask."

CHAPTER FOURTEEN

Dinner with the MacKenzies was like nothing she'd ever experienced before. The house was just as sprawling on the inside as it was on the outside, and it was obvious the large dining room was one of the newer additions to the house.

The large cherry wood table sat twenty-four, and every seat was taken. The older kids were too cool to sit with the adults, so they'd been banished to the sun porch at the large table out there. The smaller kids sat in booster seats or high chairs between their parents, and Dec had been right, there were enough kids in the room that the MacKenzie women probably spent a lot of time pregnant. But if the rest of the men in the family were anything like Declan in bed, it probably wasn't such a hardship to keep trying.

She'd once thought of having children with Declan, maybe a few years after she graduated college so they'd have time to spend some alone time together first. But she hadn't thought of bringing a child into the world since before her wedding night, and after she'd married Kane she'd made sure she got her birth control shot every three months like clockwork because she couldn't have imagined bringing a child into that situation.

But that once forgotten longing swept over her as she

sat at the center of the table next to Declan. Dane sat across from her and she watched as he took turns rubbing his very pregnant wife's back and cutting up meat for the toddler sitting next to him. Riley sat to her left and held a sleeping baby of only a few months on his shoulder while he talked baseball with Cooper sitting across from him.

It was a family that treasured the blessings they had and truly enjoyed each other's company. The men loved their wives openly—not only did they love them—they liked them. Her parents had been married almost forty years, and she knew they loved each other, but she couldn't say that they liked each other enough to spend extra time with each other. And it was a shame. If you were going to spend your life with someone, the friendship was the most important thing. Friendship survived old age and sagging body parts and illness and sorrow. She realized with clarity that's what she'd missed most after Declan had cut ties with her so abruptly. She'd lost her best friend and lover all in one fell swoop.

Declan squeezed her thigh beneath the table while he continued arguing politics with his brother Grant.

"Aw, man. You guys started the party without us."

Sophia looked toward the entryway along with everyone else, and she was caught off guard by the men who stood in the doorway. No one had run away screaming at their intrusion, so she assumed they were part of the family. She wondered briefly if the MacKenzies were related to Lucifer himself, and she hoped to God he was on their side.

"If you'd ever show up to anything on time, we wouldn't always start without you," Grant called out.

The man smiled and dimples winked at the corners of his mouth, and it almost made up for the imposing picture he made. He stood tall, several inches over six feet and his shoulders were broad and muscled. A black T-shirt fit tight around his biceps and it was tucked into black cargo pants. Dog tags hung around his neck and she could partially see a scrollwork tattoo peeking from one of his sleeves. The dimples might distract at first sight, but his eyes were as dark as night and intelligent. And he didn't look like someone you'd want to cross. Ever.

"Grab a plate and sit down, Shane," Cat, Thomas's wife, said. "There's room for you and Brady both at the table. A couple of the kids have fallen asleep in their plates."

Adjustments were made and the kids were moved into another room to bed down for the night as Shane and Brady made room for themselves at one end of the table.

"Shane MacKenzie," he said, holding out a hand as he sat down across from her. "Nice to finally meet you. I like that mole by your mouth. Very sexy," he said, waggling his eyebrows.

She burst into laughter at his boldness and felt an instant kinship with him. He was the youngest male in the family, and it looked like he'd been doing his best to needle his brothers and cousins in as many ways as possible over the years by the way everyone around them groaned at his outrageousness. Shane MacKenzie was a heartbreaker, plain and simple.

"The man standing patiently next to my Neanderthal brother is Brady Scott," Declan said. "He's Darcy's husband's brother, and he and Shane belong to the same SEAL team. They help us out on occasion."

"On occasion?" Shane snorted. "We pull your asses out of a lot of situations to just be considered occasional help. You're welcome by the way."

"It's not like you're working for free," Dec said. "If your prices keep going up I'm going to start using SEAL Team Eight out of Texas as backup. And there'd probably be less whining."

"You get what you pay for, brother."

"I'd like it noted that I have no objections with working more than occasionally," Brady said. "I've almost got my house built and paid for."

SINS AND SCARLET LACE

Shane snorted out a laugh and slapped his friend on the back. "Kiss-ass. Brady has ideas of home and hearth. I've never met a SEAL so bent on putting down roots. It doesn't seem natural."

"I think it's wonderful," Charlie said, handing her plate to Dane as they started clearing the table.

"Better watch it, Shane," Cat said, laughing. "It'll be you next. You're the last MacKenzie standing."

"Bite your tongue, woman. This MacKenzie is going to be footloose and carefree for a lot of years. Someone has to carry on the MacKenzie family tradition since all of you seem to enjoy being shackled a little too much for my liking."

Sophia felt her cheeks heat as she remembered exactly how much Declan had enjoyed being shackled, and when his hand squeezed her thigh again she realized he was remembering as well.

"How's the perimeter?" Dec asked, moving to business.

"It's secure. You've done a hell of a job with the setup, so it made our jobs easier. We added a few bonus features spanning out several miles from the perimeter of the compound, but it's ready. We've split up into teams of two." Shane laid a couple of napkins out flat and picked up several utensils that were laying nearby.

"This first napkin is the original MacKenzie land. It's a lot of space to cover, and I don't think there will be any danger to anyone outside of your location, but I have two men set up in the hunting cabin out by the lake just to be safe." He put a fork in the general location of the hunting cabin. "There's more than a hundred acres that stretches between your compound and this property."

He put another fork down where Declan had built his secured command center and his own home. "I've got another team of two set up at the cabin you built outside the walls on the southwest and another team of two in the cabin to the northeast. Brady will stay inside the gated perimeter and be backup for you there just in case, and I'll monitor the nifty electronics we've got placed around. Everyone needs to stay clear of open land areas, because we have a few surprises in strategic locations. It shouldn't be a problem since it's open land anyway, but you probably want to avoid any romantic picnics in the middle of any hayfields. That would be a terrible thing to lose a vital part of your anatomy when you're just getting to use it again."

Several of the men at the table snickered and the women rolled their eyes.

"Some day some woman is going to put you in your place, and I'm going to enjoy watching it happen tremendously," Dec said.

"When hell freezes over," he said good-naturedly. "I'm assuming that you've been doing some work on your end and haven't just been relying on the SEALs to do everything for you?"

"Whoever we're dealing with has a pretty extensive knowledge of computers that goes beyond mere hacking. I've set up some cyber-bait to see how far his curiosity about Sophia goes. As far as the money goes, that's a mystery. If Sophia had possession of accounts or the cashier's check Kane withdrew from the bank, then they'd be hard pressed to find it in the ashes of her home. Which means they think she has passwords or whatever is needed to get the money memorized."

"That's not good," Shane winced.

"Why not?" Claire asked.

"Because if they think she has the information memorized then Sophia becomes the target instead of the money itself. They'll do whatever they can to get to her, and then they'll do whatever it takes to get her to talk."

"On that note, I think I want to skip dessert," she said.

CHAPTER FIFTEEN

Sophia had never been in a place were true darkness existed. Even out on her small piece of property without neighbors for miles around, she could still see the yellow glow of city lights in the distance.

But not here. In Surrender there was nothing in the distance but stars and a sliver of moon that looked as if it were close enough to touch.

They'd left the MacKenzie house with a bag of food and a lot of hugs. It was an odd feeling, and even when her parents had been alive, that much physical contact was rare. Declan drove them down a rutted one-way road that was more trail than road, and she bounced along in the Hummer next to him, holding onto the handle on the ceiling.

"There will be rain in the next few hours." He pointed off to the northwest. "See how the clouds are rolling in? It looks like they're eating the stars."

"I'm not a fan of storms."

"I remember. This will be a short one. Just a summer shower that will give everything a good soak, though we might be isolated tomorrow if the roads flood. This is the only one that leads to my property, and you can see it's nothing but dirt." He turned on the high beams so she could see farther out in front of them.

This area was different than the land surrounding the MacKenzie homestead, and the headlights shone on nothing but flat land and tree stumps.

"We cleared the trees out here because I wanted to be able to see incomers from all directions. The perimeter wall surrounds twenty-five acres of the property. If you'll notice, we've been going uphill for the last fifteen minutes, and the altitude is a bit higher. The back of the perimeter wall backs up to a deep gorge that goes down about seventy-five feet and is nothing but rocks. I left the trees inside the perimeter because I wanted it to seem like a home, and you can't ever see the walls from where I've positioned my house. There's a small lake not too far inside the walls and there's a large cabin that sleeps several whenever I get stuck with uncle duty and the kids come hang out."

"Don't you feel imprisoned behind the walls?"

"I told you, you can see them from the house, but it's nice to know they're there. It makes me feel like I could keep my family safe. Anyone who tried to climb those walls would be in for a rude awakening."

The headlights hit the walls in questions and she leaned forward so she could see better. A heavy gate blocked the way inside and Dec hit a button on his watch and she watched as the gate slid open. They were barely through when it closed behind them.

It didn't take long for the trees to cocoon them as Dec drove along a curved road that was much smoother than the one leading in. Sophia gasped at the sight as outdoor lights came on the moment Dec stopped the car. The stone house rose up out of the ground and seemed to meld with the landscape perfectly.

"It's got two full stories above ground and another full story below," Dec said. "The command center is about a hundred feet behind the house, but I built it with the same materials, so it looks more like a guest house than secret spy headquarters."

She could hear the smile in his voice. "It's beautiful here. I could just sit and look at the scenery for hours."

"You haven't seen anything yet."

Sophia opened the back door of the Hummer and frowned as she saw her things were no longer there. "What the hell?" she said.

"Oh, that's why Shane was late to dinner. He went ahead and brought all of your things to the house and put them in your room."

"My room?" she asked. "Or your room?"

"Whose room do you want to be in, Soph? Because I've got to tell you, all I've been able to think about since I tasted you down by the lake was sliding deep inside of you until we're both begging for mercy. So my vote is for my room."

He grabbed his backpack and she waited while he disarmed security before following him into the house. Cool air met her flesh and sent shivers across her skin. He didn't turn any of the lights on, but he let his backpack fall to the ground and pushed her back against the door.

Her breath caught as he caged her in and pressed his body intimately against hers. His erection was hard against her pubic bone, and when she raised up on her toes just the smallest amount the pressure to her clit had her moaning.

"You keep forgetting about my self-preservation plan." His lips traced along her jaw and then he nipped at the sensitive skin on her neck. "I don't think sharing a bedroom is a step in the right direction."

"This stubbornness of yours is inconvenient." He suckled at her neck and then trailed up and bit gently on her earlobe. "What if you wake up in the middle of the night and your pussy is soaked and needy? All I'd need to do is roll over and slide inside."

Her fingers massaged the back of his neck and she brought her leg up so it wrapped around his hip. "That does sound more convenient," she moaned as he pushed against her.

"But I wouldn't want to interfere with your ability to make a logical decision based on your self-preservation theory." He pulled away and she tightened her leg around him to keep him close, but he untangled himself from her grasp easily and then bent down to grab his backpack. "You probably want to unpack some of your things and get a shower after the long couple of days we've had."

"Really?" she asked, putting her hands on her hips and narrowing her eyes. "We could be rolling around on the floor screaming right now, but you're going to show me to my room?"

"It's all part of my master plan."

He started up the stairs and she had no choice but to follow. The upstairs was wide and open—a large den area that split off into what she assumed were different bedrooms. If she'd been less frustrated, she would've taken the time to look around, but as it was she was having a difficult time not jumping on his back and taking him to the ground.

"A master plan of no sex? That doesn't sound like you."

"No," he said, his lips twitching. She swore if he laughed then he deserved a punch right to the nose for leaving her in such an aroused condition. "I figure if you end up coming to me then you can't blame me when you decide to forget about your self-preservation idea. So you'll have to move your things to my room if you want that middle of the night satisfaction. The master suite is in the basement by the way."

"You son of a bitch," she growled.

"That's not very nice," he said. "My mother is a lovely woman. As long as you're on her good side. Otherwise, bad things happen. That woman knows how to deliver a swat that stings."

He opened the first door on the left and ushered her in. "Here are all your things. I'm going to go grab my own shower and answer some email. If you need to find me I'll be up on the roof. Just take the stairs through that door there," he said, pointing to what looked like a closet door. "Make yourself at home, Soph."

He closed the door in her surprised face and before she could think twice her shoe hit the door after him. She liked to think she'd only imagined his laughter as he left her alone.

CHAPTER SIXTEEN

Declan brought the bottle of beer to his lips and drank deeply as he watched the last of the stars fade through the storm clouds. Thunder echoed in the distance, but there was still time until the rain hit.

On a clear night he'd sit up on the roof and stare at the stars for hours. It was completely glassed in, and he supposed it was a good place to entertain, but he'd always considered it his private space. The only furniture he'd moved up there was a double-size chaise lounge, and it sat lonely in the middle of the large space.

He'd built it for her. Because the image of how wild and carefree they'd been that afternoon at the planetarium was burned in his brain. The way she'd rubbed against him casually as they made their way through the darkened rooms or the way her hand had trailed up his thigh and cupped the erection he had no hope of hiding. The place had been all but deserted and the little sundress she wore had his imagination going wild.

Then they'd come into a room that was nothing but stars and black sky and she lifted up the skirt of her sundress so just the bottom of the round globes of her ass could be seen, and she'd pushed down the tiny panties she wore so they dropped to her feet. He'd gone crazy with wanting her, and he pushed her to the wall, anchoring her hands above her head while he freed his cock.

He'd fucked her like an animal, and the whole thing had only lasted a couple of minutes at best, just enough to take the edge off until they were home again. But that day had always stayed with him, and even now, the remembrance had him hard enough he was glad he'd pulled on sweats after his shower.

Dec took another sip of beer and then went to lay down on the chaise. He was tired, and they'd both need to get several solid hours of sleep. It was probably best for both to retreat to their own corners for the night. She needed time to think. It was obvious she still had reservations even though she was willing to share her body with him. But trust had to be earned and he'd have to give her the time she needed to come to terms with her own wants.

His body went still as he heard the rooftop door open and close again, and then he breathed in the sweet scent of soap and his cock tented his sweatpants; he fought the urge to wrap his fist around the hard flesh and start stroking. He let his beer dangle from his fingers and he didn't let his gaze shift from the turbulent clouds above.

"I found this on top of my clothes," Sophia said, tossing something hard and square onto his stomach. He almost laughed when he looked down and saw the box of condoms. A 48-pack. "It seems Shane wanted us to be prepared."

"That's the MacKenzie family motto. At least one of them. Darcy left an identical box for me back in D.C."

Declan tossed the condoms aside and finally looked at her. His bottle dropped the remaining couple of inches to the ground with a clank when he saw what she was wearing.

"I take it Darcy packed that for you too?" he asked, trying hard not to swallow his tongue. "Remind me to let her have the company credit card more often."

The nightgown shimmered in bold ruby and was the

sheerest, most delicate lace he'd ever seen. It flowed against her skin from breast to mid-thigh, and he could just make out the dark rose of her nipples beneath. She'd left her hair down how he liked it and her toes were painted scarlet to match the gown. He didn't know why that little detail turned him on, but he found himself longing to start kissing at her toes and work his way up.

"I was just thinking about the planetarium, replaying the way you pushed your panties down over that sweet bottom and let them drop to the floor. It drove me fucking insane when you did that."

"Like this?" she asked, arching a brow.

She turned so her back faced him, and he stopped breathing as her fingers skimmed up her thighs, catching on the gown and bringing it up higher and higher—teasing him—tempting him with sweet glimpses of flesh. Her thumbs hooked in the strings of the tiny matching thong she wore and she brought them down slowly until she finally released them and they fell to the ground.

Sophia stepped out of the panties and then bent down to pick them up, and he saw the sweetest sight imaginable. Her pussy lips were swollen and slick. And bare. She'd shaved during her shower, and the sight had his balls tightening against his body and come threatening to spill from his cock.

"Sweet mercy, Soph," he rasped. "Are you trying to kill me?"

"It seems to be working better than shooting you."

"Come here, baby. Let me give you what you want."

Sophia let the gown fall back to her thighs and walked toward Declan. Her body was an inferno of need, and she knew there was no changing the course of a force so powerful.

SINS AND SCARLET LACE

She belonged to him. She'd always belonged to him, and she realized something while she was in the shower. There was no shame in loving him after all they'd been through. He hadn't wanted her, but she'd managed to survive without him. And if he didn't want her again she'd keep on surviving. But there was no point in denying herself the pleasure it was obvious only he could give.

She was stronger than she'd been then, and she wanted him to understand that strength had been born of necessity, and she wouldn't run away this time. The love for him had never disappeared as she'd wanted it to, and he was in for a hell of a fight if he ever tried to protect her by sending her away again.

He took hold of her hand and pulled her close, and she lifted herself to his kiss, letting the passion take over as his lips slanted hungrily across hers. His fingers tangled in her hair, and the sharp bite against her scalp as he pulled the strands had her gasping into his mouth.

Arousal swept through her loins like a wild flame and she moaned as his tongue swept inside her mouth and mated in a way so primitive and sensual that her knees shook. Her hands found the hem of his T-shirt and jerked it up so her hands touched the taut muscles of his stomach.

He let go of her hair and ripped the shirt over his torso and tossed it aside, and she rubbed her breasts against his hot skin, moaning at the sensations as she teased herself mercilessly. He tugged at the bodice of her nightgown so her breasts popped free, plump and high, displayed for his pleasure. He filled his hands with the swollen mounds, his fingers tweaking the rosy peaks of her nipples, and she felt the tug all the way to the tight bud between her thighs.

She arched against him, crying out as he leaned down and took a nipple into his mouth, sucking it deep as his tongue laved across it. Her fingers grasped the back of his head and pulled him closer, and then she grew impatient, wanting to feel more of him.

Her nails raked down his chest to the elastic waistband of his sweats and she tugged—hard—so they pulled down below his hips and his cock sprang free. Her hand fisted around him and she groaned as he seemed to swell in her hand.

"Fuck, you'll have me coming in your hand," he said, releasing her nipple with a pop. He pushed down the sweats all the way and stepped out of them so he stood naked—his cock a mouth-watering sight as it stood iron-hard and hot away from his body. His hand replaced hers at the base of his cock and she licked her lips as he squeezed hard and a tiny drop of pearly liquid gathered at the tip.

"Mmm," she moaned, kneeling before him. His hand fisted back in her hair and he sucked in a sharp breath as her tongue licked out as delicate as a cat's and gathered the salty drops on her tongue.

"Fuck me—"

His head dropped back on his shoulders and his grip tightened as her lips wrapped around the flared head of his cock and her tongue swirled around him. One hand cupped his balls gently and her other hand gripped his thigh, her nails biting into flesh. She opened her mouth wider, took him down deeper, until her chin rested against the delicate sac. She held her breath, prolonging his pleasure for as long as she could before she had to pull back and suck in oxygen.

"Enough," he shouted. He was seconds away from shooting inside that sweet mouth, and she was lapping him up like cream. But damned if he was going to come inside anything but her tight pussy.

He pulled her back and lifted her to her feet, pushing her back until her knees hit the back of the chaise and then down so she was sprawled on her back, the red lace of the nightgown pulled down over her breast and up over her hips, exposing the bare flesh between her thighs.

"Christ, Sophia," he panted. "The sight of you is my

every fantasy. It's my turn to taste that sweet pussy and bury my tongue between those naked folds. Did you think of my tongue sliding through that sweet syrup while you were shaving?"

His finger trailed between the folds, gathering the cream of her desire so she could see the evidence. He brought his finger to his lips and sucked, moaning as the taste of her filled his senses.

"Pull your knees up high," he demanded. "I want to see all of you."

Color darkened her cheeks, but she did as he asked and pulled her knees high to her chest. He kneeled beside the chaise and inhaled her arousal before placing a soft kiss on the swollen bud of her clit.

"Fucking beautiful," he whispered, his breath feathering across the moist flesh. And then his mouth and tongue were pressed against her as he sucked and licked and tasted every delectable inch of her folds.

Her fingers tightened on his scalp, and the mewling cries she made in the back of her throat only made him want to give her more, to make her lose control until the cries turned into screams of ecstasy. Her hips rolled against him and she jerked as his teeth scraped over the hardened bud of her clit.

"Dec." His name was desperation on her lips as his tongue moved faster, building her higher and higher. He parted the bare folds with his fingers, tonguing her deep and hard before pushing two fingers into the suckling depths of her pussy.

Her back arched on a gasp and she clamped down around him, the syrup of her desire coating his fingers and dripping down his wrist. All he could think was how tight she'd feel wrapped about his cock, and he stepped up his efforts to make her come like this first—so when he finally pushed inside of her she'd be swollen and tight and still pulsing from her own climax.

Perspiration coated both of their bodies and her

desperate pants turned into wailing moans as his fingers curled inside of her and rubbed against her G-spot. The texture was different there, rougher, and he moved his fingers faster and faster over the spot until she stiffened, her legs clamping around his head, as her entire body shook with the force of her orgasm.

He drank her until the last shudder wracked her body, and then he pulled his fingers free.

"I'll buy you another," he said, ripping the gown down the middle and then flipping her quickly to her belly, removing the shredded cloth and tossing it aside. Her pussy gleamed with the proof of her release, and he couldn't wait to be inside her.

Sophia's hands clawed at the fabric of the chaise and she tried to catch her breath, to reorient herself to the present, but Dec didn't give her a chance to do anything but scream. He thrust into her in one smooth stroke, and the walls of her pussy still quivered from her previous climax.

He stroked fast and hard—forceful—and her muscles stretched to accommodate his size. His fingers bit into her hips as he slammed against her, and he pushed so far, so deep, that she felt the familiar building inside of her once more.

Flesh slapped against flesh and sweat coated their bodies as she felt pure sensation gather in her womb like the beginnings of an electrical storm—white hot and pulsing as her pussy tightened around him. Her knees gave out and he followed her down to the chaise so their bodies lay flat, but he didn't stop driving into her.

His fingers twined with hers and they both grabbed at the edge of the chaise, and if possible he moved higher and harder inside her and that was all it took to set the lightning free. It coursed from her womb down her arms and legs, and she didn't recognize her screams of pleasure as the heated jets of Declan's come blasted inside of her, every spurt increasing the pleasure of her orgasm.

CHAPTER SEVENTEEN

The intensity of their lovemaking left them both limp and weakened, and he didn't know how long they lay there, their breaths heaving in tandem and the sweat cooling on their skin. Declan groaned when he pulled out of her and felt the stickiness of his semen against the chaise.

"Damn," he said, rolling to his side and pulling her with him so she rested in his arms. He wasn't even sure she was conscious. "Condoms. There was a whole fucking box and I couldn't think past the point of burying my dick inside you to put one on."

"S'kay," she murmured. "Birth control. All good."

The rain had started to fall sometime during their lovemaking, and he stared up as the rain splattered against the glass ceiling. She rolled over in his arms so her head rested against his chest and her hand splayed on his stomach. He hoped to God she wasn't ready to go again, but he wasn't sure he could get another hard-on in the next week, much less the next ten minutes.

"I always hated that you used condoms before, even though I was on the pill. I never felt like I felt all of you. That day at the planetarium was the first and last time you ever took me without one."

His fingers glided up her back and then back down

again in a lazy motion. "That last time we were together it took every ounce of self-control I had to put one on. I thought when I came back home that I'd ask you to marry me and then I'd never use one again. That whole mission I thought about how good it would feel to slide into you with nothing but flesh between us."

"I understand why you felt you had to push me away," she said softly. "I don't agree with it, but I understand that protecting the people you love is just part of your makeup. It's in your blood. You talk about getting me to trust you again, but if you think about it, you never trusted me to begin with. You didn't trust me to love you enough or stand by you no matter what."

She felt the breath shudder in his chest, but she had more to say. "And I wasn't strong enough to tell you to shut the hell up and that I wasn't going anywhere. If we were in the same position today there wouldn't be a nurse or a relative you could throw in my path to keep you from me."

"So I guess when it comes down to it, I didn't trust your love enough either. Because I should have known you were full of shit as soon as the words started coming from your mouth." She felt the tears she'd sworn she would never shed drip down her cheeks and onto his chest. "Because if I'd been paying attention for the two years we were together I would've been positive that the love you showed me in every gesture or kiss was the kind of love that can't be turned off and on like a switch. What we had was real. And we were both stupid for walking away."

"I want a second chance with you," he said, the huskiness in his voice warming her heart. "I want to make a life with you. We've already wasted so much time."

"Ten years is a long time to pick up where we left off." She swallowed and closed her eyes against the pain. "We're different people. We might find we don't like each other as much as we once did."

His lips touched the top of her head and she felt his

smile. "I guess we'll find out. We're going to be spending a lot of time together."

Declan looked up from his laptop as Sophia came into the kitchen early the next morning. It always took her a good hour before she was ready to face the day, and she stumbled into a bar stool as she followed her nose to the coffee pot.

The sight of her wearing nothing but one of his shirts had the blood pooling from his brain to his lap, and he shook his head in wonder. After the night they'd just shared he should be more than satisfied for a long while. Apparently not.

She drank the first cup black and standing against the kitchen counter. He knew better than to say anything until she was ready, so he went back to checking the traps he'd set for their friend. The last thing he wanted to do was leave a trail that could be followed back to their location in Surrender, so he'd set up dummy trails showing their location at multiple places all over the world.

Hackers had patterns, or signatures, they used when they tried to overtake a system, and Declan was hoping he'd be able to recognize the signature by the time he'd finished taking the bait. He had his own signature as well, which is what made what he was doing risky. Whoever was on the other end of the computer had already traced three of the nine dummy locations he'd set up.

"Good morning," Sophia finally said.

He grinned and pushed the computer back, reaching for his own cup of coffee. "Twenty-nine minutes," he said, looking at his watch. "You're getting faster at waking up."

"I can recognize sarcasm when I hear it. Did you eat already?"

"That's a loaded question if I've ever heard one." His

brow quirked and he watched in fascination as she blushed as red as the nightgown she'd been wearing the night before. "I could go for a little dessert for breakfast. Why don't you come over here and let me show you what I have in mind."

It was becoming increasingly warm in the kitchen, and he watched as Sophia's nipples puckered to hard peaks beneath the cotton of his T-shirt.

"I don't know, Dec." She fluttered her eyelashes flirtatiously. "It seems to me you should have to eat a good meal before you get dessert."

"I've always thought food tasted better if you had to catch it yourself." He grinned and scooted back from the table, hooking his fingers in his shirt and pulling it over his head.

Sophia's eyes widened and she put her coffee down on the counter, moving a few steps back with each step he took closer. His thumb and forefinger flicked open the button of his jeans, and she licked her lips and took another step backward.

The air around them was thick with lust and anticipation, and he stood poised at the ready, waiting for her to make the first move. The kitchen was open on all sides and she stood just at the edge of where the kitchen met the dining room.

He saw it in her eyes before she made her first move, and he was already leaping after her as she turned to run. A shriek of surprise bubbled out in a laugh as his fingers glanced off her arms before she maneuvered quickly in the opposite direction and put the dining room table between them.

"You might as well give in," he taunted. "Maybe I'll take it easy on you if you surrender peacefully."

"Who said I wanted it easy?" She pulled off her shirt and tossed it at his face to distract him as she took off toward the foyer.

Declan leapt over the dining room table and caught her

before she made it to the stairs. She was laughing as he took her lips in a scorching kiss, going straight for heat instead of a slow simmer. His hands grasped her bottom and lifted her so she was able to wrap her legs around his waist and her nails bit into his shoulder blades.

The kiss was endless, a mating of tongues and a sensual slide of lips. His hip bumped a table and something crashed to the ground, and he cursed as he worked to get his jeans unzipped. Her back slammed against the wall, knocking a picture from where it hung and her breasts rubbed against his chest as she pushed back against him. He could smell her heat and his knuckles glanced off the slick essence between her thighs as he finally got the zipper down and his jeans shoved to his hips.

His cock sprang free and he lifted her, searching for the entrance of her pussy so he could sink home, but she rolled her hips against him just as the head of his cock found her entrance and she dislodged him. Instead she slid her drenched pussy up and down his shaft.

"Christ," he panted. Her bare skin scorched his fingers as she pleasured herself shamelessly against him. The taste of her filled him, until he was drunk from the pleasure, and he stopped worrying about how he'd find the ability to draw his next breath as her ankles crossed behind his back and she squeezed him tighter.

He stumbled back from the wall, intending to move her to the couch, but her teeth bit down on his lower lip and color exploded from beneath his closed eyelids. Something shattered—maybe a vase—and her back hit the front door just as the flared head of his cock probed at her entrance. An incredible pressure rose within her as he stretched her sore muscles, and she bit her lip as the pleasure/pain assaulted her system.

A pounding at the front door and then the insistent ring of the doorbell had them both freezing, their breaths tight in their chests.

"Everything all right in there?" Shane called out,

laughter in his voice. "It sounds like someone fell over."

Declan groaned and sank a little further inside of her as he kept her pressed against the door.

"Maybe if we're quiet he'll go away," she whispered in his ear.

"I thought we were supposed to have a meeting this morning," Shane called out. "Maybe I'd better come in and make sure everything is all right."

"If you do, you die," Declan finally yelled through the door. Sweat gathered at his temples and his muscles strained at the effort it took to hold back. "Go away, Shane."

"I could just wait here on the porch for ten minutes and then knock again. But maybe y'all should go to a different room because you're pretty loud."

"Come back in an hour or I'm going to shoot you."

Sophia's body shook in a fit of laughter and she buried her head against his neck. Every movement she made had him slipping a little farther inside of her and he felt like his skin was being flayed alive. He eased his grasp on her bottom and let gravity sink her farther onto his cock. The laughter stopped and a sharp gasp rent the air as he felt the familiar tightening of her muscles.

"An hour?" Shane asked. "That's impressive, brother. I guess you get to be king of the jungle today. And to think I woke up early for this."

They both held their breaths as they heard a car door slam shut and then an engine start before driving away. Her teeth bit into his shoulder and he realized she was just on the edge of coming.

"Remind me to kill him later," he panted. Declan tightened his grasp on her bottom once more and pushed his entire length into her with one rough thrust.

The orgasm ripped from her body and she heard herself cry out, but it sounded as if it was trapped beneath water. Blood rushed to her ears and all she could focus on was the thick shaft pounding inside of her. He kept her anchored to the door with his hips, and she clamped tighter around him as she felt his finger probe at the sensitive bud of her anus.

All it took was a touch and she climaxed hard and long around him, bucking against him as she begged for mercy. His shout echoed her own and she felt the hot spurts of his semen filling her as he pinned her to the door with a final hard thrust. It was enough for a fast and powerful climax to shudder through her once more.

Thirty minutes later they were both showered and dressed and back in the kitchen.

"I'm never going to be able to look at Shane again," Sophia said as she rummaged through the fridge for sandwich fixings.

"That would be perfectly fine with me. I'm pretty sure I'm honor bound to kick his ass for that little stunt."

"Though to be honest, we probably were being a little loud. I'm sorry you broke your clock. And the picture frame. And that table. But I'm pretty sure you can glue the leg back on."

He narrowed his eyes as she laughed at him. "You laugh now, but what you don't understand is that this family is relentless when it comes to stuff like that. My cousin Dane and his wife once pulled a towel rod free that was bolted into the wall. It flew out of Charlie's grasp and shattered the shower door. Everyone still talks about that and it's been years." He grabbed the bread from the pantry and a knife from the drawer as she started setting things out on the counter. "Also, I like how you say it was me who broke the clock. Like you weren't involved at all."

"I was just along for the ride. I've got the sore muscles to prove it."

"You know, I've got a very nice Jacuzzi downstairs—"

His phone buzzed on the table and he sighed as he saw it was Brant on the line. "Hold that thought," he said as he picked up the phone.

"Why aren't you on vacation?" he said as he answered the call.

"Because I've learned to listen to my gut," Brant said by way of greeting.

"We've got major trouble. About an hour ago a man dressed in a business suit carrying a briefcase was buzzed inside your building by your receptionist. The man pulled out a silenced pistol and double tapped your security guard in the head before giving the receptionist a single shot to the heart. I've seen the surveillance footage. It was quick and professional."

Dec stayed silent as fury boiled in his blood. He didn't show any outward reaction to what Brant had just told him, but Sophia must have sensed something was wrong because her eyes became worried and she stopped what she'd been doing to watch him carefully.

"Keep going," he said.

"The man left the briefcase and walked out. The outside cameras show him getting in a black sedan, and then they stopped beside the gate that leads down to the parking area. He tossed in a hand-held device that seemed to be on the same timing system as the briefcase left inside. The device rolled down almost all the way before things went boom."

"Who was called to the scene?" Dec asked.

"The police initially, but it wasn't fifteen minutes before Director O'Daniel was there shutting things down. I managed to slip in through your private entrance and clear out all of the classified files and set the computers to self-destruct mode."

Dec opened his laptop and checked the progress of the bait he'd set up. "How'd he find us?"

"Director O'Daniel isn't very forthcoming at the moment, but from what I was able to find out it looks like someone broke into his files. You'd think the Director of the CIA would have better security."

"Not for someone like this. Do me a favor and take Darcy on that vacation. And spread the word. I want all agents to go underground until I know how much of our personal information has been breached."

"You want me to leave you alone to fight this out by yourself? Darcy would have my head on a platter."

"I've got plenty of backup here if we need it. My best advice is to not tell her what's going on."

"So speaks the man who isn't married," Brant said, dryly. "I'll tell her what's going on, but I'll make sure we go under."

"Be safe and lock down the information you extracted from the office. I don't want any incoming information on my personal computer."

Dec hung up the phone just as the doorbell rang. "It looks like Shane's timing has improved. You're going to need to make more sandwiches."

CHAPTER EIGHTEEN

A week passed by, and the feeling in Declan's gut only grew stronger. Strong enough that he'd convinced the women and children to take a vacation into Canada for a few days, just to be safe. The original MacKenzie land was pretty far removed from where he'd set up his own stead, but he wasn't willing to take chances with the life of his family.

Unfortunately, he hadn't had the same luck getting rid of his brothers and cousins. Or his parents, who'd flown in unexpectedly a few days before. Dane had left with the women, but that was only because he needed to be with Charlie in case she went into labor, but he hadn't been happy about leaving them all behind. And Riley and his family had gone back to the other home they had in Washington State.

Despite the feeling of dread he felt, he enjoyed every moment of the time he spent with Sophia. He realized his home hadn't really felt like a home until she'd walked through the door, and now it seemed as if she'd always been there. He loved curling around her in the middle of the night or the way she looked first thing in the morning, when her cheeks were still flushed with sleep and her hair tousled.

It was the picture of the future he'd always wanted for

them, and he'd never take it for granted again.

"Maybe sometime we could do this in a bed," Sophia said. Her heart pounded wildly against his chest and he hoped the spots in his vision were temporary.

A picnic down by the lake had turned into more than just lunch by the time they'd finished eating, and he'd never been more thankful for the isolated area he'd chosen for his home, though he was pretty sure Sophia's screams could be heard up in the mountains.

"I thought you wanted to be spontaneous."

"Spontaneity was awesome when I was twenty. Now I have a deep and abiding love for mattresses. I can only imagine how you feel. You're not getting any younger either."

He pinched her backside and she giggled, wiggling against him in a way that didn't do anything to slow down his heart rate.

They'd set up their picnic blankets under a heavy covering of trees in the soft grass a few feet from the bank of the lake. Water lapped against the muddy bank and the wind rustled the tree branches above them.

"I think you broke my spine," she sighed.

"If you can't feel your legs, it means I'm doing something right. But next time I'll let you be on top. You deserve to have to do some of the work."

She laughed and rolled so her breasts were pressed into his chest and her leg was thrown over his thigh. Her hair brushed against his shoulder as she looked down at him, and he knew this moment would be another one of those snapshots of her he carried with him always.

He felt the familiar pull of arousal, and knew his body should be replete, but he could never seem to get enough of her. His hands went to her legs and he shifted her so she straddled his hips, and then he ran his fingertips up the smooth arch of her back. She purred beneath his touch and her eyes widened as his cock nudged at the still moist folds of her sex.

"I need to take out better health insurance," she said, leaning down to kiss his chin, then his lips. Her body relaxed and she sank into the kiss—gently—reverently—until time and sound ceased to exist around them.

His hands massaged her back and then lower to her buttocks, and then he shifted the head of his cock so it probed at her opening. Their gazes stayed steady on each other and neither of them seemed to breathe as she sank down all the way to the hilt.

He held her captive there, his hands anchored on her hips, filling her completely, and neither of them moved. In that moment he believed in the power of magic and he understood what the term soulmates meant for the first time, because he'd never felt more complete—more connected—than at that moment.

"I love you," he managed to get out as her muscles flexed around him. "More than I could ever say with just words."

Her breath shuddered and her eyes filled with tears that she blinked rapidly away. Her lips rubbed against his softly and the kiss was as light and fluttering as their first. "I love you, too."

The words left him feeling invincible and powerless at the same time, and his hands squeezed at her hips as he began moving inside of her, a steady push and pull that took him from hilt to tip with every thrust.

He knew he wouldn't last long, and by the rippling muscles of her pussy, he knew she'd be right there with him. Her hands pressed against his chest and he watched in awe as she rose high above him. Her hair tickled his thighs as her head dropped back on her shoulders, and her hands slid up her body to cup her breasts. He'd never seen anything more erotic, more beautiful in his life.

Then she rode him slow and steady, squeezing tight around him every time she lifted herself up. It was more than any sane man could bear, and he couldn't help but thrust upward every time she sank back down. His balls tightened and he felt the beginnings of his release at the base of his spine.

"Come with me, Soph. Come now."

Her pussy became hotter, tighter, and her orgasm washed over him as he pushed higher and harder inside her. Her scream was silent as she fell forward onto his chest and his semen erupted from his cock, draining him with every spurt, until he felt completely wrung out.

"I see what you mean about a bed," he said. It could have been a few minutes or hours later. "I think I'm laying on a rock."

She snickered but she made no move to untangle their bodies.

"I want you to make your home here with me." Her shoulders tensed and then he felt her slowly relax again. "We're right for each other, Soph. We've had our road blocks in the past, but I think we're at a place where we can move on. There's no one else I want in my life. No one else I'd want to make a family with."

"Wow. That's a lot to take in."

He could feel the nerves coiling in her spine as she sat up and tried to move away from him. He kept his hands on her hips so she couldn't disjoin their bodies and he kept his gaze steady on hers.

"You said you loved me. It seems like a natural progression to me."

"I just think this time around we should maybe take things a little slower. There's no rush for the happily-ever-after. And I want to make sure that we're both totally committed to what we have before we bring children into the mix."

"You don't trust me enough to keep loving you." He wanted to push back the anger building inside of him because he knew he deserved her skepticism and the fear that was obviously ruling her emotions, but he couldn't deny the hurt her lack of faith brought him.

He let her go this time when she tried to pull away, and

he watched as she scooted to the other side of the blanket to grab her clothes and start pulling them on.

"All I'm asking for is some time to think about it, and I'm not going to let you pressure me into doing it any other way."

Dec pulled on his jeans and T-shirt and packed up the food as his heart pounded in his chest. He didn't know how to convince her that he'd never push her away again. That he couldn't push her away without destroying himself.

"Fine," he finally said. "Take as much time as you need. As long as you're thinking about it here with me. The last I recalled you needed a place to live and you seem to like it here."

"Oh, yeah," she asked, eyes narrowing and her hands fisting at her hips. "How much is the rent? It might be out of my price range."

"I'm sure we can work out some kind of deal." He loaded up the stuff in his arms and turned his back to head toward the house. The waves of fury he felt hitting his back didn't make him feel as good as he thought it would, but he wasn't going to back down now. "MacKenzie Security could use an in-house accountant if you want the job."

Something hit him square in the back and he look down at the sandal that lay at his feet, his lips quirking. He turned around to face one furious woman.

"Don't you walk away and then drop a bombshell like that. You think you're wrapping things up nice and tidy when what you're really trying to do is put a noose around my neck."

"Do you really believe that, Soph? Or are you the one who doesn't want to tie herself down too tight? If you don't want the job then don't take it."

"So you'd just hire anyone to work for you without checking out their background first? You run what I'm assuming is a multi-million dollar corporation with government contracts and top secret information going in and out on a daily basis. That doesn't seem like very good business to me."

"It's actually excellent business. I know more about your work ethic and your brains than the partners at your old firm could ever hope to know. I know that if they'd paid attention, they would have known you'd never have been responsible for conspiring with Kane to move that money. They should've realized they were letting go their best accountant and someone who would likely be sitting as partner in another five years. Their stupidity is my gain. But like I said, if you don't want it, don't take it. Now can I go back inside or are you going to throw more shoes at me?"

Tears streamed down her face as she stared at him in complete surprise. He had no idea what he'd said to make that look appear on her face, but he knew he probably owed her an apology. Instead she surprised him with her gratitude.

"Thank you for saying that," she said, wiping her face with the back of her hand. "That's one of the things that had hurt the most. When they let me go. No one believed me. Believed in me."

"I believed in you. I just couldn't show it at the time. And I'll pay for that for the rest of my life."

She started toward him, defeat weighing down her shoulders. "Just give me a little more time to get used to this. To be with you. I do love you. I never stopped, even when I told myself I hated you."

He sighed and held out his hand. It was an offer he had no choice but to take.

"Oh, damn," she gasped, her hand going to her throat. "My necklace."

The chain she always wore around her neck was gone, and he set down the supplies and went to help her look. It was the only thing she had left of her old life, and if he had to drag the lake to help her find it then that's what he'd do.

"You had it on when we started eating lunch," he said, looking over the ground where their blankets had been spread.

"It must have come off when I took off my shirt."

"My memories are pretty vague after that, but I think your shirt landed somewhere by the tree." He walked over to the area in question and knelt down so he could see beneath the roots and wild grass that grew there. "Aha, here we go."

The cameo necklace lay face up, the silver chain crumpled beneath it. When he picked it up the chain slid out into his hand.

"The clasp is broken. We can get it fixed in town. There's a little jewelry store there."

"As long as the cameo itself is okay then I don't care. It's all I have left of my family."

"It's beautiful work." It was pale pink in color and the image was of a Victorian woman, her hair piled high and her face serene and somehow lonely. The artistry was intricate as each feature was detailed with precision.

"My parents were older when I was born, so I never met my grandparents, but I remember my mother wearing this every day when I was little. She gave it to me for my thirteenth birthday and told me to take good care of it."

He turned it over in his hands, noting the silver markings on the back and the tiny clasp to the side. "Do you have pictures inside?" he asked, working at the clasp with his thumbnail.

"What are you doing? No, it's not a locket."

"Yes, it is," he insisted. "See, you've got a clasp here. It's just hard to see the seam because it's so well made."

The clasp gave and the cameo split in two. "I'll be damned. You were right."

Declan opened it up so it lay open in his hand. A picture of Sophia's parents lay was inserted in one half of the oval, and in the other half a picture of who he assumed were her grandparents. And on top of their picture lay a tiny silver key. A lockbox key.

"What's that?" she asked, her voice barely a whisper.

"If I had to guess, I'd say half a billion dollars." He dumped the key out in his hand and handed her the cameo with the pictures of her family. "You took good care of it," he said, kissing her on the forehead as she stared down at the only photographs she had left of her family, and his heart broke as her tears fell.

CHAPTER NINETEEN

Declan started an image search of the lockbox key and numbers as soon as they made it back to the house, starting first with the banks Kane had already been known to use. The database of files he had access to was more extensive in some ways than the CIA because he didn't have to go through red tape and deal with privacy laws.

His office sat just off the kitchen and he could hear Sophia muttering to herself as she tried to follow a recipe Cat had given her for homemade bread. By the sound of the pounding going on, she was trying to get rid of some of her own frustrations.

He put in a call to his brother Cade and another one to Brant so he could update status and tell them to stay put, but to his frustration, no one was answering their damned phones. He rubbed his hands over the top of his head and left the computer search open and running.

Between the key and the way the hacker was taking the bait he'd laid, he was starting to get a good picture of the person who was after Sophia, and he knew he needed to tell her what was going on so she didn't think he was keeping things from her, but he couldn't think of a way to do it without hurting her more.

He took a deep breath and stepped into the kitchen,

wincing when her fist punched into the dough.

"How's it going?" he asked, keeping his distance on the other side of the kitchen island.

"Fantastic. I don't know why I've never done this before. It's very cathartic." She patted the dough into a ball and then put into an oversize bowl before tossing a towel over the top. "So what was all the muttering about in there? I take it you haven't found which bank the key belongs to?"

"Not yet, but it's going to be an extensive search. I think I've found out a few important pieces of information though."

"Oh yeah?" Her brow arched in question, but she could see the tension in the balled fists of her hands.

A high shrill alarm sounded from his office and his phone started buzzing at the same time. His only thought was to protect Sophia, and he pulled his weapon free. The alarm meant that there was a breach somewhere on the property, but he couldn't pinpoint where or who until he looked at the satellite.

"Go down to the basement and bolt the door behind you. You remember where the exit is that leads into the tunnels?" he asked.

She nodded and was already heading in that direction, but he pulled her back as someone pounded at the door.

"It's Shane. Open up."

Dec went to the door and let his brother in. Shane's weapon was held at the ready in one hand and the other was holding an electronic device that looked like an oversized iPad. It was still in the testing phase, but it showed a 3D projection of all satellite images and the topography of any terrain in the world.

"We've got an unidentified military transport closing in." Shane went to the table and laid down the device and hologram of the area rose up above the table.

"Whoa," Sophia said. "That's cool."

"It's in stealth mode, but those new tweaks you added

to your system worked and we can see them coming in plain as day."

Declan's phone buzzed again and Shane tossed it to him. "MacKenzie," he barked.

"It's Cade," his brother said. "We're about to land. Don't shoot us."

"You're telling me that's you that's flying toward us in an unidentified military transport?"

"Yep." He could hear the grin in Cade's voice, and his hand clenched around the phone so hard he was surprised it didn't turn to dust. "And it's a piece of work too. Still in the test phase. Gabe knows some people who owe him a favor."

"I'm going to kick your ass as soon as you land."

"No you're not. You're going to kiss my feet because I brought you something you're going to need."

"What's that?"

"Backup."

Cade disconnected the phone and Declan dropped his head down to his chest with a sigh of relief.

"He always does like to make an entrance," Shane said, closing down the device. "I think I liked him better before he started being so happy all the time. I'd finally gotten used to him being an asshole and then the man falls in love and suddenly it's rainbows and unicorns."

Sophia snorted out a laugh, and they all left through the kitchen door out to the deck, searching for Cade. If Dec hadn't felt the rush of air against his clothes he never would have known it was there. A sleek black helicopter hovered silently over his roof—one of the newest versions of the stealth helicopter that was still in the test phase. It looked like they'd finally succeeded in silencing the blades all the way.

He shook his head as he saw Gabe in the pilot seat and Cade grinning next to him like it was Christmas morning. It was large, bulbous, and obviously meant to transport a team of soldiers into a hostile area.

SINS AND SCARLET LACE

"Holy shit, will you look at that," Shane said, his grin stretching from ear to ear. "I wonder what kind of favor someone owed Gabe for this to be the payback."

"You probably don't want to know," Dec said wryly.

"Ooh, baby. I can't wait to ride out on a mission in one of these."

Gabe maneuvered the helicopter to a flat area of ground and landed it smoothly before shutting down the motor. The side door slid open and Dec put his hands on his hips, irritation etching his face as he watched his agents and brother pile out of the helicopter.

"What part of go underground didn't you understand?" he asked. Cade led the group up to the deck—Max and Jade Devlin, Cal Colter, Archer Ryan, Brant Scott and Gabe Brennan—they were all there.

Cade snorted out a laugh. "Seriously? You think we're going to let you lure the bad guys here to face all by yourself? You're not Superman, you know."

Shane was already giving knuckle bumps and slaps on the back to the new additions to the group and then he headed toward the helicopter to get a closer look.

"Don't worry, brother," Cade said. "I'm sure you'll figure out a way to pay us all back."

"I've already got it planned," Dec said, deciding to wait to tell them he was moving headquarters to Surrender. "If you guys are determined to stay, then lets get to work. Coordinate with Shane and his team and get settled. We'll debrief in an hour."

"We're going to have a problem," Sophia said. "There's not enough food in your fridge to feed all these people."

"I'm sure they'll figure something out."

"What are they going to do, go get takeout? Because I think I missed the part of Surrender where all the restaurants are located."

He let out a sigh because she was right. They were going to have to feed all these people. "We can pick up some steaks and potatoes. There are enough grills around here that it'll be quick and easy."

"Can we go after you meet with everyone?"

"I'll go. Why don't you make a list while the rest of us are meeting?"

"I don't think so, Declan MacKenzie. I'm starting to go stir crazy. I'd like to get out for a little while, even if it's just to the grocery store. And I'd like to get my chain fixed while we're out."

"I can take her while you're doing the debriefing," Shane said, not bothering to hide the fact he'd been eavesdropping. "I've got a couple of things to grab as well, so it'll kill two birds with one stone. And before you tell me I need to be at the debriefing, let me tell you that the stores all close at six and we won't make it in time if we wait until after. Also, I'll be with her and I won't let her out of my sight. Does that cover everything?"

Dec sighed and knew Shane was right. "Call me when you head back in." He pulled Sophia into his arms and didn't care that everyone stopped what they were doing to watch him kiss her brainless. When he pulled away she was out of breath and her eyes were heavy-lidded with arousal. "I love you. Don't let Shane talk you into anything that will get you arrested or banned from the stores. He has a reputation of causing trouble in this town."

"I'll try to keep him on the straight and narrow," she said, winking at Shane.

"You're killing me, Soph." Shane threw his arm around her shoulder and Dec smiled as she elbowed him in the ribs.

"She's going to fit right in this family," Cade said from behind him.

"I was just thinking the same thing."

CHAPTER TWENTY

Declan and Cade drove the perimeter of MacKenzie land in an open-top Jeep used for rough terrains. There was less than two years difference in age between he and Cade, and they'd been the closest because of it. Not that they didn't love their younger brothers and sister, but they were friends as well as brothers.

"So what was it you didn't say to everyone back there?" Cade asked.

Dec drove across a shallow stream and water splashed up on the tires. They climbed higher until they were at the top of a hill and could look down on the MacKenzie land, while the mountains stood menacingly to the east. Things were happening. He could feel it in his bones, and he took comfort in the fact that men he trusted were ready to cover his back.

"Whoever hacked into my system and followed my trails set a few pieces of bait of his own. It was clever the way he did it. More showing off than trying to be effective in doing any damage. On top of that, he knew where to look and what to look for when he hacked into Director O'Daniel's classified files. He knew to look for me first, and that led him to MacKenzie Security and the agreement we have with the government for contract work."

"So who is it?" Cade asked.

"That's the problem. The only man I know who could do all of those things is supposed to be dead."

"That's the thing with this business. Dead isn't always as dead as it's supposed to be."

"He knows we're here, and he'll come for her because he thinks she still has the safe deposit box key. He's going to need that money to set up his new life, and we're standing in his way."

"I guess he's going to be in for a surprise when he finds out we have the key and you managed to find the location of the lockbox."

"He got cocky using the bank Sophia used for all of her business. He was still trying to make her look guilty, but it was just a little too pat. We'll hand over the information to Director O'Daniel in a day or two. I'm more than willing to let the CIA clean up the rest of this mess. I've got plans."

"I hope they involve finally making an honest woman out of Sophia."

"I'd love to. The problem is she isn't so keen on being an honest woman."

"Those are my favorite kind of women," Cade said with a sigh and a smile.

They started back down the hill again and the CB radio in the Jeep crackled to life. "We've got signs of a hot spot about midway up the mountain range and tangos moving in," Brady said.

Declan jerked up the transmitter and held it to his mouth. "Shit, are Sophia and Shane back yet?"

"Negative. No response. Everyone is in position and Jade has your back from up top. It looks like things are about to heat up. Get your asses back here."

Dec floored the accelerator and the Jeep went flying down the hill. He and Cade both saw the missile launch from the hot spot Brady had warned them of in the mountains at the same moment.

SINS AND SCARLET LACE

"Fuck," Cade swore. "Clear out."

There was no time to slam on the brakes. They both opened their doors and rolled to the ground, taking cover as the Jeep went on without them. Training saved their lives. They both covered their heads and rolled towards a gulley. They'd almost made it when the missile hit its target and the Jeep went up in flames.

Heat so intense he was sure it scorched the back of his clothes surrounded them and black smoke and nauseating fumes blurred their vision and darkened their faces with soot. He and Cade both rolled to their feet and started running the rest of the way.

Declan felt his heart stop in his chest as a second short-range missile launched. He knew who the target was, and there wasn't anything he could do but pray.

"This has to be your fault somehow," Shane said to Sophia as he used the jack to raise the front of the Jeep.

"You'd better be nice to me or I'll leave you here by yourself," she said. "I can see the gates from here. I could be back home grilling steaks by the time you get it rolling again."

"He'd like hearing you call it home. He built it for you, even though I'm not sure he realized it at the time. The rest of us did though."

She sighed and handed him the tire iron when he held out his hand. "It's complicated."

"Not so much. You both have some shit to overcome. But you love each other. That's what it boils down to, right?" He took off the old tire and put on the new.

"So speaks the man who's determined be the last standing MacKenzie bachelor."

Shane grinned and shrugged his shoulders. "That doesn't mean I can't recognize something is right when it's staring me in the face. Besides, I've decided I like you okay. Not everyone can be a MacKenzie. You seem to come by it naturally."

"Only a MacKenzie would think that was a compliment," she said, laughing.

"See what I mean? You'll fit right in." Shane rolled to his feet and dusted off his hands. "Now let's go cook some steak. I've worked up an appetite."

He was about to get back in the Jeep when he heard the familiar sound of a missile launching. An explosion rocked the ground as it hit higher up above MacKenzie land, but he knew it for what it was. Someone had declared war on the MacKenzies.

"Move," he yelled at Sophia, launching himself over the hood of the Jeep as the second missile was launched. He felt it bearing down on them and grabbed Sophia around the waist, throwing her as far as he could and hoping she'd be clear of the blast.

He knew he wouldn't.

CHAPTER TWENTY-ONE

Sophia didn't remember where she was or what had happened once her eyes opened. She was on the ground, her body a mass of aches and pains, and when she moved her head she felt like she was going to throw up. She realized it was probably because her head had hit the giant rock she was currently lying beside.

Blood flowed freely from the wound in her head, and she tried not to panic when she saw exactly how much blood she was losing. Head wounds always bled badly, even the little ones.

She groaned as she rolled to her hands and knees, and she gagged as the knot on her head made her dizzy and uncoordinated. She had to find Shane. Something bad had happened, but her brain was too fuzzy to put all the pieces together. Smoke burned her eyes and then she remembered the explosion.

"Shane," she tried to call out, but her voice was weak and the effort made the pounding in her head worse. But she moved anyway because she owed it to him to help him if she could. She realized she was a good distance away from where the Jeep had ended up, and she didn't know if it was because Shane had thrown her that far or if the explosion had catapulted the Jeep.

Her ears rang and the blood from her wound made her

clothes sticky. Tears streaked down her face as she kept searching. And then she saw him, and bile rose in her throat and her stomach cramped with despair.

His body lay completely still, his torso and head flat to the ground, but his legs were at an unnatural angle. At least what was left of them.

A sob tore from her throat and she started to crawl toward him, but a hand gripped her arm and jerked her to her feet with a cry. Dizziness overwhelmed her and her knees gave out, but he pulled her up again.

"Get up, bitch," a familiar voice said.

And she did out of pure shock. "Kane?"

"Where's the fucking necklace?"

Declan surveyed the scene before him quickly and tried to assess the best way to handle Kane. He trusted his team to take care of everything else. Even as he had the thought he heard the familiar sound of Jade's rifle coming from her point location as she protected his men's backs.

He came out of the trees and into the clearing where Kane was holding Sophia with his hands raised and his gun pointed to the sky. Shane's body lay unmoving off to the side, bloodied so badly he couldn't assess the damage from a glance except for the horror of his legs.

"Drop the gun, friend," Kane Huxley called out.

Dec pushed his emotions away. Emotions would only get him and Sophia both killed. All he could do was keep a level head and pray the good guys won this round. Sophia hadn't escaped the explosion unscathed. Blood matted her hair and covered her body and her clothes were torn and dirty. Shock and pain had settled in and her reactions were slow as Kane pushed her forward so she landed on her hands and knees. She looked up at Declan with terror-filled eyes but he didn't return the gaze. If he did it would all be over. For both of them.

Kane held the gun pointed steady at her head, and Declan had no choice but to throw his own weapon to the ground. "I've got a dozen men with their scopes trained on you right this moment, Kane. There's no getting out of this."

His smile slashed cruel on his handsome face, and seeing him now, Declan wondered how he'd ever been fooled by his act.

"We'll see how many men you have left. You don't think I came without my own backup did you? I'll see you your dozen and raise you by another ten." Kane's laugh slithered across Declan's skin and he tensed as the gun he held at Sophia's head wavered. "Now I'm going to ask again. Where is the necklace? Or maybe I should just start shooting till one of you gives me the right answer."

"It was pretty clever of you to hide the safety deposit box key inside."

Kane froze and Declan prayed he hadn't miscalculated his reaction to the news they'd discovered it.

"I thought so," he said. "Found it, did you? Well you can just give it back. You're going to have to face the facts that I'm just better than you and I've won this round."

"That's what this is really all about, isn't it?" Dec asked. He saw Shane shift slightly from where he lay and breathed out a sign of relief. His brother was still alive, but with that kind of blood loss he wouldn't be for long if he didn't get help. "That's all it's ever been about. About how you never quite measured up? Second best in our military class. Second under my command when we were both recruited for the CIA. Passed over again and again for promotions because your skills weren't quite at the level they needed to be. Never quite smart enough, were you Kane?"

"I was smart enough to sell your meet location with that group of SEALs for a nice chunk of money," he said, grinning. "You were supposed to die in that Black Hawk explosion by the way, but I almost think it worked out better. I'd look at that scar on your face every day and have to turn away to keep from laughing at the realization that I did that."

"And then I was smart enough to steal your bitch and give her my name. That had to sting, didn't it, Mr. High-And-Mighty MacKenzie? I can't tell you how many times I watched our wedding video just to see the looks on both of your faces."

Dec let the words roll off of him and kept his fury banked, even though the anger boiled deep inside him.

"I don't know what you ever saw in her. She sure as hell wasn't a good fuck, but maybe my men will think differently once I've put a bullet in your brain." His boot connected with Sophia's back and a whimper of pain escaped even as she tried to make herself invisible.

"Why don't you put away your own gun, Kane? Or are you afraid to face me man to man once and for all and see who really is best?"

"You hear that, Sophia? Declan wants to fight me man to man. It seems like the least I should do considering he's been fucking my wife. What the hell, I'm game." He tossed down his weapon, but Declan made it a point to always know his enemy better than he knew himself. Kane had at least three more weapons hidden somewhere on his body.

"Sophia," Dec called out. "I know you hurt, baby. But I need you to come here."

"You're an entertaining man, Dec." Kane stood with his hands on his hips and a cocky smile on his lips. "I've always thought that about you. Yeah, Sophia. Walk back into the arms of the man who is only keeping you around for the half-a-billion dollars he wants to get his hands on. Can you really be that stupid? How many times has this man betrayed you over the years, yet you always roll over and spread your legs. You must have a magical cock, my friend," Kane sneered. "Of course, I've heard dozens of women over the years say it was true."

SINS AND SCARLET LACE

"Sophia," he said again. "Come here."

Sophia raised her head and looked at him out of shattered eyes. Kane had played with her mind for years, and he knew that training was hard to overcome, but he also hoped she'd realized by now that he would rather die than ever hurt her again. It would be her choice whether she trusted him enough to take what he offered, but even if she didn't he wanted her out of the way.

She pushed herself up off the ground until she stood shakily to her feet. And then she took a step toward him. And then another. Relief at her ability to trust him after everything they'd been through sank into his bones, and he realized how undeserving he was of this woman's love, but he was grateful just the same.

"This is all very sweet," Kane said. "I think it's going to be very damaging for her to watch me kill you. It's all very exciting."

They both ignored Kane as she stumbled toward him, though he watched Kane closely and kept his hand free to go to his extra gun if he saw him making a move.

"Thank you," he whispered once she reached him. "Thank you for loving me."

"I don't believe him," she panted, tears dripping down her cheeks. "My faith is in you, and I wanted you to know that if anything hap—"

He put his finger over her lips to keep her from saying the words. Kane wouldn't give them much time. He wasn't worried about the soldiers Kane had brought with him. Dec would put his men and their experience up against triple the kind of men Kane had brought onto his land.

"We're going to be just fine, babe." He slipped the cell phone he'd been palming into the front pocket of her shorts. "I need you to go to Shane and check on him. Text Thomas and tell him to get here as fast as possible and to arrange for a helicopter to be standing by so we can transport him."

She nodded once and wavered on her feet as she

moved back. "I'm going to be really pissed if you die. I just thought you should know." And then she did as he asked and headed towards Shane, kneeling down beside him and taking his limp hand in her own.

Declan didn't waste any time. He and Kane ran for each other and met mid-air, bodies clashing in a tangle of limbs and grunts and groans. His knee made contact with Kane's stomach and the other man let out a grunt of pain even as his fist connected with Declan's ribs. Kane outweighed him by several pounds, so their momentum sent Dec crashing backward toward the ground. His back scraped across rock and gravel, and he air left his lungs as Kane's full weight landed on top of him. They rolled several times, taking turns dealing blow after blow.

Adrenaline pumped high and Dec felt satisfaction as his palm came up and slammed into Kane's face, breaking his nose with a crunch of cartilage and bone. Grunts and muttered curses filled the air as they fought viciously, each one knowing death would come to the loser.

They rolled again and Declan ended up on his back with Kane's weight pinning him down. The prick of a knife against his throat had him stilling and looking into the eyes of a man he'd once called friend. Blood dripped down Kane's face, the steady plop landing on Declan's chin and running down his neck. Their chests heaved as they both sucked in air and not even the wind dared to move the tree limbs as they waited to see what would happen.

"You forgot one thing, brother," Kane spat, the knife cutting into the skin of Declan's neck.

"What's that?" Declan said, ignoring Sophia's quiet sobs in the background.

"I like to cheat."

His smile froze in place as Declan put a knife in his back, slipping up between the ribs to pierce his black heart.

"I remember," Dec said, pushing Kane off of him and rolling to his knees to suck in a deep breath. "Second best,

SINS AND SCARLET LACE

Kane. Just like always."

Hatred filled Kane's eyes as they clouded over with death, but Declan was already on his feet and headed to Sophia. She stumbled toward him and he caught her in his arms, wrapping his arms around her gently.

"You scared the hell out of me," she said, wiping the tears off her face. "I've never felt so useless in my life. Don't you ever do that again, Declan MacKenzie. If my head didn't hurt so bad I'd punch you in the face." A sob tore from her throat and she turned on unsteady legs to go back to Shane. He helped her before she fell on her face.

"Sit down, babe."

"I don't know what else to do for him," she whispered. "He's in shock. God, there's so much blood."

Dec noticed for the first time that she sat there in only her bra. She'd used her shirt as a tourniquet just below Shane's knee. He whipped off his own shirt and handed it to her while he looked over the rest of his brother's injuries, and he jumped as Shane's hand came up and gripped his arm. Hard.

"It's bad," Shane said. His teeth chattered, and tears ran unchecked from the corners of his eyes. Sophia had been right, shock had settled and it didn't look good. Fear clawed at Dec's insides. He'd seen too many men who looked as Shane did now just before they died from their wounds.

Dec kept his face emotionless and his voice firm. "You're all good, Shane. It's just a scratch or two. You're going to be just fine."

"Liar," he said, his breath hitching as pain wracked through his body. "Don't let—" he licked his lips before trying to get the words out again. "Don't let them take my legs. I'd rather die." His fingers pressed so hard into Dec's arms he knew there'd be bruises. "I mean it, Dec. Don't let them take them. They'll relieve me of my command. I'm not meant—not meant to sit at a desk."

Declan took hold of Shane's hand and squeezed it

hard. "Save your breath. The cavalry is almost here." The familiar sounds of a helicopter flying low and nearby had Declan looking up just as Thomas came running with his bag, his cousins and brothers close behind him.

Thomas knelt down beside them and Sophia scooted back out of the way. The other MacKenzies gathered around, talking in low voices, and she noticed Cade and Cooper were barking out orders into headsets to the men they still had out rounding up Kane's mercenaries.

Thomas was already busy running an IV and getting things set up so Shane could get a transfusion once he was airborne, but Shane's next words stopped everyone cold and silence descended in the small clearing.

"Can't feel anything now," Shane said, smiling softly. "I'm glad you finally got the girl, Dec. You deserve it." And then Shane closed his eyes.

Declan bowed his head over his brother and let the tears fall unchecked.

CHAPTER TWENTY-TWO

The waiting seemed endless.

Sophia remembered what it was like to sit in a waiting room full of MacKenzies. The way they leaned on each other and told stories of the past to fill the time. They included her just as they had the last time, but this time she had Declan sitting healthy in the seat next to her, so the time didn't go by in an invisible blur as it had once before.

"He'll be just fine," Declan's mother said for what was probably the thousandth time. "My boys have too much fight in them and are too stubborn to do anything but kick death in the teeth." Her voice wavered and her husband pulled her in close for a hug.

Mary MacKenzie didn't shed tears easily, but Sophia could tell she was close to the breaking point. She'd been holding on by a thread for almost twenty-four hours. Thomas came out occasionally with updates, but all he could say was they were doing their best to stabilize him. The last update had been six hours ago.

"She said the same thing when it was you," Sophia told Dec quietly. "She's a remarkable woman. I can see why her sons are as just as amazing."

She and Declan occupied a corner bench, sitting slightly away from the rest of the family. Thomas had insisted she be checked out as well, so her head was bandaged and all of her cuts bandaged. Her head still throbbed, but they'd given her something for the pain so it was bearable, and Thomas had loaned her a pair of blue surgical scrubs since her clothes had been ruined.

"This hell is what you went through when it was me in the operating room," Dec said. "I knew you were waiting for me. I could hear you in my mind telling me it would all be okay. And I believed you because you never lied to me." He rubbed his hands over his face and through his hair. "I love you, Sophia. I'm not sure I can ever tell you enough."

He took her hand and squeezed it once.

"I love you, too. I'm glad we got a second chance to do it right this time."

The waiting room door opened and Thomas stepped inside. He wasn't the surgeon who'd worked on Shane, but they'd let him stay and observe. The look on his face had Declan rising to his feet and pulling Sophia up with him. The waiting room went quiet as they waited to hear what he had to say.

"The good news is he's finally stable and they've replaced the blood loss. He's in critical condition, but the doctor thinks he's going to be okay. And if he doesn't have any problems through the night he can downgrade it to serious."

"Oh, thank God," Mary said, throwing her arms around her husband and squeezing him tight. Declan's dad had silver hair, but Sophia could see where Declan had gotten his looks from. James MacKenzie was a strong man, as tall and broad-shouldered as his sons, but you could see the weight of relief being lifted as he enfolded his wife in a hug and let her cry against his chest.

"What's the bad news?" Cade asked. He stood next to his parents and had his arm around his wife, Bayleigh.

Thomas sighed and looked straight at Declan. "They weren't able to save one of his legs. They had to take it or he wouldn't have made it."

SINS AND SCARLET LACE

Mary's sob was muffled against her husband's chest, and Sophia felt her own tears escape. Declan squeezed her hand so hard it hurt, but she couldn't let go, not when his pain slammed against her like a tidal wave. Declan had worried over the leg, and he understood his brother's request to not let them take it because he would have felt the same way. There was no way Shane would ever command his team again or go into the field, and to a man like Shane that might as well be a death sentence.

Mary pulled from her husband's grasp and wiped her eyes with the tissue Bayleigh had handed her. "Well, now," she said stiffening her shoulders. "What's done is done. He's alive and that's all that matters, and we'll help him deal with the rest as a family. When can we see him?"

"It's probably going to be several more hours until they have him set up in a room."

"Then I want everyone to go home and get some sleep," she said, taking charge and shooing her sons and nephews toward the door.

Sophia put her arms around Declan's waist and lay her head on his chest, taking comfort in the way he held her back.

"He's going to have a hard time," he whispered against her ear. "He's the most stubborn of all of us and the most hard-headed. Accepting isn't going to be easy for him."

"No, he just sounds like another MacKenzie I know. But maybe it'll help him work through it to know that you have a place for him in your company. Something that doesn't require sitting behind a desk."

She felt his smile against her temple and breathed in the solidness of the man she'd love for eternity. "You must be a mind reader. I was just thinking that exactly. You told me before that you needed to think about making your home here with me. Have you come to any conclusions?"

Sophia pulled back in his arms so she could look in his eyes. "I have, yes. I've decided home is wherever you are."

"Thank you," he said simply. "I've waited a lot of years

for you to become a MacKenzie."

"It's a good name, and I've waited a long time to share it with you. Let's go home."

He took her hand and winked at his mother on the way out the door. "It's about damned time, Declan MacKenzie," she called out after them. "Now go get some sleep, the both of you. We're all going to need our strength in the upcoming weeks. And a lot of prayers," she whispered, taking her husband's hand. She knew the battle was still ahead of them with Shane, but at least she no longer had to worry about Declan. He'd finally found his happiness, and as a mother, she couldn't ask for anything more than that.

"Let's go home, love," Jim said, pulling her toward the exit. "It's time to practice what you preach."

"What are we going to do? I don't even know where to begin to help him ease the pain."

"Sometimes you can't ease the pain, love. But we're going to help him by loving him and kicking him in the ass when he needs it. It's what we've always done. MacKenzies aren't quitters, and Shane is no different."

They leaned into each other as they left the hospital—a lifetime of love and laughter, children and grandchildren shared between them—knowing the hardest road was the one just in front of them.

EPILOGUE

Three Years Later...

Sophia lay down by the lake, the blanket beneath her cushioned by the thick grass, and her hand resting gently on the growing mound of her stomach.

So much had changed in the time she'd been married to Declan. She'd once given up hope that she'd ever have a home or a family. Or children. But Declan had given her all of those things and her heart was almost bursting with the gifts she'd been given—and the second chances. God knows they both deserved them after everything they'd been through.

The baby kicked beneath her hand and she smiled, soothing him with a slow rub as the breeze ruffled the limbs above her.

"You'll always have a family, little one. No matter what happens in your life your family will always be here for you and love you."

And that was what it was all about, really. The MacKenzies were a family like none she'd ever seen before, but she couldn't imagine ever belonging anywhere else. Families weathered storms and heartbreak—thoughts of Shane and what he was going through still filled her with sorrow—but families were also there through the good times and the births and weddings and Sunday dinners. It was the love that made a family work. And trusting that love would never falter.

She heard the squeal of giggles and her heart jumped in her chest at the overwhelming happiness that one sound could bring. Her head turned and she smiled as Declan walked down from the house, their little girl, Grace, up on his shoulders, her blond curls bouncing with every step he took.

She couldn't imagine having the capability to hold more love inside of her, and from the way Declan looked at her she knew he felt exactly the same way. Dec stopped beside her and plucked Grace off his shoulders and put her on the blanket.

"Hi, mama," Grace said, her smile showing two shiny teeth. Her eyes drooped despite the attempt to fight sleep.

"Hi, baby." She touched her soft curls and held out her arm so Grace could snuggle up beside her. She was out like a light as soon as she lay down.

"Hi, mama," Declan said, leaning over to kiss her softly on the lips. His hand rested next to hers on her belly and she felt his smile in his kiss as the baby kicked again. "I hope you don't mind me saying that I've been thinking we should have another picnic soon."

"The last time we had a picnic you gave me the baby who is now kicking against my ribs."

"Mmm," he agreed. "It's a good spot for a picnic. Good memories." He kissed her again, this time a little deeper, a little longer, and her heart thumped in her chest and her blood pounded by the time he pulled away. "I don't think I've told you how much I love you in the last couple of days."

"Maybe not, but you show me over and over again. So thank you for loving me."

He grinned and lifted Grace in his arms, careful not to wake her. "Why don't we go put her in her bed for a nap and you can show me just how grateful you are. I'll even make sure you have a bed this time."

She took his hand and let him help pull her to her feet. "It's hard to pass up an offer like that."

"I've told you, babe. MacKenzies know how to treat a woman right."

They were both laughing as they walked hand in hand back up the hill. Back home.

ABOUT THE AUTHOR

Liliana Hart is a bestselling and award-winning author in both the mystery and romance genres. After starting her first novel her freshman year of college, she immediately became addicted to writing and knew she'd found what she was meant to do with her life. She has no idea why she majored in music.

Liliana is an avid reader and a believer in all things romance. Her books are filled with witty dialogue, steamy sex, and the all-important happily-ever-afters her romantic soul craves. Since self-publishing in June of 2011, she's sold more than half a million ebooks all over the world. She lives in Texas with her four children, and they occasionally let her meet her deadlines.

Connect with me online:
http://twitter.com/LilianaHart
http://facebook.com/LilianaHart
My Website: http://www.lilianahart.com

Printed in Great Britain
by Amazon